AF

The Third Time He Left Me

Sarah Harris was born in 1967 and graduated from the London School of Economics in 1988. She has worked as an assistant producer on BBC Television's *Newsnight* and as a press officer for the Liberal Democrats. She now writes full-time and lives in London. *The Third Time He Left Me* is her third novel.

Acclaim for Sarah Harris:

Closure:

'Gorgeous and witty. I couldn't recommend it more – you can't put it down.'

HELEN LEDERER, Open Book, BBC RADIO FOUR

'It would be wrong to dismiss *Closure* as just another Bridget Jones clone. Harris is far too clever a writer for that, and her mix of sly observation, witty characterisation, and self-deprecating charm is scandalously entertaining.'

Mail on Sunday

'In an overcrowded field of thirty-something female writers, Sarah Harris shines out like a beacon. Terrific, funny stuff.'

Glasgow Times

'Sarah Harris's attention to detail is astounding and she manages to turn everyday situations into hilarious comedy with her biting wit. An intelligent, beautifully written and unputdownable must.'   *Sunday Post*

Wasting Time:

'As insightful as Nick Hornby's *High Fidelity*, but much funnier.'

The Times

'A debut novel of considerable confidence and élan.'

SARAH DUNANT, Observer

BY THE SAME AUTHOR

Wasting Time
Closure

THE THIRD TIME
HE LEFT ME

Sarah Harris

HarperCollins*Publishers*

This novel is entirely a work of fiction.
The names, characters and incidents portrayed in it are
the work of the author's imagination. Any resemblance to
actual persons, living or dead, events or localities is
entirely coincidental.

HarperCollins*Publishers*
77–85 Fulham Palace Road,
Hammersmith, London W6 8JB

www.fireandwater.com

A Paperback Original 2001
1 3 5 7 9 8 6 4 2

Copyright © Sarah Harris 2001

Sarah Harris asserts the moral right to
be identified as the author of this work

A catalogue record for this book
is available from the British Library

ISBN 0 00 651395 6

Typeset in Postscript Linotype Meridien with Rotis Sans display
by Palimpsest Book Production Limited, Polmont, Stirlingshire

Printed and bound in Great Britain by
Clays Ltd, St Ives plc

All rights reserved. No part of this publication may be
reproduced, stored in a retrieval system, or transmitted,
in any form or by any means, electronic, mechanical,
photocopying, recording or otherwise, without the prior
permission of the publishers.

This book is sold subject to the condition that it shall not,
by way of trade or otherwise, be lent, re-sold, hired out or
otherwise circulated without the publisher's prior consent
in any form of binding or cover other than that in which it
is published and without a similar condition including this
condition being imposed on the subsequent purchaser.

For Joe

With thanks to the family – David, Claudia, Daniel, Julie, Iris, Frank, Simon, Judith, Vivienne, and Lionel. Also, Sally Devlin; Rachel Silver; Imogen Moore; Simona Lyons; Jane Goddard; Diana Martin; Alison Tripp; Anna Buckley; Dinah Yerushalmi; Ruti Rosengart; a Rabbi who should remain anonymous; my agent at A.P. Watt, Jo Frank, and all the team at HarperCollins – Fiona McIntosh, Sally Hurworth, Anne O'Brien, Venetia Butterfield, Tilly Ware, Lee Motley and especially my editors, Rachel Hore and Jennifer Parr.

Chapter One

My husband first left me, I think, because of my cockiness, my commonness and my sluttishness, my constant yapping during our honeymoon, my argumentative nature, and my burbling on about my need for a baby. The second time, he left me because of my fat stomach during late pregnancy, my obsessive preoccupation with the baby, and my misshapen, unsexy breasts, dripping with milk. Now, he is leaving me because of the so-called accident of my second pregnancy, my cheapness, and my bloody over-confidence.

I know this because we are having another frank discussion about my flaws.

'It's your cautiousness too,' says Charlie, flexing his fingers. 'You're not at all a risk-taker.'

'You mean my caution.'

'And the way you always correct my grammar mistakes.'

'Grammatical mistakes,' I say, smiling quietly.

Half an hour ago, I came home from work to find the flat empty of Charlie's belongings.

I panicked at first, thinking that we had been burgled. Despite my panic, I was comforted that the burglars had left behind all of my possessions. They had taken only Charlie's bedside TV, Charlie's digital stereo-equipment, Charlie's latest computer, Charlie's clock with the VCR on it, Charlie's filming equipment, Charlie's cosmetics: his chamomile shampoo for blond hair; his £25 salon-conditioner for fine, flyaway hair; the £30 rejuvenating moisture capsules, all bought because Charlie believes everything that he reads in the beauty pages of men's magazines. This, despite my arguing that such magazines are largely fiction, reliant as they are on cosmetics-industry advertising.

Charlie argues that I make such points simply for the sake of starting arguments.

In the main bedroom, I closed the oak wardrobe, wondering what any thief would want with a stranger's old clothes. Yes, Charlie's clothes were all designer-made – Gaultier, Paul Smith, Versace. But they had been re-tailored to fit his skinny frame.

Then I remembered how yesterday's row had ended – with Charlie saying that he was going to 'fucking-well move out'. He had even telephoned a removals company, despite it being so late on a Thursday evening.

I had thought it a very powerful weapon, bringing in a third party to the argument, and had jokingly, and simultaneously, used Charlie's mobile phone to call a refuge for battered wives. But they had been on answering machine.

Of course, I had not taken him seriously. Charlie has left me before, yet has always returned. We have that sort of relationship. He enjoys our rows; I know he does. In many respects, arguing is our passion. Other couples shop together for sofas; we scream abuse at one another. Other couples go for rambling walks in the countryside; we look for original ways to insult each other.

That is why I had relaxed and enjoyed yesterday's argument, not thinking for a moment that it could lead to all this, just now. Charlie, moving his stuff out. Me, racing around the flat in a panic, opening cupboards. He, buzzing up to his own flat. Me, opening the front door, and saying with relief, 'Charlie. What the hell's going on? Have you lost your key? Or just your mind?' Charlie, solemnly handing me his keys. Me, saying that it was lucky that Maxie had gone to stay with Granny Oody, because otherwise she would have wondered where all of Daddy's junk had gone.

Now I ask him whether he has finished listing all that I have done wrong in the relationship.

'No. There's that look you give me,' he says, pleased to be given a chance to elaborate. 'You see, you're doing it now.'

'I'm smiling,' I protest.

I really am sleepy. Too tired for one of our fights, after a day's work. They take so long to reach a conclusion.

Charlie has never known a day's work, I think, as he sits on the fashionably uncomfortable chair – the one made almost entirely out of safety pins – that he bought to impress visitors. No-one has sat on that chair since it arrived two years ago. People wonder why it is there.

'You treat me as if I'm a two-year-old,' he says petulantly, stretching a leg over the arm of his safety pin chair.

'Don't be silly,' I say. But I want to laugh and tell him to take his feet off the furniture.

'So, you don't care that I've moved out, is that right?'

He looks towards the front door, as if terrified of what lies beyond it. And I pointedly sigh, because I know that he has not moved out. At least, not permanently. He has –

as I have repeatedly to remind myself – threatened to leave me for ever and ever, amen, before. That is why I know that he will move his belongings back in as soon as I say that he made a number of valid points during yesterday's argument. I know the rules of the game. But I am not yet ready to concede defeat. I am still niggled by the mess he left behind in the bathroom.

'I'm surprised you didn't take that so-called chair,' I say, lightly.

'I thought about it.'

'But you had a sudden attack of good taste?'

It was Charlie who chose that safety pin chair and, indeed, almost all of our furniture. He chose the paintwork – the greenish white, everywhere. It was he who wanted to change the decor. I was happy enough with the way the property developer had 're-modernized' this Georgian slum, before selling it on, at a huge premium, to me. Come to that, I had wanted to buy in Shepherd's Bush, before Charlie persuaded me to move to this flat, in Camden. We are on the ground floor – 'accessible for mothers with prams', said Charlie, trying to persuade me to buy it.

'And anyone wanting to break in,' I replied.

Charlie looks around our flat. 'I've got bloody good taste – although it *is* all a bit dated now,' he admits casually, lazing his hands behind his head, and this genuinely annoys me.

We had the flat decorated when we moved in only because Charlie thought it necessary. I felt that if I refused I would be cheating a child out of ice-cream. He was my Madame Bovary then. I thought that he would love me, if only I bought him presents. Only now do I realize that Charlie does not love me, because he is incapable of loving anyone. (It is as if he is missing something.) Only now, I

4

do not care, because I am incapable of loving any man but Charlie.

Oh, and yet, how I hate all that whitish-green paint. (Celadon, he calls it.) I hate the overpriced Camden-made 'African' statues, silently accusing us of a history of persecution and slavery. I prefer antique furniture, but we live among new. The kitchen is all stainless steel, like a school canteen. It blows dust. *And it's a bugger to clean*, says our cleaning lady. (A cleaning lady, taken on by Charlie.) The blow-up chair, shaped like a lipstick-red mouth, is a monstrosity. It vibrates when plugged in, for God's sake. Our daughter, Maxie, is scared of that mouth. I tried to explain to her that it is actually a chair. But she is only twenty-two months old, and terrified of electrical appliances.

Charlie said that if Maxie doesn't like it, then she knows where the door is.

But my concessions with regards to home improvement feel insignificant compared to those other women make, to marry. I know women who have compromised by marrying men they loathe. Men who weary them. Fat men. Bald, unsexy men. Men whom women marry purely for their bank accounts, or their sperm. Whereas I have everything in Charlie. He is, for example, so handsome that, sometimes, I want to ask him to stand still, simply so that I can stare at him. He is so sexy that I want to touch him all the time.

How many women have that?

I have everything I want. Whisper it quietly. I pursued Charlie until I knew what he wanted from a woman. (Serious discussion. Fellatio.) I concentrated my energies on delivering what he needed from a wife. (Long, flirtatious rows. Help with his homework.) In the same way

I saved hard, to pay for this flat, I worked hard to secure Charlie.

Now, I am often smug, reading Saturday supplements, realizing what I have. A job at which I rarely have to work. A child; and good childcare. A baby on the way. Family. Charlie's family money. Whisper it all quietly.

My envious friends think I have everything because I am lucky. Only I know better. Despite my education, I have a first-class degree from Oxford – and why? Because, while my peers messed about with extra-curricular activities, I concentrated on what was important. I stuck closely to the syllabus. Now, I really do sometimes fancy myself as Superwoman – or at least her less fancy, supermarket-own-brand equivalent.

'So you hate this fucking furniture too, do you?' I say, truly annoyed, but still playing the game. 'God, after all that bloody . . .'

'How come you're allowed to swear, and I'm not?'

'I'm *not* allowed. Maxie's not here.'

'One rule for you and another for me,' he says.

'Oh, don't be so fucking childish.'

'You see, there you go again. You can't win an argument by discussion. No, you have to use obscenities.'

This breaks my mood. He looks so serious; and I try not to laugh, but I often want to laugh when I am with Charlie. I want to tickle him so that he too collapses into laughter. No-one else would move out of their own home simply to win an argument.

He is – there is no other word – a dear. He is charming, never using a short – or rather, diminutive – word when a longer one would do. He goes by the principle of, Why say green, when you can just as easily say verdant? For, secretly, Charlie studies the dictionary, highlighting words like neoteny, and cumbrousness, which he can casually throw into conversation. That is why he often mispronounces words. He says epi*tome*, rhyming the tome with home. He says me*lan*choly with the stress on the lan. He has just pronounced obscenities *ob-scene-ities.*

My laughing began yesterday's argument. He had asked me to comment on an essay he had written for his Media Studies Masters degree, Special Subject: The Power Of Popular Culture. When I gave him my honest opinion, he said, 'First of all, it's not an essay. It's a dissertation.'

I held it as if it was a dirty dishcloth, and laughed.

'You mean this?' I said, cruelly, knowing that Charlie admires cruel women. The sharper, the better. The meaner, the sexier. Yes, my man likes to be patronized. Ridiculed, even. It is what keeps him here with me.

If ever I show vulnerability, he behaves as if he is bored.

He talks about leaving, or he leaves. So I know that, if I ever confessed to him how ignorant I am, he would despise me. He would tire of me. He would think me weak, and he cannot stand weakness in a woman. So I act as if he is my pretty plaything. I pretend that life without Charlie is possible.

I show strength.

Of course, as part of the rules, Charlie yesterday pretended to be hurt by my comments. He said that I was patronizing him. I had an academic cleverness, he argued, that had nothing to do with intelligence. The only reason I gained my Oxbridge degree was to patronize him. The only reason I decided to work for a newspaper (*incidentally, earning our single income,* I said) was because I wanted power.

The Media, argued Charlie, is a contemporary poison.

7

He had already argued this in essay form, urging me to read 2,000-odd words of abuse against my chosen profession and, by implication, against me. The essay included footnotes that read: *See episode 4, series 2 of the satirical comedy, Absolutely Fabulous.* He concluded that the trouble with the worlds of newspapers, PR and broadcasting was that they were run by the bourgeoisie – all of them Oxbridge graduates, and thus intrinsically ignorant.

In a verbal postscript, he added that I am lackadaisical (*lack-a-dy-sical*), and spend my life persuading strangers to take me seriously.

For my part I said that I found this a bit rich coming from the man who watched *Take the High Road* for homework.

'At least with a Masters I'll be able to pursue a proper career in TV,' he said. 'Whereas *you'll* always be working for a local newspaper.' So I reminded him that he had spent years in career analysis only to be told that he should be a temporary secretary.

He yelled, 'Well, at least I take risks with my life – and have intellectual curiosity. Oh, stop putting on that face.'

My face he said he could not stand. He walked out, and must have returned today, while I was at work, for his clothes, his maypole of ties, his unruly tower of CDs, his filming equipment. And now all I want to do is to giggle, thinking of him carrying everything out.

'I'm going to change,' I say.

'No, wait. This won't take long.'

'You bet it won't. I'm going out tonight.'

'You're always out,' he mutters; and this is true. I made an effort, after I gave birth, to keep up a social life. It is as with sex: if new mothers are not committed to going out of an evening, they never again will.

8

'Well, it's Friday night. And, anyway, how does that bother *you*? When I'm out, Maxie's always at my Mum's, or yours, or asleep.'

'Not always. She wakes up sometimes,' he says, crossing his arms, as a child would in school assembly.

'Oh well. How inconvenient.'

'Stop with the tarty comments all the time.'

'*Tart* comments.'

'Can't you just sit down?' he snaps. 'I want to talk about this.'

I sigh, theatrically; and then mutter a bit because it is too hot for an argument. In this height-of-summer heat, it is too hot to do anything except slump. I do need to change out of this woollen work-suit. The lining is sticking to my legs like Sellotape.

'Well, at least let me get a drink,' I say.

'No, you can't. For once, we're going to have a dialogue,' he says, and I feel all irritable because, from here, I can see the temptation of that bottle of white wine.

Much of our flat is open-plan. The kitchen, the living room, the dining room and the study are all knocked-through, so Charlie and I can always see each other. It is only by going into a bedroom or the bathroom that we can find privacy.

Because we share a study, I can see that Charlie – despite his insistence, last year, that he needed to come off income support and study for a Masters degree – rarely actually studies. He writes a sentence and then feels so tired that he has to go for a lie-down. Or he spends hours playing around on the internet. He hears me on the telephone. *Chitter, chitter, chitter,* he mocks – and so I affect my most superior Oxbridge accent, saying that I prefer to communicate in an old-fashioned way. By talking, say.

'Have you really gone to all that trouble of moving out just to annoy me?' I say, desperate now for a drink. Even doctors agree that one glass daily will not do a pregnant woman any harm. When I came in, I took that bottle of wine out of the fridge, and I can see it now, water dripping down its neck like sweat.

'I moved out because . . . Look, just remember, it isn't *my* fault that our marriage has broken down,' says Charlie. '*I* wanted to see someone from Relate, but you . . .'

'I don't need marriage guidance. I *have* a sense of direction.'

'We needed professional help, but . . .'

'Oh, come on, Charlie. Professional help,' I say, semi-hissing the words, because I am beginning to enjoy the melodrama. 'You just wanted to talk about yourself – at length – to someone who's been paid to listen to you. At *my* expense. Anyway, you soon lost interest. After marriage guidance, it was acupuncture, remember? And then, rebirthing.'

He lazes one leg over another.

'Just don't forget that I wanted to see a counsellor,' he smiles.

'*My* marriage is fine.'

Charlie laughs, on cue.

'OK, well, there's no point us dwelling on the past,' he says, leaning forwards. 'Let's focus on the here and now. Perhaps, if we try and have a proper discussion?'

'Yes, *sir*.'

'Because it will make things easier all round if I can have your cooperation.'

I feel – sitting there in my milky-coffee-coloured suit – as if I am his junior work colleague undergoing her annual assessment.

10

'OK,' I say, seriously, although I can feel my mouth smile at the edges. I sit upright, as if I am on my best behaviour.

'I appreciate this, Lucy. Thank you.'

His expression is so stern that I half expect him to hand me a form to fill in. *List the strengths that you have brought to this relationship within the last year . . .* Or for Charlie to say that he is having to make me redundant. *Natural wastage,* he will call it.

I tell Charlie what I am thinking, because then he might laugh and joke that, no, I am *not* being made redundant, but that I *am* being moved to another department where my skills can be utilized to the company's greater benefit. Then, we can end this argument. I can go to the pub, as planned. (That is why my mother is looking after Maxie.) Charlie can move his stuff back in.

But instead, he looks self-important and says, 'Lucy, I don't have time to piss about. I have to sign the lease tonight, on this place I'm moving to. In Kennington.'

'I hope that's a joke,' I say, my blood quickening as he does not respond. 'You're not serious, are you?'

'Oh, at last, she's taking me seriously,' he says. *'Hal-lelujah.'*

But he cannot keep a straight face. It breaks into laughter; and I relax again, realizing that the flat in Kennington is all part of some elaborate, boys'-public-school practical joke.

'Oh, well, if this is all about me not taking you seriously enough . . .'

'No, Lucy, it isn't . . .'

'You didn't have to move out, though,' I start. 'You could have just changed your taste in music and books.'

Charlie looks furious again, and stands up. He grits

11

his teeth – melodramatically, I think – and sits down again.

'No, I am not going to have a row,' he says to himself. To me, he says, 'I'm determined to discuss all this in an adult manner. *Pragmatically.*' I wonder when we can fast-forward to the scene where we are having sex. Our sex life has been worryingly deviant during the last couple of years: it has reached a stage where we only ever make love after an argument.

'OK,' I nod, knowing that this is all just foreplay.

'There are things we have to sort out.'

'The *airing* cupboard,' I say, mock-helpfully.

'No, Lucy. Things like the mortgage. Maxie.'

I am silent again, but only for effect. Silence is a useful tool in any row. It makes the husband figure (in my case, Charlie) reflect on his cruel words. It makes him go a tiny bit mad, in both the British and American senses of the word.

The only trouble with this method of argument is that it is difficult to sustain.

So I stop being silent, and start to wonder aloud why Charlie felt the need to bring up my mortgage. 'Oh, for fuck's sake,' he yells, to my satisfaction. I now want him to call me the usual names: *swot, tart, Mumsy, Yid, Essex girl, slag, ditz.* Then I can stand there looking superior. I can ask him where he took his first degree, and say that I was not aware of a polytechnic in Wolverhampton – only a few working men's clubs.

I will appear ill for a second, as if I am nauseous. Charlie will look frightened, because he never knows what to do when someone is ill. His usual response is to pretend to be ill himself, saying, 'Feel my head, Lucy; I think I've got a temperature.'

I will feel his forehead and say, 'God, yes, I think you *do* have one.'

'I *thought* I did.'

And I will sigh, and add, 'Charlie, everyone has a temperature – in your case the normal body temperature of 98.6.'

He will sulk, pretending not to listen to me, as I say, 'You have no idea how scary this is for me. Having another child.'

'How hard can it be? You'll only have two children. My mother had three.'

'Well, I'll have three children too, if I include *you*. Anyway, your mother didn't look after you lot. She had nannies and housekeepers, and sent you all off to boarding school when you were seven.'

That will make him furious.

It always does. He will pity my poor children, inheriting my fat legs. *Nice face, shame about the legs*, Billy-my-first-boyfriend, used to sing. My commonness.

Then it will be my turn to pity his poor parents, spending all that money on a boarding-school education – and for what? He will wonder what is less attractive: my natural hair colouring or the peroxide I pour in. I will say that his chamomile shampoo is hair dye too. Actually. Then I will ask after the health of Charlie's *senior diplomat* brother.

No doubt we will then throw wedding presents at each other, crashing the last of the Wedgwood crockery, smashing the £100 salt cellar. The matching crystal pepper-pot went weeks ago.

'Here's what I think of your fucking family heirlooms,' I will scream, going so far (as I did on one occasion) as to tear tablecloths and linen napkins.

'At least they *gave* us something,' he will say. 'What the fuck did *your* parents give us?'

'My *body*,' I will say, and that will stop him speaking for a moment.

'Fat lot of good that is,' he will say.

And I will push ribbons of torn tablecloth down his T-shirt. He will pull them out, and pull them out. Like confetti, they will stick everywhere. He will pull them out some more. I will edge closer to him, pushing him back, into the bedroom, and on to the bed. He will look all helpless, like a frightened schoolboy about to lose his virginity.

'You're a dirty girl, you are.'

'Yeah, that's what you love about me.' And I will prove to him that, far from being a *fat lot of good*, I am, in his words, 'fucking amazing'. So that, afterwards, he will smile and shake his head, saying, 'You have to be good at everything, don't you? That's what I fucking-well hate about you.'

But Charlie will not argue with me now. Instead, he is repeating that he has to leave. I understand that. Of course I do. I must see that these altercations cannot continue. I cannot be having much fun either. He wanted the marriage to survive. He came back, didn't he? Twice. But he is severely depressed. Even his doctor admitted that. His work is suffering.

I laugh at his idea of 'work'.

Charlie remains polite, saying that he does still love me. Really he does. The only trouble, he has realized, is that he loves me like a sister. (The only trouble, I realize, is that Charlie loathes his sister.) 'You'll make some other man a wonderful wife,' he says, and I feel my stomach lurch

14

as I think how like his mother he sometimes sounds. I feel as if he is about to say – all anti-depressant-pill smiles, à la Caroline – *'The last thing we want is unpleasantness.'*

This is what Caroline said during our wedding preparations. Specifically, when I introduced the idea of having a blessing in church from both a vicar and a rabbi. I knew that, practically speaking, such an interdenominational service would be impossible. But I have never believed in organized religion, and wanted to assert myself against all their hymns and candles and prayers.

Charlie's father, Donald, muttered that I was 'damned lucky' that the vicar would marry us at all, given that my mother was Jewish.

'What I'm trying to say is, you know how much you mean to me,' Charlie is saying now. 'I mean, I *married* you,' he laughs.

'Well, you didn't have to do me any favours.'

He knows, I think. Despite my best efforts, he knows how relieved I felt on our wedding day. Whatever happened, I was now a married woman. My marriage would succeed, I thought, if only because I had such low expectations for it. I could have children, and care a little less about waxing my legs. I could stop worrying about Charlie flirting with other women.

But I should not have relaxed, not for a moment. Because, as with any starvation diet, one takes one's eyes off the weighing scales, and the weight falls back on.

I am beginning to realize that I will not be meeting my friends at the Black Horse tonight. This row will take longer to resolve than I thought. Soon, it will be too late to go; and I wanted to watch the final of the darts competition. Despite my feigned lack of interest, I also wanted to hear how Heather's 'date' had gone. A date set up by a women's magazine.

'I think you're a good mother to Maxie. I really do.'

Yes, Charlie does sound like his mother. Caroline often speaks in code.

On meeting me: 'Well, how terribly nice it is to meet you. We're having such good luck with the weather, aren't we?' *God, what bad luck it is – Charlie dating such a cheap tart. Still, at least the sun's out.*

On hearing that Charlie and I were to be married: 'Well, what fun. So, will you go away, or have you decided to have the whole fig up in London?' *Oh fuck, and she's Jewish too. I don't want any involvement, thank you.*

On meeting her granddaughter, Maxie, for the first time: 'I always think girls are rather darling, don't you?' *I wanted a boy, damn you.*

If Charlie and I were to separate, Caroline would say, 'Do you know, there's been a spate of divorces recently. Something to do with the cost of living, apparently. And the price of property. I read it in the newspaper.' *At last you've split up. Now my son can marry someone landed, with an obscenely large trust fund.*

I tell Charlie that he is sounding like his mother, and he snorts. He swears that his connection to the Wallis family is in name only. He says that he might as well be a *nothing* – a Fletcher, like me – for all that his family has done for him.

I say, 'They give us money all the time. *Plus,* you had a trust fund which you spent on that camera, and all that editing equipment and . . .' *And,* I think, *class A drugs.*

'*Pocket* money,' he interrupts. (He even spits.) 'My mates at school got that in pocket money.'

'Caroline describes it as substantial.'

'Anyway, I'm not talking financially. I'm talking emotionally. I'm talking *values*. All those two care about is money,' he said. 'Money they don't possess, incidentally. What's the Latin word for money? Because that's been their motto. Cashum Dictum.'

I say that he should know the real Latin word for money. After all those years of a public-school education.

'Well, whatever,' he says, making a visible effort to calm down. 'I don't think there's any need for either of us to start derogating our . . .'

'Being derogatory about . . .'

'OK, being derogatory about either of our families. As you know, I like your family. But this is about us being . . . We're such antitheses.'

'You mean, we're opposites. And you're right – I'm clever, and you're thick as pig-shit.'

'Well, that's *just* why our relationship isn't functioning . . .' he says.

'For fuck's sake, can't you just say "working"? Do you have to say "functioning"?'

'I don't want to be talked down to like this any more – like a school-kid. That's why I'm going; I've just got to get away from you, woman. I don't even know why I came back to talk. We're not getting anywhere.'

'Wh . . .?'

'I *had* hoped to sort everything out today, but I see that isn't . . .'

'What, you're seriously leaving me?'

'Yes, Lucy.' Long-suffering. 'That's why I'm here, for fuck's sake.'

We both listen to the sound of my breathing.

'But you've walked out before. I thought . . .'

'This is different. That's why I've moved my stuff out

too. And I've sorted out somewhere to live. Rich lets flats out in . . .'

'Kennington.' Despite the heat, I feel suddenly cold. I imagine Rich, grinning. Rich, who thinks I am common because I wear nail varnish on my toenails.

'Yes.'

'Only I thought you might have said Kensington for a moment. But I should have known that Rich could only get you Kennington. Typical.'

I try to meet his eyes, but they are very un-Charlie-like. He is out of my reach, I think.

He is always a fraction out of my reach.

He looks so handsome. (My men always look better when they are further away.) He even looks thoughtful. *So misleading*, I think, nastily, because Charlie believes that Washington DC is the state above Oregon. He once went to Newcastle-under-Lyme, rather than to his destination – Newcastle upon Tyne.

But now he looks clever – as he did when we met. (Men always look better before they are mine. I think I change them for the worse.) And, for a few slow seconds, I feel real hatred towards Charlie. I despise him, as I did when I first spotted him – assuming that Charlie's prettiness was an indicator of stupidity. The black of his eyes against the blond of his hair was striking. I was (in retrospect, rightly) prejudiced against looks alone. But then I saw those dark eyes, so scornful of everyone else at the party. So knowing.

I, too, was scornful of the people at that party – all of whom were there purely to spot celebrities. I suppose I might have had the same motive, but I did not make it quite so clear. The women all had dyed fair hair and big breasts. But unlike them, I looked interesting.

I hoped that Black Eyes would notice this when I stood

next to him at the buffet table, and asked him about vol-au-vent fillings. He looked down at me and said, 'Vol-au-vents are *so* last decade, don't you think?'

I laughed because it was the early 1990s, and all the talk was of sun-dried tomatoes. I was glad finally to meet a man with such a well-developed sense of irony. But, when I said this, he looked confused. He muttered something about being a bit of a foodie. As he talked on, I resolved to have this beautiful creature. If only he would stop trying to talk to me about books he had not yet read.

I said, in reply to a question of his, that I had studied English Literature at Oxford. He said, 'Oh, I read all the time too.'

'Really, like what?'

'Hardbacks,' he said.

'No, I meant what *sort* of books?'

'Oh, I see. Well . . . I like the longer ones. Have you ever read any Gabriel García Márquez?'

I joked, 'Only in translation.'

'You mean the study notes?'

Charlie was something of a Hardy expert, because he was watching a *Jude The Obscure* serial, adapted for early-evening Sunday television. He thought it compared well to the book, which he found 'somewhat slow'. Charlie had not, in fact, been able to finish it, but was doing well with the TV serial.

I said that I could not compare the book to the TV show, as I did not watch much television. I found it hard, then, to suspend disbelief for long.

By then, I was keen to change the subject from books. I could see that Charlie was struggling with it. But he began to quiz me on the books I had read.

I started to see what I would have to do to attract Charlie;

and, fortunately, I had read everything, having spent much of my childhood in my bedroom with only books for company (although I often skipped the descriptive passages). This, because I had been a shy, plain child with mousy hair and NHS specs. As a result, I scored well on Charlie's quick-fire test.

He seemed impressed.

He invited me back to his place; and I thought how smart I had been, to pull such a handsome man. Wealthy, too. Or rather, his flatmate, Richard-a-schoolfriend, appeared to be. (*Rich to you*, he said, flirtatiously.) It was Rich who owned the penthouse flat in High Street Kensington.

High Street Ken, to them.

I could not wait to tell my friends about Charlie, and wanted to go straight to his bed, skipping the flatmate-introduction part altogether. But Charlie was keen to show me Richard's bookshelf, well lined as it was with Chaucer and Proust and Amis. I admired his taste, although I was more impressed, at that moment, by my own.

Because Charlie was the King of handsome.

But I had to be careful not to let Charlie know that I was interested in him only for his body. (That night, at least, that was all I wanted from him.) So, I allowed myself to be led through his record collection, and to be suitably wowed by all the 'limited edition' David Bowies. I looked at his filming equipment. I admired the many rooms in his friend Rich's flat.

Finally, Charlie showed me to his bedroom, and we had sex.

Like all former public schoolboys, he felt ashamed afterwards. (All that pleasure!) He asked me to cover myself up. He begged me to put my bra back on. He ordered a minicab to come quickly, and take me home.

*   *   *

What Charlie is saying fills me with dread. I can have the flat, he says – at least for the time being – and Maxie. He does not mention our seven-week-old foetus, growing inside me, and I wonder if he will let me keep that too.

'So, let me get this straight. You're walking out on our unborn child?' I scream.

'I didn't want this baby, Lucy. It wasn't my plan to have *Maxie.*'

I cannot speak for a moment, remembering Charlie's excitement during my first pregnancy. During those nine or so months, he looked forward to having a baby.

Someone to play with.

As for me, I truly believed that, once I was the mother of Charlie's child, it would tie me to him. If not forever, at least until Maxie left home. But, after she was born, and waking four times a night, I was constantly tired. I made the mistake of not paying him any attention. I was too self-absorbed, or baby-absorbed, even eating the occasional high-fat meal. I did not wear stockings and suspenders to bed. I allowed my vaginal muscles to relax.

So, Charlie regressed, going back to being the sulky man I had first met. He complained that my body sagged, close-up. After sex he would wonder why he wanted me. I did not have a perfect pubic triangle or pert breasts. I wore dresses cut against the bias to cover up my secret shame: I was not a real woman, like the ones in men's magazines.

Those women knew all the moves. It was just like the movies. He wanted a woman who shimmied. Not one who complained about cellulite. Or asked him to clear the table.

21

I took the pleasure out of sex by asking him to make a permanent commitment. I wanted marriage, and a man who tidied away his underpants.

It was no wonder that he left me; and, when he came back, I was patient. I made certain that I paid Charlie an equal amount of attention. I used the time when I was baby-feeding to edit his homework. I practised positive reinforcement ('you're a brilliant father . . . I still find you sexy') hoping that he would eventually wise up to the benefits of being a daddy. Or rather, that he would mature, and take a sudden interest in baby furniture.

But now, this.

'It won't be the same with this one,' I say, patting my stomach, and trying not to sound as if I am begging. 'If that's what you're worried about. I know what I'm doing now. I won't *care* as much about . . .' *It*, I want to say.

'All I'm saying is, it's not too late to . . .'

I cannot believe I'm hearing this.

'To *kill* it?' I say, wanting to tear his every hair out.

'You didn't tell me you were coming off the pill,' he says. 'I wanted to leave then. I bet you even know that. And you indubitably knew that I didn't want another Maxie. I mean, another baby.'

'It was an accident; I told you.' (I am beginning to believe this lie.) 'I came off the pill because of those scares. Did you want me to have a heart attack? Anyway, what does it matter? Don't you want us to be a family? Proper, like other . . . I wanted Maxie to have a sister or brother. Didn't you? And what are you saying, anyway? That we should get rid of *Maxie* too?'

'It's hardly the same.'

'Oh, well, don't worry about this one. I'll get rid of it if that's what you want,' I shout, uncorking the wine, and drinking straight from the bottle. 'There, that should finish it off,' I say, my head coming forward and spluttering. I will make him sorry for verbalizing so terrible a thought.

'Don't be silly,' he says.

'Well, I don't want this bloody baby either.'

And, awful as that sounds, I am suddenly speaking the truth.

I conceived this baby in a flash of insanity.

Because Maxie was no longer my baby. She had turned one, starting to walk; and she was no longer clinging to me. Six months on, and my baby girl was near-independent. She had strong opinions about foodstuffs, bedtime and acceptable storybooks. She no longer cried when I left the room.

I realized that it would not be long before Maxie was leaving home.

I needed another baby, and fast. I wanted something soft and sweet-smelling; but I should have bought a scented pillow, because my broodiness did not last beyond a positive pregnancy test.

By then I remembered it all, from birth to one-and-a-half: the unnatural 'natural' labour; the leaking breasts; the unrequited love; the unremitting anxieties; the drudgery; the need to sterilize everything; the belching baby, filled fat with formula milk; the leaking travel bottles; the need to purée everything. The guilt after serving shop-bought baby food. My clothes, all of them covered in banana paste.

I am not suffering now. I feel fine, in fact. But I know what is to come. I remember the worst, third trimester, from week twenty to thirty-eight: the weeping breasts; the need to sleep in the middle of a sentence; the shortness of breath and temper; the weeping; the addiction to indigestion medicine; the need to avoid all alcoholic drinks. The guilt after a drinking binge.

I do not want to go through this alone. I do not want to be left alone with two children. I do not want to be in a category of single mothers, my name added to a social services At Risk register. I do not want to have anything in common with any of my old schoolfriends in Gants Hill – most of them manless, degree-less, TV-licence-less. Baby-buggies, bastard-babies, everywhere.

'Well, you should have thought about that before you got pregnant,' sighs Charlie, and this incenses me. I pick up a bread knife.

'Are you crazy, woman?' he screams, ducking the knife, which I throw in the opposite direction to him. It lands in Maxie's toy-box.

It almost stabs Teddy Eddy.

Have I sunk so low? I think; and start to cry. Because Charlie has walked out on me before, but never seriously. He always left behind his bathroom products. Never before has he emptied his wardrobe. I knew that he would not go far – not without his six-speed hairdryer.

But this, this feels different – and I feel confused, as if I am playing to different rules. It is as if I am fifteen again and Billy-my-first-boyfriend is trying, and failing, to end our relationship. (If having sex, and nodding at each other the next day in school, can be defined as a relationship.)

'Lucy, please,' he says, coming over to me, his arms up in surrender.

I am crying like a child, using my whole face, but able, still, to say, 'You're lucky you're not dead. I was Wing Attack in netball.' I can feel my mascara dripping down. My foundation, washing away. The tears are falling like

Manchester rain. He puts his arm around my back and leans his head against mine.

'Don't cry, Luce, please.'

He says this gently, but seems bored. I try to stop crying as he looks around, as if desperate for escape. I go over to the mirror, pretending that I need to adjust one of my contact lenses – but, really, it is to check how attractive I am. (As my mother always says, 'Never let yourself go in their eyes.') There, I see how ugly I appear, black mascara running like Pierrot-doll tears from my eyes. Exposed, those childish freckles above my nose. My skin resembles curdled rice-water after all that crying.

Charlie hates ugliness; he cannot understand it. So I give myself a quick spit-wash – the type I give to Maxie. I do wish that my eyelashes were darker. That is the trouble with being fair-skinned. I will never look mysterious, or deep – not with blue eyes the colour of children's poster paint.

'Are you worrying about what you look like, at a time like this?' he says.

This from the man who covers up his mole, every morning, with a stick of blemish concealer. This from the man who seriously considered undergoing plastic surgery to correct his protruding navel. This from the man who calls me dirty if I miss a pubic-hair-waxing appointment.

A man who once told me to have my laughter lines surgically removed.

Charlie has often said, in the past, that I should be more natural; i.e. he hates the fact that I need to dye my hair blonde. (Notice the 'need'.) 'You're pretty enough not to have to wear make-up,' he has said. But only when I am wearing some.

The tears come again, and, for a fleeting moment, he looks as if he cares about me. 'Please, Luce, don't cry.'

'I'm not crying,' I say, wanting that caring look to come back – as if by magic – to his face. But I know that it is not as simple as that. I will have to entertain him. 'With you gone, I'll be much more tax-efficient.'

He laughs, and comes over to me, kissing my hair. For the first time, in what feels like a long time, I breathe again.

The phone rings and I steel myself to break away from Charlie to answer it. (He cannot know how much I need him.) It is Von, wanting to know why I'm late. I was meant to meet her and the others at the Black Horse at seven.

'I'm not going to make it,' I say, wiping my face. Charlie has gone over to the sofa, and is lying down, staring at our Braille-effect ceiling. 'Charlie's finally moving out . . . Ur-huh, ur-huh . . . Yes, but so what? . . . Well, he doesn't give a shit . . . He *is* a shit, yeah . . . No . . . yes . . . Look, I'll see you Monday . . . Yeah, bye.'

When I put down the phone, Charlie looks at me and smiles. *Soon, everything will be back to normal,* I promise myself. Tomorrow, all this tenderness will be forgotten about. Charlie will be back to his old, sulking self. Throwing things.

The phone rings again, and it is VD. (Vincent Derwent to his parents.) Von has passed on the good news. 'No, I'm fine,' I say, enjoying the fuss. 'Oh, you know Charlie . . . Look, I can't talk . . . Ha ha . . . OK, bye, I'll see you.'

I look at Charlie. He is lying there, his hair all ruffled.

'You don't talk to *VD* as if he's a two-year-old,' he says. 'So, why me? I mean, why d'you treat me like a child?' he whines.

'I don't,' I say. But I think how his hair needs brushing.

In fact he needs a haircut. *I must send him for a haircut,* I think, only half-jokingly, and then I remember that he is leaving me. Drily, I wonder whether to book him in anyway.

'Yes you do.'

'Well, VD isn't as cute,' I say.

I can see that he is pleased. He has always envied VD. He is in awe of his bulk. He says that VD is the type of boy who would have bullied him at public school.

'Thanks. I do think there's more to me than that,' he says, however.

There had to be, for me to have fallen in love with him.

Before Charlie, I had ached to fall in love. The modern consumer society seemed to demand it of me. But I was only ever interested in sex. At thirteen, my breasts grew, and I discovered peroxide, contact lenses, and Billy. I have been sexually active since turning teenage. Shocking, I know.

I have been told that I take a masculine approach to sex – that I am predatory. I have been told that I have a problem – although the truth is less complex. I simply enjoy sex.

When I was fourteen, I went through a shoplifting phase. I was called before the headmaster, who said he thought I was stealing for the attention. I had a problem, he said – but the truth was less interesting. I merely wanted the free cosmetics.

I was twenty-three when I first slept with Charlie. I was hardly a virgin – but, for the first time, the sex felt physical. I fell in love with him . . . when was that? Eight years ago.

It hurt that he would always chuck me out of his flat

27

in some sort of postcoital ritual. Back home, I wrapped my pillow in one of Charlie's jumpers, so that I could sleep with his smell. By lying every night on a scratchy woollen jumper, dabbed with Charlie's Gucci aftershave, I developed a nasty face rash. So, I had growing pains. I had the rash on my face. I was moody and sullen, and in love. Yes; I was at last going through adolescence.

'Well, you can have VD. I'm going to find someone who appreciates me,' he says now.

'Someone who *understands* you?' I say, all mock-sympathy. 'Like, say Heather?'

Heather, my colleague. (Charlie snogged her last year.) I overheard Heather saying that she could easily entice Charlie away from me. But I do not think that Charlie would ever have a full-blown affair. I have kept him too interested; and, besides, he is all talk – far too lazy ever to make a move on anyone. Women are the ones in the hard-rock songs he loves. Before me, if they did not want sex, they were *as cold as ice*. If they wanted sex, they were *hot for it*. If they were talking about taking in the shopping from the car, they were *dying and crying for the hard stuff*.

'Someone who's not *you*, anyway.'

That hurts. I want to hurt Charlie too – perhaps by saying that no-one could love him. But it is clear, from my face, that that is not true. Instead, I say that he won't find anyone who will put up with his habits.

'You'll find it impossible, sustaining any other relationship. I mean, bloody hell. You're a professional layabout.'

'Well, so long as I'm not with *you*, treating me like shit.'

'Fine.'

'I'll go now, in fact.' He does stand up, and I am scared. It is the threat of loneliness that feels terrible.

'Don't go.'

That was me.

I do not want to be alone. I hate it when anyone leaves. I take it personally when people want to break up a party by, for instance, going home.

If I go away with people for the weekend, I think of it as rejection when Sunday comes and they pack their bags. Until I turned twelve, I was often alone. I read too much, and it addled the brain. I spent too much time daydreaming, deciding what to call my future children.

I do not like being in this flat by myself. I hear noises, and not all of them are Maxie's. Fortunately, Charlie rarely goes out. a) he does not have any friends and b) he is addicted to the television.

I will miss the sound of Charlie's television. I had begun to enjoy watching TV too. I will miss the sly way muscles keep appearing on his body. I will miss his nipples, and the hair around them, flared up like a gas ring. I will miss his flat, brown stomach, redolent of those on a foreign beach. I will miss his virginal excitement at the sight of a dessert menu in a restaurant.

'No, I'm going,' Charlie says. 'I mean, what's the point? You won't talk.'

'I will talk. We can see a counsellor if you want. You heard me – I won't go out tonight. We can work it out. We've always worked it out. Please. You've made your point. You're right about some things. I *am* patronizing.'

'Well, there *are* things to sort out still,' he mumbles.

'No, I mean don't go at all. Move your stuff back in. I won't put you down any more, I promise. Really, I promise. I'll do anything you want. Please.' I can hardly talk for crying.

'No, I am going. I mean, definitely, that's decided. I

just came here to talk about the practicalities of a divorce.'

'A *divorce*?'

I can barely hear myself.

'Look, there's no point in pretending. A divorce usually follows a separation. And I've tried . . . Look, my father's right. For once. We should never have got married.'

'Charlie, please don't do this. I love you so much. I'll always love you.' I have never been so generous with the L word, but I will now say anything. I want to pick him up and shake any feeling out of him. But he is treating me as he always did, fifteen minutes after sex.

'I'm sorry, Lucy. I've been trying to explain for the last *hour* . . .'

I sit there for a while.

'You only married me to upset your mother.' I do not sound as furious as I feel.

'Oh, not that again. Look, if we . . . We'll only end up circumventing the real issues again. And I don't want that.'

'It's OK.' Still, small voice. 'I married you to upset *my* mother.'

That was a lie. But I will say anything now.

It was a lie because my mother likes Charlie; she always has. Her own parents stopped speaking to her when she married my father. Dad was a non-Jew. A non-person, to my grandparents. As a result, Mum was determined to approve of any boyfriend I brought home – even Enzo.

Enzo was the 'man' I went out with at Oxford. He laughed at my father's collections of newspapers. He sniggered when I told him that my father had been a bus driver. In every political discussion with my father, he always took the part of the leaders of murderous regimes, saying that he 'felt sorry' for men like Saddam Hussein and General Pinochet.

Post-Enzo, Charlie must have seemed perfect to my parents. Straight away, he saw past my father's disability. He did not offer to help him with his wheelchair, as Enzo had, all macho. He did not ask Dad what had happened to his legs. (Enzo had wanted to know every bloody detail of the accident, including who was to blame – Dad or the other driver.) No, Charlie talked to my father man-to-man. He even pretended to have the same political beliefs as Dad – agreeing with him that the Soviet experiment with Communism had been a success. Charlie even played *Countdown* with Dad.

He went so far as to lose, although my father is hopeless at quizzes.

'At last I've found someone I can beat at *Countdown*,' smiled Dad. 'I'm sick of playing against Luce. She wins every single time, *Blockbusters*, *Blind Date* . . . That's the trouble with having a genius for a daughter.'

'Hardly a genius,' I said, pinking. 'I just know how to pass exams.'

We ate in front of the TV that day. We watched *FastNews*. Dad and Charlie discussed the Kurdish crisis, and I relaxed. I did not even interrupt their discussion to tell them the real reason for the Gulf War. Or the proper way to pronounce the name of the Iraqi National Congress Party's press spokesman.

'What about my parents?' I ask, starting to cry again. 'Are you just going to stop seeing them too?'

I wish they were here now, to settle this. My mother would be able to sort Charlie out. She would be able to persuade him to stay with me.

Even when he was cheating during Monopoly, last

Christmas Day, my mum refused to take my side against his. That, despite the fact that it was obvious (even to my Communist father, who refuses to see bad in anyone) that Charlie was stealing money from the bank. No-one could have made that much money out of Mayfair and the Old Kent Road – particularly not Charlie, who has never understood the property market.

'I'm sure we'll all keep in touch,' he says lightly. It feels as if we met two weeks ago on a package holiday, and are now swapping telephone numbers at the coach depot. 'You and I will still be friends, I hope.'

Of course we will, I think, beginning to feel bitter. Because I am Charlie's only friend. Even his best man, Rich, despises him. He despises me too, but that is a different story. It is because, instead of *supper,* I say *tea.*

Charlie has trouble making friends. He was bullied at school, and at polytechnic. At school, one boy made believe he was a ventriloquist. Charlie was his 'puppet'. The boy sat Charlie on his knee, and wrapped a scarf around his mouth.

At polytechnic, Charlie was known as The Posh Twat.

By the second year, Charlie's nickname was shortened simply to Twat. He was barred from the student pub as he was unable to hold his drink. The other students banned him, too, from Socialist Workers' marches. They said that anyone with an accent like Charlie's was hardly going to be against apartheid.

'Why didn't you leave, then?' I asked Charlie, when he told me about his painful experiences in higher education.

'Well, I didn't want to be humiliated,' he said. 'My parents were horrified when I said that I was going to Wolverhampton. It would have been humiliating, coming home.' He laughed as he said this. 'Anyway, I did have some friends there.' These so-called friends all had black hair, white faces, and red lipstick.

As far as I could tell, they were all women wanting to be Charlie's girlfriend.

'You seem to have it all worked out,' I say. I feel sick, and it is not because of the baby inside of me, putting down roots. Making room for itself. Stretching my ligaments.

'Well, you know more about our finances. I'll need to know what you owe me.'

'What I *owe* you?'

He owes *me*. I have spent the last few years taking care of him and Maxie.

With barely any help from his parents, I have kept control of our finances. I have saved. I have stopped Charlie's excessive spending.

I chose the type of mortgage we needed. I completed our tax returns. *I* am the one who works for a living. By contrast, Charlie writes essays about the symbiotic relationship between the press and the PR machine. He examines the way the two bodies feed off each other *in a greedy, cynical, frenzied* way.

This is what he calls work.

'So, let me get this straight,' I say. I am all but speechless, although the survival instinct in me stirs. 'We're going to split everything down the middle even though it's *my* flat and *my* money and *my* daughter.'

'Some of that money came from my fund, remember. Anyway, I've already said that you can have custody of Maxie.'

Charlie has never taken much of an interest in Maxie. Most of the time, he treats her as if she is a small animal who might – at any moment – grow violently out-of-control, and turn on him. When I met him, Charlie said that he was the type of man that all children liked. A kind of latter-day Pied Piper, in fact. But Charlie wanted to be that type of man only in theory. He felt that children, like dogs, have an instinctive nose for likeable people.

And perhaps they do, I think, nastily.

'What about money then?' I ask.

'Well, we'll have to sort it out. I've been in touch with my father's solicitor.'

'You've . . .*what?'*

I had not thought Charlie money-grabbing. Lazy, yes. Childish, yes. Pretentious, yes.

'So, hang on. What have you been telling this solicitor then? Oh, don't tell me – let me guess. I'm out every day being greedy, frenzied and cynical, and you're in watching *Teletubbies* out of "pure intellectual curiosity".'

'There's no need to be vicious.'

'You haven't heard anything yet, you bastard.'

I want to hurt him, as he is hurting me.

I imagine a knife, bloodlessly sliding into his chest. I imagine a cricket bat, bashing him around the face. Worse, I want to tell Charlie that his deepest fears are well founded. His mother does not love him. She sent him away to boarding school. Roger was thirteen when he was sent. Charlie was only seven. *Why was that, Charlie?* I want to ask. Cruelly. *Did you wet the bed, Charlie?* But, somehow, that feels inflammatory. It would be like shouting 'Fire' in a crowded cinema.

'Lucy, please.'

'You *need* me.' But it sounds as if I am squealing: *I need you.*

Yet I am the one who pays the bills. I am the one who

conceived Maxie. I studied ovulation charts, and took my temperature each morning. Becoming pregnant this time around was also a unilateral decision. I wanted to complete our family, and simply came off the pill.

I am the one in control.

I am mother and father to my child. Charlie refused even to watch Maxie being born. He came into the labour room only when the pain was all over. He did not admire his firstborn. No, he admired the midwife. She thought Charlie charming – although his charm offensive consisted of him offering to show her *his* private parts. She giggled. He asked her to tie a neater knot in Maxie's navel.

Charlie is as interested in Maxie now as he is in cooking to a recipe. On bank holidays and bored-days he will show real enthusiasm. But, afterwards, he will leave a huge amount of clearing up (paint/puke/garlic-peel/dirty plates/tears) for me. He has never – not once – put Maxie to bed. He just stands there, saying that he wished they made Babygros for adults.

To be fair, he did once read her a bedtime story. But he came out complaining. Saying that he wished they would write picture books for grown-ups.

I am the one who washes clothes, and wakes up early, and cleans, and cooks, and washes clothes, and wakes up early, and cooks and cleans, for Maxie. I chauffeur Charlie everywhere, because he keeps on failing his driving test. He cannot handle a gearstick.

He will not even navigate when I drive. He cannot read a road map. (He always explains this away by saying that he did not take O-level geography.) I have to force him to eat properly. He does not like vegetables. If it were not for me, he would live off biscuits and strawberry-flavoured jelly. I give Charlie blow jobs and correct his essays. I fill in the gaps of his crosswords. He says that he is dyslexic, but I know that he failed the test for dyslexia.

I do the supermarket shopping, and take in and pick up the dry cleaning. I take in and pick up his daughter. He has never – not once – collected Maxie from our childminder. He just occasionally accompanies me, saying that he wished 'they' made mittens-on-a-string for adults.

'You don't know how much I do for you. You don't fucking know what I do for your only child,' I say, standing up. I turn my back on him to pour myself a glass of wine. I hope he does not realize, from my shaking voice, how upset I am. 'And it's not only Maxie. It's *you*. It's the way you depend on me for everything. You have no initiative.'

I was the one who rang Charlie after we first slept together. He *lost* my telephone number. He had mentioned that he worked at Thomas Cook, queuing at embassies for tourist visas. So, sleuth-like, I tracked him down at the Mayfair branch.

Charlie was surprised, and I think impressed, when I called him.

'Oh yes, I remember you,' he said.

'It was last Friday,' I said, helpfully.

'Yes,' he said. 'Blonde hair, brown roots?'

'*Blonde* hair, yes,' I emphasized.

'Feisty lady; yeah. How did you get this number?'

'Well, I did my research,' I said, efficiently. 'There aren't that many Thomas Cook branches in London.'

He laughed, and I asked him to the launch party of a nightclub, for which I had press tickets.

'What exactly do you do for me, Lucy?' he asks now, as I lean against the kitchen worktop, drinking wine in gulps.

'*Everything*. I fund your fucking *life*, mate.'

I bought our engagement ring, and hired Charlie a groom's suit. I acted as main liaison with Caroline for all the wedding preparations. I organized the honeymoon in Bali. I arranged the surprise bouquet for the bride.

I knew what to do. I planned the entire trip on my own. I took out the loan, which was only eventually paid off by Charlie's parents. No doubt, I think miserably, it will be me who has to finalize the details of our divorce.

That thought sobers me up.

I need a stronger drink.

I tip out the last of the wine into the sink, and go to the drinks cabinet, which also serves videos and Charlie's cereals. He always buys the multipacks. Charlie leaves the All-Bran and the Cornflakes for Maxie. He eats the Coco Pops and the Golden Grahams.

I pour myself a vodka. Neat.

But vodka mixed with the dregs of wine is not pleasant. I feel sick, although that might be because Charlie is leaving me.

He clicks open the door. As he does so, I try to remember all of the bad things about our relationship: the unrequited love; the unremitting anxieties; the drudgery; the need to bribe him. The guilt after signing yet another cheque. Those clothes of his, paid for by my overdraft.

I remember the embarrassment of being with Charlie. His restaurant orders – those shamefully large knickerbocker glories. Charlie chooses only fizzy drinks. Even at last year's office Christmas party, he stuck to orangeade. So he could not say that he was drunk when he snogged Heather. He spent the entire evening talking to her tits. He spent several evenings, after the party, talking about her tits. When I reminded him that Heather does not have breasts, he said that he loved women with short hair. Women without any meat on them.

I said, 'In other words, you love small boys.'

Then there is Charlie's indiscretion. For example, at that same office party, he revealed to my colleagues that I weighed food before I ate it. I do this to lose the cellulite on my legs. Charlie is always saying that they are fat. Yesterday, I explained that the shape of my legs was hereditary. 'What about your stomach?' he asked, looking at my slightly rounded pregnant bump. 'Perhaps you should have liposuction on those problem areas.'

There are so many reasons why I should be happy that Charlie Wallis is leaving.

* He does none of the housework.
* He does none of the out-of-house work.
* He hates all women, including his mother. All mother-figures, in fact.
* He hates me.

No, I am not suffering now. I feel fine, in fact. But I know what is to come. I remember the first time he left me, after two weeks of marriage: the need to weep in the middle of a sentence; the shortness of breath and temper; the drinking binges; the need to avoid telephoning him. The guilt after telephoning him.

'Well, I'll go then,' he says. 'I don't think I'm achieving anything by being here.'

'Oh but life isn't only about achieving things, is it, Charlie?' I say, curling up on the sofa. I am like a foetus, hugging itself. 'I mean, that's what you always say.'

'Come on. It's not as if you haven't got friends,' he says; and he glares at the photograph on the sideboard of me, in my wedding dress, next to Angela and Von. 'If anything, you've got too many friends.'

'You weren't a friend. You were my husband.'

'You'll find someone else soon,' he says, pityingly.

'Oh yeah, at this time of night,' I say, self-pityingly.

I feel more tears coming, as he pauses to look at me with sympathy. How I hate sympathy.

'I'll be in touch about Maxie and money and every-thing.'

'What about this one?' I ask, massaging my stomach.

'Mmm, yeah. Well, I'll call you,' he says. I stare at the television, wondering why Charlie has left that behind.

I hear another click, and when I turn round, Charlie has left me.

Alone.

Yet I spent so long persuading him to marry me. I warned him that, if he did not marry me, he would always be on his own. With me, he could have sex whenever he wanted it, clean sheets, a laugh, and divine sauces now that I had finished that Prue Leith cooking course.

He could have children. He could have a mother for these children. I could perform that trick with my fingers and my tongue to make him come. I do not even have to come myself. (Really, I can do without orgasms.) He did not need to pass his driving test; I could drive the two of us to the countryside if he wanted the odd dirty weekend.

I sit there like soup, thinking how I could make con-versation on his behalf at dinner parties. I could rush him to casualty whenever he had a cancerous bowel, which was diagnosed as a minor stomach upset. (Despite what the doctors said, Charlie was often dying.) No-one else can take care of him as I can. No other woman would hide his credit card whenever he watched the shopping channel, or force him – for his own good – to go to the dentist.

39

I might have sat there, in that liquidized state, forever, but the telephone rings. It is Von again, hoping that I am OK. I say that I am fine. I will be fine, alone.

But the silence of this house is so loud.

Chapter Two

My husband left me earlier this evening because of my crabbiness, my insomnia, and my meanness with money.

Von, my closest friend, is wrong about time healing. I know from experience that, when I am unhappy, time takes a long time to pass.

She came round uninvited at midnight, carrying funereal-looking flowers which she bought from a garage. There was a box of mint-flavoured chocolate Matchsticks in her bag for me.

I have perfect friends, I think, as she sits on my sofa now, complaining that she has the munchies. Von has stopped smoking, and this is the result. I tell her to eat the Matchsticks, unless she wants bread. I have bread, baby food, milk, and the Matchsticks.

She opens the Matchsticks, and I tell her that I am not going into work on Monday. I plan to be ill, as I am owed some sick leave.

Von says that Charlie was a fucker with no taste. Even with a mouth full of obscenities and mashed chocolate, she can appear feminine. She has one of those faces, often described as elfin, that stays young-looking, despite the

drinking, the drug-taking, and the ageing. It is as if someone has spent time, designing her face. Her cheekbones
have been arranged *just so.*

My own face looks as if no thought has gone into its
composition. It is as if it has been constructed by somebody
slapdash, seconds before her deadline.

Von looks pointedly at the safety pin chair.

'You did everything for that fucker except change his
nappies for him,' she says. 'Now he'll see. He's going to
have to cook his own fucking food.'

'I.e. open the tins himself,' I laugh. Because Charlie only
ever eats comfort food, like custard out of a can.

'Mind you, he will have to do his own cleaning,' I
say.

'Exactly,' says Von.

'I mean, he won't have Katie any more.'

'Who's Katie?'

'Our cleaning woman.'

Von closes the box on her lap, and says, 'Too right. Why
should he get the fucking cleaning woman?'

'He's the one who left,' I agree. 'And he's taken everything else.'

'But not your self-respect.'

'Yeah. It's enough that he took the answering machine.'

I laugh and then remember the seriousness of the situation. My laughter becomes bitter.

'I don't want to live on my own. It'll be so strange
when it's just me and Maxie here. I mean, I've always
lived with people, or Charlie. As soon as I found that flat
in Shepherd's Bush, he moved in.'

'*Seeped* in,' corrects Von.

'Yes.'

'Did he even pay rent?'

'No, of course not. He's my husband. It'd be like he's paying me for sex or something.'

Von goes into the kitchen and draws the French stick, like a sword, out of my bread bin.

'Look, Luce,' she says, coming back into the living room. 'The thing to remember is that you should never have married Charlie at all. He was – is – the love of your life; and men like that are supposed to dump you, not . . .'

She pauses to consider, and slam the lid back on the bread bin.

'It's almost the *law*. Charlie was a cruel bastard to have stayed with you. Like giving you a life sentence.'

'I could never be good enough for him,' I admit, thinking how, married to Charlie, I felt as if I was in the type of job normally filled by someone from the old boy network. I was qualified for the position (in fact, overqualified), but did not understand the ethos of the environment, or its code of conduct.

'In his opinion, no. Of course not. And the other thing is, Charlie's been institutionalized at public schools. No matter what you do, you'll only ever be a girl to him. Women to him are probably either whores or mothers.'

'Whores *and* mothers . . .'

'You'll always only be the mother of his child.'

'No, like his mother, I'll always be the whore.'

She pauses, presumably so that she can decide how to react to that.

'Well, you don't want to fucking put up with that.'

She sits down and tears my French stick in half, spraying crumbs. She says all of the things I said when VD dumped her. Charlie had no maturity, she says. He was inconsistent, she says.

'I mean, he had nothing to him. *Nothing*. He was as thick as pig-shit.'

'You're right; he was.'

When VD left Von, I was straight over to her squat with the champagne and the fresh cream chocolates. 'We should be celebrating,' I said – first rate friend that I am. 'This is *good* news.'

Von said then that she could not understand how she had ended up with such a supportive friend as me when her best friends at school were all of a type to torment her by laughing at her deaf mother, or the names of her boyfriends. Until she met me, Von thought that best friends of the type to be there for you, if you were there for them too, existed only in television comedies, or women's magazines.

But it is my opportunity to talk now; and so I talk about Charlie. I talk about Charlie's internet obsession; Charlie's shyness; Charlie's need for an afternoon nap. Like a rare-flowering plant, he is awake for only three hours a day. Charlie's protruding navel. The way Charlie takes up two-thirds of our bed. Now, none of it.

I feel depressed again, and stop speaking. Von asks me if I want any bread. I nod, and she hands me a heel.

'The way he treated you like shit?' she reminds me. 'I mean, why did you let him, Lucy?'

'Because I think, despite everything, he loved me,' I say, lying to myself with that L word again.

I nibble at the bread before realizing that I have – after all these years – finally lost my appetite.

'Charlie loved *himself*,' she spits. 'It's not enough that he was good in bed. *VD* was good at fucking, but he was good for fuck all else.'

'Charlie wasn't even good in bed,' I say, because I was

the one who studied sex manuals as if for a higher degree. 'I mean, he didn't want to move about too much, in case his hair got all sweaty.'

But, I am lying, because the sex was sometimes good. As my mother – who is always right – said, sex with one's husband will always vary. It is the same with smoking. As a committed smoker, Mum knows that every cigarette will taste different.

'I doubt whether Charlie *ever* cared about you . . .'

'He didn't. Just his bloody amateur films.'

'His fucking crappy films.'

'And his clothes.'

'His fucking crappy clothes,' she rants. 'Not you, or Maxie, or this baby coming.'

'No, because that might interrupt his skincare regime.'

'What?'

'Well, he was rigorous about that. He felt that it was important to try to reduce the visible signs of ageing.'

'Well, that shows you. So, he was probably gay anyway.'

'He *did* like the Eurovision song contest.'

Even I laugh then.

By the time Von leaves, the following evening, I am not so bothered by Charlie's departure.

Friends fill the gaps left by lovers. (As for sex, that is easily had, with any man, in any UK nightclub.) It is Saturday, and I have arranged to see a group of my old schoolfriends this evening. I still keep in touch with them, despite the fact that we have nothing in common, apart from a shared history.

'Whatever else you do, keep your friends,' my mother always says – and I do like being with the Gants Hill Posse.

With them – Tracy, Ed, Wayne, Billy, Danielle and Donna – I always feel as if I have achieved something. I was the first girl in my class to grow breasts; I was the first at my school to sit an AS level; the first to attend Oxbridge; the first to be fingered; the first to lose her virginity.

Yes, I was always in the ascendant at school. I was clever then, if only in comparison to my peer group. Had Gants Road Comp been a typical American high school, I would have had an entry in the yearbook as the person most likely to succeed.

Yet, here I am – single again. I have lost my husband to the wilds of Kennington. I am also stupid now, certainly compared with the friends I made at university – all of whom know the capitals of obscure countries in Latin America. They can offer enlightened analysis of the situation in East Timor.

I am not sure, to be frank, where East Timor is. I think it might be an island near China, but that is not knowledge enough to support my argument. In truth, I have barely read a national newspaper since 1993. With Charlie, I could not see the need. He did not stretch me, intellectually.

He did not stretch me, intellectually.

I was never very interested in the world. Just as I caught up with current affairs, something would happen. There would be a coup, or a peace agreement, and I would lose track.

Fortunately, the Gants Hill Posse do not care that I only ever thrive in exam conditions. They are wiser than my college friends, and understand that children are the stuff of life. All the women in that gang have kids now: I am used to seeing them, writ small. Only Maxie looks like her dad.

As ever, we have arranged to meet in The Case, so that we can all bring our offspring. (The owners seem intent on losing their licence.) At The Case, we buy endless pints of lager and packets of crisps, still talking, after all this time, about Mr Tartin, the French French teacher.

Tarty knickers.

I planned to take Maxie with me, so that she could play with the other children. But Caroline phoned today, offering to take her granddaughter for the night – and, although my mother has only just dropped Maxie back with me, I decided to accept the invitation.

I have not spoken to my mother-in-law since I separated from Charlie.

I am not sure whether she has been aware of our separation until now, when I see that smile cracking her skin. *She knows*, I think, staring at that long thin face, so packed with lines. There is no room left for further wrinkles. Her chin is as spiky as Shaggy's in *Scooby Doo*. Sometimes, Caroline looks like Camilla Parker Bowles. At other times, she looks as Princess Diana would have appeared had she grown old.

'*Lucy,*' says Caroline at the front door, in a manner that suggests she has not seen me for five years, and is meeting me by chance at a cocktail party.

'Hi, sorry about the face mask,' I say, pushing back the front door to allow her in. But still she stands there.

'Oh *no*. I *always* wear one.'

Maxie runs up to Granny Rine – *Ranny Rine* – and wraps her hands around her shoulders, spotting those loose shoulderpads with jam.

'I'm sorry,' I say. 'She's just had her tea.'

'Oh, don't be silly; I don't mind. This is such an old thing anyway. I bought it in Hong Kong ten years ago, and the shopping there's terrible.'

47

'It's lovely, Caroline.'

I would prefer sometimes to call her, more appropriately, Ranny Rine.

'Here's her bag. The Calpol's in the zip,' I say, because Caroline cannot make small conversation.

'Jolly good. What do I do with that?'

She is even more hopeless than me at mothering. She sends Maxie back to me with her clothes buttoned back to front. Her nappies inside out.

And she is amazed when I know how to perform simple tasks – like cutting up Maxie's tea or fitting the car-seat.

For all that, Maxie adores her. I am often surprised by this. I would have thought that Maxie would be scared of that face. Sometimes, Ranny Rine looks like a man made-up. At other times, she looks like a wolf. Then again, she sometimes looks soft, like a sheep.

Caroline so adores Maxie that Charlie is envious. He complains that her maternal instinct seems to have skipped a generation.

Maxie is the only person with whom Caroline will be honest. I overheard Caroline once asking Max whether she should 'call it a day' with Donald.

'Yesh,' my daughter said. Because Maxie is an intuitive soul.

Charlie's father, Donald, does not like children. This fact is treated as if it were a physical ailment. Caroline speaks in hushed tones of her husband's antipathy towards his grandchildren. Like an infectious illness, Maxie is kept at a distance from him.

'You won't need everything that's in the bag. Don't worry,' I say now. I am at the sink, scrubbing off my magazine cover gift of an oatmeal face mask.

'Not at all. Come on, Maxie.'

I do not want my daughter to leave me. Or rather, I do not want her to leave me willingly. This, despite the fact that I am always scheming to have Maxie looked after by someone else.

I am delighted when Ranny Rine or Ranny Oody agree to baby-sit. But I will miss her – she is going to be away until Sunday evening. It has to be worth Caroline's while, coming to collect her. She lives some way away, in a small Cotswolds village.

Caroline drops the bag, and Maxie. She then picks up the bag, and Maxie. Neither of us has mentioned Charlie's absence. Or the absence of Charlie's possessions. Only, as she goes out of the door, Caroline says shyly, 'Just keep the ball in the air, Lucy.'

As if there is only one ball.

The flat is so quiet. I want my Maxie back. All I can hear is that dripping tap, like accusing voices in the distance.

I have decided not to go out tonight. I cannot face my old schoolfriends, none of whom understands why I have chosen to live in a flat in a falling-apart building rather than a new house. Plus, I understand none of their popular-cultural references. With that posse, I often feel as if I am in a late scene from *Pygmalion*. They all laugh at my clothes and refer to me as 'the brain'.

None of them would know how to be sympathetic about Charlie leaving. They do not discuss their lives, or their relationships. They merely tell joke-book jokes and talk about TV quiz shows. I am better off like this, with my wine, and a flatful of just-bought junk food. Even the shop owner commented on the amount of chocolate I was buying. Mr Metados said that perhaps I should buy some fruit? He gave me a free apple, then asked after *lovely Maxie*.

I was forced to smile and talk about toddler tantrums. But I am back in my flat now; and I am reminded, everywhere I look, of Charlie.

So I have decided to spend the evening crying.

It is late, but still Saturday. I want the days to move on, so that it can be Monday, and I can call Charlie at his polytechnic. I know I will never find anyone to love as much as I do him. All of my pre-Charlie relationships started promisingly well but – like the flight home from a romantic Paris weekend – they wound up dull and exhausting.

I was tempted to call Caroline, to ask her for Charlie's Kennington number – *as I was on the phone* – but Angela rang to see how I was. And now she is here, cleaning my kitchen.

I told her not to, but she had found my cleaning fluids. Now, she is rearranging my furniture for Feng Shui reasons. Because Angela believes in impossible things like Feng Shui, socialism, aromatherapy, Jeffrey Archer, the tenets of all five main world religions, and Charlie.

'Charlie'll be back,' she says, firmly. 'You two belong together.'

'We do, don't we?'

I pause, to feel happier. Angela has a knack of reminding me to enjoy myself. She acts as if there is no future, and no past. There is nothing, in short, to disturb her happiness. But I cannot suspend disbelief for long.

'So why has he left me then?'

'He's just confused,' says Angela. 'Underneath that act, he loves you, you know that. Otherwise why would he marry you? Why would he have stayed so long?'

Unlike most of my other friends, Angela believes that love is far greater than a biochemical reaction which wears off after thirty months. But, then, she has had only positive experiences of love. She is a lesbian; and all of her former lovers are like schoolgirls in boarding-school novels. They do everything heartily – like eating and loving. They stay friends with their ex-girlfriends. They even giggle, for God's sake. I giggle only when I am drunk; and it is harder and harder to be drunk these days. It can take several vodka-cranberries.

'Anyway, what you should be doing, Lucy, is remembering the reasons why Charlie liked you, not the reasons why he *went*.'

Charlie liked me, I think, because of the free male grooming products which came with my job. In other words, he liked me because I came with free gifts attached. Massage oils. Hair gel. 'Cover mounts', as they call them in the magazine industry. There was an 'incentive to pick up' as people say in that same industry.

As the song goes, *Now Kitty was pretty and Jane she was plain. So, to make up the difference the Dad would explain. He'd give the best heifer he had on the land, as a sort of a bonus with Jane* . . . I came with the modern equivalent of a heifer.

'That's crap. You're very pretty,' says Angela.

'Not as pretty as Charlie, though, am I?'

Angela laughs and sits on the safety pin chair. 'Perhaps not,' she says. 'But then he is the only man to have ever made me question my sexuality.'

I slump even further into the sofa, and talk about Charlie. I talk, for example, about the sex.

But then I see Angela's embarrassed face, and remember that she loathes talking about heterosexual relationships, if there is any detailed emphasis on the sexual. The subject disgusts her, she once confessed. She said she hated to think of a man naked with a woman – a man's penis lying, like suet, between his legs.

I replied that, if one is doing it correctly, the man's penis does not lie, like suet, between his legs.

'Ugh – don't talk about it,' she squealed, all squeamish.

So now, I exercise self-restraint. I stop talking about our sex life, and so start to feel wretched again, silently remembering. As my mother would say, using her limited Yiddish, I feel it in my *kishkes*.

Angela appears to see my happiness drain away. She shakes her head and says, 'You don't believe me, do you? About Charlie coming back?'

'Not this time, no.'

'But you're pregnant, Lucy.'

'He didn't want this baby. I just came off the pill, without telling him.'

She tries not to look as if she disapproves.

'It's still his baby.'

'His foetus,' I say, looking at my stomach. 'In fact, no, it's just an embryo. Not even a foetus yet. Still get-riddable.'

'You wouldn't?' she says.

'I have thought about it.'

'But not enough to . . .'

'No.'

Angela looks relieved. Not for the first time, I wonder how someone so big can look so fragile. I suppose it is because she does not look fat. Rather, all-breasts.

'Anyway,' I say, standing up and stretching. I go into the kitchen. 'D'you want tea?'

'Have you got any herbal? It helps the digestive system.'

I rifle through my tea tin.

'Blackcurrant . . . forest fruits . . . chamom . . .'

'Forest fruits.'

'Anyway, enough about Charlie,' I say, remembering that Angela did not simply come over to talk about me. My friends have needs too. 'I want to hear about your new woman. So she's famous, no less?'

'*Felice*,' sighs Angela, and I remember that feeling. When I first started seeing Charlie I wanted to find a context in which I could say his name, over and over.

'Is she French?' I put a teabag into a mug, and switch on the kettle.

'No, her original name's Felicity. But she thought that a French name would help her career in TV. Oh, Lucy, you're going to have to tell me how to be in a relationship. It's been so bloody long.'

'Don't take *my* advice,' I say, watching the steam smoke up from the kettle. 'Unless you want it to *fail* with this Felice.'

'Lucy, a) your relationship with Charlie is fine. You've had a row, that's all. And b) he'll probably be back tomorrow. You'll be round at mine, whinging about the way he never does anything.' I take the mug and pour in the hot water. It colours up, reminding me of a tampon advert. All that string hanging out.

'But what *about* that?' I say. 'I mean that I do everything for Charlie? Isn't Von right – that it's not healthy?'

'Who cares? It works for you, doesn't it?' says Angela.

'I suppose.'

'You're Taurus and cusp-of-Capricorn. Perfect together.'

It is useful, having a friend who happens to be a lesbian. I have the benefit of her alternative perspective. She believes in romance. She has faith in Charlie. Experience has not taught her to mistrust men.

She believes that women have the bigger problem with commitment. But really, she lives in an alternative universe, where men are irrelevant. In Angela's world, no-one cares about failure. Success is a male term. There are no rules. Only feelings.

I met Angela almost eight years ago, in the local library. I was sitting in Teenage Fiction, and embarrassed to see her glancing over. I did not want anyone to think I was reading adolescent literature. So, I tipped my book up against my stomach to show her that the book I was reading was adult, but that this was the only chair available.

I hoped that she would conclude all this from my smile.

I was surprised, seconds later, to see her standing next to me, commenting on the layout of the library. She was telling me about the confusion of corridors leading to the Feminist and Lesbian literature section.

She looked at me as if we shared a secret, and I returned the knowing look, glad to find a fellow feminist in an age when women were rejecting the fight for women's liberation in all three worlds, in favour of the dull boardroom battle for equality in the workplace.

She thanked me, a touch too profusely, and I returned to my reading.

It was almost two hours later, as I was studying the corridor paintings by local artists, that I met her again.

I was wondering whether to buy a watercolour. I had no art on my walls then – only posters, weighed down by dry Blu-Tac at the corners. Those campaigning posters – *Free John McCarthy; Wanted for crimes against humanity – Margaret Thatcher* – showed not that I was a concerned political activist, but that I had been inactive, and unconcerned, since circa 1989.

I had been skim-reading children's books, and knew that I was now an adult. (Hence, my need for proper artwork.) I knew this because, in all of the books, I had taken the part of the villainous grown-up.

I had wanted to stop those heroic children having fun.

In my opinion, the bumbling PC Goon should have arrested Enid Blyton's Five Find Outers, and locked them away until menopause. William Brown's parents should have had him removed by social services. Never mind Ballet Shoes For Anna – I would have force-fed her hard drugs and taken her joyriding. She spent more time than was healthy, pirouetting.

'That one's good, isn't it?' said a voice, smiling at my side. It came suddenly, and without any warning, and I actually jumped, as characters do in children's books – possibly because I had just finished an Enid Blyton, and had subconsciously adopted the childish mannerisms. Without knowing it, my mouth was probably agape and my eyes agoggle.

I looked at the watercolours. The trouble was, I did not know much about art, and I did not know what I liked. More importantly, I did not know what other people liked.

'Yes, it is.'

'It might even be worth money some day.'

I was persuaded in that instant to buy that painting by Jackie Clayton, year twelve. I nodded, until I realized that she was joking. Then, I continued to nod, but ironically.

'Is there anywhere to get coffee in this place? I need caffeine,' she said, shyly, and I explained that the only chance of a café was out of the building, after a right-turn, and a block of shops up.

'Oh, OK. Thanks,' she said. But I felt that she wanted more from me.

I found myself walking just behind her, on my way to the bus stop. She seemed to slow down, and we began to walk together. I learned that Angela was from Kentish Town, liked acting and astrology, and was a receptionist at a GP's clinic. She talked non-stop, in a giggling-girlie way.

I, too, am friendly. Charlie thinks of it as a fault. I often strike up conversations with strangers. Usually with public servants. I talk, for example, to bus drivers about the sheer heavy weight of traffic. I ask busy shop assistants if they are tired. I have a friend of sorts in the local lollipop lady. We chat about the weather, the size of her lollipop, and the price of sheer tights. It makes me feel less mortal. If people care about me, they will not let me die easily.

But, friendly as I am, I had never been as friendly as this Angela, who asked me whether I wanted to come into the café too. Perhaps because she looked so hopeful, I said Yes, OK, What the heck.

It sounds ludicrous now, but it was only inside – after our orders had gone in – that I realized Angela was a lesbian. It clicked when we chatted about the attractiveness of movie stars such as Isabella Rossellini and Nicole Kidman. I was quite happy to talk about Jennifer Aniston's body, but only in a bitchy way.

'She has lost far too much weight,' I said.

'Oh, but imagine waking up every morning with that body.'

'I suppose,' I agreed.

'Just *lying* there, next to you.'

I must have looked as uncomfortable as I instantly felt. She asked me what was wrong, but it was then that

Angela's sticky bun and our coffees arrived. As the waitress left us, I told her about my new boyfriend, Charlie. She spooned three sugars into her coffee, and winced, visibly. Several bunches of black hair stuck out of the top of her head, like curlicues. They made her appear even more surprised than she was.

I continued to talk about Charlie.

It crossed my mind that, had Angela been a man, I would not have allowed myself to be picked up like this. Certainly, I would not have agreed to coffee in a public place. Not that any man had ever tried to pick me up, cold like that. It crossed my mind: *Why not?*

Then – I could not help it: Angela might have been a lesbian, but she was also a woman – I poured my heart out to her. How my new boyfriend was good-looking. But he spent too much time snorting his namesake. His flat was a mess, and he always asked me to leave after sex.

Angela looked less embarrassed. It was as if she was on more certain ground. She told me that I should end the relationship. First of all, he did not sound as if he was committed. Secondly – and like most men – he did not do any housework. Thirdly, he was a man.

I told her that I liked men.

I explained to her that I was straight – although I felt as if I was saying that I was a pompous half-wit. She went all embarrassed again, bit her upper lip, and said that she did not normally pick up strange women.

I said that I was not that strange.

Angela laughed, and said that she thought I had been trying to pick *her* up. She looked thoughtful. She had never been wrong before, she said. She did not normally like straight women.

I asked her why she thought I was a lesbian – deciding that, once home, I would change my wardrobe and hairstyle. But she said that she could see now – 'it was so obvious, in fact' – that I was not one.

The way she said that made me want to look like a lesbian again.

But not enough to sleep with a woman. Ugh – all those orifices. So I actually joked, 'Can't we just be friends?', and because I said this with a relaxed, wry smile on my face, she looked less worried. She peeled the sticky bun off her plate, and took a bite.

She said, 'I don't think I've ever been friends with a *straight* woman before.'

I laughed too loud at that.

The truth was that I had too many friends, and not enough time to see them. The last thing I wanted was another telephone number in my address book. But I did like the idea of having a gay friend. *A gay man*, because I liked the idea of a man liking me purely for my personality. *A lesbian*, because I liked the idea of a woman liking me for more than my personality.

And I wanted a friend who looked foreign, as Angela did. She had that shade of fat brown skin that announced she could be from anywhere, and nowhere in particular. It appealed to me, because I was so unexotically English, and had only thin-plain-white-people friends. Angela was brown and pretty and massive like one of those delicately embroidered African floor cushions. Angela was confident and focused enough to be her size in today's world of eating disorders and spinning classes.

Yet I did not phone her, and she did not phone me. Two months later, I saw Angela again. At the issuing desk of that same public library. She was behind me in the queue.

She grinned when I turned round. She said that I did not have to worry this time. She had a girlfriend. We went for coffee, and swapped telephone numbers – although I doubt that I would have phoned her. It was only that my editor had recently given me a weekly health and beauty column. He had said that I would need to find a media-friendly doctor to help me answer readers' queries. I remembered that Angela was a GP's receptionist, and called her on the number she had scribbled down. She put me in contact with her boss, Dr Strom, who was 'delighted' to be quoted. She had always wanted to be a media pundit. And I could quote her on that.

Several weeks later, Angela phoned *me*. Her girlfriend had ended their relationship. She needed to talk to a woman who would not try and make her feel loved by making love to her. So we became friends, I think, because she liked the idea of a woman liking her purely for her personality.

I have benefited from having a friend like Angela. She taught me how to behave with Charlie's posh-lot of a family. (Ange was an actress trapped in a GP receptionist's body.) She had appeared in a Noël Coward, and so knew the form. She told me to speak rarely. When I did speak, I was to be careful not to say anything.

I was to carry myself stiffly, like a virgin.

After being in Angela's company, I feel more like a human being. So much so, that I arrange to meet some university friends for Sunday lunch.

Sophie, Ysanne, and Ruth.

Straight as we all are, we always meet in this same, gay pub, in Soho. Ysanne says that, here, we will be left alone.

The men won't hit on us. But I think that that would be true of any pub.

I always wonder why we meet in a place where the music is played at club decibel-levels. We cannot talk; and only Ysanne fits in. She is flat-chested, and dresses like a gay bloke. Her clothes are so skin-tight that they look like a permanent part of her body. Mind you, Ruth looks more out of place than anyone. More and more, these days, she looks like a Conservative politician.

By the time she is fifty, Ruth will look exactly like Ann Widdecombe.

At least, unlike my schoolfriends, these three are prepared to discuss Charlie. Albeit, academically. Sophie will insist on sourcing all of her comments to psychological journals. Ruth is always in charge of the conversation. She is the same as she was in tutorials – i.e. fiercely competitive.

'Angela says we fit together,' I say, daring to interrupt her monologue.

'Oh, *Angela*,' says Ruth, dismissively. 'She has such a warped view of the world.'

Ruth thinks that Angela is a lesbian only to be competitive. Lesbianism, in Ruth's opinion, is the highest form of feminism. She cannot see that Angela loathes any form of competitiveness, and even feels pity for the loser in, say, general elections.

But Ruth thinks that Angela parades her lesbianism. In her eyes, Angela 'became' a lesbian in the same way that she herself became a vegetarian. And vegetarianism for Ruth, although ethically correct, is a constant struggle. Meat, a daily temptation.

I try to keep these three away from Angela. Ruth, for obvious reasons. Sophie, because she intimidates Angela with the way she quietly intellectualizes everything from relationships to world affairs. And Ysanne, because she describes herself as the opposite of a lesbian – as if that is a positive attribute.

Perhaps I too should keep away from these three. I only ever understand about half of Sophie's high-cultural references. Ruth corrects my pronunciation of foreign cities. And Ysanne laughs at the way I dress. I feel, with these friends, as if I am in an early scene from *Pygmalion*.

And yet, if I lose these three, I will leave behind a part of me. I was once as close to Sophie as I am now to Von. I was as ambitious as Ruth. Like everyone else at college, I wanted to *be* Ysanne.

Besides, they offer useful advice.

Ysanne says that, if I want to win Charlie back, it will be easy enough. Men want the woman every other man wants. All I have to do is to make another man fall in love with me.

'Yes,' I laugh. 'That'll be easy enough.'

Even louder than the music, Ruth says that she does not understand why women talk endlessly about relationships when there are four basic points which close the subject:

* If a man is unreliable, one will think him unpredictable and like him all the more.
* If a man is reliable, one will think him dull and like him less.
* If a man is not telephoning, it means he does not want to talk to you. It does not mean that his phone is not working.
* If a man is cruel to you, it does not mean that he is interested. It probably means the opposite.

Men confuse lust with love, says Ruth. They are pro-grammed to fall out of lust quickly.

Women fall in love as regularly as they ovulate, says Sophie. Love happens only to women experiencing a surge of hormones. According to Sophie, love comes to women like clockwork – although some need their machinery oiling. After falling in love, or ovulating, physical changes take place. The woman's temperature rises. Her vaginal mucus becomes wet and slippery. (Ysanne guffaws at this.) Some women experience a pain or ache low in the abdomen. (I laugh, bitterly, at this.) In ovulation, this pain is the result of a slight leakage of fluid as the egg ripens and bursts from the ovary. In love, this pain is because . . .

'Charlie was gorgeous,' I finish.

'Men are only interested in penetration.'

I dispute that. Whereas other men with whom I had relationships before Charlie were legs men, or breast men, or, indeed, men interested only in penetration, Charlie liked every bit of women's bodies.

'Every *slice*, you mean,' says Ruth.

By the time I leave that Soho pub, I am angry not only with Charlie, but with the whole of mankind.

I am still in a 'men, who needs 'em?' mood when Caroline delivers back Maxie – her skin dried-in with chocolate. My evening is spent with my daughter, who is full of energy, glad to be released from her car-seat, after a long, sleepy journey.

I put my child to bed after a midnight bath, realizing that nothing feels nicer than kissing the skin of one's own clean baby. I still have so much, I think, as Maxie stares up at me sleepily.

'Wheresh Daddy?' she asks.

'He's gone to live in another house.'

'No cry.' She touches my lower lip, to stop it trembling.

'I'm fine,' I say, recovering. 'The thing about Daddy is that he loves all women, but can't live with them.'

She pauses to consider this.

'Wheresh Postman Pat?' she asks.

'At the postal sorting office.'

I read her a story about Postman Pat and she listens, rapt, as if, until that moment, I have locked her up alone in a small, dark room without entertainment – so that I feel guilty for not reading to her more often.

Then I remember that children are like that. They can make one feel guilty for drinking tea, or going for a pee. They are unable to understand that the mother has needs of her own. Like my husband, Charlie, in fact. He found it hard to understand that I needed his help reaching orgasm, or the top shelf of the airing cupboard.

But, as I turn off the light, she says, 'Love nice Mummy.'

And I realize that, once you have loved a Maxie, men are far less loveable.

Chapter Three

I wake up feeling wretched. Judd is here, and I tell him that I am not going into work this morning. I feel too ill.

He picks up an empty bottle of wine from my draining board and says that it might explain the sickness. But I say *No*, I have not had a hangover in almost a year of alcoholism.

It is a joke, but Judd does not smile. He puts down the bottle, reminds me that I am pregnant; and asks me whether I am going to get dressed today. I say that he is not *my* childminder but Maxie's.

'*You* need more looking after,' says Judd.

I used to avoid walking past this building. The Camden Leisure Services Community Centre. There was always a group of hard-faced women outside, pushing prams. They seemed to be a fixture, and I wondered who forced these women to assemble here, day after drab day, waiting for those heavy doors to unlatch and open, slowly. Now, of course, I know.

The under-twos are incapable of being indoors: pottering, and pining for Charlie. No – Maxie needs to go somewhere

where she can run, relentlessly and pointlessly, albeit within the confincs of a baby-safe play area.

Usually, Judd takes his son, Solomon, and my Maxie to a daily playgroup at the Camden Synagogue. There, they teach the children songs such as, 'God is here, God is there, God is always everywhere.'

Maxie sings, 'God is almost everywhere.' *God is almoshe ewhere.*

I would have agreed to go there, but that crowd feels it is their right to ask me personal questions. Usually, I like talking about Charlie. He is more attractive than all of their husbands. But Charlie has left me – and I do not want to face those over-familiar faces. So I persuaded Judd to come here with me instead. Here, nobody knows me. I am also curious to see inside this metal hut.

We wait for the doors to be opened.

Judd, uncomfortably.

At the Camden Synagogue he is accepted, despite the fact that he is a man. The mothers there revere him. In their world, he is male and handsome, and that is enough in a world where women barely remember their sexuality. He is attentive, and that is enough in a world where women barely bother to change out of night-clothes.

Judd is their hunter-gatherer. They ask him questions about current affairs, as if he is the only person in the group able to read a newspaper. Yet, in this interdenominational playgroup, the other women look at him as if he is about to steal their baby accessories.

The doors open from the inside. We walk in, and the women turn to see whether he is still there. They clutch their formula bottles and changing bags. They hold cartons of orange juice close to their chests.

Judd thinks that this is because they have seen his skull-cap. 'What are we doing here?' he mutters, uncomfortably, parking the twin buggy at a table inside the cordoned-off coffee area.

This area is roped off, because, if we wish to purchase beverages and/or snacks, we must do so without disturbing the pleasure of our children. Judd unbuckles Maxie and Solomon, and they burst out, running towards the play area, as if we have been cruelly imprisoning them for weeks.

'This place is so depressing,' says Judd, as we sit at one of the metal tables.

It is grim. The walls are trying to be cheerful, but they are plastered with grotesque collages. Someone has painted a sky on the ceiling. *Someone with postnatal depression*, I think – as there is barely any sky bleeding through the clouds. More than any normal ceiling, it makes me feel claustrophobic.

Behind us, I hear the gunshot sound of a metal hatch going up. A woman peers unhappily out of her hole in the wall.

'D'you want anything?' I ask Judd.

'It's all *treif*,' he snarls, because Judd is the only man I have ever met, who snarls. He is the only snarling man I have ever met.

'Well, tea can't be unkosher, can it? It's just hot water and a bag.'

'No thanks.'

I buy a spilling cup of coffee and a packet of chocolate Bourbons. As I sit down, I can feel Judd's disapproval. So I hide the unkosher biscuits on my lap.

We are almost able to watch our children from here. They do disappear from view, but reappear quickly, their bodies intact and unmolested by paedophiles. It is lucky that we are able to see them from our table, as I am in the sluggish seventh week of pregnancy.

Now that I am sitting comfortably, I am unable to stand up.

'Hey, Maxie, he's not interested,' calls Judd, and I see that my daughter is busy following a boy around. Following, following, dementedly. She turns round and sees Judd. Giggles, girlishly.

'Maxie laughs at jokes she doesn't get,' he says, turning back to me. 'No doubt she'll end up in the media, like you.'

'Nothing wrong with that.' I think I should say something to Maxie too, but I cannot think of anything apart from, 'Where's your hairband?'

She was so pretty when we first arrived. But why did I make all that effort?

What thanks do I get? No-one knows how long it takes for me to fashion Maxie after a child in a shop-window poster. No-one knows how difficult it was for me to grip her hairclips into place, flannel her face, brush her teeth, wash and iron her dress, pull on her tights, and polish those shoes a patent black.

Before Maxie came, I presumed that dressing up a doll-like child was a definite perk of motherhood. Yet, I truly do not care what my daughter looks like. I cannot see her sometimes, blinded as I am by mother love, and weariness.

I listen to the conversation between the women on the next table. There is great excitement because someone they know is appearing on TV tonight to talk about the breakdown of her marriage.

One of the women is young enough to be my daughter

– had I decided to have children sooner, rather than wait for my career to establish itself. She is wearing a stretch top that has stretched as far as it is going to go. Its fur rim looks tired from all that stretching. One more meal, and her beaks-for-breasts will poke out of that top – like newborn birds out of their nest.

'She's gonna be famous now,' says Beaks-for-breasts.

'Yeah,' says the pretty, dark-haired woman beside her. She is wearing a cut-off T-shirt, and the sleeves look as if they had been chopped off in a hurry – just in time for this season.

'Clo-*eee*,' shouts Beaks-for-breasts at her charge. She and T-shirt are clearly nannies, rather than mothers. They are too thin to have squeezed out babies, and are not half-watching their children for signs of gross motor development.

'They're all right.' The woman bags out her T-shirt as if to empty it of sweat. 'D'you think she'll get to meet *Shelley*?'

I turn my chair to face the play-area, and watch in slow motion as a boy pushes my daughter out of the playbus. Maxie falls on to a soft mat, and I stand up, my arms outstretched, as she comes crying to Judd.

I try not to care that she seeks comfort from Judd, rather than from me, watching her eyes squirt real tears.

I am just pleased to see that her body works. In all honesty, I like it even when she defecates. I am filled with wonder that she operates properly, like a real child. She is mine – and thus should be defective. All of my possessions break, sooner or later. The video camera broke down before the end of my honeymoon. When I was a child, all of my dolls were missing limbs.

'Buus,' cries my fully functioning daughter. Judd pulls

Maxie up on to his lap. As a diversionary tactic, he gives her a kosher rice cake.

I did not know that rice cakes could be unkosher.

Solomon must have smelt the word *snack*, because he runs over. His face is half-stuck with wet sand, but Judd does not clean him up. Solomon is often dirty. Sometimes, I suspect that Judd orders him to roll in the garden, if only to prove what a great childhood he is giving his son. 'Children shouldn't be clean all the time,' he once said. 'Filthy play's good for them.'

I replied that this is true, but it is not good for one's soft furnishings.

The children run off again, spilling crumbs, and I say, 'What do *you* think, Judd – I mean, about Charlie leaving?'

'Well, you know what I think.'

'No, I don't.'

I do not know what Judd thinks, because he suffers from conversational interruptus. Every time I bring up an interesting subject, such as my personal life, he changes it to one that is more obviously political. Judd tries to relax into his hard chair. But he looks even more uncomfortable than usual, as I wait impatiently for his answer.

'Charlie's non-Jewish, that's what I think.'

'Oh, not that again.'

'Well, it's important. I mean, he's from a different world. How can he possibly understand you – your history, your culture? The upper classes are *notoriously* anti-Semitic. I'm surprised he was allowed to marry you in the first place.'

'Charlie wasn't upper class. He's more upper upper-middle. Or maybe lower-upper.'

'No matter how much you believe you're assimilated, Lucy, you have to accept that you're Jewish.' He tuts as

I take apart my unkosher Bourbon, scraping the cream centre with my teeth.

'Stop looking at me like that,' I say. 'I can eat what I want. I'm only half-Jewish anyway.'

'Your mother's Jewish. So, according to Jewish law, you are too. The truth is, assimilation's useless. The Berlin Jews tried that. A lot of them were salon Jews; they were barely aware of their religion. Lawyers, bankers, businessmen. But Hitler soon taught them that they were Jewish – rounding them up, transporting them in cattle trains, starving them and their children, stripping them naked in the ice-cold, prodding them into gas ch . . .'

'Yes, I know,' I interrupt, embarrassed. He is talking so loudly. Whenever he becomes aggressively anti-racist, I feel as if he is inciting racial hatred.

Judd once said that he would never again marry out of the faith. 'I'd just be finishing off the job for Hitler. Marrying out is the fastest way to kill off the Jewish people.'

That sounds quite racist to me. I was surprised that my mother disagreed. She has suffered so from Jewish laws of purity. But she likes Judd. She thinks that he is 'a natural' with Maxie. 'What's wrong with him wanting to marry a Jewish woman?' she said.

I only wish Judd would be less loud in public places. But he is anxious to uncover any anti-Semites and blame them for the Holocaust. That was what he tried to do to me when I first met him at the Camden Liberal Synagogue Toddlers and Tiny Tears group almost two years ago.

Maxie was six weeks old that day.

I was on maternity leave from the *Chronicle*, and bored. (Motherhood was meant to be anything but dull.) I wanted to be with adults, and the synagogue group was the only daily 'babies welcome' event in my *Camden Children's Directory*. I wanted to be with other mothers, to enable them to admire my baby's genius and beauty. But I now realize that they were all doing the same, with babies that looked exactly like my own – i.e.: fat and bald.

Besides, I am Jewish. (My mother is Jewish.) I had every right to be there, having been brought up eating Jewish soul food. *Gefilte fish, kneidlach, matzo brei,* and *lokshen pudding.* I even know some Yiddish. *Mensch, macher, schvitzing,* and *schmaltzy.* (Gentleman; leader; sweating; and cheesy.)

But, really, this is all I know of Judaism. Fattening food, and a smattering of the vocabulary. So I felt pretty fraudulent that day, at the synagogue Toddlers and Tiny Tears session.

My Tiny Tears was colicky that day, and vibrating in my arms like an electric toothbrush. When I walked in, I was half-scared that somebody would spot me as unorthodox. I would stand out, I thought, as non-Jewish looking. I am naturally fair, for God's sake, with an upturned stub of a nose.

Never had I seen so many women, in one room, who did not appear to care about their appearance. They were all fat and stuffed into black leggings.

I immediately felt at home, going over to one smiling woman who asked me what Maxie's name was. Then, why. I explained that her father named her after a violent, if mischievous, female character from the Australian soap opera, *Prisoner Cell Block H*.

The woman pretended to smile, and sidled away. She joined a group of cross-legged women, all competing over the pain they had suffered during labour. There was a tie-break between two of them. Both had almost died during their deliveries.

Their nursing breasts had been sucked, they said, to look like shrivelled bunches of grapes.

But it was clear from Woman One's expression that there was to be no camaraderie until a clear winner emerged. Woman Two raised the stakes by announcing her incontinence. But this was nothing. I knew, from Woman One's triumphant smile, that she had long since lost all control of her bowels.

Women Three, Four, Five and Six gazed at her with a new respect. Meanwhile, their babies crawled around and over them, like bugs. Occasionally, one or other would be swatted.

'BEN-JEEE.' 'LOU-EEE.' 'ZAAAAK.'

Woman Two had not quite given up. She laughed that she had had her baby six months ago, and was still not having sex with her husband. Woman One saw the seriousness of Two's statement, and laughed even louder. She had not had sex, she confessed, since her first child was born, four years ago.

'How did Daniel happen then?' asked Woman Five.

Women Four and Six looked at her as if to say: *Where have you been?* How could she not know that Danny had been conceived after artificial insemination? (There had been all that fuss over whether she should consult the rabbis to check the sperm's origins.) Woman One had been talking about it since the day they went to that clinic to have her husband's sperm sorted. 'Washed', she called it. Good from bad. Unfortunately, more bad than good. Woman One had had to visit a sperm bank.

I felt that I had no right to this information. I had

not even been properly introduced. They only knew my baby's name.

I did not then know that that was enough.

I sat there, wondering where all the men were, post-feminism. I felt as if I was with Angela's group of friends – although there were subtle differences. Because Angela and her friends often talk about men. Or rather, they ridicule them. Angela might say that men smell of horses, or sheep. One of her friends might respond, 'Yes, like red meat.' But, with the synagogue women, it was as if men did not exist. Or rather, it was as if there was no reason for their existence.

Maxie was crying unnecessarily. I had tried all manner of scream-prevention methods, feeding, rocking and soothing her, but still she screamed. So I made my excuses and rushed my baby to the bathroom, where I changed her from a clean nappy to one half-drenched in a leaking carton of formula milk.

I had breast-fed for a while but I have size 32F breasts and it had felt unseemly.

Only those women whose breasts are all nipple look natural with a baby attached. It looks vulgar if the breast-flesh bulges out of the baby's sucking mouth. It is like fat bulging out of knickers.

I had wanted to breast-feed only to separate myself from the common masses (I abandoned my Essex accent for the same snobbish reason), and it seemed pointless to continue, if it made me appear more coarse. Plus, it felt far too erotic an act to perform on a three-hourly basis – no matter what government health department pamphlets say.

I was still in the tiny Ladies. It was studded with panty-liner and tampon machines, but had no baby-changing mat. I almost cried as diarrhoea oozed out of the sides of Maxie's nappy. I do not like diarrhoea; it makes me feel that my baby is faulty.

'*Shit,*' I said aloud, wondering why I had been left with so much responsibility.

It was the biggest responsibility I had ever been given. I had never gained any position of authority. Even as a Brownie-Guide I did not make it to be sixer. Miss Jackson felt that I was irresponsible. So I was always the seconder, assisting Danielle Carruthers.

Yet I was suddenly being left in charge of a human being. A human being entirely dependent on me for her wellbeing. I felt certain that it would not be long before my baby was taken from me. By Miss Jackson, or her doppelgänger, in the guise of a kindly health visitor.

In the toilet, my hands were covered in excrement. But there was no time to cry – I had a baby in my arms. In those days, I had neither the time, nor the energy, to do anything – even if it was to attend a course of classes for women with postnatal depression.

It took all of my energy to lock Maxie into her car-seat.

Despite my six weeks of motherhood, I still felt like a man-in-a-movie, left for the first time in charge of a baby. In charge, and incompetent. It was like being back in primary school arts-and-crafts. No matter that I had the most imagination and zeal, I still came away with a papier-mâché project that was more mâché than papier.

Nothing was ever worth taking home. 'Whose is this?' Miss Roberts had once asked, taking out of the kiln my cracked china mask. It fell apart in her hands, and she added, 'What's left of it.' I had had to watch dull and plodding children produce perfectly formed masks, while my own was sadly disfigured. I came home crying to my mother, who complained to the teacher. From then on, I was allowed to sit reading a book, as all the other children made a mess with brightly coloured stars and glue.

In the synagogue Ladies, I wondered whether – left in my hands – Maxie would inevitably grow into a broken and half-cracked adult.

It was ridiculous. I had always been considered a maternal person. I had been expert with my Gants Hill friends' kids, brimming over with good ideas for their discipline. Plus, during my pregnancy, I had studied the baby manuals as if for a GCSE. I could recite the way a newborn's faeces changed colour. It was just like school chemistry. Brown to green to black and back to green.

Yes, I was fine in theory. But the practical part of motherhood was too repetitive. Feed, change, rock, pat on the back. It was as if I was having a recurring nightmare where I needed to take an exam I thought I had passed. Feed, change, wind, rock, feed, change, wind, rock. No time for sleep.

I was so tired that the bones around my eyes hurt.

I had no time to shop, let alone use the toilet. Mum offered to take care of Maxie, but I could not be without my baby. I felt as if I had left a part of me behind. When she did start to sleep through the night, I myself could not sleep.

I worried that my daughter would not wake in the morning.

I needed to be with my baby, but there were times, I confess, when I fantasized about throwing her off a cliff. Her organs, floating down. Me, running down fast to rescue her. Because I loved my daughter so much. If that was love; it hurt so much.

In that synagogue Ladies, I buttoned up her designer

Babygro. Coffee stained the designer's name. I looked in the mirror, and mouthed the word *Help*, wondering what had become of that sexy, young columnist that had been me. Was she still out there at parties? Having fun, as I sat hearing screams – not knowing whether those screams were mine or Maxie's.

I no longer knew why people wanted to be out having fun, when they could be at home, catching up on their sleep.

So many myths surround motherhood, and I perpetuated them all in those initial weeks. I set up the blissful picture of Mother-and-Daughter before greeting any visitors.

I put Maxie – scrawny, and with a nappy half falling off – in her cot. I Hoovered the house and cleaned and scrubbed, and cooked something that smelled delicious. I sloshed baby-oil over Maxie. I fed her full, cramming her into an all-in-one pink outfit, with mittens. I half smothered her in a hat.

I played classical music. I brewed a smell of fresh coffee.

Picture the scene. A house immaculate, and a mother-in-make-up. A husband, albeit asleep, in the next room. Baby smells, baby sounds, baby smiles everywhere. Mother, generous, passing baby around. Baby, attractive in other women's arms. Mother, more motherly. Baby, more attractive, further away.

My friends all bought into the myth that I had it all. 'Oh, you're so lucky, Lucy.'

Lucky Lucy could have stared in that Ladies mirror for hours. But for how long was it dignified to stare, in public, at one's reflection? *Not this long*, I thought, and bent down to pick up Maxie from the bathroom floor, my body weak and painful after childbirth. Torn, down there.

When I went back into the assembly hall, I decided to join a different group of women. To that end, I circled the hall for a while, feigning interest in the Passover posters. I then sat down underneath a collage of The Red Sea Parting.

I tried to find an opening into the group of women, but they were tight-knit. Central to the group was – surprisingly – a man. He was wearing a pale-pink skullcap, which fell from the side of his head. The skullcap was made out of fine wool. A name was knitted around its edge.

Judd.

His blond hair was thick and dirty looking. He had a slightly broken nose, like a boxer's, slightly spoiling his (very) good looks. Blue, pale eyes, so probing that my eyes glanced down instead at his lower half.

I found myself staring at his Chino'd crotch, creased from sitting.

A serious toddler was attached to him. He did not toddle, this boy, but listened to Judd, who was holding forth about a film he had seen the night before. Was it right, he was asking, for a satire to be made about the Holocaust? So many innocents, dead. Their surviving relatives alive to witness such a mocking, mockery of a movie.

'Did any of your family die in the Holocaust?' I heard myself asking.

I am trained as a journalist, and good at infiltrating groups of people. But this works best at parties, and when everyone has been drinking. It also works best with groups of men, all wanting to have sex with me.

I was still on the outside of Judd and his mother-disciples.

77

'Why?' he mumbled, as if he found the question inappropriate.

'Well, I just wondered,' I said, and he looked suddenly scornful.

'Try, six million of our people.'

I looked down quickly, pretending interest in my baby.

I wonder how I might have reacted then to be told that this man would become my baby's childminder. ('Well, *my* people anyway,' he added.) I think I would have been horrified. ('I am *half*-Jewish,' I said – so he looked at me as if I had failed his test.) Throughout that Toddlers and Tiny Tears session, Judd patronized me, ridiculed me, and argued with me. He turned the mothers against me.

I confided in one, for example, that I found life difficult with a baby. But the woman stared at me and said, 'Well, I see you've had time to put your make-up on.'

After the session, I sat at the wheel of my car, listening to my colicky Maxie. I would have turned the engine on, but I could not see for crying.

There was a knock at my window, and it was Judd. I quickly wiped my eyes, and wound down the window. 'Are you OK?' he asked.

'Mmm,' I said, still wiping.

'You don't look it.' He stood back from the car, and smiled. 'Can I come in?' he asked, and I opened the car door.

'Mind the formula.'

'That's fine. You coming in, Sol?'

Solomon climbed on his lap. He was sucking something ragged.

Judd said, 'It's hard with a newborn, isn't it?'

He said this with such genuine sympathy that I did not tell him I was crying about my husband, who had left me.

I nodded and said, 'The last thing I needed was that group of women. I really don't know why I came.'

'They're OK. It was only because you walked in looking so glamorous.'

'Hardly,' I said, pleased. 'They're just judgemental. *You're* judgemental,' I added, candidly.

'Oh, am I?'

'All that crap about how children need their mothers at home with them. What the fuck do you know? Mothers are better off fulfilled at work, in my opinion.'

I was yearning to be back at work.

I wanted once more to wear the badge of the working woman: the suit.

I wanted to be on a train, patting my swollen briefcase. Or at my desk, in that womb-like office environment – surrounded by my computer, address card index and telephone. My paperweight. At lunchtime, spilling out on to the streets with all the other suits. Pampering myself in the gym. Raising all my concerns at staff meetings. I wanted to be with colleagues, careful not to hurt my feelings. Bosses, caring about my welfare.

'What I said was that mothers ought to *live* with their kids. Not be with them twenty-four-seven. I meant, Solomon just might have been better off, had his mother not left him and his father to live with some yok at the office. That was all.'

I digested what he had said. It took a few, surprised, seconds.

'I'm sorry,' seemed appropriate.

'Why?' He grunted. 'Did you help arrange her escape?'

'I don't think you should use words like yok,' I said. 'My father's a non-Jew. A *yok*, to you.'

He said, 'So's mine, actually.'

79

I smiled.

'So, you were a fraud in there too? Only *half*-Jewish? Oh dear; what would your women worshippers say?'

He laughed as if I had hit a nerve. He pretended to think about the question, then said, 'I'm sure they'd say that being half-Jewish was good enough. But then, my women worshippers are all optimists.'

'Or pessimists, depending which way you look at it.'

– Again, he laughed that gruff laugh of his.

'Look, I'm sorry about my attitude in there,' he said. 'I get pissed off sometimes. With everyone.'

'I'm sorry too. So do I.'

'It wasn't me who upset you, was it?'

'No.' I decided to be honest. 'My husband's left me, that's all.'

'Oh God, really?' He tutted, and paused. 'I mean, bloody hell. You've just had a . . . Mind you, it's what Clare did to me.'

'Yeah, well. I'm sure we're part of some national trend. Anyway, no doubt he'll be back tomorrow. This isn't the first time Charlie's walked out. And it's not as if he's taken any of his stuff. Look, d'you want to come back to my place for coffee?'

'That,' he said, 'would be very nice.'

En route to my flat, I learned that Judd lived two blocks away from me, in Mornington Crescent. He was writing a situation comedy. His wife had left him because of Judd's born-again orthodox Judaism. But was that any reason for her to have left Solomon?

Judd asked me who was going to take care of Maxie when I went back to work. I confessed that I had not thought that far ahead.

I watched him holding Solomon and my six-week-old

80

Maxie. He had soothed Maxie to sleep, all the while entertaining Solomon. So I asked him, on an impulse, to be Maxie's nanny.

Judd looked down at the sleeping, shyly breathing, Maxie.

He tried to smile, but his face fell back into a sneer.

'I suppose someone has to teach your daughter that she's Jewish,' he said. 'Or she'll find out that she's been living a lie all her life – like I did.'

'So you'll do it?' I was surprised how right the agreement felt. I had not been this confident when I employed Katie as my cleaner. 'I mean, I'll pay you the going rate.'

'I could use the money.'

Judd Drexler became my childminder, and, shamefully, I did not even ask for references. Unashamedly, he outlined his religious restrictions. He would not cook in, or eat in, my unkosher flat. He could not work on the Sabbath. So, if I wanted him to take care of Maxie after Friday's sunset, he would have to do so unpaid.

I was happy to go along with his specifications – although it sounded to me as if he made up the rules as he went along.

I asked him to tell me more about himself. And so I learned that Judd had reached the grand old age of twenty-nine when he discovered that, according to Jewish law, he was Jewish. His mother, Eva, had been three years old when Hitler came to power. She had escaped Nazi Germany on the *kindertransport* – an evacuation programme of Jewish children.

By the time the war had ended, and the horror of the Holocaust became generally known, Eva barely remembered her Jewish parents. They were a haze. They were *best forgotten*, according to her adoptive parents – Judd's 'grandparents' – who had taken Eva to church throughout her childhood. They had had her converted, baptised, confirmed.

Judd's parents had taken him to church throughout his childhood. They had had him baptised, confirmed.

He had married Clare in a church. It was only when she was expecting Solomon that Judd began to quiz his mother about her family. At first, Eva refused to answer. But he wore her down with his questions. Eventually, Eva revealed that her birth parents had died in the Holocaust. But that he should keep his origins a secret. 'It's not something you advertise,' she said. 'Being Jewish.'

Her son was horrified that she should have kept such a secret from him. He said, 'So, my entire life is a lie?' He studied the Holocaust, and his Jewish-Czech origins. He joined an organization that sought to bring irreligious Jews 'back' to orthodoxy.

Judd sought answers in the Jewish religion, and learned how to kosher a chicken. He was taught the Talmud. One year later, and he had changed his name from John Lester to Judd Drexler. Judd Drexler, after his maternal grandfather, who had died in the gas chambers at Birkenau, with his two sons, Solomon and Sam.

He went to Israel, and found out more about his mother's family.

Judd told Eva that her parents had tried to escape Czechoslovakia with Eva's brothers soon after she was evacuated. But Hitler's troops invaded before the Drexlers managed their escape. Only Eva's aunt had survived the war. She had emigrated first to the United States, and then to Israel. She lives in Tel Aviv. It was from this great-aunt that Judd learned about his origins.

Eva's first cousin died in Terezin – the concentration

camp where they were first taken. Her father and two brothers died in Birkenau. Her mother, Chana, (*Don't tell me, I don't want to hear*) was taken from Auschwitz to Bergen-Belsen. There – three days before the camp was liberated – she died of typhus. April 12. (*Anne's my mother, full stop. Enough.*) Chana's brother-in-law died after the war ended. He ate too quickly after liberation. (*John, why are you doing this?*)

Her son had said, 'My name is Judd.'

Now, I watch Judd building a tower of bricks for his son to bash down. Maxie is scared of the sound of bricks crashing. Her fears are far more logical than my own. She is scared of aeroplanes falling out of the sky. She is scared of being sucked inside a vacuum cleaner. She is scared of flies; Big Ears; strangers smiling; and of people leaving, when they go, forever.

'Mummy, Mummy,' shouts Maxie.

My daughter runs over to me. She stops and wraps her arms around my legs. I feel her small arms around my knees, my faith in mother-love restored. Maxie has such edible hands. They are so fleshy. I take a moment to contemplate resigning from my job, so that I can spend my days being hugged. The nannies at the next table look at me approvingly.

Not for the first time, I think how sanctified mother-hood is.

And rightly so.

'Did you understand what Maxie wanted?' asks Judd, coming over.

'Oh yeah; of course.'

I look at my daughter, understanding her completely. She has my way of attention-seeking. She has my allergies.

To cats and to peas. She has my addictive personality. I am addicted to alcohol and stationery. I cannot stop buying new lined notepaper. She is addicted to cranberry juice and Flumpy. She has my legs. No knees, just fat thighs down to the ankle.

'I told her that if she asked you nicely you'd give her a biscuit,' says Judd. 'The Grodz ones, in my rucksack.'

'Oh yes, of course,' I say, looking at my daughter.

I misunderstood her completely.

I search through Judd's bag – all of those Jewish-studies books – for biscuits. As I hand one to Maxie, I realize how unlike me she is.

I did not imagine I would have a child like that – with sleek hair and dark eyes. I thought that she would look like me, writ small. A mess of wavy, fair hair. Pale blue eyes. But Maxie has not even inherited any of my hereditary illnesses. She is in perfect health, like all of the Wallises. Because that is what generations of money can buy you – genetic superiority.

It is as with my flat. Before I moved in, I had imagined my ideal home, but Charlie came along, and I compromised. His furniture. His gadgets. His idea of style cluttering up my flat. Now it looks less mine than his. His, frankly.

'What do you say, Max?' asks Judd, helping his son into a chair.

'Tank shoo.'

'Good girl.'

'OK, go and give half to Solomon,' Judd says.

Sometimes I feel that my daughter is less mine than Judd's. His, frankly. I feel sometimes as if I am going through the business of pregnancy, simply to give him another child to play with.

We watch Maxie running off, as if she has somewhere

to go, and Judd asks, 'Will Charlie go for custody, d'you think?'

I snort, and say, 'I doubt he'll even want access.'

Judd looks angry.

'How can he feel nothing for his own child? Even *Clare* wanted to see Solomon; and she was postnatally depressed. I think she realized that you can't just pop in and out of motherhood; so I persuaded her to leave us alone. She was pregnant again anyway – by that computer salesman.' He sighs. 'We should never have got married. She even drove a German car. I should have seen . . . I tell you, anti-Semitism's never far below the surface.'

'Does Clare want access now?'

'She lives in the States with her new husband. And their kid. So, no.'

'Angela says Charlie'll be back.'

'Well, she could be right, I suppose. What do you think?'

'I think I agree with Von. He's not worth having back.'

'Mmm.'

'But that doesn't stop me wanting him back. I want him back,' I whine, realizing again that I am a soon-to-be divorcée in my early thirties.

I look at the teenage nannies at the next table. Beaks-for-breasts has her arms folded tight, bandaging her chest; and I wonder how I can possibly compete with such young women.

I will have to spend even more time exfoliating my dead skin.

'D'you think Maxie'll be OK?' asks Judd, interrupting my thoughts. He looks even more anxious than he usually does. 'With her Dad gone?'

'Oh yes,' I say, wondering whether I will be OK, feeling

like Solomon's stacker toy. If you remove one piece too quickly, the whole edifice is at risk of falling apart. 'She probably won't even notice,' I say, grimly.

'Well, you never know with kids, do you? They don't exactly express themselves in the way we do. She might start having awful tantrums.'

'*I've* had those,' I smile, watching my daughter laugh with Judd's son as Solomon takes her hand.

'I'll keep an eye on her,' says Judd, and I think, if only other women knew how easy it was to be the perfect mother.

Excellent childcare.

The phone rings, and I race to it, knowing that it will be Charlie.

But my mother's voice says, 'Is he back yet?'

'No, I told you when you dropped off Maxie, he won't be coming back. Not this time.'

'He will, Lucy.'

'No, I told you on Saturday, he's taken his stuff.' My voice shrinks to a small: 'He's talking about divorce.'

The receiver feels huge, sucking up my voice. But my mother is there, telling me what to do. I might be thirty-two, but I am still her child, and her responsibility. I need to:

   a) give it time.
   b) see him, as if by surprise, looking perfect. Make him realize what he is missing.
   c) give in to his demands.

Chapter Four

I am sitting on the tube, on my way to work. There is a ticket inspector four people down, and I feel that familiar sense of panic and guilt. This, despite the fact that I have a valid season ticket.

'Tickets ready, please.'

I had this feeling throughout university. Punting, public-school, Pimms-drinking students looked at me suspiciously. I felt as if they were about to expose me as an interloper. This, despite the fact that I had the four A grades required for entrance.

'Thank you, love.'

The inspector leers at my ticket. He has clean hair and a strong, cowboy jaw, so I weigh him up as a potential next husband. Since Charlie left my life, a month ago, I have been looking at all men as prospective partners. Only half-jokingly. The man who allowed me into his lane of the motorway, maybe. Or the bloke who stopped me in the street, this morning, to ask me several personal questions – because he was conducting a survey about pedestrianization. Or, perhaps, the man opposite me, who is reading a foreign-language newspaper. Two stops ago, delays to all destinations were announced on the Northern line, and that clever man with an interest in current affairs smiled at me, in camaraderie.

Clever he may be, but he does not realize that he is treading in a pool of pee, or apple juice. It is streaming through the grooves in the tube floor, forming a puddle at his feet. It smells sweet, in among the usual train smells of dust and sour breath. I prefer this smell to the one I have at home, of baby lotion and excrement.

But I cannot afford to be too picky about husbands. The truth is, Charlie could not have left me at a more terrible time. I am hardly going to find another love interest now. Men treat pregnant women as if they have opted out of womanhood for the duration.

Yes, I am eleven weeks pregnant; and beginning already to lose sight of what is important. My dyed-blonde hair desperately needs retouching. My cheeks are puffy. But I do not have the energy to shop for beauty products.

It is as if a tree is growing inside me, spreading its roots. I feel sick every time I walk past Mothercare and see those car-seats hanging in the window. The bars on the cots. The child-safety locks. But there is no-one to blame but the baby.

My first pregnancy was different. It felt exciting, if nothing else. It was a way to feel alive without having to take mind-altering drugs. Those forty weeks passed so quickly – perhaps because I was with Charlie.

I still miss him. Charlie. He took up so much space, and the flat seems empty without him. His toothbrush-holder in the shape of a tooth. His entire collection of Mr Men books. His dirty, stainless-steel juice-press, which resembles an alien. Even the kitchen is different without my husband's smeared plates piled up. Blobs of ketchup on big, greasy dishes.

It is all over, bar divorce proceedings.

I am not even looking forward to taking maternity leave. I enjoy working. I enjoy being a part of working London; and this is my favourite part of the day. Travelling to work. Travelling home is not the same. Then, everyone is tired, and creased. Then, there are never any seats.

The tube is a great leveller; I could be anyone important in this outfit. No-one need know that I am a mother – although Maxie's fingerprints are all over me.

I keep finding pieces of Fuzzy Felt sticking to my suit.

No-one need know that I am pregnant. The jacket of my suit covers the fact that my zip will not fasten. This weight gain is the result either of pregnancy, or of eating too many refined sugars.

I have been trying to explain to my daughter that I am pregnant. Because I feel as if I am betraying her by having another Maxie. I put her hand on my bloated stomach, saying, 'There's a baby in here.' But she looks at me sceptically, as if to say, 'No, Mummy, just fat.'

The woman sitting in the row of seats opposite me is talking to herself.

I cannot help but smile; and the woman sneers at me, acting as if I am the one who is strange, for smiling. Suddenly, I realize why. The woman was not talking to herself, but to a hands-free mobile phone.

So, I look out of the tube window, seeing Mrs Leslie's face, staring back at me.

Mrs Leslie lived in the basement flat below mine.

Oh, Mrs Leslie. Two weeks ago, two men came through her window. One black, one white. One taller than is average. They were seen escaping with a 24-inch colour TV. They must have found nothing else of value.

One of the policemen who came to interview me said,

'Mrs Leslie's window was open. There was no forced entry. When they found her in there – an older lady – they probably pushed her. She died from a wound to the head. I'd say it was opportunistic.'

He said this as if he himself could not have resisted such an opportunity.

'They wouldn't have meant to kill her,' said the other policeman – as if he knew anything. (They both seemed so stupid.) He had a photofit of a face. It was so even that certain features did not seem to belong to him.

Usually, I suffer from insomnia. But I am pregnant, and so was deep asleep in a three-am-at-a-nightclub sense. I heard nothing.

Thank God Maxie was at my parents' house.

My father, who can never see bad in anyone, says he pities the lads who killed Mrs Leslie. He can only imagine how they must be feeling. They would not have wanted much more than a colour TV. Yet, poor things, now they have blood on their hands.

My father is like that. He finds excuses even for the Holocaust. In the 1920s – as a result of their defeat in World War One – the Germans suffered terrible economic depression. They were looking for a leader to give them back their pride. They were looking for a scapegoat, he said.

'They're not excuses, they're reasons,' I said.

'They're not even reasons,' said Judd.

I told Dad that it was Mrs Leslie I felt sorry for.

Oh, lovely Mrs Leslie. She backed my planning application to paint the window-sills. She offered me unlimited access to her back garden. Maxie needed fresh air, she said. So I was to treat the lawn as communal. Mrs Leslie heard the rows between Charlie and me. She always took my side against his. She told me that I should leave him before my beauty disappeared.

I cannot believe that Mrs Leslie is not merely dead, but murdered. A News In Brief. Norma Leslie.

It is no wonder that I am so scared. My home feels like Dorothy's windblown shack in *The Wizard of Oz* – all walls off. I have been bunkering down. On police advice, I added window locks. But it does not prevent the fear. It does not stop me thinking about the murder. The fist slamming into Mrs Leslie. I imagine the blood. I picture her face. At night, that frightened face morphs into my own.

I spent years saving up to buy my own flat. I spent weeks persuading the building society to lend me triple my worth.

I breathed with relief when the contracts were exchanged. I thought that, whatever happened, I was now a homeowner. Now, I could buy lifestyle accessories without worrying that they clashed with the wallpaper.

I could tear down any wallpaper.

I could stop worrying about my renewal of short-term leases for flats such as the one in Shepherd's Bush, where everything was shabby. The wallpaper was striped, the carpet floral. There were so many clashing patterns that it resembled a roomful of Albanian refugees.

Even the pouffe had lost its puff.

The curtains were so old. They had been a backdrop to too many terrible lives. The lining fell out of the bottom like an old lady's slip. I always felt that those curtains would be best put out of their misery – allowed down, and shoved in a box at the back of some sofa.

By the time I moved out, everything needed throwing out. Even the kettle. The element had gone. I was having to boil up water in a pan. The crockery looked as if it had come straight out of a charity shop. It was covered in food stains.

But then the mice came to my newly bought, and redecorated, home in Camden. They ignored the traps I set for them. They multiplied inside the airing cupboard. They defecated inside my bread bin. I could only relax after the men from the council had killed them all, by laying down poison. I made myself comfortable again. I made myself at home. I even bought a throw.

But, Mrs Leslie is dead; and I am now stuck in a building where someone was murdered.

I immediately called my mother. She is my mum, after all, and always on call. Besides, she has always taught me the key stuff of life – such as the application of toenail polish, and make-up. She was my birthing partner, telling me not to push Maxie out.

It's too soon, she said.

My father answered the phone, saying that, if I was that scared, perhaps I should move 'home'. Then, my mother came on the line. She said that I was not to worry – Dad was being ridiculous. 'You're stronger than he thinks,' she said. To Dad, she added: 'She's more of a Fine than a Fletcher.'

But I am not strong like my mother. She brought up more than one child without the benefit of a washing machine, disposable nappies, a nappy bin, videotapes, a dishwasher, ready-to-drink formula milk, a bottle-warmer, a Magimix, a travel cot, computerized toys, childcare, a baby-bath, Marmite-flavoured rice cakes, baby massage, National Childbirth Trust support groups, a full-time job, pop-up books, homeopathy, grandparents, equal-opportunity legislation, and an able-bodied husband.

When her children were at school, she started a slimming

business. She worked from home, and built up Slimco, which now employs a staff of 25. Women phone my mother all the time, asking for advice. Throughout my childhood, I heard Mum on the telephone, telling fat women what to eat. Her company had its own stock rhyming lines:

'Chocolate biscuits are a sin. Now don't you dare go near that tin.'

'Go easy on the sugar – otherwise you'll end up bigger.'

Her business enabled her, three years ago, to buy a mock-Tudor detached house. I tease her by calling it the Slimco house. She calls it her dream home.

My mother's dreams kept her going, through the rows she had had with her parents. They said that my mother would never amount to anything – not by marrying a non-Jewish bus driver with no money.

I have not met my mother's parents. To them, my brother and I are the Unborn, because our mother had married out of the Jewish faith. When Mum married Dad, my 'grandparents' declared her dead.

When I was twelve, Mum's father died. Her mother phoned to tell her about 'Jack's' death.

'Your Grandma Ellie; you have her face,' Mum said to me, playing and replaying her own mother's answering machine message. 'I shouldn't be calling you he would hate me to do this but I thought you should know anyway that your father's dead it's your mother.'

So, that's my grandma, I thought. She did not pause for commas, or full stops. No matter how many times my mother played back the message, still I could not detect any feeling.

Still, Mum took me and my brother to the synagogue (*shul*, she called it) in Gants Hill so that she could say *Yizkor*

– the prayer for the dead. 'He would have loved you, your Grandpa Jack,' she said to me, with wet eyes. 'You have his brains.'

But we left before the service ended. We left before the best bit when everyone got to eat the peanuts and fishballs that were laid out, on trestle tables. My mother said that she felt uncomfortable surrounded by so much hypocrisy. 'And I'm schvitzing in this suit.'

I could not survive without a mother. Without Mum. She is so perfect a role model that I am sometimes tempted to ask her to raise Maxie.

Cut out the middle woman.

In the seventies, Mum set up a successful business. In the eighties, she spent several weeks occupying Greenham Common. In the nineties, she helped to organize a Bosnian aid convoy, feeding refugees from Srebrenica. She has built up so much. The business. The children. The handsome husband. (Dad is still almost entirely dark-haired. The few silver streaks looked painted on, as if by a make-up artist.) She pushed one of her children through college, and another through a fast-track, retail training course, while taking an Open University degree in English Literature. She knows far more than me about life and sixteenth-century poetry.

'It is scary,' I said to Mum, on the phone, after Mrs Leslie's murder.

'But that woman lived in the basement.'

'And I'm on the ground floor. It's even easier to break in here.'

'But what do you have for them to take?'

She would not be scared, my mother. When she saw that mouse in my flat, she strangled it. I watched her. She caught it in a beaker. Then, she picked it up and squeezed tight, her hand around its neck. She said that she was sick of waiting for it to eat the chocolate on the trap.

'That's not the point. Mrs Leslie didn't have anything either, but she . . .'

'But you can't live that way. Scared all the time of dying.'

My mother does not live her life scared all the time of dying. She refuses to wear a seatbelt in a car which urgently needs servicing. Despite the Government ban, she eats beef on the bone. Despite her parents' ban, she eats non-kosher food, and married a non-Jew. She smokes sixty cigarettes a day, all of them socially. True, the smoking, and the drugs, have spoiled her looks. My mother was once as pretty as the young Marianne Faithful. But now, she looks like Marianne Faithful, today.

'I'm on my own,' I said to Mum. 'Perhaps I should get a flatmate.'

'You mean, until Charlie comes back?'

My mother believes that Charlie will come back to me. Like Charlie, she had to fight her family to marry the love of her life. Like Charlie, Mr Darcy, and Romeo. And, yes, there have been times when she has been tempted to walk out. Dad is no saint. Neither, she supposes, was Elizabeth Bennett. No doubt even Juliet had her moments. But women have to work at their husbands. If they do not want to lose them.

I say, but Charlie is not like Dad. For a start, he has never loved me. He married me to embarrass Caroline and Donald in front of their friends. Our wedding day was nothing more than a celebration of Charlie's status as family black sheep. Or family maverick, depending on which of the guests one overheard. Charlie spent part of the day sulking because old friends of his, when asked

95

by ushers whether they were friends of the bride or the groom, said *bride*.

I explained that it was not a competition; it did not matter that the guests preferred my speech to his. He should not have insulted his mother – it was embarrassing for everybody.

The truth is that it would have been a real leap of feeling for Charlie to have kept his marriage vows. How could he hope to love, honour and comfort me? It took him years to accept that we were in a relationship. We started living together only because I was adept at oral sex – and because I finally agreed to move out of Shepherd's Bush.

He persuaded me to buy my ground-floor flat in Camden. And now, he has left me all alone to its terrors. This flat is easily accessed by murderers. I might as well be living in a public space such as a bus-shelter. I might as well be living in a tube carriage such as this one, constantly surrounded by a cross section of the working public.

'Charlie's not coming back, Mum,' I said, on the phone. 'Anyway, I need someone to help me pay the mortgage. I can't afford Judd's salary on what I'm earning.'

'Well, why don't you ask *Judd* to move in?' suggested my mother. 'That'll be a saving.'

Thank goodness for Judd, who has agreed to move in for a while. And only if he can put up *mezuzahs* (Hebrew scrolls) on all the doors. Only if he can kosher my kitchen. I will have to boil my pans clean. I will need to bin all my *treif* food. He and Solomon will sleep in the spare room.

'Will you be OK? The two of you in there?' I asked.

Judd laughed, and said that I should try sleeping on stone ground, with no space to turn over, as they did in the Nazi concentration camp, Majdanek.

*   *   *

I climb the seventeen stairs leading to my local-newspaper office. The first eight are littered with junk-mail, just as in a shared student house. They smell of the tandoori takeaway, below. The carpet stops dead at stair sixteen, as I do.

'Come on Lucy Fletcher, make the effort,' says the receptionist, holding the door open for me.

'Morning.'

'I don't know. Is it?' asks Fred, who reminds me of a dirty white van. His face could be upside down, it is that round and even-featured.

His T-shirt looks slept in, and I wonder whether he has spent another night at his desk, reading grubby back issues of the *Sun*. He has a hygiene problem, does Fred – i.e. he sometimes smells of old towels, left wet in a drawer for too long.

At other times, he smells of dead people's clothes.

Fred stretches down his turquoise T-shirt so that it almost covers his navel. He pulls up his yellow trousers so that they almost cover his behind. So colourful are his clothes, against the white of his flesh, that they look painted on by an incompetent decorator.

He disappears back behind his counter, where he has only his computer for company. That, and a *No Smoking Zone* sign – there, despite the no-smoking policy for the whole building.

Fred lives alone, in Bayswater, which is all I want to know about him. I do pity him, however. Perhaps that is why I sympathize with him when he ritually complains about the weather, work, and artificial breasts.

'I mean to say, what's the point of putting them tits in if they're stuffed with silicone?' he is saying, lazing his hands behind his head, to reveal patches of grey sweat on his armpits.

I nod in agreement, as Fred's face settles into chins, like a fat woman on a sofa. Perhaps it is because I pity Fred – but I always agree with whatever he says. Socialism is an evil; the world was a better place when Thatcher ruled the waves; French beef is made out of excrement; women should be stopped from selling their eggs over the internet – oh, and working; chocolate should be made an illegal drug; young men need a war to fight; *Coronation Street*'s Ken Barlow should be put away for being so boring; Jews always take the best jobs.

'Yeah, absolutely.' I smile, my hand wrapped around the door handle.

'So, I'll see you at four, then,' says Fred, who will say anything to prolong our conversations.

'What's happening at four?'

'Hen's called a staff meeting.'

'What about?'

'New filing cabinets, I think.'

'It's about time,' I say, opening the door to the office.

It is about time we had somewhere to store the promotional material sent to us by local restaurants: the rubber pizzas; the life-sized cheques. Those depressing, deflating balloons. We need a place to put those boxes of dead newspapers, waiting to be taken away by men in brown coats.

It is about time we had new office furniture, to replace our desks, which are made of Victorian-schoolroom wood. The umbrella stand is drooping with the weight of the editor's golf umbrella. The filing cabinets are over-stuffed with rotting newspaper cuttings and old typewriters.

Oh, but it's home.

I will never stop appreciating my job, I think, sliding behind my desk near the door. As the paper's health and beauty columnist, I have the freedom to write whatever I please – however fictitious. I do not need to worry about breaking news.

I receive free products in the post.

I can relax, I think, switching on the computer, which starts up like an orchestra in the pit of a theatre. After all, I worked hard to reach this position – standing in the rain interviewing local politicians. I attended night after night of late council meetings.

I have done my bit, covering fete after charity fete.

I smile back at these familiar faces grunting Hello every morning, or – in good weather – Good morning. Most of them have normal names, made strange – like Vinnie Derwent changed to VD; or Derek to Derky; Cleo to Clay; Yvonne to Von; Lorraine to Rainie; Shirley to Shirl; Henry to Hen. I suppose that the pet names make us feel like more of a family – albeit a dysfunctional one.

'Luce. How are you?'

Heather greets me like this every day – as if we are meeting after many years at a school reunion. She is the only downside to my job, routinely scrutinising me, to check that I have not lost weight, or bought a flattering haircut.

'Fine, and you?'

Heather thinks that she is a close friend because of the proximity of our desks. I have tried, over the years, to make it clear that all we have in common is a stapler. (We are only alike in that we are both forever rushing to the toilet. Me, for ante- and postnatal reasons. Heather, because she drinks eight healthy glasses of water a day.) Yet, despite our differences, and the fact that she once snogged my husband, Heather still pretends that I am one of her best buddies. But I know that she loathes me. So much so that she named her cat after my child.

She talks about her cat all the time. Now, people laugh when I mention my own Maxie.

'Well, I've got so much to *do*,' she wails, pouring some granulated saccharin into her takeaway cup of skinny cappuccino. But she says this only because she is being shadowed by a girl on work experience.

'Yeah, it's hard labour here. I mean – having to cover everything that's happening in the whole of Archway and Highgate. God, it could take all morning.'

I become facetious around Heather. But, really, she should not define herself by a job that cannot take more than two daily hours of her time. She should not have forced herself on to Charlie at that office Christmas party. She should have apologized to me even more profusely, and blamed herself rather than the evils of alcohol.

She was sober enough when I overheard her saying she could easily take Charlie from me.

'No, I'm doing this epilepsy feature. It's going to take forever,' says Heather.

It takes me two hours to write my health-and-beauty column – although I do work the odd evening. It is not compulsory for me to attend those PR launch parties, but I am half-Protestant, and so have a degree of that work ethic.

When I started at the *Chronicle*, I resented having to work out-of-office hours. I was bitter about working through my long, student summer vacation. But I have since become institutionalized, and no longer feel that I should be paid for taking part in office pub dart matches, or staff Christmas parties.

'What, just to rewrite their press release?' I say.

'I have to phone the centre too.'

I imagine that, when one reaches a senior level, most workplaces are like this. Not much work done. After ten years in any job, one does not have to work hard. For some of my college friends, it is not any different. Ysanne is a PR officer, Ruth an MP's assistant; and Sophie, a solicitor with a city firm – yet all of them spend their time photocopying.

I did try a real job when I first graduated, assisting a scheme to help deprived children on council estates. But the children threw stones and sniffed glue, and I was scared of them.

When I was a child I felt certain that I would grow up to do something important and caring. I was once walking across a footpath that ran like a bridge over a road, when I saw a small box lying on the motorway. Like any good citizen I ran to the nearest telephone box, from where I called the emergency services.

The rules were clear then.

Afterwards, I felt like one of E. Nesbit's railway children. I was interviewed by our local newspaper. The police said that I had probably saved many lives as a result of my 'spirited action'.

Originally, the *Chronicle* was meant only to be a short-term job before a lofty career, perhaps in politics, the bar, or one of the bigger charities. For many years, I wanted to be a judge. Or to head a company such as ICI. During my first five years of work here, I sat, waiting for someone to encourage me to leave. I thought that someone might recognize my ability as a first female president, a chief of the NSPCC or a director of, say, public prosecutions.

I used to wonder when it all went wrong and I stopped having potential.

I felt that if everything was equal I would have been among the UK's top ten most powerful women. At the very least I would have been a leading campaigner for prisoners' rights abroad – although I suspected that such jobs are not advertised.

No-one, it seemed, went through the proper channels.

Only now – after ten years at the *Chronicle* – do I realize how lucky I am, writing a column in the name of the mythical Louise Bennett. I watch my other friends-who-are-mothers trying to combine high-powered jobs with having children, and realize how perfect is my own, low-flying, career.

I type, *A Beautiful Life, by Louise Bennett.* How I now love the tap-dancing sound of my keyboard.

How I envy my alter ego, despite Louise's facial hair, flat chest, irregular pubic triangle, eye bags, thread veins, large breasts, unwanted tattoo, excess fat, skin tags, thin lips, big cheeks, no chin, and rotten teeth. Lucky Louise with such minor concerns.

At least Louise is not pregnant and feeling sporadically comatose. She is never pregnant. At least she is living with a husband – albeit one who criticizes her dry, flaky skin; her flyaway hair; her large nostrils; her flabby upper arms; and her sideburns.

My husband has finally spotted those thick, green vari-cose veins, so I suppose I will have to invest in one of the creams on the market. I thought my flabby backside had gone unnoticed by my husband – until, that is, he suggested liposuction! So, I have decided to explore the less invasive alternatives . . .

Lucky Louise, who spends all day nursing her neuroses.

'So, what did you do, Saturday?' asks Heather, nibbling the end of a pen stolen from the offices of the Imperial Cancer Research Fund.

'I stayed in, alone.'

'You didn't?'

'I did.'

'You are so *weird*.'

According to Heather, I am weird because I stay in on the odd Saturday evening; I eat vegetarian bread; I have a male nanny; I did not hear a woman being murdered in my house; I read biographies; I once wrote a letter to the letters page of a national newspaper; I do not like jungle music; I have been known to wear a jacket indoors; I drink wine when I am in the bath.

Heather thinks anyone weird if they do not fit her idea of a national average. She is always quoting surveys about women.

* Did you know that the majority of women under thirty enjoy a plain biscuit with their afternoon tea?
* Did you know that more than two-thirds of women have sex six times a week?

In Heather's opinion, it is fine for a woman to wear, say, lipstick to work but weird for that woman to wear, say, mascara.

I am weird because I wear mascara (well, I have pale eyelashes); I have four A levels; I do not wear a watch; I weigh food before I eat it; I lost my virginity before it was legal; my daughter has a knitted hat in the shape of a strawberry; I take sugar in my tea; I gave my child a cat's name; I have a born-again-Jewish childminder.

Heather might think this weird, yet she flirts with Judd. All single, childless women do. He is attractive. Plus he has a way with children, and so with women who desperately

103

want children. Heather is desperate for a child – but only for a girl, because she wants someone to shop with.

She thinks that if she is ever bored by this mythical daughter, she can put her aside, to play with later.

Judd remains uninterested, and that is a tantalizing enough challenge for Heather – although she should know that Judd judges all non-Jewish people on what he presumes they would do in a Holocaust.

He approves of Von, for example, because he could imagine her lying on his behalf. He likes Charlie, but thinks that he would be too much of a coward to help even Solomon. Angela would confess to being a lesbian and – thus interned – would be in no position to protect anyone. My university friend, Ruth, would make a great big show of organizing her attic to hide us, Anne Frank-style, but then would be too self-absorbed to remember to 'organize' any food. Heather, he thinks, would steal all of our possessions, blackmail us, and report us to the SS.

Yet, still, Heather continues to be interested in Judd – because he ignores her. VD, too, is not sexually attracted to her, so she is besotted with him. She finds Judd and VD 'refreshing', because most men chase Heather, particularly moneyed-city-men-in-suits types. They try to pick her up when we are all out together, drinking in the Black Horse. Men so good-looking that it is a surprise to hear them speak.

These men pursue Heather, although she is so thin, she looks like a strip torn from an average person. Personally, I think her un-pretty. She wears far too fashionable clothes. The blonde in her hair has been over-highlighted. (It looks as if she is making too big a deal of it.) Her eyes are silver, as if they should belong to an animal. Plus, her face is spoiled by those enormous, impractical teeth. Impractical, because

Heather does not eat. She snorts cocaine and drinks diet packet-soups.

Her face looks, in fact, as if it has been pinched, hard, into features. Her nose is tiny and tight. *Pinch.* Her silver eyes are poked in. *Pinch.* She has too many edges to her face. *Pinch, pinch, pinch.*

Yet, the common consensus is that Heather is pretty. *Certainly, Charlie thought her stunning,* I think, bitterly.

Good-looking men like Heather, despite the fact that she has an ugly nature. She has ugliness written through her, like a stick of Bognor Regis rock. The woman is cruel.

Personally, I put this down to the fact that she is always hungry. Because Heather is always dieting – although she calls these diets 'allergies'. Right now, she is allergic to everything except mushrooms and cabbage soup. Soup that she brings into work in a fashionable aluminium hip-flask.

Last week she was allergic to carbohydrates.

Irresistible men pursue Heather although she lies about who she is. Perhaps *for* that reason. Her biggest concern is her self-image. She cuts out the chain-store labels from her clothes. She adds celebrity interviewees' telephone numbers to her personal address book. She talks about her 'first degree' as if she has a second. She described her new flat as trendy but filled with original classic touches like cornicing. I later found out, from Von, that she bought these from a newly opened shop called Classic Touches.

When Heather finally showed me around this flat, I saw her out on the patio, peeling B&Q stickers away from her garden furniture.

'These are antiques,' she later lied.

'So, what did you do at the weekend?' I ask, because I am

irritated by the sound of Heather waiting for that question. Plus, she thinks I have long since forgiven her for sticking her tongue down my husband's throat. She thinks I am duped by her mock friendship.

'Second date with Dominick,' she breathes out. She nibbles her stolen pen in a manner that I expect she believes is sexy.

'Well, I won't pry.'

'Oh no, that's fine. I am *so* loved up.'

I do not like myself when I am with Heather. I use words such as *pry*.

'Well, let's cut to the chase. Is he gay?' I ask Heather.

'*Noo,*' she insists. 'He's from New *Zealand.*'

I despise Heather, and not only because she appeared triumphant when she heard that Charlie had left me forever. Not only because she has big teeth and laughs too late – seconds after I have told the joke. Or because she is always buying the same clothes as me, but with knobs on. Tiny silver knobs on her designer black skirt, for example. No, it is because she is a liar. This is a woman who draws freckles on her nose, and pretends to like me. This is a woman who was dishonest about her A levels.

She pretended that she had three, mocking me because I had four, and went to Oxford. When I found out the truth, she said that it was not that she had failed her examinations, but that the examination system had failed her. I had only gained entry to unfashionable Oxbridge, according to Heather, because I had a privileged background and the right accent.

I explained to Heather that, in fact, my father was a bus driver. I said I went to a state comprehensive. So she began to criticize me for shrugging off my Essex accent.

I reminded Heather that she had gone through years of

106

painful speech therapy to rid her voice of all memory of Birmingham.

She said that her parents had forced her to do this. *As I knew*, she had reclaimed her Brum – although, to me, Heather's voice sounds as if she has claimed someone else's.

'Well, if you don't want to *know* about the date,' says that light voice, rearranging the press releases on her desk. (I am certain that she thinks I have forgiven her for trying to steal away my husband.) She turns to Work Experience. 'Lucy's never interested in the things everyone else is.'

'Oh, go on then,' I snap. 'What was your – what do you call it – "date" like?'

Unlike most women I know, Heather 'dates'. Her relationships with men have a definite beginning, middle and end. So she thinks women weird if they have a relationship history which involves aspects of drifting-in, inconclusive sex, and drifting-out again. Women are weirder still if they have such a marriage.

'Excellent. He took me to Bar 8000. We got off our faces.'

'Oh, what's that like? I've never been there.'

'You've never. Been. To Bar eight *thousand?*'

Sitting next to Heather is like being forced to sit in the front row of a comedy club. It is all a matter of *when* one will face public ridicule, whether for the weird size of one's lager or the potency of one's odd partner.

I am weird because I have never been to Bar 8000; I have a chair made out of safety pins; my husband keeps leaving me; I do not buy organic milk; I never see 'must see' TV programmes; I find bits of Plasticine inside my shoes; I become tired by 3am in a nightclub; I do not do drugs.

I do not do drugs because I have an addictive personality.

Whereas Heather, Von and VD can be satisfied disappearing into the office toilets to snort a line of cocaine before a night out, I know that I would be in there every coffee break, lunch hour and regulation fire practice.

'Coke isn't a *drug*,' says Heather.

Whereas Heather and Co. can deal with careers, marriages, and cats on a diet of class A drugs, I know that I would be the one coming apart – losing my job, my child, and my mortgage endowment policy. Eyes rolling around my head, I would ultimately be the homeless one, bedding down for the night in Waterloo's Bullring.

Years later, while Heather and Co. were graduating from local to national newspaper journalism, considering schools for their children, and buying detached houses with dining rooms, I would be hanging around sink estates in Sheffield, selling crack-cocaine to ten-year-olds. Heather would call me weird for taking part in a Government-sponsored drug-recovery outreach programme.

So I argue that drug-taking destroys brain cells – although I am aware that my mother spent most of the sixties tripping and speeding, and has spent the three decades since, over-achieving.

'So, what did you do on Sunday?' asks Heather, willing me to say that I was in alone then too. She once said that I was weird for having so many friends. That was when she began to add the phone numbers of famous people such as Zoe Ball and Gail Porter to her personal address book.

'I saw Ange.'

'Oh. And her girlfriend?'

'Yeah, and Felice.'

Angela's girlfriend is a children's-television presenter. Hence, the interest. For Heather is biding her time at the *Archway and Highgate District Chronicle* before becoming a

108

celebrity. She wants so to be a celebrity, believing everything that we read in the showbusiness pages of popular newspapers. This, despite my arguing that celebrities are rarely celebrated – they are there for us to read about, and revile, like car clampers and serial killers.

'Felice Elessier,' explains Heather to the work-experience girl.

'The one on kids' TV?' asks Work Experience, sniffing glamour.

'Yeah,' says Heather. 'She's lovely.'

When Angela last week brought Felice into the Black Horse, Heather monopolized her. Indeed, I was not surprised to see Felice and Heather bonding, as they had a shared interest in slimming. They discussed the number of kilocalories in everything from toothpaste to semen.

I call Angela. It *is* work, as I want to speak to her doctor about liposomes. Angela asks me whether I still miss Charlie, reminding me how much I miss him. I say that I certainly miss the sex, and Angela says that she does not know how. Straight people's sex reminds her of maggots drilling holes in apples.

Ugh.

She asks me whether I want an appointment with Dr Strom. I might well be suffering from antenatal depression: something that Angela says Dr Strom knows a great deal about, having recently taken a weekend residential course in the subject. Angela still believes in the healing power of the general practitioner. This, despite my arguing that they are at the bottom of the medical-professional ladder, and useful only as conduits for a specialist referral.

But Angela believes in medical people, horoscopes, multivitamins, and denying herself things like dairy products, red meat and men.

It was a female specialist doctor who persuaded Angela on to antidepressant tablets. (She is never depressed.) I tried to tell her not to listen to the psychiatrist, who probably wanted additional funding for some research project. But Angela, although easily led, will not be led by me.

I can picture her at her surgery desk, squeamish about each medical complaint that comes in. She tells me that she finds it hard not to laugh when women talk about their cystitis. She cracks up at the faintest mention of discharge.

She asks the other receptionist to handle all urine samples.

Yet she is not above handing out advice of her own. Indeed, Angela has been in trouble with Dr Strom for telling patients about the benefits of alternative medicine. She is big, for example, on lymph-node massage.

Angela prescribes this for a range of disorders, from a prickly cough to throat cancer.

'Hey, before I put you through to Dr Strom, I wanted to tell you something,' says Angela.

'Oh yeah?'

'You'll be pleased to know, I've decided to dump her.'

'Felice? Oh, I *am* pleased,' I say, because I loathe Felice. She has a Dalmatian dog that goes with her everywhere, like a coat.

'No, not Felice,' says Angela, sounding hurt. 'My therapist.'

She talks about her new therapist, then puts me on to chat with Dr Strom about the benefits of Retinol. VD comes over. He sits on my desk, playing with my paperclips, and pretending to flirt with me. Only it is clear that he is, in fact, flirting with Work Experience. He might be looking at me, but his body is pointing towards her.

I know that VD would not flirt with me; I have an absent husband, a child and – albeit unknown to him – a growing foetus.

'Did you get my message, Luce?' he asks, after I put down the phone. He is sitting, legs splayed open. 'About your P45? You have to collect it this afternoon.'

'Oh, I do, do I?'

'Well, it's only that you've been working here so long . . .' He looks at Work Experience. 'Don't you think she looks jaded?'

Work Experience seems to collapse under his gaze. She even lets down her guard, and smiles.

Girls such as Work Experience are a perk of VD's job. I sometimes wonder whether he would come into work at all, were it not for these willing girls, hungry for experience. As for me, I enjoy office romances, and, if not my own, then other people's. So I sit back, watching VD flirt so easily.

'Where does she have to pick up her P45?' asks Heather, trying to join in the flirtation. She does her best to make her eyes all doe.

'From the accounts department. If Derky sitting in that attic room can be called a department.'

Every office has its VD. He is attractive in an academic sense, with thick hair and American-white teeth. From far away, he looks like the plastic grooms caterers place on wedding cakes. Close-up, he is all fat muscles and soft features. It is as if his body has been fed on the hormones in beef. The sort of body that might be tanned all over. His hair is as black as a London taxi. Smooth as gel.

He has won a local newspaper journalism award, and is handsome. So, the *Chronicle* clings on to him, as if, at any moment, he is going to be headhunted. But I am suspicious of VD's good looks and talent in the same way that I am suspicious of the 99 dishes served 24 hours daily in cheap Chinese restaurants.

'From Derky?' I say, distractedly. Distractedly, because I am half writing my column: *Twenty-four-hour turnaround cream? I can't wait that long! And, more importantly, neither can my husband!*

'Derky?' says Work Experience. 'Is someone actually called that?'

She can no doubt feel VD's attention half focused on her, and is crossing her legs so tightly, she is probably doing herself permanent gynaecological damage.

'Haven't you met our Derky?' asks VD of Work Experience.

VD has the ability to smile without using his mouth.

'Derky's the accounts manager,' says Heather.

VD says, 'Derky's job is to disapprove our expenses, and a good thing in Heather's case, because she puts down her bill for sweets at the newsagent.'

Heather pokes VD with a ruler, embarrassed that the object of her affections has noticed how often she snacks on low-fat confectionery. VD picks up a protractor to poke back.

We have enough stationery in our drawers to enter the entire office for a GCSE in geometry. Why do we need hole-punchers? I would send Hen, or his secretary, Shirl, a memo about such needless waste, but that is not part of my job description.

'I need sweets for energy,' she blushes, the pink of her face blending in to that skullcap of strawberry blonde hair.

'Yes, but how do you justify the need for energy?' I ask, and VD laughs.

He is close enough for me to smell his spearmint breath.

'I wouldn't joke about redundancies anyway, VD,' says Heather.

'Yeah, why not?'

'Well, what d'you think this four o'clock meeting's all about?'

'What?' says Susanna, who has a habit of slipping unnoticed into groups of gossiping people. She is holding a magazine called *Looks* and I cannot help but bitchily think that she should be reading it more closely – because her skin is as bumpy as a badly painted wall.

'Well, I just think it's odd. I mean, Hen never has meetings like this. He divides and rules, doesn't he?'

'Isn't it about office furniture?'

'Lucy, you are weird sometimes. Office *furniture*?'

'This meeting's going to interrupt everything. That's the time I've been given to phone Maureen from that docu-soap. There's rumours she's moving to Archway.'

'I know; I'm doing epilepsy.'

'Clay, did you hear this?' says Susanna.

'What? About Maureen from *Driving School* . . .?'

'*No, about redundancies. There's this meeting today.*'

'*God, what?*' *says Clay, in her usual hormonal way. Sometimes, I feel as if I should make a note of Clay's menstrual cycle. It is only safe to talk to her once she has ovulated.*

Oh, but I bitch, because Clay is lovely. Like many at the Chronicle *Clay is such a good colleague that she doubles as a friend. I forget that VD, Von, Clay, Rainie and Susanna were once mere colleagues. I feel lucky having my favourite gang work alongside me.*

If I took a new job, I would no doubt come into this office every day, anyway.

113

'Well, you know about this meeting?'

'Four o'clock?'

'Heather says it's about redund . . .'

'I didn't say that.'

'No, I think it's about the internet. Finally, we're all going to be on the net. Not just Fred.'

Our receptionist, Fred, has been logged on to the web since the days when it was all rubbish and porn – but only for the porn. He often asks me whether I want to have a look at obscure sex sites (Fred discovered these because he 'knows his way around'), but I do not see the point of pornography. For this reason, I always skip the sex chapters in books, or fast-forward the scenes on videos. They do not touch me. Watching a sex scene is like watching someone have a baby or a bowel movement: repugnant for anyone not involved in the process.

I like the credits to come up long before any messy exchange of bodily fluids.

'God. Great.'

'All of us on the internet?'

'Wow.'

Only I disagree. I do not understand why the *Archway and Highgate Chronicle* needs to be linked to a global marketplace. Besides, I do not approve of the internet, believing that it will go the same way as the Sodastream and the sandwich toaster – up in the loft with all of those other technological inventions.

Man is a social animal. He does not want to interact via modems, any more than he wants a ready-made toasted sandwich. Man does not want to shake up his own fizzy drinks when there are drinks sold with the fizz already in them.

'Lucy, you are so weird,' says Heather.

Chapter Five

Heather thinks me weird because I spend my lunchtimes lunging with Von in the gym – a giant concrete building, beside an always-empty church. She could be right on this one.

'Make sure you're back for the meeting,' she says, over-excitedly, as we leave. Heather untwists her aluminium hip-flask, and I smell the sulphurous stink of cabbage soup.

'The notice said four o'clock.'

'Mmm, but I was wondering . . . Do you think we should have a pre-meeting meeting?'

'*No,*' I insist.

Von persuaded me along to Leotards Gym last year. She implied that, if I joined, I would eventually become her doppelgänger. At the very least, I would have her figure. There is no sign, however, of that happening. And I am beginning to suspect that Von's metabolism has been speeded up – not by the lunchtime aerobics – but by the drugs.

Nevertheless, I continue to attend, because my Slimco mother has made me superstitious about exercise; and I believe that if I stop my aerobics class now, I will turn suddenly into Shirl, the editor's secretary, who is fat to the point of hyperventilating.

I would rather face the suffering of the fit than that of the fat.

Besides, now that women have so many labour-saving devices in the kitchen, this is the only exercise I have – although, personally, I would rather go back to a time pre-microwave, intensive-farming methods, and the spinning jenny. I would have been a Luddite during the industrial revolution.

Women, I think, were much happier hand-weaving. Women would prefer to exercise usefully, by chasing chickens, or children.

Women would prefer to change into my gym kit in a cubicle. I loathe these communal changing rooms, as I have to concentrate on appearing uninhibited, as Von is. She thinks it peculiar to worry about what is – when all is said and done – just a body.

In your case, perhaps, I always think. For Von is unburdened by her body. It is there merely to bring her pleasure. Bits of it will not have disgusted her in the bath.

It is unusually hot outside, but unhealthily cold here in Hall One. I suspect that the gym's new management is anxious to show off its air-conditioning. Von is warming up by stretching her calf muscles. I am warming up by shivering. We are interrupted by the official warm-up.

'Right, are we ready to go?' says Craig, our instructor, who is in Barbie-doll pink leggings. 'Lucy, Lucy, legs closed please.'

There is clearly an element of double entendre to his constant correcting of my position.

'Lucy, come on. You could fit a bull between those legs.'

'Oh, *please*,' I say, but I smile as I say it.

He likes me because I once asked him about the benefit of legwarmers.

In here, smiling is obligatory. Certainly, our instructor is all grim enjoyment. 'Come on, put a bit of life into it,' he says; and I feel as if I am in some Orwellian world where office exercise is mandatory. All natural light is shut out, and music with nursery rhyme-style lyrics is piped down to dull the minds of we proletariat.

'Come on, Lucy, enjoy it,' the instructor demands. But I only enjoy exercise in retrospect – i.e. during breaks.

The instructor calls a break now, using it as a commercial one to promote his Wednesday evening class of kick-boxing.

'How does he know your name?' asks Von, as we swig bottles of purified tap water.

'He fancies me.'

'No, seriously,' says my closest friend, without even a question mark.

'Lucy, back smiling please,' the instructor interrupts.

I am unsmiling in that wall-to-wall mirror, opposite. Jumping and punching thin air. It takes six sets of jumping and punching before it is time to cool down, and I can buy low-fat bars of chocolate from the gym fridge, because I missed lunch.

I wash my sweaty leotard in the Ladies, hanging it to dry on the window peg.

Shirl comes out of one of the toilets. I am surprised because I thought I was alone. I have, after all, been in here for several minutes.

Shirl has left behind a bad smell, and I suspect that she was waiting for me to leave the Ladies before coming out

117

of her cubicle. She is that type of woman. I can imagine her sitting in there, waiting for me to wring dry my leotard.

I am tempted to tell her not to worry – I am used to the smell of Maxie's nappies. But she is the sort who would be upset, and I do not want to upset so powerful a woman as Shirl. She is, after all, the editor's secretary. So I smile, and ask her why Hen has called a staff meeting. At first, she tries to deny that there is going to be a meeting. So I remind her that there is a notice on the notice board. *Staff meeting today – all attend. 4.00.*

She tries to smile, but fails.

Shirl is wearing the same expression as when she was caught, three years ago, stealing office supplies. When Derky asked everyone to empty their bags on the desk. Out of Shirl's handbag came four rolls of toilet tissue and a glue gun.

Hen behaved as if Derky had been at fault.

He said, 'I'll see you in my office later, Derek.'

'Right-o,' said Derky, looking straight at Hen. 'What time will that be?'

'Oh, I don't care. Three.'

'Fifteen hundred hours. Right you are, sir.'

Shirl now goes to wash her hands, and I ask her gently if the meeting is about the net.

She asks me what that is.

I am surprised at how coy Shirl is being. She has always confided in me, even when her husband had his vasectomy. She told me about her daughter having leukaemia. She asks for my opinion about her purchases.

Shirl likes me, because we have a shared interest in shoes.

I ask Shirl to give me a clue, but she refuses. She plays with the pen she often wears around her neck.

Her expression then changes; and she looks as she did last year, when I asked after the health of her (dead) cat.

It is as if she is about to disappear, leaving behind only her clothes; and I imagine those lipstick-pink suits, carved to fit the fuller figure, lying in a heap on the floor. Thick, tan tights – the type used by armed robbers to disguise their faces – peeled off. Large, lacy underwear, writhing.

I change the subject, making small talk about filing cabinets. But Shirl cannot hear me above the sound of the hand-drier. So I decide to go, because Shirl is the sort who will stay until her hands are bone dry.

At least I now know that this meeting will be interesting. (I did not pursue six months' journalism training in Leigh-on-Sea for nothing.) I go into VD's office, to tell him about the significant meeting.

'If it was that significant, Hen would have talked to each of us individually,' he says, throwing balls of paper into the bin. 'Score!' he screams, as each one drops in.

'So you don't think it's anything sinister?'

'No, Lucy, I don't.' He smiles at me.

I like being in VD's office. It has the same sacred atmosphere as my elder brother's bedroom. I look at him, as he swivels back to his computer. His big body, squeezed on to a stool.

His cowherd hands, tip-tapping away on his computer.

The atmosphere in here is important. So important that I do not often come in. Perhaps, because I feel I will be asked to leave at any moment. There are maps on the wall. There are lists of telephone numbers, stuck up in a hurry. There are fresh sandwiches, lying half-eaten on his desk. It is as if this room is the nerve centre for the outside world.

'So why is Shirl so upset?'

119

'Probably remembers you asking after her dead cat.' He offers me a mint-flavoured Tic Tac, the lid snapping open.

'Oh, don't remind me.' I hold the Tic Tac. 'I just didn't think.'

'I disagree. Your trouble, Lucy Fletcher, is that you think too much.'

He presses save, and shuts down his computer, as I laugh, my eyes drifting to his dirty rugby-kit, stuffed into a Sainsbury's carrier bag in the corner.

VD is a rugby player. When I first started working for the *Chronicle* I thought he was crass, imagining him singing sexist rugby songs in the showers after every Sunday's game.

Oh, his manners, in public, were impeccable. Not for nothing did he enjoy a public-school education. But he made cruel jokes at the expense of weak people like Susanna. (He invented the word SusannaLowried as a description for being cornered by a bore at a party. 'Oh, you weren't SusannaLowried, were you?' *Chronicle* staff would ask.) But no gentleman would corner a woman in the stationery cupboard, attempting to snog her – as he did me when I started at the paper.

Yet. And yet. Perhaps because he has been one of the crowd for so long, I do like him. I now like him so much that I am angry when his name is used to describe a sexually transmitted disease.

I sit on the corner of his desk, snapping open and shut his box of Tic Tacs, as he gazes at me. 'How are you anyway?' he asks, suddenly shy.

'Oh, not so bad – considering I'm all alone now.' I still cannot say that without the tears coming. 'God, how embarrassing. Have you got any tissues?'

120

I wipe my face with one of his man-sized, glad that I am wearing waterproof mascara.

'You don't have to be embarrassed with me.'

'I know.' I smile at him, willing myself not to cry.

'D'you think he'll be back?'

'I don't know. His mother says that he needs time to think. She says he still loves me. But I don't know.'

'Well, I think he's fucking stupid.'

'That I know. But I reckon it was part of his charm.'

'No. What I mean is, he was stupid to have left you.'

I smile, embarrassed.

'Thank you,' I say. 'Things must be bad if you're being nice to me.'

'I am more than just the office clown, y'know.'

'I know you are,' I say, in the tone I use to soothe Maxie when she is having a tantrum. 'So, how're the redecorations going?' Because VD last month moved into a new flat, and is having it re-designed.

'They're halfway through,' he says, soothed. 'You should come and see it.'

'Yeah. Why don't we all come round on Saturday?'

'Why don't *you* come round?'

'Yeah, that'd be nice.'

'Why don't you come round *tonight*?'

'Tonight?'

For some strange reason I feel as if VD is asking me out.

'I know that Von and Rainie'd like to see the flat . . .'

'Yeah, but I'm not asking them. I'm asking you. On your own.'

'Oh, VD . . .' I start, but then I see that he is serious.

'Just for a coffee. You don't have to worry.'

'Are you serious?'

121

'You can't take me seriously, can you?'

'Well, yes. I mean . . . I'll have to ring Judd and ask him to stay on, with Max. But, well, OK.'

I do not know why he is asking me – *all alone* – to his flat. Perhaps he wants us to have a closer friendship. But I should have said No. (It was only that he took me by surprise.) No matter that it is now all in the past, VD last year hurt my best friend, ending their relationship by saying to Von, 'I don't think you're the one.'

Heather was delighted, because she thinks that she is the one.

I should invite Von along to VD's flat tonight, I think, going up to her desk, in the attic. As I climb the collapsing stairs, I remind myself that Von and VD are just friends. She could not possibly believe that VD is interested in me in any other way beyond friendship. *Plus,* since then, she has been out with Jon and Nibs. (And Tom.)

Yet.

Von is not alone. Work Experience is with her, learning how to transcribe tapes. Von is having a sneaky cigarette. I can smell her yellow-stained fingers from here.

'Do people still *do* that?' says Work Experience, staring, with amusement, at the cigarette. Von tells her that, despite her incessant smoking, she is officially a non-smoker.

'You're doing a good *impression* of one,' says Work Experience smugly.

'No, I've given up,' insists Von, tapping the cigarette ash into a dirty champagne glass. 'That's why I'm able to have the odd cigarette.'

Work Experience presses a button, hard, on the tape recorder. Von's voice plays, *I couldn't help but notice how*

you're always cast as the good-looking friend in a film. Does this
mean that . . . ?

Von grabs the tape recorder, to stop her interview with
the movie star, who has recently bought a house on the
Archway border. She had a battle with Hen who did not
want the interview. In our editor's opinion – and according
to his map – the celebrity's house was in Tufnell Park.

'There was nothing about that man worth celebrating,'
says Von.

'I told you he wasn't worth . . .'

'You coming out next Friday?' she interrupts. 'Rainie
and Heather were talking about going to that new club-
night at Stormont. Fuchsia Girl. It's supposed to be . . .'

'Does Heather *have* to come?' I say sulkily, playing with
Von's pencil sharpener, and wondering whether my finger
is delicate enough to fit into the smaller hole. But, no.

'Of course she does. Don't be such a bitch, Luce,' she
says, smiling. 'What's Heather ever done to you?'

'Ooh, I don't know,' I say, exaggerating my ignorance.
'Snogged my husband, perhaps?'

'Oh, that was ages ago – and she was out of her head
on coke and Es. And you know what Charlie's like. Give
her a break.'

Work Experience begins to pretend not to listen, as I
tell Von that Heather might be cited in my divorce from
Charlie . . .

But the truth as to why I despise Heather has nothing to
do with her snogging Charlie. I simply have a better time
without her there – in the same way that I prefer salads
without apples. She always finds a way to make me feel
shrunken. She laughs at me in that I learned at university
how to tolerate opera, people such as Ruth, bracing walks,
and Melvyn Bragg. She regularly calls me an elitist; and

implies that – ignorant as I am – I must have taken up not my place at Oxford, but her own.

Yet Heather is the one with private health insurance. *She* is the one with a showroom-clean flat in West Hampstead. So 'showroom' that I always expect the books to be glued together and empty.

Hard Work Experience now asks Von whether there is anything she can do. She is anxious to be put to use. I know this because she told me, pointedly, that she was worked hard at her last experience-work with Save the Children. It was 'good for contacts', she said. She found it 'really useful' working for a charity – although what she really wants to do is to edit a tabloid news-paper.

'So, what did you say about tapes?' she says.

Like every work-experience person who has ever passed through the *Chronicle*, Hard Work cannot understand why Von and I are seemingly satisfied by such undemanding uninteresting jobs, when she is certain to become an editor of a national newspaper if only she will put in the hours. Only I know that I will meet her, in years to come, when she is a secretary for an insurance firm along Holloway Road.

I know this because I was fleetingly like Work Experi-ence in the mid-80s when I truly thought that my fly-posters might free Nelson Mandela.

Like every work-experience girl, Hard Work has ideas all of her own. The rest of us know that a legitimate feature idea for the *Archway and Highgate Chronicle* stems either from a press release, or from the London *Evening Stand-ard* – with any reference to either Highgate or Archway highlighted. Once a week, we are obliged to hand these press releases or cuttings to the editor. He will then – if

124

he likes the idea – hand them back with a Post-it note attached saying *Check*.

Hard Work Experience still thinks that local reporters are there to ferret out information about corruption in council offices, or among estate agents. She does not yet know that we cannot print such stories, reliant as our newspaper is on local authority briefings and property advertisements.

'Isn't this a non-smoking building?' asks Hard Work, waving away the smoke.

'Well, I'm sorry if I'm giving you lung cancer,' says Von.

She does not sound sorry. She exacerbates Hard Work's chances of contracting cancer by sending her to do some photocopying.

When Hard Work leaves, she says, 'I'll stop if you want,' remembering my pregnancy.

'No, no,' I say, reminded of the fact that I am pregnant.

'You should be looking after yourself.'

'God, I don't want it.'

I realize, suddenly, that VD has indeed asked me out. I was naive to think otherwise. Why else would he want me to come alone to his new bachelor flat?

(I cannot possibly invite Von.)

It was only that I had not realized, until now, that good-looking men would ask me out. I envisaged years of loneliness, followed by my forcing Von to introduce me to men who would, over the years, become less and less acceptable to me. Bald men. Fat men. Dates sprinting to meet me – a flower in their buttonhole – like a fat father on school sports days.

Their hands, all over me, would be all flesh.

But I would have two children, and aged skin, so could not afford to be too picky. Eventually, I would have to

marry a man with a round, begging bowl of a face –
pretending to be happy. I imagined having to have sex
with this fat, bald man.

His puff of a body on top of mine, breathing fast.

But now I feel that life could be as fun as it was when
I was twenty-one. Of course, I will tonight tell *VD* that I
could never go out with him. But if *he* is asking me out,
so will other handsome men; and, suddenly, I want to go
to child-unfriendly places, like pubs. Like clubs.

If only I was not pregnant. If only I did not have this
baby-to-be, scratching around inside of me. If only I did
not soon have to go back to wearing a sling.

'I suppose it's not the best time for you to be pregnant,'
says Von, sympathetically.

'I can't cope with this *as well.*' As well as Charlie going.

Von stubs out her cigarette.

'You know, you don't have to have it,' she says.

I feel myself breathing.

'You're not saying what I think you're saying, are you?'

'Well, yes, I am. People only ever tell you about the *bad*
side of abortion. "Oh, you feel such guilt". But I didn't. I
found it a relief. I really did. Yeah, getting rid of it was the
best thing I've ever done.'

'You've had an *abortion*?'

'Mmm.' She lights another cigarette.

'Why have you never told me?'

'Well, it's not something you talk about. Certainly not
to you. Miss Babymother.'

'When did you . . . ?'

'At university. And I'm glad I did; I mean, what did I
want with a *baby*? It would have killed my career. And I'm
still waiting for my maternal urge to kick in. But maybe it
just won't. People always assume women want babies. But

126

I don't. I didn't. I must be weird, but I've always preferred cats. Gerbils, even.'

'And you didn't feel any guilt at all?'

'For a day or so. But only because of the hormones. What's the difference between an abortion and taking a morning-after pill? When does an embryo become a baby anyway?'

I think about those advertisements that I have seen, so many times, on the side of the Underground escalator. *Discreet, reliable, confidential* . . . All I had to do was to ring. One phone call, that was all. These people took the hassle out of pregnancy. Or was that *We take the hassle out of banking?* (We take the hassle out of bonking.) One advert morphed into another when you were going up an escalator.

'You can afford to go to some nice clinic, with carpets, and biscuits,' says Von, whose body was not designed to bring displeasure. 'Those sodding *Country Life* magazines. You'll be in and out in a day. Back at work the next day.'

'Really?'

'It's as easy as fucking.'

I am sick of being stretched by babies. All I have to do is dial a number. Eleven digits to liberation.

'But it's still killing, whichever way you look at it. I mean . . . I'm not saying that that's what you did. But I've *had* a baby. It'd feel like I was getting rid of another Maxie. And I'm not being judgemental or anything, but I kind of feel that getting rid of it would be going against nature.'

'Is it going against *nature* to get rid of a blackhead?' she sneers. 'No. You just fucking steam them out, don't you? I tell you, Luce, an abortion's like a facial. You're getting rid of the muck under your skin, that's all.'

'And you didn't feel guilty, say, a year later?'

'No,' says Von, grinning that grin of hers. 'I thought of it more as a mercy killing.'

Hen is about to arrive, and make his announcement. Everyone has gathered around my desk, for some reason. There is a palpable sense of anxiety, I think emanating from Susanna.

We are an odd-looking bunch, and so unlike the newspaper teams typically portrayed on television. Susanna has giant spots the size of small volcanoes; they drip molten rock, or something equally repulsive. (Her skin is as nicked as a school-desk.) Clay's breasts are the largest I have ever seen; they appear modelled on the designs that schoolboys graffiti on to toilet walls. Derky has a huge growth on his forehead, which we all try to ignore. And Hugo, a sub-editor, wears his hair Hitlerian.

If this group existed away from the *Archway and Highgate District Chronicle*, it would be the subject of a secret services investigation.

Hen comes in, sits on Heather's desk, all informal. But Hen could never seem casual. He always wears stiff clothes which appear to restrict his movement. Perhaps that is what lends him the air of an old-fashioned gentleman.

Now, he says that he will, ahem, get straight to the point. He is going to sell the *Chronicle*. To the *Post* group, owned by Tobu Frazer.

There is the kind of collective gasp that in retrospect sounds amusing.

Nothing will change, he says. Except that we will all be relocating. Beginning of November. To central London. (Shirl's bottom lip collapses. She probably thought that she *was* in central London.) Tobu Frazer does not think it necessary to have local-newspaper offices dotted about London doing nothing. Of course, that is not what Hen believes, but . . .

Hen interrupts himself to ask for questions, and VD says that he is sure he is speaking on everyone's behalf when he says that he is sorry the *Chronicle* is being sold. And he is sure that he is speaking for everyone when he says that he cannot believe that nothing will change.

Hen clears his throat, theatrically. His adam's apple looks like a pinball stuck in a bonus-score pocket. As he talks, it tries desperately to free itself.

'I have been given every assurance that the *Chronicle* will stay the same. Every guarantee. Tobu Frazer is happy with the way things have been run here. There's to be a new layout, that's all. A different masthead, of course. Of *course*, there are no guarantees. There might be a slightly different style of management, for example. And perhaps some voluntary redundancies. But that is called progress. Now, are there any more questions?' The ball in his throat stops trying to free itself.

I want to ask why there has to be progress.

There is a meeting postmortem at Pizza Hut. Clay rounds up the gang, and Heather telephones in advance to order six pizzas with her favourite topping. VD is trying to calm everyone down. But we all know that – should we be made redundant – we are unlikely to be employed elsewhere.

'Lucy, you are so weird, not liking mushrooms,' says Heather, when the pizzas arrive.

Susanna says, 'I can't remember what Hen said about redundancies. What did he . . . ?'

'He said that there *might* be . . .'

'He said that there *would* be . . .'

'He didn't say anything about redundancies,' says Derky, who we sometimes invite along with the gang, if only for him to approve our expenses.

I wish we had not invited him out to eat. He is worse than a child, eating with his mouth open. He resembles Helen Keller before Annie Sullivan arrived, grabbing food off other people's plates.

Trying not to look at Derky's mouthful of pizza, I tell everyone the good news: we are so accustomed to not working, that unemployment will be a natural next step.

I am able to joke because I have seen enough changes in my lifetime – from school to university to job – to know that everything stays the same. Same desks, for example. Same rules.

'That is such a weird thing to say,' says Heather, not eating. Instead, she scrapes away the fatty sauce from the mushrooms, and sucks on their stalks.

'No, it's true.'

Nothing ever changes. I treat Hen as I did my headmaster at school. I treat my computer as I did my manual type-writer. Everything remains the same. I remember when we lost our primary school teacher, Miss O'Connors. There were small children everywhere in tears. Yet Miss Roberts was just the same as Miss O'Connors. In awe of me, and my brain.

I am glad that Miss Roberts is not here to see me now, writing about such superficial subjects. She is no doubt retired now, and expecting to see me pop up on *Channel Four News*, discussing the state of the nation's economy with Zeinab Badawi.

Clay says that it is all right for everyone else to joke, but she has a child to support. I say that I do too, but she rolls her eyeballs almost white, and reminds me of the Wallis fortune. I say that Charlie and I are separated, but again she rolls those eyeballs, and says, 'for the moment, maybe'.

I have known Clay for a long time, and through my meeting Charlie; her meeting and marrying Tommy; my marrying Charlie; her anxiety about Tommy's business failures; my separation from Charlie; Tommy's departure; my pregnancy with Maxie; her endometriosis; Maxie's birth; her gynaecologist giving her a short window of opportunity to become pregnant; my second separation from Charlie; her pregnancy with Abel; Maxie's first birthday; her having to take out a loan to pay for Abel's childcare; Abel's first birthday.

No wonder she considers herself an expert on my relationship with Charlie. When he left, this time, she gave me advice that sounded as if it had been lifted straight out of a childcare manual. I should give him boundaries, she said. I should ignore his bad behaviour. If I praised him for his good conduct, instead of punishing him for his bad, I would soon see a new Charlie.

'I don't think he's coming back this time,' I say quietly.

'No. The wanker's gone for good,' agrees Von, eating only the middle of her pizza.

'How's Maxie reacting?' Clay asks. She is scraping the pizza base of its topping.

'D'you know – she's barely noticed.'

'Maxie's *funny* like that, isn't she?' says Clay, still scraping. 'I mean, she doesn't even mind you going off in the mornings. Abel screams his head off when I leave for work.'

'Really?'

'Sometimes I wish he didn't love me so much,' she laughs.

Before Abel arrived, Clay was a sweet type of woman who talked in T-shirt logos. Whenever someone left the *Chronicle*, she would say, 'Don't worry. There's enough success to go around.' When that someone was seen, years later, reporting for national television, she would say, 'Don't worry. It shows it's possible for all of us.' She was as funny as VD. But – unlike VD – Clay's jokes were always at her own expense.

'I'm the same weight as when I got married,' she would say. *'Unfortunately.'*

But as soon as she was pregnant with Clay, she began to brag. First of all about his frenetic activity in the womb. 'He's going to be an athlete,' said one of the nurses. Then, about his presentation. 'Congratulations. He's head first,' said one of the nurses. When the baby's head engaged, Clay was beyond proud.

'He's *engaged*,' she screamed around the office – as if her son had announced he was about to marry into money.

After Abel was born, she bragged about the results of his apgar test that confirmed his expert heart rate, breathing, skin colour, muscle tone and reflex ability. She boasted about his sight, his hearing, his grasping, and his firm stools. She talked about his good looks, despite the fact that Abel has always been a baby quite determined to look simply like a baby, with no discernible features. He had as much hair as a peach.

But, 'Isn't he like the boy in those food adverts?' she would ask. *'Edible.'*

Clay has long since given up on her own appearance. She is now fat and plain, with a middle-of-bread face and fried brown hair. She dresses like a long-term prisoner who has at last been given back her own clothes. Really, she has not bought anything new to wear since the last decade. It is as if she has given up.

Of course, Clay has never been beautiful but, before Abel, she was at least this side of pretty. Even with those dirty strands of premature grey, and the increasingly unfashionable clothes. Now, she is repelled by what she sees in the mirror. Flabby bits. Grey skin to match the hair. Tired eyes. She confessed this, begging me to recommend a turnaround cream that would turn around her life. Of course, I said that she looked fine. The last thing she needed was cosmetics.

Clay laughed and said that there was no hope for her, after that labour. Because she blames everything, from the weight gain to the smoker's cough, on childbirth. Besides, all she has to do is to lose a little weight. If she lost weight now, she would have a perfect model's figure. If she could only control her appetite, she could learn to control her life.

But this is the sort of gobbledegook that my mother comes out with when persuading people to sign up for the Slimthin diet.

She tried, and failed, to lose weight; and, now, she really does not care. Not one jot, she says. It is all Abel now, anyway. All we hear is Abel showing signs of memory; Abel pushing himself up; Abel making a variety of different sounds in his babbling.

'Unlike his mother,' Von added, privately, to me.

Clay's child drinks purified water; mine drinks cranberry juice. Her child sleeps. Her child understands the concept of giving. (Not even I have yet reached that stage of development.) Her child is a good smiler, a good communicator – in fact, a good all-rounder. She will allow me only the fact that my child is a good eater.

133

She thinks I am negligent because I have not made a note of my child's baseline respiration rate. In fact, she has become the sort of woman whose every utterance implies that she is a wonderful mother.

I never let him watch videos *because I'm a wonderful mother*.

He's very gentle *because I'm a wonderful mother*.

He's never ill *because I'm a wonderful mother*.

'God, I am such a pig,' says Heather, ostentatiously eating the head of a mushroom. 'I can feel this going straight to my hips.'

'You're the size of my right leg,' says Clay, and I look at the diamond ring, still squeezed on to that thick finger. Like a farm girl in a boob-tube. Even from here, I can see its sparkle.

'Not the left one?' jokes VD.

'Can we talk about Hen selling the *Chronicle*, please?' says Susanna, desperately.

'Well, what can we do? We can't exactly *stop* him.'

'He's sold the paper anyway. He was just keeping us informed.'

'Sold *out*.'

'Sold *us* out.'

'I don't think anything will change. But I wonder how it's going to affect my maternity leave,' I say, without thinking.

'What maternity leave?' VD asks me.

'Are you pregnant again?' asks Rainie. She has a slice of mushroom stuck to the cracked corner of her mouth.

'Not *again*?' says Heather.

'But I thought that you and Charlie were separated,' says Susanna.

'You're having *another* one?' says Heather, staring at

me, as if I am not having my own baby, but stealing hers. Because I know how much she wants one. She has even talked about having artificial insemination. I thought, *What's wrong with having one in the old-fashioned way? By having sex, say?*

For some reason, everyone looks at VD, who appears suddenly anxious.

'Is that why he left?' asks Heather. She is the only one still looking at VD.

'No, of course not.'

'How many weeks are you?' asks Clay, who appears to be mentally calculating whether one Abel is worth two of my Maxies.

'Eleven.'

'Seventy-seven days?' asks Derky, typically irrelevantly, eating Heather's pizza. He has just eaten all of Von's crusts.

'So you'll be going on maternity leave soon?' asks Rainie, our crime reporter.

Rainie is sceptical about everything from charities to maternity leave. The former she thinks of as a sop to the middle-class conscience. The latter she thinks is a term invented by lazy people to give credibility to their career breaks.

'Yeah, erm, you've got mushroom on your mouth. There . . . no, there . . . yes, that's it.'

'How old's Maxie now?' asks Rainie, wiping ferociously.

'She's two next month.'

'God, isn't it funny how they just grow, without you having to do anything?' says Susanna, without malice.

'I don't think you quite underst . . .'

'So you're pregnant, are you?' says Derky, gravely. I feel

as if he is wondering whether it is his duty, as our accounts manager, to inform the editor.

'Aren't you telling people too early? I thought you were meant to tell people at twelve weeks?' says Heather, with malice, looking at me as if I am pregnant purely for the attention.

'What are you implying, Heath?' says Von. 'That Lucy's not actually pregnant?'

'No,' she tinkles. 'That would be too weird, even for Lucy.'

How I wish I had not said anything. VD is looking at me as if I have betrayed him. It is soap-operatic; and I feel less secure about my position on the *Chronicle* if it is under new management. Hen was delighted when I fell pregnant with Maxie. He bought champagne. Whenever he walked past me, he pretended to fall asleep.

'Better sleep now, Lucy,' he said. 'You won't get any when the babby's born.'

But the *Post* group management might have a different attitude to pregnant women; and I cannot cope with being a mother *and* being made redundant, on top of Charlie leaving. I love my job; and no-one else would employ me to write their health-and-beauty column.

Their obituaries, perhaps.

'So, Charlie knows you're pregnant, and he still left?' asks Susanna.

'Yeah.' I know that Susanna, who makes her own tapestries, would never understand. She is married, but still I doubt she has had sex. At least, not with her underwear off.

'Bastard.'

That was VD. He appears to have lost his appetite – and that is a first for VD. He has an enormous capacity for food.

He has entered pub eating competitions, and won against people who eat pub food competitively for a living. His second pizza is lying whole on his plate. He is looking at his other, empty plate as if he ate that first pizza by mistake. He looks sick, in fact.

I wonder whether he still wants me to see his bachelor flat. But, oh, I have to go now. Otherwise, VD can pay Judd's overtime.

Heather is smiling, because she takes every opportunity to feel schadenfreude. I watch her, picking at her mushrooms, and think how like a shark she looks. Such big teeth. As the waitress comes to take our plates, she says, admonishingly, '*Lucy*. You've only eaten the fatty bits.'

'So, can we discuss this redundancy thing again?' says Susanna, worriedly. 'Because I'll need to tell Jonathon something. He's always been very pro me working.'

'As has my bank manager,' says VD.

'As has your *dealer*,' says Von, watching Derky reach for VD's spare pizza.

'I wouldn't worry, Susanna,' I say, thinking that Susanna has nothing ever to worry about. She is always taken care of by her husband, Jonathon-with-an-O.

There are advantages to plainness, I think. One settles for far less much earlier. The plainest girl in my school was the first to be married – albeit to a clerk in a building society.

Yes, she found it hard to settle into our office gang. VD was particularly cruel to her. When she confessed, in the coffee room, to having a problem with spots, even at her – tinkly laugh – age, VD said, nastily, 'They're not spots, Susanna, they're breasts.' But VD says that he could sleep with her now – if he was drunk, and the lights were out.

'It's *me* who should worry,' I continue. 'I'm sure I'll be the first out. Being pregnant.'

'No. That's illegal . . .' says Rainie, but she is interrupted by a small, hard voice from the far end of the table.

'Well, I'll be *second* out,' it says. 'Being only on work experience.'

I am mentally designing my dream house, and have just reached the guest bathroom, when VD returns with a mug of coffee for him, a tea for me, and a plate of Jaffa Cakes.

'You said milk, yeah?' he asks, deftly closing the living-room door with his right foot. (It is as if he has been practising that move for several years.) I am sitting on a spotlessly cream sofa, in his new flat.

'Yeah, thanks.'

'Is that sofa comfortable?'

'Fine, yeah.'

'Well, thank you for christening it.'

'It's lovely. The whole flat's lovely.'

I have just been given a guided tour.

'Is it what you expected?'

'The bedroom, maybe.'

It was exactly the bedroom I thought VD would have. The bed, discreetly folded against the wall. It so reminded me of a men's clothing store – dark suits hanging in lines – that I would not have been surprised to see a bottle of aftershave standing on a marble pillar. A shop assistant sneering at one's husband, 'Can I help you, sir?'

'Yeah, it's the only room that's finished,' says VD, sitting beside me.

'Pleased to see you've got your priorities right.'

'Well, a bed's pretty important,' he says, and I avoid

looking at him, hoping that he will not see the heat rising to my cheeks.

It feels strange, being alone, and away from the office, with VD. It is like seeing a schoolmaster away from the classroom. (Mr Tartin in Miss Selfridge.) I am pleased that VD knows about my pregnancy. At least I know that the coffee will not now be a prelude to sex. That would have been embarrassing.

It feels strange, seeing him in a flat he has chosen. It is the first place VD has ever owned, and very different to the rented flats he shared with other rugby-players. Those places were always a mess of underwear and cigarettes. The window-ledges, piled high with board games. There is a trembling pile of books on this window-ledge. There is a fresh smell of paint.

'Are you seeing a new side to me?' he laughs, watching me as I stare at those books. Biographies of Harold Macmillan and Michael Heseltine.

'I did in the kitchen,' I admit, because that room was gutted. There were holes everywhere. It looked like a body about to undergo a surgical operation.

He breathes in, hard, and stretches out his legs. 'So. You're pregnant again?' he says.

'Unfortunately.'

'You don't want to be pregnant?'

'No.'

I sip the strong tea.

'Charlie's such a cunt,' he says, but his swearing sounds artificial. He has such a plummy accent; it is as if he is practising for the outside world with his public-schoolboy friends.

'He is. But you shouldn't use the c word.'

'Why not?'

139

'Because it's used by men to humiliate women.' And I blush again, because we are, after all, alone in his flat, talking about female genitalia.

'There you go again, with your feminism.'

I put the mug on to the table. Firmly. Decisively.

'Oh, come on. Everyone's a feminist now. You are too. It's just that my Mum and her mates did such a good job, with all their campaigning for equality, that "feminism" has become the norm; and you *expect* women to have choices now. I mean, you wouldn't marry a woman who wanted to stay at home and darn your socks, would you?'

'Depends how big her breasts were.'

I laugh, saying, 'Seriously,' and sitting cross-legged on the sofa, so that I am facing VD.

'Seriously,' he says, affecting a grave expression. But, spoiling it by dunking his coffee with a Jaffa Cake. The chocolate peels away, like burnt skin.

'You don't think it's right that women have choices now? That they can choose to have a career, or to stay at home? To have abortions?'

He dunks again.

'You're not going to choose to have an abortion, are you?'

'And why not? It's easy for a man to be "Pro-Life". It's not your bloody body being hijacked.'

'But imagine if you'd had an abortion with Maxie?'

'It's impossible to compare Maxie with this one,' I say, my hands gentle on my stomach.

'In what way?'

'I don't know . . . When I found out I was pregnant with Maxie, it was as if I knew her.'

'What d'you mean?'

'I felt I knew everything about her. Even her name.'

'And you don't this time?'

'No. I can't even imagine it.'

I have known VD for a long time, and through my meeting Charlie; his series of one-night stands with cheerleading-stereotype-blondes; my marrying Charlie; his promotion to news editor; my promotion to columnist; his buying the MG; my buying the flat; VD appearing on a Saturday morning kids' TV programme, after his step-brother, Ben, won a competition; my becoming pregnant with Maxie; his sleeping with Von; my daughter's birth; his father dying; Charlie walking out for the second time; his minor sports injuries; my mild mastitis; his disintegrating relationship with Von; my disintegrating relationship with Charlie; his winning Local Newspaper Journalist of the year; my daughter's first birthday; Charlie leaving me; his struggle for a mortgage; my fear after Mrs Leslie's murder; his crashing the MG.

But I have always been suspicious of VD, whose looks could earn him a place on the cover of a men's magazine. I have been suspicious of him, ever since his clumsy pass at me, on my third day at work, inside a shut stationery cupboard.

I have suspected him of God-knows-what, until tonight, when we talk for the first time about his father's death; my mother's disappointment in me; his mother's grief; my father's accident; my love for Charlie; his lack of love for Von; my rejection of him that day in the stationery cupboard; his embarrassment; my suspicion of him, ever since; his quiet crush on me; my sneaking fancy for him; his secret love for me; my unrelenting love for Charlie; his losing his virginity at thirteen, to Donna Hennessy.

Donna, who showed her knickers for cash. It was as if she had no alternative but to stand there, skirt up. VD remembers her legs. They were ceramic cold; the colour of a school toilet. He remembers those lacy knickers, and the sounds of the other schoolgirls, surrounding her, screaming, 'Slag.'

He remembers making the mistake of looking up at Donna's face. So that, when they had sex that one and only time, VD could think only of her face.

Sad. So sad, that it took all the fun out of it.

VD smiles. We have been talking for so long that his coffee is soupy from being dunked. The table is scattered with our remains. Half a Jaffa Cake. Crumbs, everywhere. My mug of greasy, stewed tea.

Bits of biscuit float around in his mug.

He asks me if I mind him lying down. I do not have to move, he says. It is only that he is tired after all that business at work. He will just, *that's it*, put his feet on my lap.

If I wanted to, I could give him a foot massage. *That's nice*, he sighs, as I rub his soles. *You're a good masseur. Could you do my back?* He sits up in a jerk, pulls off his heavy-knit jumper (heavy-knit, despite the weather) and turns his back to me. I hear myself speak. 'I can't, VD. I can't do it to Von.'

I don't want you to do it to Von. I want you to do it to me.

Oh, that's lovely. Paradise, he says.

But, we'd be much more comfortable in the bedroom.

Chapter Six

Judd has clearly found the butter. He has been kneeling down at my fridge for minutes now. I cannot see what he is examining, but it must be the butter I bought from the 24-hour shop, where VD bought me chrysanthemums to celebrate our month-long anniversary.

Unkosher butter.

In a life-or-death situation, a Jew is permitted to eat unkosher; and I have decided to tell Judd that that butter could save his life. It contains virtually no trans-fatty acids, and so can contribute to the fight against heart disease.

Of course, Judd will say that I am being ridiculous, as most foodstuffs contribute in some way to the fight against disease. But at least it will prompt a discussion, during which he might forget that I hid the butter inside an empty tub of Snowcrest ice-cream – so was clearly intending to deceive him.

'What's this, Lucy?' he asks now, and I can almost smell that butter.

'What's what?' I reply, lightly. I put down the magazine I am reading, and go to the kitchen counter. Leaning against it, I see that he has found, not the butter, but my beef. I had forgotten about that. Grease has melted

143

the paper bag in places. Judd's hands are damp from it.

'Salt beef.'

'From where?'

'Jewish Mommas.' I can smell it from here.

'Since when was that place kosher?'

'Jewish Mommas? Isn't it?'

I knew the rules, of course. Judd's rigid set of rules. I bought the salt beef thinking that I could trick Judd into believing that it came from Rafis – a delicatessen in Golders Green. If a Jew genuinely believes that a foodstuff is kosher, then he is not committing a sin by eating it.

But I am a hopeless liar. When Derky searched everyone's bag for stolen office stationery, I confessed that I had at home two Pritt Sticks and a permanent marker pen. So, Judd can probably hear how fast I am breathing. He can no doubt see my lying eyes.

'Jewish Mommas is for non-Jews who think they're tasting Jewish culture by eating bagels with lox. No, Lucy, it's *not* kosher; and I've asked you not to keep meat in the fridge anyway.'

'Oh.' It is as if I have murdered his mother.

'It's *milchik*. That's why I buy all our meat from Rafi's.'

'OK, OK. Don't shout at me. I'm four months pregnant.'

'Well, I'll buy all the food in future.'

He pedals open the swing bin, and throws in the beef. It lands with a flat thud; and I want to ask him whether it is *halachically correct* (according to Jewish law) to throw out good food. Some poor animal was slaughtered – albeit in the wrong way – for us. I want to mock him, and suggest that he calls the Beth Din to check whether it is halachically correct for him to waste food.

144

He is always telephoning this Beth Din. It is a Jewish court, but I am beginning to think of it as a woman. He calls with questions, such as, 'Are gummy bears made with beef gelatine?' Or, 'Is it OK to eat bacon-flavoured crisps if the bacon is only flavouring?'

I want to ask, mockingly, whether it is halachically sound to place unkosher meat into a kosher dustbin, but I cannot risk losing another argument to him. After that last one – about the existence of God – he threatened to move out.

I begged him not to. I cannot stand the idea of being alone in the flat. I feel safer now, him living here. I had considered buying a dangerous dog, but Judd is a better deterrent to thieves. He has a mad look in his eyes when he is angry. Like now.

'You really wind me up sometimes,' he says, tearing the end from a loaf of challah bread.

'I know; I'm sorry.' I am also worried that he will want to butter that bread. Of course, there is kosher butter in there too, but he might ferret around until he finds my Buttery Buttero. He eats the bread plain, however. He eats it fast, swallowing quickly.

'It's not a game, OK?' he says, slamming the bread bin shut. 'This is my life. It's what I believe in.'

I go back to the living room, sitting in the armchair and realizing the truth: that if Judd caught someone breaking and entering, he would probably call that Beth Din of his. *'Is it halachically correct to hang a thief from the kitchen ceiling?'* Beth would reply, *'Is the thief Jewish?'*

'Perhaps this isn't working out,' says Judd, moving Solomon's Brio train set away from the sofa, and sitting down. 'You can't do it, can you?' I can see the outline of his arm muscles, like plaited challah bread, through that white shirt. He always wears white shirts. Black trousers and white shirts. They are lined up, like waiters, in his wardrobe.

'Of course I can. I lapsed, that was all. Remember, I am learning. I'd never even heard of this *Beth Din.*' I hope he does not hear my facetious tone. Which I cannot help. I really do not want him to move out and leave me to my empty flat – the telephone's echo. The sound of Maxie sleeping. Now that Judd and Solomon live here, we are a kind of family-of-four. There is always the smell of roasting chickens, or children in the bath. There are ornaments on the sideboard. Jewish candlesticks and Hebrew-etched wine goblets.

Before Judd moved in, I had only the one ornament. It was a piece of the Berlin Wall. When he saw it, Judd said, 'You do realize that that wall was Germany's only punishment for their Final Solution? You do *realize* that it should never have been pulled down? You do *realize* that it came down on the anniversary of Kristallnacht – a night of state-organized terrorisation, and murder, of the Jewish people?'

I said that I would start campaigning for the Berlin Wall to be resurrected. As a joke. But I did throw out that brick. *'If it's going to upset you that much . . .'* I did not want to upset my new house-guest. I like having Judd around, flushing the toilet. Switching off the lights. Filling the flat with comforting sounds. Using me as a thesaurus.

'What's another word for "coarse"?' he asks now.

'Well, what's wrong with "coarse"?'

In the evenings, Judd becomes a writer. When I met him, he was writing a situation comedy. But he could not sell it, I think, because it had neither a situation, nor any comedy. Now, he is working on a screenplay. It

146

is supposed to be a light romantic comedy. But it is about anti-Semitism in the Baltic States – set in 1988.

'I'm trying to describe one of the characters.' He kicks off his shoes.

'And this character is coarse?' I ask.

'Yeah. He's like your boyfriend.'

'A) VD's not coarse. b) He's not really my boyfriend. We just see each other occasionally.'

'Seem like lovers to me,' says Judd. Smiling.

'We haven't told anyone about us. Not even Von – because it's only a fling.'

Judd has a hole in his right sock. I want to offer to sew it up, but I cannot remember even blanket stitch. Even if I could sew, Judd would not allow me to do anything for him. He does all of his own cooking.

All of his own laundry.

It is strange, living with a man who knows how to change a lightbulb. Charlie said that he knew *how* – it was only that he was scared of dying by electrocution. He was scared of dying by electrocution, drowning, burning, ill-health, a car accident, strangulation, suffocation and grievous bodily harm.

By contrast, Judd is prepared to risk his life by driving a car, using household detergents, walking past pollutants, taking Maxie swimming, fixing a plug, walking along Camden's canal after dark, going to a playgroup full of infectious children, and wheeling a double supermarket trolley.

'You might think it's only a fling.'

'Yeah, well so does VD.'

'Why aren't you with the oaf tonight anyway? Or do you only see him *en famille* these days?'

'I'll pardon your using French,' I say.

147

'Oaf,' mutters Judd, because he does not like VD.

Or rather, he does not like the fact that Maxie adores my boyfriend; or that my boyfriend adores Maxie. I think he feels that VD is trying to come between them. Because VD insists on taking Maxie out with us at the weekends. He says that she and I come as a package.

'A perfectly formed package,' grinned VD, last weekend, pushing Maxie on her swing.

'Thank you,' I said, shyly, sitting on a park bench.

I still feel shy around VD. I cannot quite work out why he wants to be with someone who comes with the baggage of a child, and a pregnancy. I do not want him to help with my childcaring, in the same way I do not want hotel porters to take luggage to my room. I never know how much to tip.

In truth, the more I come to know VD, the shyer I am. I feel, with each date, as if I know less and less about him. By the time our relationship ends, I will not know him at all.

Before, I thought I had the measure of VD. I knew this of him: above everything he liked fast cars, fast women and fast food; he was an expert at cunnilingus; he shaved his chest hair; he would not date a woman over thirty; he read four newspapers a day; he had a stepbrother, called Ben; he played rugby in an amateur league every weekend; he always had in his wallet wads of cash, a tube pass with a picture of him looking silly, a membership card of a drinking club, and the now defunct SDP, as well as a photograph of Claudia Schiffer. I knew that he told jokes at anyone's expense.

After our first week together, I knew this of VD: he liked fast cars, fast women, and fast food above everything; he was an expert at cunnilingus; he had a stepbrother

148

called Ben; he played rugby in an amateur league every weekend; hc always had in his wallet a tube pass, two credit cards, and a photograph – tucked behind the one of Claudia Schiffer – of his dead father. I knew that he did not think cancer a laughing matter.

Now, I only know this of VD: he has a stepbrother called Ben, and is an expert at cunnilingus.

I remember now, how much better sex is with a stranger. As my mother says, it is like smoking a cigarette after a twenty-four-hour stoppage. So, the sex is great, yet I sometimes feel awkward with him. I cannot work out why. It is not as if we don't talk when we're together. It is only that all of his likes and dislikes – even his jokes, for goodness' sake – cancel out the VD I have come to know over oh-so-many years.

In his place is a virtual stranger.

Yet, I was aware – that Sunday in the park – how perfect a picture we must have formed. Daddy figure pushing child on swing. Pregnant Mummy, relaxing. By contrast, I was always the one to push Maxie's swing – not Charlie. He sat on the park bench, sneering at the park keeper, and saying that he wished they built children's playgrounds for adults.

In some ways, it does not surprise me, having VD. I knew I would not be alone for long, because I have not been properly single since the age of thirteen. Since before Billy.

I have always had someone. (HOW TO GET A BOYFRIEND: Cleanse, tone and moisturise with *Anne French*. Face pack at weekends. *Immac* for legs. Earrings. Slim body. *Shaders* hair lightener.) My boyfriends have always overlapped. After Billy, there was Carl.

Carl was almost a Cockney. He said Behave all the time,

as if it was two separate words. *Be. Have.* I was fifteen when I met him at a disco. I was there with Billy, but he had been trying to give me the push for weeks, and was snogging a skingirl with a violently short haircut. (At first I thought he was snogging a boy.) Carl said that he went by his instincts about people, and that he liked me. He said this staring at my breasts. Then, he said that he liked me a lot.

And his gaze went down to my crotch.

We snogged in an alleyway. The same alleyway where, two years later, I discovered Carl having sex with a girl from my sixth form. But I did not care; by then, I wanted an older man who had, not merely common sense, but sense. (I wanted Hamish.) Carl was not sensible. He smoked dope all the time, and had a police record for TWOC. Taking Without Consent.

Hamish would never take anything without consent. He was twenty-one, and a Cambridge graduate. Hamish asked me out on an all-American date. Bowling and a burger meal. On our first outing, he had a written list of the qualities he required in a girlfriend.

He liked a girl who grew her hair straight and long, like an American cheerleader. He liked a girl who wore skirts. He liked a girl who enjoyed musical theatre. He liked a girl who took her studies seriously. He liked a girl who could not say no.

I pretended to be all of these things, and more. I spent all of my spare time studying. I grew my hair beyond beautiful. I saw all of Andrew Lloyd Webber's oeuvre.

I pretended to be able to see the stage from the back row of the theatre. (All the time, his hand up my skirt, then up me.) But I was not happy sitting in the gods – and my hair looked like a burned, white rug. I had started university, and Hamish could see that I was not working.

He had to think of his future, he said. His ambition was to be a backbench Conservative MP. He had to think of his image. So he ended our relationship.

Luckily, I had another man lined up. Enzo. As far as the opposite sex went, there was not a great deal of choice at my university. Not if you liked men like Enzo. Too many of the men at Oxford had spent too much of their time sitting behind books, or in front of computers. Their skin was as dirty and pale as the sand on an English beach. They held sherry parties.

That was not my scene. As soon as I left college, I realized that there were many Enzos – of Mediterranean origin, sneering, cosmopolitan. *Cosmopolitan*-reading. There was Jahid, from Turkey. He was, initially, a more interesting Enzo. I will always remember his eyes, two clear green marbles. He was, however, terrifying during sex. Jahid said that he was an actor – his body was a tool.

I thought that he used it more as a weapon.

I discovered that he only 'acted' in porn movies, when Hamish telephoned, out of the blue, to ask me how I was. I said, 'Not fine,' and told him about Jahid. Hamish laughed, and asked me out to a party. I quickly finished with Jahid – although, perhaps I had been too hasty.

This time Hamish did not bring along a written list of qualities he wanted in a girlfriend, but he had put on an incredible amount of weight. He had also developed adult acne – although those spots looked stuck on for attention.

No wonder Hamish had given up on his American dream girlfriend. He looked as if his face had been squashed, whole, into a sesame-seed bun. But it was not simply his appearance that was unattractive. Hamish had become a Member of Parliament and whined on and on about his tiny majority.

151

'VD's not an oaf,' I say now.

'Oh no. It's just that, if you want Neanderthal man, he's your closest approximation,' Judd sneers.

'He's a gentle giant.'

'Hardly. He takes the piss out of everyone. Nothing's serious to him.'

'I thought that when I first met him.'

'Just don't be fooled by those puppy-dog eyes.'

'What?'

'The way VD looks at you.'

'Nah, his eyes are like that with everyone. They're naturally puppy-dog.'

'Just take it from me, Lucy. Every time he sees you he wants to rip your clothes off . . .'

'Well, I know *that*.'

'Yeah, well that's what I'm saying.'

'Oh, fine, yeah. No, I thought you were saying he was serious about me.' I laugh, peeling my right sock off. I want to see if my toe-nails need re-polishing. 'It's just sex.'

Judd grunts, and says that I should respect my body. Or no man ever will. I laugh, saying that he has an exaggerated respect for his own body.

'It's not just sex for VD. He's serious about you,' says Judd, ignoring my comment.

'Well, I can't be serious about VD. I can't be serious about anyone who has such a low income,' I joke.

'Or Polish blood.'

Judd judges every nation by the role they played in the Second World War. Poles, he loathes. He thinks them worse than Germans and Austrians for anti-Semitism. Poland, he says, actively fed its Jewish population to the gas chambers.

Heather was once proud of the quarter of her that is

152

French. She would behave as if at least a quarter of her had natural French chic.

Until Judd said to her, 'You French couldn't wait to see the Jews murdered.'

'No, not *me,*' said Heather. She had thought that Judd would like the Parisian in her. 'You don't understand. I mean, my *grandparents,* maybe. But I barely know them . . .'

'I thought you were *very* close – always staying in their flat in Paris. You know the city better than you do London. It feels like home to you, you said.'

'Lucy, d'you have to be so sarcastic all the time?'

'How can you trust a Frenchman? I mean, after Dreyfus . . .'

Judd said this with only half a smile. The other half of him is seriously suspicious of the French, the Italians, the Greeks and the Slovaks.

He approves of Von only because she is half-Danish. Judd adores Denmark and all things Danish (except for bacon). The Danes he considers honorary Jews – because, in 1943, when the decree came in Denmark from Nazi-occupation headquarters – *All Jews must wear a yellow arm band with a Star of David* – the king said that he too would wear a Star of David; and that he expected every loyal Dane to do the same. The next day in Copenhagen almost the whole of its population wore Star of David arm bands. The Danes evacuated its entire Jewish population north, to the safety of Sweden. Non-Jewish Danes, said Judd, insisted on wearing yellow stars when the order came in from the Nazis. So there was no way of telling them apart from their Jewish neighbours.

'So, thank you,' said Judd when he met Von.

'Well, I don't think it was quite my . . .'

'No, seriously. There were only a few like you.'

'You really should tell Von about VD,' says Judd. 'It's not right.'

'Von doesn't need to know,' I say, putting on my sock. 'We're going to have to stop sleeping together, for practical reasons, anyway. I mean, I'm sixteen weeks pregnant. My stomach'll get in the way soon.'

Judd has the same expression that Caroline wore when I tried to talk to her about Charlie leaving. *Please*, it says, *there are some things I will not discuss.*

'Your stomach's as flat as a board,' he mutters at last. Staring down.

'All I'm saying is, I won't be with VD for much longer. And at least that'll give Heather hope that he'll shag her. It might stop her bursting into tears every two minutes and rushing to the loo. Because she's convinced herself that she's in lurve with him. Not that Heather knows the *meaning* of love. She has exactly the same feelings for any member of a boy band.'

'And you know the meaning of love, do you?'

'Yes,' I say. Quietly.

'Oh yeah? So, what is it?'

'Well, I'm not exactly a virgin in that department, am I? It's the way I feel about Charlie.'

Judd pinks; and I suspect that he is thinking about Chava.

He is in love with a woman called Chava. I know about her from Judd's private diaries. I skim-read them last week, when Judd was out at a Jewish study meeting. I felt it my right, as Judd's employer, to explore his deepest private thoughts. Besides, I was bored.

Volume one was dull stuff. Repetitive. Soul-searching.

Rabbis' opinions, all of them conflicting. There were footnotes, for goodness' sake: *See Rashi: 1/2*. I was halfway
through volume two and about to give up reading, when,
suddenly, the pace quickened. A new character was introduced. Chava. The daughter of Rabbi Scheur – who runs
Ba'al T'shuva, an organization which converts Jews back
to orthodoxy.

I didn't think I could like anyone after Clare, wrote Judd. *I
went through a period of misogyny. But that was before Chava
– a woman I met today at the Scheurs. She was about to go out
on a shidduch* [a blind date] *and so nervous her hands shook.
I have never seen such delicate, feminine hands.*

I looked at my own large hands, the nails chewed to
their cud.

*Clare had great big farmer's-wife hands. Ironically, they were
workmanlike. But Chava had pretty, delicate hands, like a
peasant girl from the nineteenth century . . .'* And so on,
and on.

Poor ex-wife Clare could not compete with Chava, who
was prepared to discuss with Judd all of life's largest
questions. And keep her hands dainty. How did HaShem
allow the Holocaust to happen? Are children born without
blemish? Should an unmarried woman be allowed to talk
freely to an unmarried *ba'al t'shuvah* – born-again Jewish
– man about her deepest concerns? What would her father
say if he knew they sat alone, without a chaperone?

*In shul today, I looked up at the women's section. I saw Chava,
peering through the gap in the white lace. She's so unlike other
women, in that she doesn't know or care that she's beautiful. God,
I can't bear to think of her with one of those fat men with food in
their beards. It would be like watching a child being swallowed
up by a . . .*

That was when I heard a noise. Someone turning a

key in the door. Judd, turning his key in the door. So I shoved the journals back under the bed. I came out, fast-breathing, and Judd saw my lying eyes. But he presumed it was because of the unkosher cheese he had found, that morning, hidden in the egg-tray.

'There's no need to look so guilty,' he said. 'I know about the Gorgonzola.'

'Why do we always have to discuss *my* private life?'

'Since when did you keep your private life private?' says Judd, picking up my newspaper. He reads the *Guardian* only to criticize its anti-Israel stance. He thinks its leaders have an anti-Zionist agenda even when they concern, say, Zimbabwe.

'Well, can't we discuss *your* private life for once? Are there any nice enough Jewish girls for you out there?' *Say, Chava?*

'Nah. I'm not at that *shidduch* stage.'

'But you will be soon?'

'You'll be the second to know, Lucy.'

'Who'll be the first?'

'Probably Rabbi Scheur,' he says, only half-jokingly.

He turns the pages of the *Guardian*. Roughly. I see that he is dangerously close to the leader pages.

'Of *course.*'

'Well, he'll be the one introducing me to women . . .'

'The Jew's Cilla Black?' I interrupt.

'Ha ha. *No. He* doesn't have one eye on TV ratings.'

'Well, I'd go for it now, if I were you. Just think of all those blushing virgins out there, all waiting for Judd *Drexler* to seduce them.'

'Yeah, I wondered how long it would take you to bring the subject back to sex.'

I sigh heavily, picking up the magazine I borrowed from Heather. But I cannot concentrate for wondering. What is the difference between an embryo and a missed period? When does a foetus become a life? Is it ever appropriate to terminate a pregnancy? After all, my baby will not have a father.

Not that Maxie ever did.

Judd is more of a father to Maxie, than Charlie. Especially now that Maxie has him living here. Her Mummy and Judd have become like a married couple without the usual marital pressures of mortgage payments, sex and emotional needs.

I always felt the need to entertain Charlie, in the evenings, by having sex, or an argument.

It is a relief tonight – just Judd and I in the flat. No children about to wake up next door. No Solomon having nightmares about the Holocaust. He and Maxie are staying overnight with my mother. She said that it was as easy for her to have two as one. She would make sure he said his prayers, and ate only kosher food.

Of course, it is not as easy to have two children as one. But my mother can juggle any number of tasks. Last year, she was awarded the accolade of 'Essex Businesswoman of the year'. She is a magistrate. She delivers meals-on-wheels to the elderly in Gants Hill. She takes care of my disabled father.

I look up at Judd. It is surprising how comfortable I am, living with him. This, despite the rigid rules of Jewish orthodoxy now governing my every waking moment. I am too comfortable, according to my university friend, Ruth. She says I should show him who is boss.

In Ruth's opinion, I should treat Judd as if he is representative of all mankind. I should rule over my 'live-in

157

au-pair' as men have been ruling over women for centuries. Sophie said that, at the very least, I should assert my role as Judd's employer. She has recently been promoted to partner at her law firm called Saks Kerwin. Ysanne said that I should assert my role as Maxie's mother.

So, I say now, 'By the way. Judd, could you stop giving Maxie semi-skimmed milk.'

'Why?'

'Well, she needs full-fat for bone growth.'

'Well, that's OK then, because Maxie already has bones.'

I tell Judd there is plenty he can learn from me about childcare.

'What d'you mean?'

'Well, look how lovely Maxie's suddenly being.'

'She *is* lovely,' he says.

'Yes, because of me.'

'Because of *her*.'

'No, seriously. Listen to this.'

I pick up a bulky childcare manual, *Nanny's Handbook*, and flick through to the tantrum pages. They are lovingly battered. I read aloud, in an actressy way:

'Always offer your child a choice, so that he thinks he is in control, but let the choice be a narrow one. Otherwise, you – the nanny – will be the one to lose control. For example, ask, "Would you like milk or water?" therefore offering two, healthy beverages. You win whatever choice your child makes.'

Judd laughs. He says that we are all offered the same narrow choices by a nanny state. For example, we can choose *either* to obey the law, *or* to go to prison. We can choose *either* to dress according to a strict code, *or* to be ridiculed by our peers. We can . . .

'All right, all right.'

'Perhaps you should leave the childcare to me,' he says,

smugly. Because Judd is always suggesting that I leave all domestic tasks to him – from creative writing to emergency plumbing.

He runs my household like a military machine – all the while messy-playing, cooking, and storytelling like any children's-television presenter. He believes in honesty with children being the best policy. Hence, his answers to Maxie's What's This? questions.

Qu: Whash this?

Ans: That's money, Maxie. The game is you need to get as much of it as you can and then spend it on meaningless, useless objects to impress men.

Qu: Whash this?

Ans: That's a taxi, Max. It picks up anyone who can pay for a ride except black people.

Hence, his answers to Solomon's Why? questions.

Qu: Why is the sky there?

Ans: Because it was the only beautiful thing that prisoners could see in a concentration camp.

Qu: What is a Mummy?

Ans: Someone who leaves a Daddy for a computer programmer.

Qu: Why do I have to eat it?

Ans: Because any Jewish child in a Nazi ghetto in the 1940s would have given anything for this potato. Even if it was stale and shot through with bullets.

Yet, despite Judd's brutal honesty, I have never seen my daughter so happy, since Judd moved in. She is so well-behaved that I have to pretend to other mothers that she does not like the bath, or broccoli.

But she does, I think, smugly.

Finally, we have the perfect mother-daughter relationship. Yes, and this is the start of the so-called 'terrible' year. But I feel as if I have come into my own, now that my daughter is able to speak and use the potty.

Before, I did not have the time to enjoy being a mother because I was too busy performing all the tasks normally involved with motherhood. I was too busy doing the washing, the nappy-changing, the feeding, the rocking-to-sleep, the keeping-her-quiet-in-supermarkets.

I thought my life had ended post-motherhood. But, if Judd has taught me anything, it is that life has, in fact, begun again. I am back to babyhood and enjoying the pleasures of bouncy castles and building bricks. Soon I will be vicariously going through adolescence, and crying over some boy in Year Ten.

Indeed, now that Maxie is bigger, and responds to my jokes, I resent the fact that Judd has her all day to himself. At times, I even envy him. My daughter is such good company, I want to be her constant companion.

When Charlie was here, Maxie knew that she was in the way – no place to be during our more physical arguments. Charlie would compete with Maxie for my attention. If she screamed, he would scream louder and for longer.

'I win,' he would say, if she stopped first.

When I once praised Maxie for repeating the word *laughing*, Charlie asked me what I thought of a word he had learned that day. *Disintermediation*. 'Great word, isn't it?' he said. 'It's not bad,' I replied. 'But Maxie's word can be used more often and in a much wider variety of contexts.'

On another occasion – when I admired Maxie's chalk drawing – Charlie took possession of her blackboard to draw a landscape. 'What d'you think?' he asked me. 'I was always good at art. That was one thing . . .'

'Is it an abstract?'

'Well, you do something better,' he said. So I rooted around in a cupboard, and showed him the sketchbook I had kept from my Art O level. 'They look better further away,' said Charlie. 'Like you.'

Maxie does not ask after her father any more. In many ways, I think she is relieved that he is no longer here, playing with her tank engine.

Her two favourite people now live together. Judd and Mummy. She is happy that there are two people to pay her more attention than they do the television. It is as if Maxie is aware that the majority of my conversations with Judd are about her. As for Solomon – well, Maxie adores him. She tries to imitate him. That is why she has begun to say morning prayers, and to use the potty.

It is a good time for her to be potty-trained. As I am pregnant, we both need to be within constant running distance of a toilet. It is a good time, because I am now a more patient person. I do not have the constant threat of Charlie leaving. And I have a live-in au-pair – so I can go out whenever I choose, with VD.

I like seeing VD – although he is so good looking that I feel as if I am dating the lead singer in a boy band. In the streets, teenage girls gaze at him. But the relationship means nothing. Neither of us wants commitment. That c word has not come up in conversation.

But I do like being with him.

We talk about our careers; and VD has made me see the advantages to the *Chronicle* moving into central London. The truth is that I do love London's streets, because they fill up so quickly with people wanting to give me things, like makeovers, or magazines. I love walking through the ground floors of department stores. There is always the chance, there, of a cheese or wine-tasting. The women

161

in the food halls, with full trays, and too much cheese, are always glad to see me. Their job, after all, is to get rid of cheese.

In essence, nothing will change.

'I'm feeling so lousy,' I tell Judd. 'I never felt like this when I was pregnant with Maxie.' I want to know whether he thinks I have options. Should I abort this baby? Or rather, this foetus? This embryo?

This missed period?

Yet, I know exactly what Judd would say. His very new faith does not allow him even to masturbate, because sperm should not be wasted. Sex should not be purely for pleasure's sake. So I can only imagine the strength of his opinion against a termination.

I have been feeling more and more pregnant lately. My bladder bursting. My stomach stretching. My urine is pink – the colour of Maxie's milk shake – but the midwives put that down to the possibility of thrush.

It is not just sometimes that it is hard to be a woman. Womanhood is always about feeling uncomfortable. My big bits pushed into a bra and string knickers. My big baby pushed through my bits. When I turned thirteen, I knew that it was all going to be downhill. I could no longer run for a bus, so self-conscious was I about my breasts.

Von has given me the number of an abortion clinic. 'It's one call, she said. 'And you can close a chapter on Charlie.'

But VD talked me out of phoning. In his opinion, it was murder by any other name. He could not understand a woman trapped with an unwanted pregnancy. It is not like a bad marriage: one cannot simply leave it. One cannot take a break from one's body, with some lover in Brighton.

162

No, the thing, the foetus, the *mistake,* is growing inside you. Every day, bigger.

Every day, more organs. A beating heart; a throbbing liver; a brain, even. It is a fact that – inside you – there is a person. A person with – according to my thirteenth-week scan – a penis. A foetus. A baby.

A child. A man.

The truth is, I do not have the option of abortion. It feels as if there is something inevitable about this baby inside me. The way it grows daily, notwithstanding my state of mind.

'Is something wrong?' asks Judd, now, staring at me. With those pale blue eyes of his. Eyes that look as if they belong in a laboratory jar, to be closely examined.

'No, I'm fine. Why?' I flip a few pages of my magazine, on to the celebrity-focus pages.

'You were looking very strange.'

'Was I?'

'Is this about the butter?'

'What?'

I think I might have actually jumped.

'Is this about the butter you'd hidden inside a box in the fridge?'

'To save you from a *heart* attack,' I say, angry now.

'What d'you mean? Oh, don't worry; I'm not going to have a go now. Seriously; don't look so worried. I threw it away yesterday.'

'So why bring it up *now*?'

I turn the magazine pages until I find my favourite section: the one where long camera lenses go inside the homes of famous people, and sneer at their furniture.

'Because I only just remembered it,' he smiles.

'Well, I think that's small. That's really small, and . . .

Petty. I'm still learning the minutiae of Jewish legislation, remember? I mean, this is worse than Sophie's law finals. You're always giving me bloody spot tests.'

Frankly, I am relieved that he found that butter. It had grown mountainous in my mind. I only bought it because I loathed the taste of the kosher substitute. But I am glad that everything is now out in the open. Perhaps I can buy another fridge for my bedroom.

'Perhaps I can buy another fridge for my bedroom.'

'Oh Lucy, don't be ridiculous. God. It would be far easier if I just moved out. You don't feel vulnerable any more, anyway – so I don't really have to be here at all. It must be hard, living with me.'

'Oh, don't start that again. I like you being here, eccentricities aside.'

'Says the woman who weighs her food before she eats it.'

'Well, I'm not religious. It's my way of coping with impending death.'

I am a Slimco child, I think, as Judd smiles and goes back to reading his newspaper. I turn to the last page of my magazine.

'Hey,' I say.

'What?'

'Sindy Patchitt – you remember, that child star?'

'No.'

'Oh, you *do*. She's the same age as us.'

'Well, what age'll that be? I'm years older than you, remember.'

'All of three.'

'Lucy, I'm just not interested.'

'You'll be interested in this. She's just committed suicide after the pressure became too much.'

'Ah, well. No doubt someone'll make a musical about that.'

'Oh, why do people have to die?' I say.

'I take full responsibility,' says Judd.

'For someone so *uncynical* when it comes to mass orchestrated religion, you really are cynical.'

He turns to the sports pages and I hear his breathing relax. I ask Judd whether football is kosher. He looks decidedly guilty, and says that his love for sport is a hangover from the days when he needed to fill the void of meaningless living.

I say that that sounds to me as if he is post hoc rationalizing.

He sighs and picks up a book. A fat, fact book, about the Catholic Church's conspiracy with the Third Reich, because Judd despises novels, in the same way intellectuals did in the nineteenth century. I appreciate his books around me. I feel as if, one day, I will simply absorb the words inside, as if by osmosis.

'You're not going to bed, are you?' he says, as I stand up.

'No, only the toilet. Or do I have to check that that's OK with the Beth Din?'

To his credit, Judd does laugh.

I am bleeding. I look at the toilet paper, covered in red blood; and I know that this cannot be connected with thrush. I look at it for a long time.

When I come back in the living room, Judd is asleep on the sofa. I telephone my midwife, who says that I am to go straight to casualty. As I am writing a message for Judd, to tell him where I am, he wakes up. His eyes open quickly, and he seems startled.

'Oh, it's you,' he says, smiling.

'Who did you think it was?'

'I have bad dreams. About Clare in an SS uniform.' He yawns. 'Why have you got your coat on?'

'Well, I was just leaving you a note, actually. I've got to go to casualty.'

It takes me some time to convince him that I am serious. It then takes Judd some time to convince me that he should accompany me. So it is ten minutes later that we leave. And it takes more time for Judd to convince me that he should drive.

'It's not even as bad as a period,' I say.

'You shouldn't be having a period, Lucy. You're pregnant.'

He drives me to the nearest hospital. We go in his car, although grey steam comes out of the exhaust. It is less a car than an offensive weapon.

He refuses to let me direct him. I wish I could convince him that I am only bleeding mildly, and that it will take more than a bit of mild bleeding to upset this baby. So far, the foetus has grown to the size of a small melon, despite the trauma of his father leaving him. He has posed happily for scan photographs, despite the upset of his mother loathing him. He will grow up to be either a leader of men, or one of those serial killers who cannot feel empathy.

We park on a double yellow line and run into Accident and Emergency. The receptionist takes me to see a nurse. Her hair is pinned up into a cottage loaf. Despite the situation, I am still able to enjoy the drama, and the attention.

'How many weeks pregnant are you?' asks the nurse, wearily.

'Sixteen.'

'And how much have you been bleeding?'

'Well, it's difficult to tell.'

'A teaspoon?'

'More than that.'

'A tablespoon?'

I settle for a soup spoon of blood; and she gives me a yellow card, saying, 'I'm afraid it might be a couple of hours' wait.' I sit down opposite Judd. He is staring at the wall-chart.

Red cards: for people who need to be seen immediately.

Yellow cards: for people who need urgent attention.

Blue cards: for people who need non-urgent attention.

My tramp-neighbour has blood dripping from his bottom lip. Yet he is holding only a blue card, and I feel a mild sense of victory.

Judd seems even more troubled than is usual. He is standing, agitated, like one of those men, in films from the 1950s, who are waiting for their wives to give birth.

'You go home,' I say. Soothing voice. 'I'll get a cab back.'

'No, I'm fine.'

'But it could be a two-hour wait. You heard what she said.'

'So, we'll wait. I'm not in a hurry.'

'I *want* you to go.'

'I don't care what you want. I'm not going anywhere.'

'That's right, you stay with your lady,' says the tramp-man with the bloody lip and the blue card. There is the melting smell of alcohol on his breath, and he has hair growth everywhere. Nonetheless, I smile at him, and ask him whether he has been in a fight.

167

'*Lucy,*' says Judd, because – like Charlie – he cannot bear the fact that I talk to strangers. But if I am going to be here for two hours I need some entertainment.

'No, let the lady ask,' says Bloody Lip. 'I wasn't in a fight so much as a dispute about money.'

'Aren't all disputes about money?' I say.

'Aren't all disputes about money?' repeats Bloody Lip, although not mockingly. It is as if he has not had a conversation in a very long time, and wants to savour every moment of it.

Judd makes irritated noises. 'You're not going to have a political discussion *now* are you?' he asks; and I wonder whether he wants me to pretend to be ill, merely because we are now in casualty. If he does, he will find out that I am a terrible liar: I pretended to be sick on countless schooldays, yet was never able to fool my mother, who does not believe in illness. She walks around with achingly high temperatures.

'Are you going to have a political discussion now?' repeats Bloody Lip. His head then rolls sideways on to his shoulder. He is either asleep or dead. But still I do not think I should trouble the nurse. I have read the notice board, and he only has a blue card.

A fat woman comes in, handcuffed to a female police officer. Every womanly bit of the WPC had been stuffed inside her uniform. As she and the fat woman sit down, next to Judd, her black trousers almost split at the seams. Her face is so dry that it looks as if it has been grated. Hard. Flecks fall off that pink skin.

The fat woman's face is covered in real dirt – the type that is used in stage musicals such as *Oliver!* so that those in the cheap seats can see it.

They are joined by a policeman, hat in hand. The three of them are lined up opposite me. Their expressions say that they are prepared to wait for a very long time.

I know that I look guilty, as I always do around policemen. Indeed, around all figures of authority. This, despite my desire to help these people to keep law and order – hence my act of social responsibility, when I was eleven, with that object on the motorway. I always feel like telling police officers that they have an ally in me. I obey their laws.

Policewoman asks Policeman whether he wants a cup of tea. He blushes, peach-pink.

'From that machine? No, thank you,' he says, and I think how smart his uniform is. It is as if his mother has freshly pressed it for his first day at work.

'Yeah, you could be right,' says Policewoman, looking round at the machine. She crosses her fat calves.

'I had one yesterday and it tasted of soup.'

'Maybe it was soup?' says Policewoman helpfully; and I think of my soup spoon of blood.

'No, I pressed the right buttons.'

'I'm sure you did,' says the filthy, fat woman to Policeman.

I am surprised to hear her speak. She is like a saucy postcard, talking. I wait for Policewoman to tell the fat woman not to be so cheeky, but they do not appear to mind such a lowdown, dirty criminal interrupting their conversation. Policeman merely blushes cranberry.

'Why wouldn't they question me before?' the fat woman asks. She does not appear to be cold. Yet she must be. Even though it's October, she is wearing a T-shirt under that thin cardigan.

'I don't know,' smiles the policeman. It is as if he is

trying to remember his training. Should he discuss a case with a woman on the wrong side of the law?

'They said I was drunk, but I wasn't. I'd only drunk a bottle of gin.'

The PCs exchange smiles.

'Are you from Kentish Town station?' asks the fat woman.

'Me? No,' says the policeman. He would clearly rather be talking to someone more senior, such as the policewoman. But the WPC appears bored now. She wants to be in her warm, albeit empty, home. She wants to switch on the central heating, taking off that uniform. She wants to hang it on a wooden hanger behind her bedroom door. She wants to drag on her brown corduroy trousers and phone her father. Hearing his proud voice. Proud of his chip off the old block.

'I could've sworn you were.'

'No. This is my first job.'

'Oh, I was goin' a say. I know them all down there. There's one that I've known since I was that high.' The fat woman holds her hand flat and low, as if she is patting a small child's head. 'He's been arrestin' me since I was a kid.'

I look at Judd, and realize that he is writing down dialogue between the fat woman and the two PCs. He has on his lap that notebook, which he takes everywhere.

He was advised by his creative writing evening-class teacher to keep a notebook. Once a week, I baby-sit Solomon so that Judd can learn how to write, creatively. He comes back bursting with other people's ideas. Last week, he learned that – for a character to seem real – every characteristic must fit to make up a whole, except one. There must be one ill-fitting characteristic.

170

I laughed, and asked Judd what he thought my ill-fitting characteristic was. He said I ruined the theory, because I have two ill-fitting characteristics.

'Two?' I said, pleased, despite myself. He said that:

1) He had been surprised to find out that I was a beauty columnist. Given my acid tongue, he thought I should be an embittered biology teacher.

2) Given my personality, it does not fit that I am so pretty.

'You think I'm pretty?' I said, as he went into his bedroom.

'I think you should get rid of that acid tongue,' he said, closing the door.

I now go to sit beside him. I want to see what he has written in his notebook. I whisper, 'You can't use this. People don't talk like this in real life.' But he shushes me, because Policewoman has stood up with her fat prisoner.

'I'd shot up, that was all,' says Fat Prisoner.

'Is that right?' asks Policeman, as if he could not care less. He stands up, awkwardly.

'Come on love, we'll go through now,' says Police-woman; and they disappear through the green door. Into casualty's inner sanctum.

I am disappointed. I cannot understand how a junkie, alcoholic prisoner takes precedence over me in the queue for casualty. Plus, those police officers talked to her as an equal.

I realize now that they are all in this together. Establishment and anti-establishment. *I* am the one excluded from society because I do not break, or uphold, the law. I am outside of the class structure. I am passing through life without upsetting or participating in any societal organ. In other words, I am a parasite, and good for nothing.

'Have you thought of a name?' says Judd, stuffing the notebook into his pocket.

'What?'

'For the baby.'

For a moment I think he is talking about Maxie.

'Why? Have you got a good name for it?' I want to say that it is not a baby. It is a cluster of cells.

'For him.'

'Well, for him, then.'

'You could call him Sam. I mean, if you haven't got a name yet. That was my uncle's name. The one who died in . . .'

'I remember you saying, yes.'

'Well? What d'you think?' He looks so hopeful, that I haven't the heart to tell him that I might as well be carrying a melon as a baby.

So I say Yes.

Like most doctors, this one has very even features. His name is Dr Armstrong, and he cares about me in a way that my husband never did. He wants to go straight to the heart of my pain, like a headache tablet. So it is no wonder that I find him attractive. Even in the run-up to sex, men do not normally ask questions such as:

'Are you in pain?'

'Have you been in pain at any point before now?'

He really seems to care. He finds my heartbeat, without even trying to. I am embarrassed, because it is beating faster than is medically normal.

'I need to find the baby's heartbeat. Not yours. Ah, yes. That's it,' he says; and we both listen to Sam's tiny heart, beating on – as I knew it would be.

'I knew it would be,' I say. 'It's just a bit of spotting.'

'Well, it's worth checking these things. Now, can you give me a sample?' he asks, handing me a Tupperware pot.

He has the same pleading expression I have when putting Maxie on her potty.

Like Maxie, I am anxious to perform, but the toilet is so filthy. There are drops of pee on the toilet seat. There is wet toilet paper stuck to the floor. The corridors outside are cleaner and shinier than any I have ever seen; there is a woman out there in a blue uniform whose job it is to keep mopping no matter what. Yet, in here, it stinks like a men's public urinal.

When I return, with a proud amount of pee in the pot, my doctor is not there. On his chair is a book, rather like my *Family Health A-Z* at home. It goes through every possible illness, listing the symptoms. By the time Dr Armstrong returns, I have lost all confidence in him. For the book was open at a page marked Miscarriage; and I feel as if he has been doing some last-minute studying whilst I was out of the room. I want to quiz him when he comes back in with a nurse.

'I hope you don't mind, but I've brought Nurse Kelly in, to witness the internal examination.'

For a moment, I think he needs Nurse Kelly for a second, more expert, opinion; but then I realize that he needs her in case I sue him for sexual harassment. I want to say that he should feel free to sexually harass me. But his metal spatula is up me by then, and it hurts.

'Sorry, this does cause a bit of discomfort,' says Dr Armstrong, using that medical term for extreme and agonizing pain.

'No, it's – ow – fine.' I am suffering, but at the same time pleased that I checked my toenail polish.

173

'No, you're all right, the os is closed.'

'Oh good.'

I do not know what he is talking about, but I am pleased, nonetheless. It is clearly better to be closed than open. I feel as if I am being congratulated.

Prematurely. I have another five months of this to go.

'I can't guarantee anything, of course,' says Dr Armstrong, as if he has read my mind. We are talking through the plastic curtain. Nurse Kelly has gone. I pull on my black jeans. Button up the fly. 'And you should come back in for a scan tomorrow. But, as your os is closed, I doubt you'll miscarry. Well, not in the next twelve hours, anyway.'

'But I could still miscarry?' I ask, coming through the curtain.

'I wouldn't worry. It was only a bit of bleeding. Probably due to a low-lying placenta. Or a tiny blood clot.'

'You think?'

I sound as if I am putting my faith in Dr Armstrong, but only to give him more confidence. I know that Sam would not die, even if I did.

'Yes, we see this every day. Often, it's just a warning sign. Try to take it easy. You work?' He is wielding a pen, presumably to make himself feel important.

'God, yes. Full-time.'

I tell him about my job, stressing the demanding nature of my senior position; and the doctor nods sagely, all the time staring down at his medical dictionary. It is still open at the Miscarriage section; and I wonder whether he is sneaking a quick look in the event of my asking a difficult question. I want to tell Dr Armstrong that it will not help him to cheat. Not in the long run. One day, he will find himself performing a major heart operation, and there will be no notes to help him. *Will there?*

174

He says, 'Perhaps this is your body's way of telling you something.'

'Like what?'

'Well, to appreciate the fact that you're pregnant.'

As we drive home, Judd says, 'This might be God's way of making you appreciate this pregnancy.' And I tell him that the doctor said the same, only with less faith.

Chapter Seven

It is my mother at the door. Groomed, as ever. Never a blonde hair brown. Even her buttons match her shoes. Ten denier tights, because my mother does not fear the cold. Stiletto heels, because she does not care about comfort. Expensive make-up, because, to her, a naked face is common. Her lips are perfectly outlined, yet there is no sense of edge to them. They are filled in, rose pink.

'Maxie. Hello. Solomon. It's Granny *Oody*. Hello, Lucy.'

'Hello, Mum.'

But she has no time to stop. Maxie and Solomon have to be put into her gold tank of a car, double-quick. She has to do some supermarket shopping. She has to brief the Staines Slimco Rep.

'I have to rush if I want to get to the supermarket. There's a new one opened up, underground. It's *won* . . .'

'You don't *have* to take the children,' I say, handing my mother two mini-coats. I bought Solomon's: he had been wearing a two-year-old's jacket for years.

In truth, I was looking forward to a weekend free of Maxie's needs and Solomon's nightmares. Judd is out tonight too, at Rabbi Scheur's. In other words, he is with the Rabbi's *perfect* daughter, Chava.

So I have the rare pleasure of a night in, alone. It is a pleasure because it is rare. I am out all day tomorrow. It is Heather's birthday, and I have been invited to her place for a celebratory lunch. We are all finally going to meet the man she met through a women's magazine. Dominick. Does he know that he would be dumped in seconds for VD? In the same way one peers into blackened limousine windows, Heather still holds out hope for VD.

My man, VD. I dread to think what she would say if she knew I was sleeping with him.

I prefer not to think what Von would say.

In the evening, I will be appreciating high culture at the theatre with Ruth, Ysanne and Sophie. But, tonight, I am in, and set to spend the entire time watching television. At least Charlie taught me how pleasurable it can be, to lose oneself in a TV programme.

I am enjoying two documentary-soaps. One is set in the Accident and Emergency department of a hospital. The other, in a women's prison. There is a better spirit in the high-security women's prison than there is in my own community. Any community spirit in Camden used to come from a 24-hour grocery store that has since closed down.

I knew the Greek-Cypriot family who ran the store. They remembered Maxie's birthday, and I remembered which child in the family was having which operation. We had reached a stage where we were exchanging presents.

But Mr Metados said that he could not afford to turn down the offer from the hypermarket. In order to construct their car park of a building, the hypermarket needed to bulldoze All Stores, S.J. Household Goods, the NHS dentist, Flowerville, and that nameless shop which sold items that nobody needs.

Mr Metados said that profits were down, anyhow. Restricted parking had harmed his trade. No-one shopped in the area unless they were resident.

At the brand-new hypermarket, there is free parking, and they have built-in people to wash your car for you. Everything is under one roof, and there is a place for everything. Everything is in its place. It was not like that in Mr Metados's shop. He piled sanitary products on top of boxes of fruit.

The hypermarket has an aisle of three hundred different varieties of savoury snacks and sixty-two brands of juice. I know this because Solomon is going through a counting stage. I have teased Judd that – despite all the moral teaching – Solomon will grow up to be an accountant.

I do not bother to strike up conversations with the shop assistants in the hypermarket; they are all too tired. There is no such thing as society any more. Not in Camden, anyhow. Even that last vestige of a bygone era – our lollipop lady – has gone. There is now a computerized pedestrian crossing.

Yet, in the prison docu-soap, there is a real spirit of camaraderie. So much so that the inmates find it hard on release to adjust to life on the outside. Inside, there are women who help illiterate inmates to write letters home. There is a set time for fresh air and exercise. There are karaoke evenings. Prisoners go to church on a Sunday.

Angela, Von and I would love it on Block B. Angela, for the thriving lesbian community; Von, for the drugs; and me, because mothers have it easy in prison. Unlike the majority of women, jailed mothers are taught how to look after their newborns. In fact, they have the equivalent of a £400 a week maternity nurse, because new babies are looked after by someone else. Someone trained. Inmates have only set hours in which they may visit their babies. The rest of the time these mothers can catch up with their sleep, and allow their bodies to heal. They are not under pressure to breast-feed.

Yes, I would be more at ease, locked up in an institution like school, or prison, where the rules are so clear; and I am only half-joking.

'I'm not saying I don't *want* to look after the children,' says Mum now. 'I'm just telling you what I have to do tomorrow.' Because my father needs driving to the dentist. My brother needs taking to his therapist. He has been depressed since his wife left him. Mum needs to research treatment for Dad's arthritis. She has to do her meals on wheels, and practise her salsa steps. All this, and still she has to fit in those sixty daily cigarettes. She is smoking now – a Silk Cut to the butt – and buttoning Solomon into his coat. Solomon, who is singing, rather than speaking, like a child in a light opera.

It's time to go. It's time to go to Granny Oody's.

'I want to start reading my new book as well,' says Mum, proudly. 'I ordered it over the internet, and it's just arrived. *The Outsider*. Isn't this New Media exciting?'

'Haven't you read that yet?' I say lightly, but I am delighted that I have found a book I have read before my mother, whose bookshelf would put a city-centre library to shame.

'Only in English. I want to read it in the original French.'

'Oh.'

On this, we differ. I do not understand why my mother wastes her time in this way. I do not see the point of reading, unless the book is part of an examination syllabus and on a compulsory reading list.

179

'Is this for your French course?' I ask, unpeeling Maxie from my legs. I divert her attention by telling her to look through Granny Oody's handbag. Louis Vuitton, naturally.

'No. I just think that my French is good enough now. What are you reading?'

'Mmm. Now? I'm in the middle of *Tatler*.'

I have not read a novel right through since circa 1993. After Charlie, I could not see the need. Our culture had become so atomized that it was rare to find anyone – let alone my badly read husband – immersed in the same book. Charlie always argued that, even then, it was likely that the book would be dramatized, at some stage, for serialization. Why read a book, he said, and spoil the ending of a television show?

'Oh Lucy. I thought I'd *taught* you,' says Mum in that voice. 'You should be in the middle of two books at any one time – one fact and one fiction. Have you listened to nothing I've ever said? You *must* read *Birdsong*. I've just finished it, and it's wonderful. I'll give you ten quid if you do,' she smiles, and raises a trim, dusted, eyebrow.

Throughout my childhood, Mum bribed me to read the classics. She would not let me watch more than one hour of television per week. Even then, it needed to be informative, and educational.

My mother does not believe in entertainment, so I had to wait until she went out, so that I could beg my father. *Please, Dad. Just one programme. She'll never know.* When she came home, Mum would check whether the telly was warm from watching.

If it was, she would scream at Dad that he was encouraging me to be unambitious, like him. She did not want me to end up driving buses. Like him.

Dad would simply smile. He does not raise his voice, my father – unless he is on an organized demonstration against the evils of capitalism. Even sitting in that wheelchair, he is so tall a man. His size forces people to notice him. Everyone listens to my quietly spoken father – apart from my strident, forceful mother.

Dad thinks that I was worked too hard in childhood. He believes strongly that I should have been having more fun, as he did, hanging around on street corners, with a gang.

Yet, Dad did not realize what it meant to be a girl in a gang. If he had seen me with Billy and the others, he would have changed his mind. I think he thought that we went fishing.

'I'll take ten quid to finish *Tatler*,' I say, with half an eye on Maxie, who is going through Granny Oody's bag. She is trying to unscrew Mum's multivitamin pill bottle. But if Maxie has inherited any (in)abilities from her father, she will not be able to open childproof bottles when she reaches middle youth.

'I wish *I* had time to read magazines,' says Mum, and I tell her that she could make the time if she really, really, wanted to.

She smiles at the children and says, 'Even with grand-children?' because she is starting to see Solomon as one of her own.

Secretly, I think Mum wants me to become romantically involved with Judd although she has still not given up on Charlie. This, despite the fact that Judd is a religious zealot. I wonder whether she is nostalgic for her parents' bigotry. Perhaps Judd's rigid orthodoxy reminds her of her childhood in the same way that huge trees, salad cream and the royal family do me. Certainly, she goes through my food cupboards now with a childlike enthusiasm.

181

Borscht, she says, her voice like warm cream. *Matzo meal. Oh, lokshen.*

'Well, they could have gone to Caroline's,' I tell Mum, because my mother-in-law phoned earlier this evening, begging to take Maxie. I explained to her that, this week-end, I also had responsibility for Solomon.

Caroline fell silent, which is her way of shouting. Then, she said, 'Oh, I see. Jolly good.' In other words, *Oh fuck; another man's moved in on my grandchild.* The most she would say, when Judd moved in with me, was, 'Well, it's not ideal. But then, what is?' In other words, *Well, I suppose I'll have to suffer it, my son being the bastard that he is.* She said that she had once been in a similar position with her gardener. Caroline had had to offer him something 'live-in' too.

At the time, all sorts of obvious, Charlie-type double entendres floated around my head, but I pushed them to recede. I do not want to think of life with Charlie. (Lucy, formerly Lucy-and-Charlie.) I have not seen my husband since he left. He checked I would be out before coming to pick up the *Radio Times* bath-towels.

Judd allowed him in. Judd allowed him to take the safety pin chair, my liquidizer and the cutlery that we saved for dinner parties – i.e. still a new set.

I still do not mention Charlie to Caroline. It is as if her son never existed. Sometimes I wonder if he has even spoken to her since our split. I was always the go-between, relaying messages between them.

Do tell Charlie to bring a tie if he's coming down this Sunday. Donald is refusing to . . .

Tell the old bag that I'm not coming to stay if Helen is. And if Roger's there, I'll . . .

Certainly, Caroline did not mention him when she

182

called. When I said that my mother was taking Solomon as well as Maxie, she said, 'Oh, I can take the little boy as well, you know, Lucy. In many ways, I'm easier with boys anyway.'

'I don't know,' I said. 'Thanks, and everything. But Judd's an orthodox Jew, and he had to be persuaded to let Mum have him. Even then, Sol brings his own food.'

'Oh, you don't have to worry about that. I'm just as easy as Judy is, around Jews.'

I crushed a laugh, knowing that Caroline only offered to take Judd's son because she will do anything to compete with my Mum, who intimidates her, what with her Jaeger and her Escada.

As my father-in-law says, Caroline cannot wear clothes. She has an especial problem with accessories. Donald is cruel like that. Because of him, Caroline assumes that she cannot sew, dress, or wear make-up. 'You look like a tart's pair of knickers,' said Donald when Caroline once wore red lipstick.

Because of Donald, Caroline thinks that she cannot sit exams, pass exams, concentrate, prepare a decent cheese sauce, read a broadsheet newspaper, talk quietly, serve canapés, oil-paint even amateurishly, learn a foreign language, use a computer, listen, ride, wrap a parcel, address an envelope, find another oven setting other than *high*, sing, look womanly, or make conversation.

All women are useless, in Donald's opinion – but it is not only women. Children, coloureds, homosexuals, journalists, socialists, teachers, ticket-sellers, road-sweepers, neighbours, pop-music stars, writers, artists, stockbrokers, air hostesses – all of them, in Donald's opinion, are good for very little.

The bottom line with my father-in-law is that he thinks people are fundamentally evil. My Mum says that the quicker Donald's generation of men dies out, and their way of thinking with them, the better.

'I'm not completely hopeless,' said Caroline to me, on the phone.

'I know you're not.'

'I can look after an extra little boy.'

'I know you can.'

'And I've just started a French class too. French cuisine.'

Caroline is always competing with my mother. She asks for Mum's recipes and then adds an odd ingredient, like cherries to soup. She copies my mother's clothes and then adds unnecessary accessories, like bows or sequins. Caroline wants to make it clear who is the richer. But, despite all that old money, it is she who ends up looking nouveau riche.

Caroline should simply accept that she and my mother have different values. Mum is a liberal, for example. Caroline thinks that she is, because she can 'see that some people are homosexual, poor things'. My mother is intellectually curious. Caroline believes that she is, because she occasionally reads fat biographies about the wives of presidents.

'French cuisine; that's good,' I said to Caroline, absent-mindedly.

'Although I don't know how I'm going to fit it in, what with my business,' she added. For a moment I thought that she was referring to the business of her marriage – for being married to Donald is a full-time job. But then I remembered the shop. Because Caroline owns a shop. *It's really only a hobby,* she once said. *So it's just lovely when someone wants to buy something.*

184

The shop appears to specialize in lace doilies. Of course, Caroline has someone to run the shop for her: a mannish woman who does her utmost to make Simply Gifts unwelcoming. The (man)-woman has made it into the sort of shop that asks you not to bring in food, or children.

'It's hard running a business,' said Caroline, on the phone. 'Your Mummy's so lucky having all those representatives running hers for her.'

I am caught between Mum and Caroline. They always disagree, particularly about childcare. My mother believes that I am far too soft on Maxie. She thinks I should give her sweets only on national holidays. Caroline thinks I am too hard on Maxie. She once said, 'Maxie's surrounded by No's, isn't she?' because I refused to allow my daughter to eat mouse poison.

Mum argues that I should have potty-trained Maxie at ten months. Caroline wonders why I want to deny Maxie her babyhood by forcing her out of nappies. Mum believes that I should do more handwashing – it will preserve my finer fabrics – and apply for a place on a national newspaper's training scheme. Caroline thinks that I try to fit too much into my time. She says that I am heading for a breakdown. Women try to do too much these days. It is hard enough, keeping staff.

'How's the pregnancy going?' asked Caroline, on the phone, earlier. Brightly, because I did not tell her about last week's scare.

'Oh, fine.'

'How do you manage it all?'

'With difficulty.'

'You poor thing.'

I often feel that I am closer to Caroline than my mother,

185

in opinion at least. But if I were to follow my mother-in-law's advice, I would end up wasting far too much of my time in butteries.

When the door closes on two colourful children, I feel such a sense of peace that I do not move away for a few seconds, but stand there, leaning against the door. Since Judd and Solomon moved in, I have started to appreciate the value of silence.

I am like a child in a toy-shop – or Charlie in an electrical-goods store – in the empty flat. I switch on the dishwasher, then play with the radio dial, finally turning on the television at a news report. It is about five Asian people dying in a house fire after a lit newspaper was shoved through their letterbox. Police were not ruling out a racial motive.

I switch over to a gritty, contemporary film about how terrible life is. I want fantasy, so I change channels, wondering when Pauline Collins aged so. It seems like yesterday when I was watching her as a young floozy in *Upstairs, Downstairs*. Yet, there she is – a middle-aged woman with stretch-mark problems.

I have seen this film before, so I try the last-chance channel. There, I find a programme about interior decorating. It lulls me into a feeling that I have re-decorated my whole flat. It is the same feeling I often have after pressing the snooze button on my morning alarm clock. In the haze of half-sleep, I think that I have washed and dressed and fed my child. But everything is as it was when the alarm went off.

I tell Angela this when she phones. She laughs. Then, she stops, saying that she has nothing to laugh about. It was reported in the gossip columns that her celebrity girlfriend was seen feeding ice-cream in a public place to another celebrity lesbian. I say Not To Worry. Celebrities have to invent gossip about themselves. Otherwise they cease to exist.

I feel such a good friend, making Angela happier in a single phone call, when I spot the bouquet of flowers I forgot to give my mother. They were to thank her for taking the children. They are sitting there, smugly wrapped in cellophane. Thank goodness that flowers are made to last these days. Of course, they have no smell. But who cares when they stay pretty for weeks?

I phone Von, then VD; then I go to the toilet and find a blood clot in my knickers. It is the size of a small animal.

I cannot think, so I telephone my midwife. I have saved the blood clot in a piece of toilet tissue, in the same way that I saved my tooth when it fell out. I am always practical like this.

When Peter Billings chopped off a piece of his finger in craft, design and technology, I kept the piece. Before our primary school teacher, Miss O'Connors, left, I asked her for the Roman projects we were halfway through. In this way, I could hand them on to Miss Roberts.

I telephone the midwife, because I am efficient like this. I make sure I study a set number of hours before every examination. I assiduously fill in my tax returns.

'How big is the clot?' she asks me, and I study it.

'About the size of a small mouse.' The size of the one my mother strangled with her bare hands.

'Are you alone?'

'Yes.'

'Lucy, your os is open. I think you're about to miscarry.'

I can hear what she says. But I have saved the blood clot,

and I know that there is a lot that doctors can do these days. Babies are born without heads but doctors mould working brains from foot cells. I know this, because Caroline read about it once in the newspaper.

'No, it'll be fine.' I can still feel Sam moving about inside me. Besides, I believe in my body. It has never let me down. I conceived easily; I started my periods, trouble-free, at thirteen.

'If you've passed a clot, that probably means you'll miscarry, Lucy.'

'I can't,' I say, beginning to believe her. 'I mean, I'm all alone.'

I cannot be alone for this. I cannot be alone for this, or for a World Cup final, or for any New Year's Eve. I could not be alone for the General Election results. I could not be alone when Princess Diana died.

'Is there anyone you can ring? Your husband, maybe?' and I actually laugh, as I imagine Charlie in this situation. He was no use when the dishwasher flooded. He was no use on that car journey to Wales. And then there was the egg incident.

'I'm better off alone than with *him*.'

'Well, then you must call for an ambulance.'

'What – 999?'

'Yes. And Lucy, I'm sorry.' She is being so kind. She has not even met me, yet she cares about me in a way my mother has never done.

'But I'm not in any pain. My urine isn't irritated,' I say, trying to remember what I read in that stack of pregnancy manuals.

'Well, if you don't want to go through this alone?'

'*No*,' I say.

And I cry, barely able to hear that beautiful, dislocated

voice of the midwife. Her voice is as soft and as strange as a hotel bath-towel.

'Shall I keep the blood clot? Will it help?'

'Yes. Take it with you if you want,' she says. But I can hear her thinking: *if that helps you, Lucy;* and I say Goodbye, crying, dialling 999.

'Did you dial 999?' asks the ambulance man when he arrives. I am standing there, carrying my labour bag – the huge holdall that I took into hospital with me, when Maxie was born.

'Yes.'

'I'm not used to picking people up like this. We're not a taxi service.'

He is looking at me in disgust.

I am horrified. At the very least, I was expecting sympathy. I packed my wash-things because I am practical like that. I even left a note for Judd saying that if he needed me I would be at the hospital, miscarrying.

I do everything – as Caroline would say – 'by the book'. At school, I pretended to be stupid, and to listen to Ska music. At university, I pretended to be clever, and to appreciate opera. At work, I pretend to be interesting, and to forgive Heather.

'The midwife told me to dial 999,' I say, but my righteous indignation is spoiled by those pink tears, dripping down my face.

I do as I am told, I want to say, following him downstairs, and out to the ambulance. I have eleven O levels and four A levels and a first-class degree from Oxford, because I do the right thing. I married, on the advice of my mother. I had one child. One is on the way. I cover all the books on

189

the reading lists. I follow washing instructions. I even dry clean if necessary.

But to this uniformed man – his mouth half-hidden by a moustache – I am wasting ambulancemen time. In the time I am taking to walk to his ambulance, he could be rescuing children from burning buildings.

I climb into the ambulance and lie down on one of the surprisingly soft beds, because I do what I am told. And it is then that the pain starts. Contractions that are the opposite of orgasms. I am crying white tears, and screaming. I am holding on to the ambulance man.

I am told to breathe into a machine – gas and air, I think – and the moustached man turns suddenly kind, even turning on his siren. He tells me that it is not far to the hospital.

He is being so kind that, between contractions, I ask him whether he wants to see my blood clot, but he tells me to keep it. I clutch it hard as the contractions keep coming, and coming, and coming.

I think: *At least I have the blood clot.*

I am inside an ambulance with flashing lights and noise; and it feels as if it is taking me to my death. Cars pass my window, uncaring, as if they had always known death was among them.

Only I was ignorant of everyone's mortality. I was too busy worrying about which butter to buy, or office relocation.

Cars pass my window as if they do not care that I am screaming, and dying. I used to point out ambulances to Solomon and to Maxie. Solomon would be excited, especially if the blue light was on. Now I know that, as I was busy laughing and pointing, there was someone screaming inside the vehicle.

I feel as if I am in a limousine. I can see out, but no-one can see me, lying here, screaming.

There are some crises that no-one can turn into a drama and enjoy. I am too scared even to want my mother. I am too scared to think.

People are asking the ambulance man questions, but the bottom line is that I have a wounded womb.

No-one wants to look at the blood clot that I had prepared earlier. I feel as if they are not interested in any part of me.

I am through the door of casualty, still screaming. The screaming does not feel as if it is coming from me.

I realize that I have not been given a coloured card. I was pushed straight through the door to the other side. Obviously, if there is really something wrong with you there is no need for a card system.

I feel like yelling this through the curtain at the patient people, waiting. *They're lying about their card system . . .*

I am on a bed in a corridor, but soon I am wheeled into a room behind a curtain. I am a movable feast. This is fortunate, because I am making too much noise to be left in the corridor with the ill people.

The pretty young Irish nurse who so obviously has no idea of sex, or birth, or death (she is so clearly thinking of one of the handsome doctors with even features) takes my temperature and then my blood pressure, but she will not take my blood clot.

I am still holding it, beautifully wrapped up in a tissue, when she asks me, in that lovely, lilting, accent whether I want any pain relief.

'Please.'

She tells me to change into a hospital gown. It is the sort

with no back that takes away anyone's dignity – even that tall, elderly man's in the corridor. He looks like a landed squire, but we are all equal here in casualty. We are all semi-naked under these white gowns.

I am hooked up to a machine. They are giving me laughing gas. I am being given laughing gas; and I think of Von and her amphetamines.

'Do you want a top-up?'

'How do I *know*?'

'The gauge goes down to empty, look. You let me know when you do.' She points to the ugly machine next to me.

The Irish girl, slip-of-a, leaves; and I suck in that gas because it really does make me feel happy. *All I need to be happy,* I think, *is the relief of pain.* Von knows this; why did she not explain it to me?

The curtain opens – rather dramatically, I think, in my drugged state – and Judd comes in. It is so wonderful and strange to see him here. Strange, because I assumed that everyone living had been left behind.

There are only dead people here, I think, but aloud.

'I don't think you're dying, Lucy. Not yet, anyway,' says Judd, his skullcap loose. It is such a pretty pink. He is pretty in pink, with a yarmulke that Chava knitted for him.

'I am. They don't tell you anything here. They just leave you alone. It fucking hurts so much, Judd, will you look after Maxie for me?'

I now know that this is how my own death will be. It will be a shock; and I will lie there, bleeding profusely, and wondering when the real moment will come. I will be so scared. Despite the nurses and Judd, I will be on my own.

Judd: 'When d'you want me to look after Max?'

Me: 'During my funeral.'

Judd: 'Will you pay double rates?'

I laugh hysterically at that. But I tell Judd not to judge his jokes by my reaction. This is an artificial situation; and I am drugged. I am sucking and breathing in laughing gas and screaming in between the breaths. I do not know what is tighter: the contractions or Judd's hand, squeezing mine.

'You're my childminder,' I say, suddenly remembering. (What would my mother say?) 'You shouldn't be seeing me in my knickers.'

Judd raises an eyebrow, looking at my silk Agent Provocateurs.

'I hope they can be cleaned in a forty degree wash,' he says, because he does the laundry.

I laugh, because of the gas, singing, 'Little Sam, little Sam, who do you think that I am?' to the tune of Little lamb, little lamb; and that might have been a poignant moment, but I am laughing like a drunken tramp in an alleyway.

I can hear the nurses outside, laughing too. They are ignoring my screams, and all the other screams I can hear too, coming from behind the curtains. I realize that it is a competition for casualty patients to see who can scream the loudest.

'I win,' I say, to Judd's obvious confusion.

'What do you win?'

'I've got the loudest voice; and I give the best head ever. Tell that to the gorgeous Dr Armstrong,' I yell, in my drugged state. 'Perhaps then he'll save my baby.'

'Lucy, please.'

I had not thought Judd sentimental. But then I have not seen him cry before.

Although he is not really crying. He has wet eyes. That is all.

Charlie cried properly. He was always crying. He cried loudly during weepie movies. He used to cry his way through televised Danielle Steel novels. 'I don't care what you say,' he would whimper. 'This is really moving.'

Typically, I have become addicted to the laughing gas. It is more effective even than drink. The jokes are coming thick and fast. I joke to Judd, between screams, about Dr Armstrong, and my blood clot, and the Irish nurse with the mole on her neck.

But he has stopped talking. He is simply sitting, squeezing my hand.

Perhaps I am paranoid, but I am worried. I am worried that the laughing gas is running out. As I say to Judd, I am sure that the gauge is empty.

'It's not. It's fine,' says Judd. 'It's full.'

'No, it's running out. *Please.*' I breathe it in. 'Please get Dr Armstrong. I want filling up.'

I laugh, and then wriggle in agony. The pain has started up again; and I do not trust Judd about the gauge. He is the same in a car. He waits for the orange light to flash before filling up with petrol. I prefer a full tank.

'I want a full tank.'

'Lucy, calm down. I don't think you should be using it like that. It's for when you're in agony, not . . . You've got such an addictive personality.'

But I am not listening. I am concentrating on breathing in the laughing gas. I am breathing in – the way they told me to in those antenatal classes, ante-Maxie. If I breathe deep, the pain will go.

'Don't you think this room looks like a gas chamber?' I say to Judd.

194

'Don't be . . . You've never been in a gas chamber. Don't be glib, Lucy.' He seems weary, despite the fact that he has nothing to do. I am the one in premature labour. Premature, because I do everything first. I was the first girl at school to be fucked. The first to be entered for Oxbridge.

'I've heard enough about them from you.'

Only a gas chamber would not have those three tissue boxes, lined up on the wall. One is full of rubber gloves, the fingers sticking out like lots of limp condoms.

'Get a nurse, Judd.' I suddenly, desperately, need the toilet.

'You'll be all right, won't you?'

'No, I won't. *Get a nurse, Judd.*'

I can still hear those nurses outside, laughing. Laughing, while my baby is dying. Through the haze, I try to remember that I did not want this baby. But I cannot concentrate on what I want.

The least they can do, those guards outside, is to help me to a toilet.

But Judd has gone out through that green curtain. When he comes back, he is with a male nurse.

The nurse is holding a bed-pan. He sends Judd out, referring to him as my husband. I try to make a joke, but I cannot reach the punchline. I am in desperate pain. In my back, and stomach.

I ask the nurse to leave too. I climb off the trolley-bed and squat on the cardboard pan, feeling Sam slip out of me. Slip.

Like jelly sliding out of a bowl. Slip.

I cannot look down. I simply stay on that cardboard potty, screaming, 'It's all over,' because I remember this line from films; and it seems appropriate. 'It's all over.'

195

As I repeat this, over and over, the male nurse comes back in and helps me back on the bed. He has covered up the bed-pan.

'Do you want to see the baby?' he says; and I yell *No*. Because I do not want to see my faeces and goodness knows what else. I am squeamish about seeing dead bodies in ordinary times. I do not even go to see horror movies. Because there is enough that is horrific about real-life documentaries on the television.

'Are you OK?' asks Judd, coming in.

He is grey, his skullcap hanging off his head by a thread.

'Everything's OK.'

'What d'you mean?' He stares at me. 'What's happened?'

'I've had a spontaneous abortion,' I say half-laughing.

I want him to tell me what to do, according to his Beth Din, to stop this happening. But he simply stands there, in shock, saying: *'You've . . . ?'*

I am disappointed in him, as I say, 'Well, I'm unpredictable like that. You never know what I'm going to do next.'

Judd sits down, and covers his face with his hands. 'Oh God.'

I wonder where the laughing gas has gone. I want it back. I want to take the machine home with me. Perhaps Von and Heather mean that sort of pleasure when they discuss their drug-taking? The male nurse is standing there with that bedpan. It is as if he is awaiting further instruction.

I realize that the nurse knew that I was going to miscarry. When I asked for the bedpan, he knew.

'Did you know that that was going to happen?' I ask the male nurse.

'I thought it might. It often does.' He is so young. So white that I can see his veins.

'Why didn't you tell me? You just left me to . . .'

'There was nothing I could do. I'm so sorry.'

'So you just left me to squat, and dump like an animal. To shit life. Death.' I am still drugged – hence the melodrama. *It is such a short link to madness,* I think. I could drift off it into it, like sleep.

Judd is sitting there, staring into space.

'I ought to phone your parents,' he says, eventually, and his face is as soft as it can be.

I feel as if everyone, apart from me, is speaking to a script.

Me: 'They'll be pleased. Sam was never meant to be.'

Judd: 'I very much doubt that Judy'll be pleased.'

Me: 'You don't know how much my mother likes order.'

Judd: 'Lucy, stop it.'

Me: 'It's neater this way.'

The male nurse repeats his invitation for me to see the contents of that bed pan he is carrying; and, in my drugged state, I think how much like a sonderkommando he is.

Judd had taught me about sonderkommandos. How, during the Holocaust, they were the Jews forced to clean out the gas chambers of dead people. They carried out dead bodies – stuck together sometimes, and babies – knowing that they would one day soon meet the same fate.

'Poor you,' I say to the nurse. 'You poor thing, like a sonderkommando. Coming in to take my dead baby away.'

'I'm so sorry,' he says, like a TV nurse in *Casualty*. 'It's terrible for you. This is awful.'

'No, someone has to do it. It's an awful job, but someone has to do it.'

'I'll go away now,' says the nurse. 'The obstetrician's coming.'

'What for? Don't they deal with *live* babies?'

'To see what happened. They'll want a postmortem.'

'Got to tick those boxes,' I say with a tinkle-laugh.

He looks at Judd, all confused, and Judd shrugs his shoulders.

'I'm sorry,' says the nurse. He is so sweet-looking.

'No, you're a good man. You do this every day without complaining. And you probably don't tell anyone either, do you?'

'I'll go now. You can see the baby later if you want.'

'*No.*'

This was a scream. The nurse goes out, carrying the contents of my womb. Judd takes my hands in his. He has such rough hands, I think. There is so much dead skin. I realize that, before now, he has not touched me. I have never felt him.

'D'you want a coffee?' he says.

'He was goodness itself, don't you think?' I reply.

'Or food? You must be hungry?'

'You mean after all that effort?' I pause, then say, 'I doubt they'll have a kosher counter.'

'That's OK. Really. It's . . .' He tries to think of something to say, and settles for, 'I've given up on you, anyway.'

His voice is so gentle, and I know now why Maxie calls out his name when she falls over. I know why my own daughter prefers him to me. His voice is so soft. Mine is loud and rasping.

Before he goes out, he says: 'Lucy, I'm really so sorry. I feel sort of respons . . .'

'Look at it this way,' I interrupt, to cheer him up. 'I get

198

to go through labour but don't have the agony of those sleepless nights.'

I laugh, and lie there alone, feeling hungry. Starving, in fact. Staring at a sign on the wall that says the hospital's casualty ward accepts no responsibility for any loss of personal belongings.

The male nurse comes in with the Irish nurse. They start to clean up. *So soon?* I think. (Maybe the next person in here will be giving birth.) I have to sign something saying that I agree to them conducting a postmortem examination.

They do not call Sam my baby. They talk about him as if he was a very heavy period. But I know from my pregnancy manuals that he had human hands, and fingernails, and a head, and eyes that opened and shut.

I wonder if he was able yet to cry. Judd comes back with a trayful of unkosher food and drink. I am ravenous, quickly eating the doorstep of a sandwich. Drinking the orange juice. The male nurse is asking me whether I want a burial, and I feel as if he is asking me whether I want a doggy bag to take home.

'No,' I say.

The obstetrician comes in. He reminds me, with that accent, of Charlie's father, Donald. They probably club together – gentleman-like. He says, 'Right, what's happened here, then?' and this makes me angry.

'What do you think's bloody happened?'

'I don't know.' I can see that he is bored. 'That's why I'm asking.'

'Put it this way. What d'you think was in that bedpan?' I look at the male nurse for moral support. But he is too much in awe of the obstetrician even to look at me.

'Why don't *you* tell me?' he asks with exaggerated patience.

'My baby; my bloody baby. I miscarried, for fuck's sake. It was stillborn. Born still. Still. Born.'

'How many weeks pregnant were you?'

'Eighteen.'

'You've had a miscarriage. It's only much later on that it would be described as a stillborn.' In other words, *you've failed even to have a stillbirth.*

Now I am crying too much to argue with him. It is always the way with me. Self-pity takes over. As a suffragette I would have been too busy crying to chain myself to any building. Blubbing, 'How could men have treated women like this – it's so *unfair.*'

'So, I miscarried. Whatever. My baby died. Either way, you're a bit fucking late, aren't you?' I say again, but still crying. Judd has my hand again. But he feels elsewhere, and too far away to support me against this cruel doctor.

'I have to examine you now,' says the obstetrician. He is so clean-looking. He is staring at me with revulsion. It is as if he will later say to his wife, *'You should have seen the dirty thing I had to examine today. Horrible.'*

'No. I don't want you to. I know my rights,' I lie, thinking of my mother, who always says, 'Never let yourself go in their eyes.'

I try to stand up, but feel too fragile. I do not have a middle to me.

'Well, that's OK. It was for your benefit.'

'Oh, well OK then,' I say, ever so weakly, wondering why doctors refuse to take control nowadays. It is not as it was in Victorian times, when medical people had confidence in their leeches. Now, even specialists know nothing.

No-one is in authority any more.

There is a rush then of urine tests, and metal rods shoved up my vagina. Judd asks me whether I want him to phone Charlie; and I say No. Right now, I hate Charlie. Right now, I feel that he killed my baby. By neglect.

That stops me thinking about who really killed Sam. Me. My arms ache. The pain of emphasis has moved from my uterus to the crook of my arm – the ache in my shoulder an unbearable strain from not-carrying. I am primed to hold a baby. My breasts feel as if they need a role too. Judd asks me whether I want him to call VD; but I say, 'Why? He wasn't the father.'

When he leaves, I whisper, 'Sam didn't have a father.'

Something beeps loudly.

'What was that?' I ask, frightened that, perhaps, someone else has died.

'It's my pager,' says the obstetrician, sticking the biggest needle I have ever seen into my thigh. It is like the needle in Solomon's toy doctor's bag. It is being used to stop me haemorrhaging. The result is pain, the size and shape of a sticking plaster.

I am wheeled up to a ward. I want to be carrying something, anything. I wonder whether Judd will find me here. I am not sure that I care. I do not want him here any more.

He has a habit of bringing God into everything.

Chapter Eight

It is the middle of the night, and black outside. Judd was forced to leave the hospital hours ago. The doctors discovered that he was not my husband.

I have a whole ward to myself, and a view of London from the window. Outside, the top of a tower flickers like a lighthouse.

I am unable to sleep, trying to work out what they have done with my baby.

I wonder whether they have thrown Sam into a hospital incinerator. If a patient says that they do not want a burial, what happens to the baby? Is he shoved down a waste-disposal chute? Is my dead son there now with all those empty syringes and medical waste?

A nurse comes to see how I am; and I pretend to be the same as I was before my baby slipped, dead, out of me. Slip. I ask her how much blood I can safely lose. This is something I ought to know.

'You'll bleed for some time. It's like having a baby,' she says.

'But not.'

'I didn't mean . . .' She blushes a soft pink.

'I know.' I smile, so as to comfort her.

'You'll have a scan tomorrow. We'll need to check that there's no more retained products.'

So Sam is now being referred to as 'retained products'. She is saying that I have bits of baby left in my uterus.

'What'll happen to my breasts? Will they leak colostrum?'

'How many weeks were you?'

'Eighteen.'

'Probably too soon. They'll hurt, that's all. Now, why don't you try and get some sleep?'

I do try.

I actually hurt in the spot where Sam used to be. That exact uterine place where he lived and died. That is why I rang the bell for the nurse. I need to know where my baby is. I need to rescue him.

Perhaps there is a chance that I will find him still alive in that wreckage of syringes.

'Have you thrown him out?' I ask her.

'Who?'

'My son,' I whimper. 'Have you thrown him out yet?'

'No, Lucy. We wouldn't do that. He was your baby.'

She has been trained for situations such as this one, I think. She goes on to say all the right things: she says that of course he seemed real to me; he *was* real. She suggests that I bury my son properly.

I want to grovel at her feet. I want to beg this angel sent from heaven for my son. I want him back. I made a mistake, that was all. It was only that I thought I did not want him.

If they would only give me my son back, I would do anything. I would believe in Judd's God. If he was the one with the ability to give me my Sam, I would worship him, and follow his laws.

I would never buy unkosher again.

I know why this has happened. I think bad thoughts about sweet, dull people, such as Susanna. I was pleased when Heather cut her hair short, revealing her odd shape of a head. At school, I victimized Mel Amphrey; and I drink too much. (I was drunk when only seven weeks pregnant.) When planes crash, I am pleased, because there is a smaller statistical chance of such a horror happening to me. And I am not a good mother to Maxie. My idea of good childcare is to buy children's outfits from Ralph Lauren.

'Where is he now?'

'He's in a fridge,' she says in that gentle voice.

'A fridge?'

It does not seem strange to me – that Sam should be in a fridge. I think about that fact for a few seconds. Then I ask, 'Where's the fridge?'

'Along the corridor.'

'He's along the corridor?'

I am closer to him than I thought I was. I am almost close enough to touch him. He is not in a rubbish bin, but in a fridge. Near me.

'Do you want to see him?' asks the nurse. 'You can if you want.'

'No.' I know that that would be too much. I cannot even picture him without crying.

I have been crying throughout this conversation. The tears will not stop. But, at least they are noiseless. I wonder whether they will take as long to dry up as the bleeding.

'Can I see the fridge?'

'You want to see the fridge?'

'Yes.'

I climb out of the bed. 'Please,' I say, glad that I can do something for Sam. At least I now have something to do.

'I want to.' I feel weak from the drugs. But I follow the nurse to a room that is labelled Dirty Utility.

She points out which fridge he is in. I am so happy to see it. I can imagine him inside that fridge. Opposite it, is a sign saying Vomit Bowls, Toilet Paper Only, Waste Products Only. It makes me think of the time we buried my father's mother. We were all crying, apart from Mum, who was angry at Grandma Pinny for dying on my brother's wedding day. But the rest of us cried. Even my brother. Even Sally, his new wife. There were gravediggers there. But I was the only one who saw them laughing at us all. When I told my mother she said that it was in my imagination. She said that I always see the black side to everything.

I ask if I can be left alone – although I have seen the sign on the wall, saying: Gynaecological Staff Only. I wonder why they want to keep patients out of here.

'Why do you want me to go?' asks the nurse in that sweet Scottish. Probably Edinburgh.

'I need to be alone.' *With the fridge.*

'Are you going to open the fridge?'

'No,' I say patiently.

'I don't want you to open the fridge.' Her face is all concern.

Perhaps my baby is not in the fridge, I think. Perhaps she is worried that I will open it up to find shelf upon shelf of cold cuts and vegetables.

'Why not? Is he not really in there?'

'Of course he's in there, Lucy.'

Perhaps my baby is not the only baby in that fridge. She is concerned that I will open it up to find shelf upon shelf of dead babies. The nurse will not be able to identify my baby, because at that age they all look the same.

205

'I just don't think it's good for you to be in here on your own. I don't think you should be alone right now.'

I cannot be trusted in here, on my own. Perhaps, given the state of the NHS, she is worried that I will pilfer the large-sized, extra absorbent sanitary towels, piled up on that counter. Or the boxful of disposable panty liners. But she does go – although I think that she is listening outside. I sit next to my fridge looking around me. At the large black polythene bag with a sign attached to it that reads:

FOR DISPOSAL OF:
Non-infectious rubbish
i.e. paper hand towels
Dead flowers
Newspapers
Disposal = Buried wherever possible.

I am sitting down with my back next to the fridge. In this way I can be close to my baby. I am so close to him like this. There is only the fridge door between the two of us.

I think of him lying there; and I sob. Gut tears that come like Maxie's. From the stomach. I think of Sam alone and lonely in that fridge, wanting his mother. Needing me. *I'm his mother, for fuck's sake.*

Why are they taking him away from me?

I wonder whether – if I called up an ambulance – the moustached ambulance man would come and take me away for a few weeks in the country. Me and my fridge.

I want to be alone in a field with my fridge. Or I want to be in a land where they do not think it strange to see a woman walking everywhere with her arms around a fridge.

Outside, I can hear the Scottish nurse saying: 'I hope she's OK. I don't know what to do. Shall I leave her in there?'

206

It is so cold in here. People think that I am mad, wanting to be near that fridge, but I know the truth. *They* are the mad ones. They do not seem to care that we all die . . . slip. Besides, I do not care what they think: from now on, I will go everywhere with my fridge. Cold as it is. I sit so close to the fridge door that he can probably hear my heartbeat.

'Can you hear me, Sam?'

'I love you, baby.'

'Only you knew that I wanted you.'

'I always wanted you.'

'You'll always be with me, my lovely. I won't let them move you.'

'I won't ever leave you.'

But of course I do.

I was so tired and cold that I came back to my bed. But I am unhappy here. I was happy with my fridge.

The Scottish nurse was so helpful, suggesting that I see my baby, suggesting that I have a burial. She was so kind, that I asked her whether Sam could be moved next to my bed. I said that I wanted him in a box by me.

I said that I wanted him in a box, but really I wanted him back inside me.

She said No to the box idea. She said that we had to keep Sam at a certain temperature. Fridge temperature.

Now I want him so much. But they are keeping me away from my fridge.

I am sure that there is someone I can complain to. But I have not got the energy.

The nurse comes and offers me sleeping pills. But I will not be fobbed off with drugs again. They got me like that before – with their laughing gas. I did what they said. I laughed and laughed as Sam died inside me.

Only I do not want to go to sleep, because I do not want to wake up in the morning all empty, knowing that I have lost my baby.

She comes in later, to see me staring; and she asks me again whether I want a sedative. I want to ask whether that is all she has for miscarriages. Only half-jokingly.

Nothing feels different in the morning. Only the ward. When I wake up, I feel like a madwoman for having sat by the fridge.

The ward is full of morning sounds and smells. Breakfast for the ordinary. I feel like a madwoman among them, because I am the only person attached to a fridge.

There is an invisible cord between me and it.

I can hear people in the corridor; and I want my son, the fridge, so much that I am jealous and bitter about the nurses who are walking past that room, unmoved.

They would think me odd if I went in that room now. *Gynaecological staff only*. I suppose that the Scottish nurse has ended her shift, and gone home. It feels as if she was the only one with access to the room.

I should have stayed in there last night. I should have kept vigil, protected my baby. I did not do a good enough job while he was in my womb. Then he died, and I allowed my tiredness to get the better of me. It was too cold in there for me.

What must he think of *me* – his mother? I should have sat there forever, or at least until they agreed I could take him home. It is only a fridge to them, after all.

My breasts are so sore. I can hear too many people; and the lights are full-on. I know that I will never reach that fridge – not with all these people around.

I think of him, all lonely. Cold.

Neglected. An unsmiling woman offers me tea. I order a cup for the hell of it. It comes in the sort of china that my grandmother served. Thick and patterned Braille.

Judd comes in, smiling like a madman. I am not used to seeing him grin so profusely. I thought he could only smile wryly. He has a bagful of food that I work my way through. I am so hungry. I open the Kit Kat and eat all four fingers at once.

It is clear that Judd is determined to behave differently today. As if he has not seen me in such a state. I am relieved; I was embarrassed and ashamed, knowing that he had seen too much of me.

He is rushing around, looking at everything. He is like someone who has just been presented with a key to his hotel room. He is opening all the cupboards. He is admiring the swivelling bedside tables, and the view. 'Wow; that's the Millennium Dome – like a giant pin-cushion.' I eat the Frosties; and he goes next door to the bathroom.

'You've got a private bathroom, Lucy,' he says. 'This is great.'

'Yeah; aren't I lucky? I'm really enjoying myself.'

I cannot help but be facetious – although it is true that I have been treated well. The ward where I gave birth to Maxie was full of helpless women, crying in that half-light that is new motherhood. The bathroom was soiled with bloody towels. Having just given birth, I could barely see my reflection in the dirty mirror. Yet visitors were due any minute – I needed to brush my hair, and apply make-up. 'If you look good outside, you'll feel better in,' Mum said, as I tried to remember the lower half of my body.

Upstairs, in a different postnatal ward, the nurses were dismissive. I remember walking along the corridor towards the payphone, and a midwife whipping off Maxie's blanket, saying, 'You're boiling that baby to death.' On my way back from the phone, a different midwife screamed at me for freezing my baby to death.

They did not once change my sheets, although they were covered in my blood. There were germs enough to kill my Maxie, too.

Here, in a different death-ward of the same hospital, I have a clean, private bathroom. 'Can we have you up, dear?' asks a nurse now. 'I'd like to give you fresh sheets.' The hot tap works. But my baby is in a cold fridge, surrounded by sanitary towels. He, not me, should be having special treatment. I effectively killed my baby, yet I am being rewarded.

I eat the cereal bar. But I cannot fill my stomach fast enough.

Judd is talking on. He is trying to ignore the fact that I am desperately unhappy. I have never known him to talk so much. So much rubbish. While the orderly changes my sheets, I look at the objects on my bed-table, as if I need to remember them later. One glass of water. One tissue. One cup of half-drunk tea. It helps me to focus my mind away from the fact that I had a little boy who died inside me.

'What d'you think, Luce?' asks Judd; but I am not listening. I am staring at the *Strictly No Smoking* sign. I am wondering why I have stopped crying. I feel so lumpen.

'Think about what?' I ask, in a haze.

'About what we've arranged? I'm going back to the kids . . .'

'Yes, of course.' For a moment, I had forgotten that I had another child, alive.

'And then your Mum's coming.'

'There's no need.'

Maxie will die soon. I steel myself for that inevitability.

Slip, when a fat nurse comes over and smiles. The nurse has a face like a bruised apple. 'I expect you couldn't manage any breakfast,' she says, looking at my half-drunk cup of tea. The milk, now scummy.

I hide the plastic carrier bag that Judd brought with him under the bedclothes. It is pretty much empty now, apart from the fruit and the sweet wrappers.

'Hard to eat after such an ordeal,' she says, kindly; and I feel guilty because I have managed a big breakfast consisting of chocolate and sticky buns and sugary cereal.

The fat nurse leaves me with a form to fill in. It asks me whether I want a burial for my baby. It does not allow me space to say that I want him to stay in the fridge.

It queries whether I want to leave something with the nurses to put in the baby's grave. I wonder what they mean. A tooth? A flower? Some bedroom furniture?

I pull out a snatch of hair, sharp, and put it on the bedside table. It looks like spun gold, lying there, and I am pleased. It is all I have to give him. *If I can't be with him*, I think. So the tears start again.

'I want to be with him,' I whisper.

'Who?' asks Judd, coming back from the toilet.

'Sam.'

For a moment, he looks as if he is going to perform his usual conversational interruptus. But he pauses for such a long time that I wonder whether he will say anything.

Then, 'I shouldn't have suggested a name,' he sighs.

'What d'you mean?' I half laugh. 'That if he was nameless I wouldn't care as much?'

'You don't want to listen to me,' he says, and is sadder than I have ever seen him. 'What do *I* know?'

'More than me.'

'Maybe I've got it all wrong.'

211

I panic, waiting for him to say that he no longer believes in Judaism. If he says that, I will lose it. The only Judd I have known is certain of everything. Certainly, after checking with the Beth Din.

But he says: 'VD called, by the way.'

'Oafish VD.'

'He was actually very sympathetic.' He smiles, gently. 'You could do a lot worse.'

I think of VD and the way he tries to pretend that his feelings for me are meaningful. Despite his thirty-four years, he is so young. Give him a few minutes, and he will be pursuing another, equally vulnerable, woman. He will say to me all of the things he said when dumping Von. *I have a problem with commitment*, he will say. *I can't cope with your needs*, he will say.

'That's very gracious of you,' I say to Judd.

'Well, maybe I misjudged VD,' he sighs.

'So, does this mean you now forgive the Poles for the way they behaved in the Holocaust?'

He grins and stands up suddenly in that Judd-furious way.

'One step at a time. All I'm saying is, perhaps you should take the relationship more seriously. With VD. He really seems to care about you.'

'Almost as much as his MG,' I joke. 'So, I have your blessing?'

Judd is reading the folder of medical notes pinned to the end of my bed.

'I think you need Von's, rather than mine,' he says, distractedly.

I will goad him to be himself again. 'Since when were you interested in Von? Are you training to be a rabbi or something?' I want to hear him tell me what to do. But

212

he won't be pushed. The smile is still fixed on to his face. It is as if it is detachable.

'It's not hard to see that you should have told your best friend you're seeing her ex-boyfriend.' He returns the notes to their plastic folder. 'Otherwise, things get very messy.'

'Well, I would've. But it's only a fling.'

'Whatever you say, Lucy. But.' He stops and stretches his chest. 'I can't stand here chatting about your love life.' His expression says *Little love life*. 'I have to be back at the flat ten minutes ago. To relieve your Mum. She wants to see you.'

'It's not necessary. She's got a lot to do.'

I say this sulkily. But thinking that I fall between *Florist* and *Further Education Institute* in her personal address book. *Fletcher, Lucy.* I feel betrayed by Mum, who was not here last night to stop my baby dying.

She was there for Maxie's birth, but that was easy. If she was mother enough, she would have been here to organize Sam's death.

When Judd leaves, I go to the bathroom to bleed. I return to find that they have put a woman in the opposite bed. *So*, I think, *my special treatment is over.*

I wonder what the opposite-woman is in for. I had presumed that this was the miscarriage ward, but that woman does not appear to be at all upset. She is laughing, in fact.

I draw the curtain around my bed, because I still want privacy. I hear a nurse whispering to her that I have just had a miscarriage.

'Oh no, poor thing,' says the woman, and I want to undraw the curtains, dramatically, announcing to the ward at large that I have a living, breathing, born child at home.

I do not need their pity; I am not only a mother of dead babies. I have a fit, Slimco body. My mother made sure of that. Twenty minutes aerobic exercise three times a week. Simply follow the positions on the laminated Slimco exercise card.

The nurse pops her fat face around my curtain to tell me that I am needed in another room for blood tests.

'Can I ask you something?' I say, before she leaves.

'Yes, of course.' She has the same bedside manner as the Scottish nurse had – i.e. she sits down and looks into my eyes. Her voice is sweet; it barely disturbs. No doubt, she is following instructions in how to behave.

I say, 'There's something I did. I think it could have killed the baby.'

'What's that?'

'I drank.'

'You what?'

This is worse than I thought it might be. I believed that, if I confessed everything, I would be absolved of all sin. I look down at my hands, seeing my wedding rings there. Second finger, left hand. I wonder briefly why I did not throw them at Charlie when he left. I always miss my dramatic moment.

'I drank,' I repeat.

'What did you drink?' she asks, confused.

I wonder whether my Sam would still be alive if I had married another man. A man who was not Charlie. As Von implied, I have been self-indulgent, marrying the man I loved. I should have married a man who would have made a good father. Someone who would have supported me. A man such as VD.

'Vodka. And a glass of wine. But, vodka. I got drunk on

214

vodka when I was pregnant. My husband had just walked out on me,' I say, in my defence.

'Oh, Lucy.' I can hear her breathe out. 'Of course that didn't hurt the baby. Whatever you did, you would have miscarried. Nothing could have prevented it.' When I look up, the nurse has glassy eyes. I wonder how she can do her job properly – if she is so easily upset.

She is upsetting me, with her tears.

I thought that, if I was absolved of all sin, I would feel better. But I do not.

I am in the blood-test room. Finally, I feel useful – my arm outstretched. This is like pregnancy, being treated like this. I adored the attention that came with pregnancy. All those doctors, prodding. People asked questions about what went on inside me.

When I come back to my bed, my knot of hair has been cleared away with my cup of tea. My Mum is sitting there, smiling. She chatters on about how desperate she is for a cigarette. How Britain is becoming like America – i.e. a fascist state.

'You can carry a gun,' she says. 'But not a cigarette.' She talks about Maxie and Solomon. How Maxie told my father that he was useless, because she had learned the word *useless* from my mother. She tells me that in the space of 24 hours she has increased Maxie's vocabulary by 100 per cent. She tells me that she has taught Solomon how to complete jigsaw puzzles.

She says that she cheated and gave Solomon Smarties, and I tell her that she was wrong to do that. All Judd asked was that Mum fed him the food he gave her – all those silver-foil cartons of kosher meals.

But she says that I was not to worry: Smarties are kosher.

She took out the *treif* red ones. She laughs as she says that she *did* remember which foods had the stamp of the Beth Din. Besides she says that – according to the Halacha – if a Jew genuinely believes that a foodstuff is kosher, he is not committing a sin by eating it.

Mum talks about Solomon's suppers; and I think how funny people are about life-changing tragedies, preferring to discuss the merits of boil-in-the-bag rice. If she was mother enough, she would have warned me that babies are easily killed.

She would see that this was killing me.

But people pretend that painful death is not inevitable. They know nothing until they have given birth and death. They are blank faces.

I wonder how I will explain to the blank faces that my baby has died.

'How's the pregnancy going?' they will all ask.

'No, er, I lost it.' *But too trivial.*

'No, er, he died.' *But too serious.*

'No, er, I'm not pregnant any more.' *But, too dismissive.*

Mum sees that I am not listening to her. She changes the subject, saying I should take my hair out of the bunch. I would feel better if it was loose, she says; and I realize that my mother has come to my miscarriage in the same way that she came to my wedding – to rearrange my hairstyle.

'*God*, I want a cigarette.' She looks around. 'Never mind. Oh, I brought you your make-up.' She says this as if that will make me feel better. But I feel very removed from Mum, and Maxie. I can think only of that fridge. That is why there are tears again.

'Come on, Lucy. You can't fall apart over this. You have to be strong.'

But I am not strong like my mother. I could not believe it when I read about what she had seen in Bosnia. She gave birth to both of her children in a bath at home. Without any pain relief. She stood up to the taunts of men when she organized that rally for the women's movement. She fought her father, physically, before she eloped with Dad.

'You have to fight back,' says my mother.

She has always been able to identify her enemy. Her orthodox Jewish parents. Men. Pain. The Bosnian Serbs. But I have no-one to fight. Most states are run as liberal democracies. Even men such as VD are, secretly, feminists. Sometimes I do believe I am fighting my mother.

Certainly, I feel girlish and weak in front of her, for crying.

When the nurse comes to take away my form, I want to cross out my answer to the question: 'Do you want to see a chaplain?'

I had said that I would like to see a rabbi. But I do not now want to see a rabbi. The whole idea feels ludicrous. I no longer want to ask questions about the nature of death and life. No, now that my mother is here, galvanizing me, I want to know when my stomach will return to its former shape.

It was a good thing it happened really, I think. *I was sick of people patting my abdomen.*

Mum is rummaging around in her huge handbag. Eventually, she hands me her mobile phone. 'Call your Dad,' she says. 'You know what he's like. He's so worried. He wanted to come, but I couldn't face the journey with two kids and your father in the back.' She smiles. 'Or rather, two buggies and a wheelchair.'

'You can't use mobile phones in here.'

217

'Don't worry – we're behind a curtain.'

'*Mum*. It might interfere with the machinery.'

'What machinery?' she asks, looking around. 'You're not hooked up to anything.'

So I do phone Dad, and he is too kind. One can be too kind; and he makes me weep like an old woman when he says that he wishes he could have gone through it for me. I want another sticky bun.

'So, when d'you think they'll let you go?' my Mum asks, as I hand her back the phone. She ignores the fact that I am crying.

'I don't know,' I say, lying down on the bed. I stare up at the ceiling, which is tiled like a floor. Mum says that she will find out for me. She opens the curtain, and sweeps out. Dramatically.

Melodramatically, I think.

It is as if she believes that assertiveness will change the inevitable. I see the opposite-woman staring at me. I feel as if I have a sign saying *Yesterday, I had a son* stamped on my forehead.

My mother comes back with a nurse, who is all sympathy.' You can go whenever you want, Lucy,' she says.

'Thank you.' *What about my fridge?*

'Do you have someone to be with you?'

'Yes.'

'She'll be fine,' says my mother, who is all Slimco smiles.

In a terrible metaphor, the flowers I bought for my mother have died. They are the first things I see when I come into the flat. A cellophaned bunch of dead roses.

'They were for you,' I tell my mother.

'Oh, why?' She is all bustle, picking up Maxie, putting on the kettle.

'It was the least . . . You're always looking after my child.'

I cannot say my daughter's name aloud. I cannot even look at her. I feel that, if I did, I would be betraying Sam. *Little Sam, little Sam, who do you think that I am?*

'That's what mothers are for.' But she is too late, telling me this. I should have sacrificed myself for Sam. If I had stayed indoors more often, he would not have died. If I had stayed away from alcohol. (But even doctors allow a certain number of units.)

I switch on my new answering machine. There are five messages. I wonder what to say if someone rings now, without warning? The truth, perhaps? That my baby died, and I see everything in different, darker, colours now?

The first message is from Motherstore. I had ordered a bed for Maxie. She is too old now for a cot. They want to deliver it today. The second message is from Heather, who wants to know why I am not there, to meet Dominick. Not that it matters, she says, now that she's split up with him.

The third message is from Ruth, who needs to know why I stood up her, Ysanne and Sophie. The fourth message is from VD. 'Remember I'm here,' he said. The fifth message is from a chaplain, who wants to discuss Sam's funeral arrangements.

This sets off those same, dribbly, tears. I forget about phoning Heather, or Ruth, or VD, and go straight into my bedroom. I do not want to see my mother, or Judd. As I close the door, I hear them all stop what they are doing – even the children.

I pick up a panda-bear puppet, that Maxie must have left in here, and hold it in my still-aching arms.

'Lucy?' says Judd. He comes in with my daughter, who

219

is pushing a doll's pram. Judd is wearing a new skullcap today, and I wonder whether Chava knitted another one for him. A green one, this time. I feel so unwomanly. I cannot even have a baby properly, let alone crochet.

'Go away,' I say, cradling the panda. But Judd sits next to me, with Maxie on his lap.

'One thing's for certain,' he says, trying to laugh. 'I don't think Sam was a panda-bear puppet.'

I think that this is funny, but I cannot laugh.

He puts Maxie on my lap. 'She wants you,' he smiles. The way he leaves the room, makes me feel as if I am taking part in an experiment. Maxie sinks into my lap. She is so warm, but I deny myself a hug. She is too big; and I want a wee baby. A newly born.

I resent her for not being my baby. All I want to do is to return to the hospital. It is dark now, and the Scottish nurse will be back on her shift. She will allow me to sit vigil at my fridge.

Maxie climbs off my lap and pushes the pram around the room. Watching her, I feel so lonely. I was never lonely when pregnant. I carried around company. Even when Maxie was born alive, I mourned being pregnant. I missed her being inside me. I resented my new daughter for being independent of me. She had betrayed our special, private, relationship by being born.

But at least she was there. I cannot stop wondering where Sam is. Are they cutting him open, painfully, for their postmortem, as I speak?

Maxie takes the doll out of the pram. 'No want doll. Take doll out,' she says.

'Yes, you do that, Max,' I say, grabbing the doll. 'Take the doll out and put it in a fridge. Then, when the baby's cooled down, put it into an incinerator and burn it up until . . .'

I am interrupted by my mother, coming in. She makes it clear, by her expression, that she has been listening at the door.

'Come on Max,' she says, looking helpless. (My mother, vulnerable.)

'You look after her,' I say, dully. Right now, I will only look after babies that are newly born and male. Sam only.

As soon as the door closes, I peel away the doll's clothing and put it to my huge, milk-sodden breasts. I want to go out; but everyone will think me mad if I am carrying a doll. I will be known as the mad-doll-woman. I want to be in a land where it is perfectly normal for women to carry around baby dolls.

My boy baby doll is butt naked, lying in the crook of my arm. He is like my son, with human-like hands, and fingernails, and a head, and eyes that open and shut.

I lie down, and it is then that I start to cry. I start small, but, after a while, I am wailing, like Mr Rochester's mad first wife.

I must have fallen asleep, because when I wake, I can hear Caroline's voice in the living room. My mother's voice is no longer there.

Judd is saying, 'The hospital let her go this morning.'

Caroline: 'Well, that *is* an early release date, isn't it?'

I go into the living room, carrying my baby doll. Holding the doll relieves the pain in the crook of my arm. But I doubt that anyone would understand that – least of all Caroline.

'Oh, Lucy,' she says, when I come out. She is all wrinkled skin and sympathy, and I realize that I am a stereotypical daughter-in-law, always looking for her to criticize me.

'Hello.'

'I bought you this,' she says, and hands me a badly wrapped parcel. There is Sellotape everywhere. I help Solomon to open it. Inside the bubble wrap is a bottle of expensive, cheap-smelling perfume.

'I didn't know what to get. But I thought you'd want to smell nice.'

'Of course,' I say, sitting on the sofa.

Caroline props up the perfume.

'Daddy,' asks Solomon, popping the bubble wrap. 'Why did Lucy's baby fall out of her tummy?'

'It's God's will, Sol. Human brains can't cope with the concept of infinity. That's why we don't understand death,' says Judd, absent-mindedly, sorting through a pile of skullcaps. He is back to his old Judd self, having talked at length to Rabbi Scheur. But I have watched him lose faith for a second, and I no longer see Judd in the same, fixed, way. 'And Lucy's baby didn't fall out of her tummy. It fell out of her uterus. D'you mind if I go out for a bit?' he says, turning to me.

He clips on yet another skullcap.

'You don't have to ask my permission.'

'I just need to talk to the Rabbi.' He just needs to see Chava. 'And if you're OK with Caroline . . .'

'She's not going to eat me.'

'*No,*' interrupts Caroline, as if she would not dream of doing such a thing. 'Look, I brought you these.' And she hands me a pile of leaflets. The top one is entitled *Coping with Miscarriage*. 'I got them from the clinic. I hope they . . . Oh, this really is your annus horribilis, isn't it, Lucy?'

This is what the Queen said after a year which involved Princess Anne entering divorce proceedings against Captain Mark Phillips, the publication of an account of the

Princess of Wales's bulimia and suicide attempts, the Duke and Duchess of York's announcement that they were to separate, the printing of photographs of a topless Duchess of York sucking the toes of her 'financial advisor', and a fire at Windsor Castle that caused £55 million in damage.

'See you later,' says Judd, slamming the door behind him.

When the Queen called her year an annus horribilis, it was as if she was putting a lid on misfortune. Likewise, by calling my year an annus horribilis, Caroline was saying that I could sink no lower. But I could not help being reminded of the years which followed the Queen's annus horribilis, during which the Prince and Princess of Wales divorced, and Princess Diana died.

'Oh, just get to the point, Caroline. Say it. My baby's dead. Donald's probably having an affair. Your son's a bastard. *Both* your sons are bastards. Life's shit, and then you die. Slip.'

'Oh,' says Caroline, looking around, frightened. 'That's right, Lucy. You say what you feel. Better out than in, that's what Donald always says.' Seconds later, she realizes what she has said. She covers up her mouth with both hands. Her eyes are huger, and unhappier, than ever.

'How can we hope to understand why these things happen,' she goes on, helplessly.

'Oh, that's easy. We're given leaflets.'

I am harder now. I can feel it. Meaner. The experience has toughened me up. I am no longer as vulnerable. To be too open leads only to misfortune. And I now understand why my father-in-law, Donald, is so closed-up and tough. He was sent away to public school, at the age of seven, after his parents split up.

'Made me what I am today,' he always says, proudly.

Now I know that people like Donald, with pursed mouths, are unhappy. The only reason their lips are set in such a straight line is because if they were to open up, even fractionally, they would start to sob, uncontrollably. Irreversibly. Perhaps they have it right, living by their Latin school mottoes.

'I, er, I told Charlie, Lucy,' says Caroline, smoothing down her skirt. 'What happened.'

'And did he give a toss?' I cannot bear hearing his name. Not now that he has killed my baby.

'Of *course*. He's not so . . . He still loves you, you know. He says, if you could only be less . . .'

'Of a failure?' I spit.

'*Controlling*. That was what he said. I think. He doesn't believe you love him, Lucy; and I'm sure he'll come and see you. Between you and me, I think he wants . . .'

'I don't want him fucking near me.'

She smooths down her skirt again; and I stand up, sharply switching on the kettle. *Click.* 'D'you want tea? And you two. D'you want juice?' I ask the children.

'Want juish,' nods Maxie.

'No, thank you,' says Solomon. He is building a house out of old sheets. Maxie is arranging her Barbies inside the 'house'. He is pretending to be his father, sounding just like Judd, telling Maxie that she should choose only two dolls to take inside the house. There is room for just two dolls. It is the policy of the ghetto.

'*Is the polishy of the ghetto, Maxie.*'

I feel a sudden, overwhelming warmth towards him. It is like a fire. Sam would have grown up to be Solomon. Despite my shag of blonde hair, and blue eyes, Sam too would have had dark hair, and big, brown eyes. Long lashes. He too would have looked old-fashioned – as if he has stepped out of a sepia photograph.

'So. Tea,' I say, remembering.

'No. *I'll* play Mummy.'

Caroline always finds the wrong words. Donald is right: she does not think before she speaks. She talks, and blushes afterwards.

'I can make tea. I'm not disabled.' The last time my mother-in-law made tea for me, it was mostly milk. Caroline said that she did not want to leave the bag in for too long; she was afraid that that might upset me.

'Of course you're not disabled. I pity those poor people; they should never have been allowed to live at all. All that happens is they're herded into institutions in our village. No, you're just very weak – although you can have three miscarriages before it becomes a problem.'

Three strikes then you're out.

I put the doll on to the counter, so that I can pour the water from the kettle into two extra-large cups.

All I want to do is to go back to the hospital. I want to go up to the fourth floor again, and into the fridge-room. I want to be back at my fridge. This doll is not enough, I think, pouring an excessive amount of cranberry juice into Maxie's cup. Handing it to her.

Even the smallest task seems a chore. I use a tablespoon to sweat tea from the bag. Then, the second cup. Then, milk. Then, sugar for Caroline.

'Sorry,' she says, as I spoon in three sugars. 'Donald always says it's because I'm not sweet enough.'

'Don't worry.'

'Well, thank you,' she says, upsetting some tea into the saucer. 'Although I'm here to look after you.'

'I don't need looking after.'

225

'You'll feel better over time, I promise.'

'Oh Caroline, how do you know?'

'Well, I've had one.'

'What d'you mean, you've *had* one?'

'A miscarriage.'

I pause, to regulate my breathing.

'You've had a miscarriage?'

'Oh yes,' she says, stirring her tea. 'It runs in my family, I think. Babies just fall out of us women like . . .'

'At what week did you miscarry?' Because I do not want her to finish her simile.

'Eight, I think. Maybe ten.'

'Oh, well that's early,' I say, relieved. Caroline knows nothing. 'I'm eighteen weeks gone. I *was* eighteen . . .'

'Well, what's the difference?' She stares at me, genuinely confused. 'It's the same thing. You go to the toilet and it drops out. My *mother* had late miscarriages. She was six months gone when she had her second . . .'

'Her second miscarriage?'

'Oh yes. *So.* You'll feel very strange for a while, but then life will go back to normal.'

So that is why Caroline talks in euphemisms. The doorbell rings, interrupting whatever I might have said. I buzz up the Motherstore delivery men.

'What are you expecting?' asks Caroline, as I open the front door.

'What did you have, love?' says the man with a pen behind his ear.

'What did I *have*?'

'What was it you ordered?' he asks, patiently. The other man gears up his clipboard.

'Oh – a bed. A child's bed.' A Barbie bed.

'Oh. Right. I thought that was strange.'

'Why?'

'Well, you're down on our list to deliver. But the van's empty. Damn, they didn't put the bed in.'

'They didn't put it in?' I ask, unable to cope with any more terrible metaphors.

'I'm sorry.'

'So you've arrived all empty-handed?' says Caroline, tinkling with laughter, trying to switch on some charm, but, as ever, unable to.

''Fraid so.'

This causes commotion, and Maxie cries. She so wanted that Barbie-doll bed. She runs to me, hugging my right leg. I feel as if I have a frisky dog.

'It's only a bed, Max,' I say. But still she cries. 'Want bed.'

'S'only a bed,' says Solomon, sitting on the floor. Shaking his head.

'I'll buy you two beds,' says Caroline. 'Three, if you'll stop crying.'

'No. Want bed.'

'Is there anything you want me to sign?' Caroline asks the delivery men.

'Please don't have a tantrum, Maxie. I can't cope right now.'

'She can have my bed.'

That was Solomon, coming to stand beside me. I kneel on the floor, and hug him to me. The noise Maxie is making zips through my head. She is having a tantrum now, and shuddering. In the past, I have been known to find her tantrums amusing; but that was in the past.

'Sorry, love,' says Delivery Man, as I release Solomon.

'We'll get out of your hair then,' says Other Delivery Man. He is wearing a T-shirt which reads, *I survived the*

Nutra Sweet London Marathon. From the look of it, it has not been washed since then.

'That might be for the best,' says Caroline.

'*You're* a good boy for your Mummy, aren't you?' says Delivery Man to Solomon, as his colleague turns to go, revealing a map of Europe in sweat on his back.

'Yes,' he says.

I look at him in surprise. I might have said something, but I am holding Maxie tightly. 'Want bed. No want Mummy.' The noise she is making is terrible, and she is kicking me hard. But, still, I hug her to my knees. For I will never again complain about motherhood.

The opposite is far worse.

Chapter Nine

I have almost recovered from my miscarriage. I was able to dress this morning. Wash, dress, buy food, run home, unlock door. Change into my night clothes. Wrap myself in a duvet. Switch on TV. Say goodbye to the children Judd presents to me, in the manner of a Victorian nanny. Answer my doorbell.

Buzz in Best Friends. (Von: 'Hey, we've turned up at the same time.' Angela: 'You don't mind, do you, Luce? I just had to come round when I heard.') Make tea. Von's with sugar.

Von opens a packet of kosher biscuits, describing the press launch party she has just been to. Well, why else did I think she was wearing this awful outfit? The jacket is made out of a diaphanous white material, which makes her look to me like an angel with wings.

Angela sits, like a cushion, on the hard chair.

'Is Judd here?' asks Von, taking off her wings.

'He's out with Maxie,' I say, explaining that Judd is concerned about the effect my miscarriage has had on my daughter.

Angela says that she is more concerned about the effect my miscarriage has had on me. Von swears about men in general, and Judd in particular.

'I'm fine,' I say, staring at the television. A cookery programme. *'Just add three cupfuls of flour, and voilà . . .'*

'You can't be fine. It only happened three days ago,' says Von, in a sixty-a-day voice like my mother's.

'Does it feel like it happened a long time ago?' asks Angela, gently.

'Everyone sends their love, but you know who's being amazing?' asks Von. *'VD.* He says he keeps calling, but you won't talk to him.'

'I think you should talk to Charlie,' says Angela. 'I was reading your tarot cards and . . .'

I stop listening, thinking how I am the whore, having lost my virginity to Billy at thirteen, and cunningly used sex to lure Charlie into marrying me. I am the whore, having slept with VD, because I am unable to resist taking a chocolate when the box is being passed around.

'Are you OK, Lucy?' asks Angela.

'OK; yeah. I mean, fine. I was in a bit of a bad state yesterday.'

'I told VD you wouldn't want him here. What use is a fucking *man* at a time like this?'

Even with a mouth full of obscenities and dunked biscuits, Von can sound like an angel. It is as if someone Godly has spent time teaching her right from wrong; she has such a clear set of principles. She knows what she wants, at all times.

My own moral training has left me confused. It is as if I have been cramming, days before an ethics exam. As a result, I can sleep with a man who last year viciously told Von that she was too good for him, leaving her to go on a month-long drinking, drugging binge. It is only that I have never known how to stop sex.

'Why does VD care so much?' I say, loathing myself for the lies.

'Heather thinks he's interested in you.'

'Until Saturday I was *pregnant*,' I say; and I am crying again. Tears which disappear halfway down my cheeks.

'You're still with Charlie,' says Angela, sitting on the floor so that she can put her arm around me, to comfort me.

'I'm OK,' I insist. 'Anyway, the crying's hormonal. You must have felt like this, Von, after your abortion.'

'Thanks for broadcasting that fact,' says Von, looking at Angela, whose face spreads with sympathy.

I freeze.

Von cannot stand to be pitied; and I know now why I rarely see Von and Angela together. They see the world from such clashing vistas that it is difficult to focus on either of them. In company with the two of them, I veer from one Von viewpoint to the other Angela opinion without pausing to consider my own perspective.

'I'm sorry,' I say, quickly.

'Anyway, Lucy, you can't compare . . . That was so sodding different. I wanted an abortion,' she says, for Angela's benefit.

'I don't see why that changes anything.' *A baby dies, however it is killed.*

'I didn't tell you this, but last week . . . You picked the death card,' says Angela.

'Did I?'

'And you know that the death card's good. It means new beginnings. Now you can . . .'

'No. No. Nothing good can come out of Sam's death. Nothing.'

I did not realize it, until now, but there are limits to my friendship with both Von and Angela. I try to make them comfortable by changing the subject back to the more certain one of star signs.

'Would he have been a Scorpio?' I ask.

'Oh Lucy, d'you want to talk about it?'

I say No, and more tears come. I am hoping that Angela will realize that I want to talk about Sam all the time, without pause. But neither of them are textbook friends. We do not breathe the same air.

'OK, no. Of course not; I'm sorry,' says Angela.

'We shouldn't talk about it,' says Von, as I stare at the television.

'Oh, love.'

'I'm not crying because of the *miscarriage*.'

I am crying because of a chocolate commercial. Phrases such as 'a glass and a half of milk' set me off, as do babies' limbs, babies' newborn yells, and the floppiness and fatness between babies' limbs. I cry after making a list of things To Do:

* *Ring office to tell them I won't be coming in.*

* *Reply to building-society question, the bottom line of which is: Do you believe in mutuality or simply want some quick cash?*

* *Call chaplain and arrange burial.*

I cry after radiographers triumphantly tell me that my womb is clear.

'You should be pleased,' said Radiographer Woman. 'You might have had to have a D&C to scrape away all traces.'

Of the baby.

But I had felt until then as if my baby might still be inside me, struggling to survive. Because miracles happen; and Sam could have survived the trauma of my miscarriage. One reads about such miracles all the time in tabloid newspapers. Babies surviving outside of the womb. Living on, in lungs or hearts.

'You're bound to be emotional,' said Radiographer, studying her notes, as I wiped my cheeks with a mess of toilet paper. 'You're in mourning, you know. Grieving for the baby.'

I do not know what my baby looks like, so I picture him as the young lad on the front cover of one of Judd's books about the Holocaust. *The Yellow Star*. When I said this to Judd, he said that that boy came to represent the haunting image of the Holocaust itself; and that it could be my way of mourning all Holocaust victims.

Von watches as I wipe my face with a thin string of toilet paper. Angela says that she is going to find me some tissues. She is certain that I have scented tissues somewhere.

'That was Charlie,' I mumble. 'He took them with him.'

'You know Jonathon's left Susanna,' says Von, brightly.

'What d'you mean he left her?'

'Yes. Fucking bastard. Just as she'd finished the house.'

'Because he's worried she'll be made redundant?' I say. But then I remember my vow to be kinder, and add: 'Poor Suse.'

Von laughs, wrapping herself in half of my duvet.

'This smells terrible,' she says. 'No. Jonathon told her on Saturday that he'd been having an affair.'

'Bloody hell. Poor *Suse*. I thought *they'd* always be together.'

'So did Susanna,' she says. 'He left her this *note* saying he still liked her as a person.'

'As opposed to what?'

Von laughs, and I unwrap myself a little.

'God; so what other gossip is there?'

'Hmm. *Gossip*. Well, OK. I slept with our aerobics instructor.'

233

Even I laugh then.

By the time my friends leave, that afternoon, I am completely recovered. So much so, that I have decided to go
into work. Archway cannot do without Louise Bennett's
column. I am putting on a trouser suit when the telephone
rings. It is the hospital chaplain. She is choosing her words
carefully.

I want to tell her to hurry, and not to worry – I miscarried
days ago. So much has happened since then. Jonathon has
left Susanna. The planets are clustered below the horizon
of my chart, which means domestic and personal matters
are more important to me now than anything going on
in the wider world. Von is sleeping with the aerobics
instructor.

Just have a laugh.

But the chaplain is being unnecessarily kind, saying, 'I'm
sorry to have to throw all this at you, but there are legalities
to arrange. Sorry. You have an option to buy a burial plot.
Otherwise, the baby will be buried in a *general* area.'

'A common area?'

'A common area, yes.'

'But I can buy a special plot?'

'Yes, sorry, you have that option. But there's no need.
The general burial will be done . . .'

'He gets a plot of his own?'

'Well, no, there are four in each plot. Because they're
so, sorry, small and . . .'

'But it's a proper plot, that someone's dug out?'

'Oh no.' She laughs, like an elderly virgin – pleased
that she has found a subject with which she is familiar.
'Nowadays they don't do it *manually*. They do it with a
digger.'

I tell the woman that I am too upset to finish the conversation. I will ring her back. (*Yes, sorry.*) I apologize for crying. (*Of course. I'm so sorry.*) She says that I have all the time in the world. When I come off the phone, I sob. Big, nasal tears, which dry up only when the telephone rings, and I pick it up to hear my editor, Hen's, voice.

He has called to say that I should not come into work. I should take the rest of the month – even year – off as compassionate leave. I laugh, and say that a week will be fine. As I put down the phone, I hear a key turning in my lock. I stiffen, wondering whether it is Mrs Leslie's murderers, coming to finish the job.

But it is my cleaning woman, Katie – as surprised to see me as I am her.

I had forgotten that it was her day to clean. I have not seen her since my maternity leave two years ago. I am at work when she comes; and the house seems no cleaner after she has been. It smells of eco-liquids, that is all. I have to re-clean surfaces afterwards, using environmentally unfriendly cleaning products.

Now, I am trying to appear occupied, tapping on my computer – *working* – as Katie does the ironing. I stare at the date on the screen – 3.50pm, Wednesday, October 8 – in order to convince her that I am thinking. Or rather, to convince her that I am not thinking, *Please leave, so that I can do nothing.*

But I cannot lounge around as another woman irons my clothes.

'I hope you don't mind, but I borrowed one of your books. Only I wanted to read some Sebastian Faulks,' says Katie, thudding the iron on to its stand. Steam hisses out of the boat of her iron.

'Oh, that's fine,' I say, ever-so politely, thinking how badly she smells – of vegetarianism. A fusty smell of staple grains and scratchy jumpers.

Charlie hired Katie after he saw her advertisement on the student notice board. *Need a cleaner? Call Katie on . . .*
 I made the obvious scrubbing jokes. I was happy cleaning up after myself. And I did not want a student peering down my toilet bowl. But I would have done anything to make Charlie happier in my home.
 Inevitably, Charlie joked about running off with the clever maid. So I said that Katie might appear brighter than me, but only because she regularly read a newspaper.
 The truth is that most of Katie's topics for discussion are beyond me. She makes me wonder why issues such as nuclear dumping and expressionism were not on my O-level curriculum. Because Katie has no exam passes, yet can talk knowledgeably about anything from classical music to Bill Gates's monopolistic business strategy. Whilst I spent my formative years sitting in a big and draughty exam room, she was out educating herself. Yet, still, Katie kids herself – as I once did – that exam passes are key to survival in the millennium. That is why she is at college as a mature student.
 I want to tell her to treat university as Ysanne did. Because Ysanne might only have a third-class degree but she realized early on that university was less about studying, and more about drinking eight pints of snakebites-and-black in one evening. That, and initiating discussions with Sophie, Ruth and myself, about the meaninglessness of living.
 I want to tell Katie that, for all my formal qualifications, I am qualified to do very little. Only ignorant men like

Charlie – to whom academia is a mystery – are impressed by my degree. Charlie is so ignorant that he thinks China's cultural revolution was nothing but a backlash against high culture, comprising popular demonstrations against German opera and the type of books I have on my shelf – i.e. those with no action.

We should never have been together, Charlie and I. I realize that now.

We were worlds apart intellectually.

Oh, it was all very romantic when he proposed to me in a gondola. But, married life was different. Charlie, sitting pretty, while I worked. Charlie shopping for ready-to-build furniture, then asking me to put it together? Me, finding his mouth stuck to Heather's at last year's office Christmas party?

'D'you mind if I don't come next Wednesday?' says Katie now. 'Only I've got to finish my dissertation by the end of January and I haven't even *started*.'

'Oh yeah, that's fine.'

Because, really, I have no need for a cleaning woman anyway. Not now that Charlie has gone for good. He was the one who wanted servants. He wanted everything ironed, even his Calvin Klein underpants.

Besides, Judd does most of the housework. I did not ask him to. It is only that he thinks I am sloppy, and incapable of reading a washing label. I questioned the political correctness of his taking on every domestic role, like a 1950s housewife. But Judd said that if he does the ironing, there is a higher chance our clothes will not burn.

Nor will he let Katie do his ironing. When Judd started taking care of Maxie, near the end of my maternity leave, he was forever arguing with my cleaning woman

Caroline said, 'It's always that way with *staff*. They

squabble amongst themselves.'

Katie thinks that the way an animal is slaughtered, according to the Jewish religion, is a cruelty. Judd argues that the Jewish method of slaughter is the most humane.

'You have to have a firm hand with them,' insisted Caroline.

Judd is suspicious of Katie's veganism. He says that she cares more about animals than people. (She once helped break into a restaurant to rescue a lobster.) So I asked Judd to leave money for Katie, out of his housekeeping, and be out of the house when she came.

'If firmness fails,' said Caroline, enjoying being an expert on something. 'Keep them separated.'

Katie says now, 'I just can't do my dissertation. God, I wish I hadn't started this degree. I'm just not clever enough.'

'Of *course* you are.'

I sound patronizing, when what I want to tell Katie is that, for all my A levels, she is cleverer than I am. I want to tell her that she has no need of a degree from a minor polytechnic.

Well, it must be small-time if it accepted Charlie.

But if I say that, I will lose my authority. I will be unable to look her in the face when I ask her to clean out my fridge. It would be like Lady Bellamy telling Mrs Bridges, in those repeats of *Upstairs, Downstairs,* that she has always been her intellectual superior. It would upset the natural order of things.

Caroline said, 'Don't ever be friends with the hired help. They'll only take advantage.'

Besides, Katie would probably argue that my degree has helped me to afford a cleaning woman. Without whom I would not have that smell of hot, pressed clothes.

That sturdy tower of folded tops. She would say that my supposedly useless degree has put me in a position where I can afford a cleaning woman, and a generous set of stainless-steel kitchen units.

In truth, Charlie's parents helped to pay for it all. Dirty Wallis money. Yet, for all my refusals, I still seemed to need it.

Money is still coming from Caroline's account to my own. Despite my prudence, I am never able to save enough to pay for our lifestyle. As I said to Judd last night, I am not paid a great deal more than the minimum wage.

He replied, 'Well, that's the trouble with those fun, glamorous jobs – they're badly paid.'

'My job isn't glamorous *or* fun,' I said.

'Yeah, that's the other trouble with those jobs,' he grinned.

So, I receive handouts. From Caroline. Recently, too. I have become dependent on them.

'Think of it as money for Maxie,' said my mother-in-law.

Hmm. Yes. According to Caroline, I am still a Wallis, despite the fact that I have kept the name Fletcher. Despite the fact that my Wallis husband has left me.

Donald probably cannot understand why money is leaving his account to go to me. No doubt, he thinks Caroline is unable to disentangle herself from the Fletcher family.

I presume that he thinks it a good thing all round that Sam, his grandson-to-be, died. But he did pass on his condolences via his wife. Because not for nothing did Donald have an expensive gentleman's education.

The phone rings, and I go into the bedroom to take the call.

'I was just thinking about you,' I say, because it is Caroline.

'*No?*' she squeaks, delightedly.

'Yes.'

'Why are you speaking so quietly?' she asks.

'My cleaning woman's here. I think she listens in to my conversations.'

'Oh, well, you don't want that. You have to show her who's boss. My mother's last words to me were: "Caroline, keep your staff."'

'So, how are you coping?' she asks as I pause to allow her to think about her mother.

'I'm OK now.'

'I was telling Charlie how that miscarriage business knocked the stuffing out of you,' says Caroline.

'You told him what?'

'Oh no, I didn't mean that,' she says, and I hear her hand go, like tissue paper, to her mouth.

'So, you spoke to Charlie?'

'He came up. He's furnishing this flat of his, you see. Took some old furniture.'

I smile, because, for Caroline's old furniture, read expensive antiques.

'What did he say?'

'Oh, this and that. He's chummed up with some old friends from school. Richard something. I can't remember any other names.'

I cannot resist saying, 'Has he got a girlfriend?'

'Oh, Lucy. *No.* I mean, he mentions girls' names. Someone called Catheter, I think it was. No, it couldn't have been catheter. But it wasn't Catherine.'

I cannot say anything for thinking of Catheter/Catherine.

'But,' says Caroline, filling the gap, 'he really only talked about you.'

When Charlie was around, I disliked Caroline almost as much as Charlie did. But now we are both on the same side. It is still awkward, of course, between my mother-in-law and me. We are like Russia and the US after the end of the Cold War. We cannot work out who our enemy is. We suspect it might be Charlie, but cannot yet speak freely about him.

'About me?'

'Oh yes. He misses you. Asked about you and Maxie. Well, just you, actually.'

'What did he ask about me?'

'Well, really, just whether you were missing him.'

'I saw your husband this week,' says Katie now. She folds a jumper, flicking under the arms.

It takes a long time for me to speak. But when I do, all I say is, 'Oh yeah?'

'In the caffy at college. He wanted to know whether I was still working here.'

'*Oh?*' I can feel each of my organs tightening.

'He wanted me to clean his place too.'

'Really?'

'But I said I'd stay with you.'

She squirts water over one of Maxie's tops. *Spritz.* I feel as if I ought to play Lady Bellamy and praise Katie for her long service and outstanding loyalty. But she would probably hear shades of my old Essex accent and laugh.

'*And,*' she says, smiling a secret smile, 'he wanted to know if you had a boyfriend. I think he misses you.'

'Sit still woman,' says Judd, cutting my hair.

I did not know, until I saw Maxie's new bob, that – as

well as everything else – Judd cut hair. But I should have known. There is nothing he cannot do.

'Sodding scissors,' he says, looking at my nail scissors.

'Aren't you going to ask me where I'm going for my holidays?'

'I don't do conversation,' he says, bluntly cutting.

I think how he manages to make all his activities, from childcaring through housework to hairdressing seem so masculine, despite all three jobs being the usual preserve of the female.

'These are for cutting nails. I need those choppers. What's that Katie person done with them?'

'Tidied them away, perhaps?'

'Well, these are shit.'

'A bad workman blames his tools.'

'Yeah, well, you wouldn't expect a surgeon to operate on your bowels with a Hoover, would you?'

'No.'

'*No.* So stop using clichés.'

'How do I look?' I ask, when he finishes. I stand up and turn to face him.

He quickly looks away.

Saying, 'Don't be so bloody vain.'

I have absolutely recovered from my ordeal, four days ago. Judd's haircut has helped. At least I now look human, but Maxie still thinks I am behaving strangely because on Sunday I stole her doll and ripped off its clothes. I cradle it sometimes when I think no-one is looking.

I look like Maxie's Mummy, but I have been different somehow.

'Put Flumpy in the basket,' I earlier said to Maxie. Politely – because, the angrier I am, the more polite I sound.

'Bas-ket in Flumpy.' She dropped the toy rabbit she loves more than anyone in the basket.

'There's a place for everything and everything in its place.'

But I cannot take care of Maxie any more. I broke down, because everything reminds me of Sam. Even Flumpy. Even the baby ducks in the bath. We are bathing the children. Judd is washing Solomon's hair, and I am sitting on the toilet, pretending not to cry. Judd massages in the frothy shampoo, pouring water over Solomon's head, who wails on cue.

Judd pours over another cupful, and tells me that he has talked to the Rabbi about Sam's burial. He says that, because I am not a member of a synagogue, a Jewish burial will cost me three hundred pounds.

'But that's disgusting,' I say.

'Everyone has to pay for burials, Lucy.'

'I don't have to pay for a *Gentile* one. The hospital will bury him for free. Although I still have to talk to a chaplain about it.'

'Well, he needs a proper Jewish burial.'

'So I have to make a moral decision about whether to pay three hundred pounds for the chance that there's a Jewish God or not?'

'No, it's not like that.'

'It's a huge amount of money. I mean, I'd pay it if I thought that Sam would benefit.'

'He's Jewish. He needs a Jewish burial. End of subject.'

I pretend to be silenced, but I will have to think about this one. I have always sat on the fence about my religious beliefs. I have said enough of The Lord's Prayer and the Jewish grace after meals to persuade whichever God is sitting in judgement of me that I deserve a place in Heaven.

243

I have been awed by mosques and Hindu temples. But it now feels as if I am being asked to choose – because three hundred pounds is too much stake-money to fool around with. I cannot be half-anything.

'I've got someone coming round tonight. She wants to meet you,' says Judd, interrupting my decision. He is multi-tasking – towel-drying Solomon's head, and tickling Maxie.

'Oh yeah? Who?'

'Rabbi Scheur's daughter – Chava. Maxie, don't do that. You'll fall over.'

'Oh really?' I pause to think. 'Well, you can bloody well cancel her, because I'm not in the mood to meet anyone, let alone some pious moralizer . . .'

I stop, because I am surprised at how bitter I sound.

'Chava doesn't moralize.'

'Some religious *nutter* woman.'

'She's hardly a nutter. I've never met anyone more sane than Chava. D'you think *I'm* a religious nutter?'

'Yes, of course I bloody do. You pray. Three times a day. You won't wash your hair with unkosher shampoo,' I continue, picking up Solomon's bottle of shampoo, which is covered in Hebrew lettering.

Judd looks thoughtful, then sighs.

'Well, you're not completely wrong. I do think I've been a bit fanatical. Yeah, I admit that. The Rabbi said as much. I've been going too fast. But, apparently, that's pretty typical of people who come late to Judaism. I wanted to know – to do – everything at once.'

'*Mummy*,' wails Maxie.

'Oh, baby.' I take her wet body out of the bath. She has such a slippery body. She keeps slipping out of the towel. Away from me.

'How you can believe in God now that we know about evolution and –'

'Why should that stop me believing in God?'

'*Daddy,*' wails Solomon.

'You're just ignoring logic.'

'The reason why Einstein was a religious Jew was because faith isn't *about* logic.'

'No, it's about money, as all organized religion is. Guilt Money. Milking three hundred pounds out of people for a burial. At a time when people are vulnerable and not thinking straight. It's emotional blackmail.'

'If you were a member of a synagogue, the burial would be free. And it's *men* asking you for money. Not God.'

He is speaking so calmly that I am determined to rile him.

'Some God after the Holocaust, and my miscarriage.'

'A) you can't compare the two.'

Judd does not reach b) because he is riled. According to him, I need to put things in perspective. He knows a woman who lost her baby when she was nine months pregnant. He knows a woman whose newborn baby died. He knows a woman whose twins died, days apart. Judd had a mother whose whole family was killed in the Holocaust. He has relatives who were murdered in gas chambers. By the time he has finished listing my blessings, the children are in their pyjamas, cowed into silence.

'And how many *Holocaust* survivors believe in God?' I ask, because I am not as easily cowed.

'Many of them, actually.'

'So, is that why you thought I needed my hair cut? Because this *Chava's* coming round. Why's she coming here, anyway?' I ask, changing the subject, because I do

245

not have the statistics to hand to disprove his point about God-fearing Holocaust survivors. 'I wouldn't have thought a rabbi's daughter would be allowed to visit the home of a single man.' *With dirty thoughts,* I think.

'Well, for a start, she doesn't know that I've moved in with you.'

'What?'

We are in the living room, and the children have started playing. In other words, they have turned the toy-boxes upside down. I can hear the spill of bricks and chalks.

'Well, she thinks I still live in my flat. So don't tell . . .'

'What?' I am almost, but never quite, speechless. 'It's your dirty secret, is it?'

'It's just that I haven't told anyone I'm living here.' He laughs, drily. 'You might have noticed no-one calls for me.'

'I just thought that you were unpopular. Or that socializing was against the Jewish law.'

'Very funny.' He ruffles Solomon's hair. 'Anyway, now you know. And, no, it wouldn't be approved of. Me, living here with you.'

'God, you talk about my unkosher cheese and you . . . You *hypocrite.*'

I pick up a struggling Maxie because it is time she went to bed. She is trying to climb out of my arms, but I am hugging her too hard. My daughter smells of pink lotion and white towels.

I take her to her bedroom, and she allows herself to be lain down, laughing. Demanding, *'Shtory.'* Judd stands at the door, leaning against its spine.

'I was only going to move in for a couple of weeks. You *know* I only moved in because you were scared after that woman was killed. And I don't think you should be left

246

alone right now. Not after your miscarriage.'

'What you mean is that you don't think I should be left alone with Maxie.' Now that babies die on me, I feel as if everyone is waiting for me to kill my daughter.

'Don't be ridiculous. I don't mean that.'

'Well, you can just fuck off with this Chava. You probably think it's so *romantic,* meeting secretly, behind the Rabbi's back. But I think it's very sad.'

'She's coming here to see *you,* actually.'

It is then that the doorbell rings. We both stand there. Me, hovering above Maxie's bed. Judd, still at the bedroom door. In the other room, I can hear Solomon's commentary as he builds a tottering tower of bricks.

'Well, aren't you going to get that?' I ask. 'Or are you not meant to be here?'

The bell rings again – a fraction less politely.

I laugh at his scared expression and say, 'Quick – hide in the airing cupboard.'

Chava is a saintly version of me. Or rather, she looks like me, with that rough blonde hair and spongy bosom. She is me in disguise, her body modestly camouflaged in high-collar, shoulderpadded blouse and long blue skirt.

She is here, sitting on the uncomfortable end of my sofa, because I miscarried. I almost pity her, watching those pads squirm about the shoulders of her blouse, like small animals.

But she has come because she thinks it a *'chesed'* – a blessing – to visit poor, barren Lucy.

I imagine that she has a *chesed* sticker chart at home. No doubt it is like the one I made for Maxie, who is potty training. Presumably, she has a blue sticker for every small *chesed.* A yellow one for real acts of kindness. And a red one

247

for emergency cases, like me. One hundred red stickers and she probably has a place automatically reserved for her in Heaven.

She is looking so smug, sitting on the sofa. Her bony hands, crossed on her lap. They are all knuckles, those tiny hands.

I can see that she is thinking of that red sticker, as she preaches to me about the nature of 'Hashem'. Or God, to me. She is half speaking ancient Hebrew. Gobbledy-gook, to me. I imagine her reaction if I were to say that I was only half-Jewish.

'*Half*-Jewish?' she would say – a Yiddish Lady Bracknell.

She tells me all about God's will, and I nod, noticing that she has no use for full stops. It is as if she alone is privy to His intentions.

'*Of course nothing can be known here by us but, baruch hashem, we all think . . .*'

The extremely religious irritate me. It is as if, because they have come to a decision about God's existence, they are the only ones to have thought about such matters. The rest of us mere mortals live decadent, shallow lives. Our Gods are shopping malls.

'*I know from Judd, of course, that you aren't as frum as perhaps he would like but, please God, maybe now that this has happened . . .*'

I want to tell this Chava Scheur that I too have thought deeply about matters immaterial, and have come to the conclusion that organized religion is largely baloney. It is only that I am too polite to pour my baloney argument down the throats of happy-clappy Christians or extremely orthodox Jews (although that could be because I have some residual doubt about my argument).

Uh oh, now she is talking about her Great Father.

'We all look up to him, he always has the answers, perhaps because, as he says, we always have the questions, but he is so modest like that, I . . .'

I think at first that she is still talking about God, but then I realize that she is referring to her Dad, who is – according to his daughter – a Very Big Rabbi. So much so that she is trying to sell me his 'bestselling' lecture tapes.

'Well worth listening to, really good shiurim, if you want I could . . .'

I resist the urge to joke that I have them already. They were sold to me, bootleg. I resist the urge to tell her about my own father – a Very Big Atheist. I do not want to upset Judd, so I tell fibs about his socks that are lying, like banana skins, over the radiator. His white shirts, slung over the back of the chair.

'Oh, they're mine,' I say, seeing her stare. 'Men's clothes are warmer in this cold.'

'It is, you're right, so cold.'

Judd appears as relieved as he is able. Chava sits there, pinkly. Her face looks as if it has been scrubbed hard with soap.

'Yes, so cold and, you know, I was sorry to hear about your husband, so many things sent, but, baruch hashem, I hope . . .'

I look at Judd, who is gazing at Chava, and think about the fact that he does not laugh as loudly at my jokes. He does not look at me as if I am glass, about to shatter under his stare. He does not try to persuade me to stay, as he is with Chava. He will say anything to have her there a moment longer.

'No, no, time to go, it's only that when Judd told me about what happened to you . . . I thought it would be a chesed to come over . . .'

She is looking around, at my computer and proud CD collection. Meanwhile, Sabbath candles, prayer shawls and challah covers hide inside chests and drawers, the tassels anxiously peeking out. And I feel like strangling her with that tight collar of a white blouse. Or taking her to a clifftop and pushing her off. I would watch that billowing skirt of hers struggle to inflate as a parachute.

'Oh, it is. A *chesed*, as you say. It really is.' I see Judd following her gaze around the room.

'As much for me as for you, you know?'

'Of course.'

'Thank you for letting me use your toilet.'

'That's fine.'

'I'll come back with you, see you're safe,' says Judd to Chava, adopting her patterns of speech.

Naturally, I think.

Nothing makes me feel better. Not Ysanne; not Ruth; not Sophie. When Judd went out with Chava, I phoned these three.

'They only want to speak to you,' said Judd when he took their messages. So I spent ages on the phone to them, trying to make them feel better about what has happened to me.

It does not feel as if a week has gone by since I lost my baby. But that time has passed, somehow.

It is Monday; and, to all the world, I am recovered, because I no longer carry around Maxie's naked doll. I have stopped wailing in the shower. Only I know that I will always remember how I felt, Sam slipping away from me.

At least I am going into work. Nothing changes on the

Underground. There are too many people crowded like cattle into carriages, and hanging from straps on the ceiling.

We all stare longingly at the adverts offering isolation in Scotland.

Those seventeen stairs leading up to my office seem even longer today. I am anxious to be back in the bosom of work. Fred is there, smelling of wet dogs. He smiles when he sees me, asking me what I think of Bill Hempsall coming this Friday to address us all.

'Who's Bill Hempsall?'

'Our new boss, Lucy Fletcher. Or will be, next month.'

'Is he from the *Post* group?'

'One of Frazer's own, yes.'

'Oh God. He's coming here?'

'Yes, and, oh, Lucy, I downloaded this for you.'

He clears his throat and hands me an information sheet from a miscarriage website. 'Thanks,' I say, unable to respond appropriately. 'I'll er read it inside.'

I go to my desk, trying to avoid Heather's stare, which drags me towards her. She is the sort of woman with no shape who is able to wear dungarees. Whereas I look in them as if I am wearing giant Babygros.

'How *are* you?' says Clay, all motherly, as I switch on my computer. I look at her, gratefully, as if I might absorb her sympathy.

'Yes, how are you?' says Heather, trying to echo Clay's concern, but more intent on fixing the strap of her dungarees.

'I can't think how awful you must feel,' says Clay.

'But at least you *have* a baby,' says Heather, in a soft voice.

I know what she is thinking, because Heather makes no

251

secret of the fact that she desperately wants a baby. But she makes no secret, either, of the fact that she desperately wants an iBook laptop. In Heather's opinion, women have babies because they are bored. It is something to do. To her, it is a choice between becoming pregnant or buying a glossy monthly magazine.

'And you've got Judd living with you now, haven't you? How's that going, by the way, Lucy?'

'I've told you, it's not *going* anywhere. We're friends,' I say, severely.

I want to be melodramatic, and tell Heather that death is an ever-present hurt – unlike, say, not being able to find a husband.

'I'm amazed you're back to work so quickly,' says Clay, nervously, her cheeks stretching like dough.

'I love being back,' I say, so that Clay can relax around me.

'Well, I suppose it happened ages ago,' says Heather.

For Heather, who has no patience, *ages* is anything over fifteen seconds. That is why she enjoys watching breakfast television.

I am having lunch with Ruth, Ysanne and Sophie, in the House of Commons.

I can take all afternoon for lunch, as I have pretended that I am going on to a press launch. Diol are bringing out a new range of beauty products, created especially for people who care about the active ingredients in their day-creams.

Ruth shows us around the House. She makes a point of saying that there are corridors only *she* can enter, and I pretend extreme disappointment at being excluded from these dark, menacing hallways.

Ysanne tries to sneak down them anyway, giggling.

Ruth pulls Ysanne away from the red carpet, smiling at famous MPs, like Edward Heath, who do not smile back. She says that they are very busy, but great friends.

She keeps shushing Ysanne, who is talking about her internet fashion site that is attracting millions of pounds in investment. Sophie says she does not have long for lunch; she has a completion meeting on a major reverse takeover.

I see Hamish – my old boyfriend, now a New Labour MP – who has put on even more weight. He is as fat as a fat American. His suit could fit two average people and a small pig. I take comfort from this: it is as if Hamish's story is moving towards an obvious conclusion.

Ruth tries to introduce him to us, smilingly, although he is clearly interested in impressing, not Ruth, but me. He goes about this in the wrong way, however – by talking about the amendments he has made to a bill currently going through Standing Committee.

I am so embarrassed by his ignoring Ruth that I say, 'Er, Hamish, you know Ruth Campbell, don't you?'

'Ruth *Campbell*?'

'No relation,' she giggles.

'Henry Berwick's researcher?' I add, quietly.

'Oh *no*, then,' says Hamish, dismissing Ruth with his eyes. 'I wouldn't know her.'

Despite Hamish, Ruth remains impressed by Hamish. She refers to him as *Mclure* all the way to the cafeteria, and says that he is in line for the cabinet, come the next reshuffle.

She taps her nose when she says this; and I resist the urge to laugh and remind her that she is talking about Hamish. We go down the stairs, and she makes a point of telling me that we can only eat in the Strangers' cafeteria. I feign awe that she has access to Members Only eateries.

The Palace of Westminster it may be, but the cafeteria is a glorified canteen. Sullen women slop fried food on to our plates, as Ruth avoids eye contact with an out-of-favour MP she cannot be seen talking to.

She eats something that looks as if it has been chewed up by my brother, as Ysanne ignores her food to tell us about her fashion site. 'It was only a hobby, but we're getting so many hits,' she says. 'I think I'm going to have to leave work. If we want proper investment, I'll need to be serious about it.' I look at Ysanne who is not able to be serious about anything any more – except trivial subjects such as fashion.

'I really should go now,' says Sophie. 'I'm working with the senior corporate partner.'

'I thought you said you had millions from investors?' I ask Ysanne.

'Exactly. Barely enough to buy advertising on buses.'

'It's all easy money. It doesn't mean anything,' says Ruth, going on to discuss my miscarriage using all the correct medical terminology. Ysanne insists that I go for counselling.

'Nah,' says Ruth. 'Counselling doesn't work for some people. I think it would actually make you worse, Lucy.'

'Sorry,' says Sophie, standing up. 'But the whole team from the client sponsor and the merchant bank are convening at three.'

'It's only one,' I say, pathetically. But they cannot veer from their career paths.

I have learned a lot about people by their reaction, this

week, to my miscarriage. Heather, for example, appears to be gloating. She made no secret of the fact that she did not think I deserved another baby. Not when she wanted one so. Not when her own need for a baby had turned into a craving. She keeps asking me lots of prying questions about the number of units of alcohol I consumed during pregnancy.

Did I eat soft cheese?

I am beginning to feel as if the miscarriage was not mine, but the office's. Everyone is using it to colour their own lives. Rainie, for example, wants only to hear about the blood, the guts, and the gore. But I suppose that this is what makes her a good crime reporter.

Was the foetus intact?

I have not seen VD all week – he's been away on a rugby tour. When I do, his expression is difficult to read. I can only imagine what he is thinking: 'I'll have no excuse to get rid of the woman now that she's lost that baby.'

'Hiya,' he smiles, sitting on Heather's desk.

'Hello.'

'How are you?'

'Great now, thanks. Better. I er I'm sorry I didn't take your calls.'

'That's fine,' he says, being polite in a disingenuous, American way. Usually, Heather would be desperately trying to overhear our conversation. But she is a shriek of nerves because the man from the *Post* is coming to address us all today.

Bill Hempsall.

His only outstanding feature is his chin. It is so sharp that it looks as if it should point to a beard.

'Thank you for being here,' says our editor, Hen, as if we are usually all out of the office, busily chasing a story. 'In

255

a moment, I'll hand you over to Bill, but I wanted to say, first that, ahem, as I did mention, I am offering voluntary redundancy to anyone who, yes, wants it. There has to be . . . yes. But the offer won't last for ever, so please do take advantage of what will be, yes, quite generous severance packages. Now, most of us won't be working in this building after November . . .'

'*Shame,*' interrupts someone from the classifieds section.

'But I know I'm speaking on behalf of you all when I say to Bill here how happy we all are to be relocating to the *Post* building.'

He pauses for an interruption, but no-one says anything.

'And now. Bill.' He looks at Bill Hempsall, and brightens.

'Thank you Henry.' He smiles a lazy smile, staring over our heads at the wall. 'I hope I'll be able to give you some idea, today, what it will be like, working for the *Post* group, and Tobu Frazer . . .'

Tobu Frazer made his money from porn, but will sue anyone who says so. Because, two years ago, he used the money from his small empire of sex websites to buy some local newspapers. Gifts to himself. He now owns sixty such publications – from the *Gunnersbury* to the *Grimsby Post*s.

'Your column er Lucy Fletcher will be renamed *A Post Beautiful Life*, and reproduced in every *Post* newspaper. You'll be famous,' Hempsall says, smiling through me. 'Read by your Granny in Grimsby.'

Last year – inspired by a business trip to America – Frazer set about changing the way these newspapers operated. He moved them all into penis-shaped buildings which he bought up in London, Manchester, Edinburgh, Birmingham and Cardiff. Then he standardized the content of all the *Post* newspapers, cutting the local news and

256

sport pages, and bulking the rest with regulation features, columns and advertorials. I know, because I looked him up in the newspaper cuttings library, filed under the heading *Libel Actions*.

'So, in short, we'll be expanding the lifestyle sections and slimming down the news pages. Now, any questions?' Hempsall asks, stirring a cold cup of coffee which Susanna made for him.

So I query, 'Just one page for news?'

Admittedly, I say this because I feel confident. Hempsall has already made it clear that my type of column is in the ascendant.

He opens his mouth into a toothy Tony Blair smile, and asks, 'So. You think there should be more pages for news, do you?'

'Well, yes.'

The teeth disappear then, and Bill Hempsall says that no-one is interested in local news. Does anyone really want to read about the MP visiting a home for the deaf? Or the cat stuck up a chimney?

The editorial team stares, scared of redundancy. Susanna's eyes bulge as prominently as her spots. I turn to look at our editor for support. But Hen is sitting in Hempsall's shadow. He looks so deflated in one of those kagoul-like jumpers. It is as if Bill Hempsall has pulled Hen's cord, hard, to let out all air.

'Why do people buy the paper then?' I ask. 'If they don't want the news?'

'Good question,' said Hempsall, baring those teeth, as if he wants to bite me. 'What does everyone else think? Why *do* people buy local papers?'

'For the crime reports?' suggests Rainie.

'You sure it's not for the news?' asks VD.

'Out of habit?' says Clay. 'Because they always have?'

'No,' says our new boss, looking at us as if he is a secondary-school teacher who cannot believe how badly we had been taught at primary level. Behind him, Hen sinks out of view.

'To feel part of the community?' tries Susanna.

'Because they're well displayed in the newsagents?' asks Heather, opening her mouth to display teeth bigger than Bill Hempsall's.

'No,' says Hempsall. Extensive market research and focus groups have informed him that people buy local newspapers for the advertisements.

But Bill Hempsall ignores our reaction. He might be amused by it; at any rate, he ignores Von's swearing, VD's muttering and Rainie's tutting, saying that most people do not bother to read news. If they read the features, it is only because they are there, in front of them. Any editorial space is purely for show, he says. Hempsall explains that he is motivated – like most people – by profit.

'The world's smaller,' he says. 'You might live in . . .' He looks down, and sees the *Chronicle*'s masthead. 'You might live in *Highgate*,' he says, 'but you can buy your baby's shoes in Utah. Children at a sink school in Wigan can study with kids from Atlanta. Students can buy lectures from professors in Australia. Patients can speak to doctors in Pennsylvania.'

He pauses, as if his script requires it. I feel that Hempsall had made this speech many times. He is pause perfect. I time his next silence. It is six seconds before he says, 'So. Where does that leave us? What do you all think? Do we continue to put out the same old press releases, rehashed . . . ?'

VD's face is as passionate as during a game of rugby.

'I don't think we're *quite* that . . .' he starts, interrupted by Hempsall.

'I tell you what . . . Why don't you break with the habit of a lifetime and forget what you've been taught,' he patronizes. He turns to face VD, which is when I notice acne scarring his left cheek. 'Forget your journalism handbook for one moment and *think*. Think about the fact that the *Chronicle*'s sales have been going down . . .'

'Typical September st . . .' starts Hen, our editor.

'Yes, yes. Find any number of excuses. But the fact is, we need to sell ourselves. We're competing with the net for readers in an electronic age. And the way to keep readers reading is through advertising. Marketing. Free offers. Who cares? We're a *business*. That's all you have to remember. And it's the classified section that pays your wages.'

He smiles in a straight line, as if to underline what he is saying. 'The internet is soon going to replace local newspapers. What will be the point of reading about stuck traffic lights in Acacia Avenue, when you can just click on to the Acacia Avenue website and ask questions online to the chair of the Neighbourhood Watch?'

No-one says anything.

'*Exactly*. And no-one's going to advertise in local papers when all the readers have gone elsewhere. Not when online advertising is so much cheaper. So, we have to keep ahead. Eh?'

'Yes,' whispers Hen.

'Yes,' says Work Experience, who has been made a permanent member of staff.

Hempsall comes to a full stop. There is an embarrassed silence, as he bends down to pick up his robot-silver laptop computer.

We all stand up and prepare to mingle around plastic cups of white wine. (Hen's secretary, Shirl, thought to buy the wine. She said that we *ought* to greet Bill Hempsall properly.) No-one speaks to Hempsall – although Work Experience stands grinning at him, like a lovesick teenager. So Susanna behaves as if the man is being bullied. She asks him whether he wants some wine. Or perhaps another cup of coffee? He smiles, and says, *Bill, please*, and that coffee would be lovely.

If I did not think it impossible, I might wonder whether she is making a play for him. Because, although Bill Hempsall is middle-aged, and middle-management, our Susanna has never set her sights high.

That is why she married Jonathon.

He was at least twenty years Susanna's senior, and favoured paisley tank-tops. They met in our local work pub almost eight years ago. Jonathon was the miserable, monotonous one of that group of solicitors who bought us drinks and played us at pool. It was little wonder that he had so much in common with Susanna. That evening, he talked to her at length about conveyancing, as she had been in the process of buying a rundown flat to renovate it.

A few years later, Jonathon moved into Susanna's flat. By then, it was no longer rundown.

By then, Jonathon too had been modernized. He wore designer suits and hair gel, and had been taught not to make comments, in public, such as, 'Susanna bleaches her moustache.' Or, 'Susanna's pubes look like grated cheese.'

They moved into an empty shell of a house. They married. Susanna set about redecorating her new home. For years, all she could talk about was curtains. Only last week all that changed when Jonathon confessed to being in love with another, more upholstered, woman.

I remember, at Susanna's engagement party, overhearing her asking him whether he loved her.

'Well, erm, yeah, whatever love is supposed to mean,' said Jonathon, in a reply reminiscent of Prince Charles's when asked if he loved his new fiancée, Lady Diana.

So I knew that it would not be long before Jonathon found himself a Camilla – although Gaby was as dark-haired and as beautifully pale-skinned as Snow White. That was how a distraught Susanna painted her, anyway. *She* had been the one to invest in Jonathon. *She* had put all that work in. And who benefited, but *Gaby*? A cartoonist's idea of a dream woman!

Susanna has recovered enough by now to flirt with a fiftysomething ex-pornographer's sidekick. Bill Hempsall. Not that Hempsall's plainness or dullness would bother a woman like Susanna. Her hobby is to improve houses, and men.

'Ah, just before I go, I forgot to mention that we'll be sending you all on a week-long induction course,' says Hempsall, tapping his laptop keyboard. 'It'll be, yes, this month. Two weeks' time.'

'Oh, I was thinking of having a moving party that week,' says Hen, sadly. 'It'll have to be the week before.'

'Will we be able to bring children?' asks Clay; and Hempsall stares at her as if she is part of another, much less interesting, life form. I, meanwhile, am grateful to Clay for speaking out on behalf of we women disabled by children. She is a real woman's woman, of a type usually found in textbooks, whilst I skulk around, pretending to be childless, so that everyone can feel more comfortable in my company.

'Of course not Clay,' says Hen, embarrassed.

'Oh, that would have been soo sweet,' says Heather, looking at VD. 'I *love* babies.'

'But that's such short notice. What am I supposed to do with my son?' asks Clay.

'Can't his father do it?' asks Hempsall, helpfully.

'There is no father,' she says, looking to him for more helpful solutions. But Hempsall says *You should have thought of that before becoming a single mother* – and all with a raise of his right eyebrow.

'What sort of things will the course cover?' asks VD; and Hempsall says that we will learn about *Post* policy, and utilizing the world wide web.

I express quiet surprise, asking why we have to know about the world. Our job is surely to cover events in Archway, Highgate, and some crossover streets in Tufnell Park.

VD hear hears.

Von *fucking* hear hears.

Hempsall says that we will also be learning survival techniques; and I joke, 'Now we're talking. I don't know *how* I've learned to survive Highgate up till now.'

I am ignored by Hempsall, who describes the various techniques we will be taught, to survive.

I would ask, *But why do we have to survive?* if Heather was not looking at me as if I am Margo from *The Good Life* – because I do not like the idea of skinning a rabbit, or walking marathon-long distances.

Before VD leaves the newsroom, he stops at my desk to read last week's *Chronicle*. I think how much he needs a shave. His skin is as gravelly as Caroline's driveway.

'How're you doing?' he asks, finishing his article about an explosion in Archway.

'Really OK,' I say, shyly. So much has happened since I last saw him, and I feel as I did when I was twelve, and saw Wayne.

Wayne, my teenage crush.

I knew this of Wayne: he performed impressions of Frank Spencer; he liked ska music and strawberry Fondant Fancies; his Mum worked in Tesco's. I knew that he liked cheese-and-onion best. I knew his telephone number. And that he was a Sagittarius.

'That was a good piece,' I say of the explosion-Archway article.

'Thanks. Listen, erm . . . Any chance of us going for a drink?'

'What. Now?' I had forgotten this former life. In it, everything is made hazy by drink.

'We could sneak out.'

I look over his shoulder, at Hen laughing at everything Hempsall says. 'I suppose we could.'

I need to tell VD that – despite the sex – we cannot go on having sex.

'I'll meet you in The Punch,' he says, in the manner of a small boy playing at being James Bond.

'OK.'

It is only when I look up that I see Heather overheard. But she waits for VD to leave before gasping.

Chapter Ten

I watch the barlady cleaning the pumps. Expertly. The
pumps shining, she swirls clean the oversized glass ash-
trays. Brilliantly. 'A pint of Ruddles and a vodka-tonic,'
says VD at the bar. He looks round at me, smiling, as if to
check I am still there.

The barlady hands him an overflowing pint. Froth
everywhere. VD picks some coins out of the puddle and
pushes them towards the barlady.

'Do you do food this early?' he asks, one big, lazy arm
on the bar.

'On the board love,' grins the woman. She seems so
very comfortable in her role of barlady. I cannot imagine
her worrying about her career – although, on a Friday
evening, the pub is empty apart from VD, myself, and an
old man. He looks as if he has been dragged in from the
street in order to make the place seem more crowded.

Four doors away, The Black Horse is so packed that the
owners are considering introducing a door policy. But it is
not hard to see why this pub is unpopular. The Black Horse
has a snooker table and a competition-size darts board.
The Punch has a game of Scrabble. The Punch stinks of
thick smoke; The Black Horse smells of pine wood. The

Black Horse has a happy hour between four and five. The Punch's Scrabble board is missing most of its letters.

The Punch docs not have a happy hour.

'Right. Great. I'll have erm the beef and salad thanks.' VD flutters a ten-pound note towards the barlady.

'I'll bring it over.' She has a hard face, despite all that smiling.

I watch VD coming towards me and wonder why he is with me.

'Did you want to order food?'

'No thanks,' I say, taking the glass of vodka from VD. He sets the bottle of tonic beside my glass and sits opposite me.

'*So*,' he says.

'So.'

The head on his beer is huge. He brings the pint to his mouth, and slurps. I add the tonic to the vodka, and sip. I always feel so feminine with VD. It would be difficult to feel otherwise. Next to him I am fragile. I am a wisp of a woman, sipping my spirit.

'Heather overheard us saying we were going to the pub.'

'What's wrong with us going the pub?'

'The Punch?' I lower my voice. 'No-one comes here unless they have to. Well, unless they're having a sordid affair.'

'It's not *sordid*,' he says, hurt.

'I've had to ask her to keep it quiet,' I say.

'Well, she will, I'm sure.'

The froth from his beer is forming the beginnings of a fake moustache.

'I don't know.'

'Why have you got it in for Heather? She likes you.'

'No, she doesn't,' I say, grimly. 'Er, you've got beer above your lip.'

He wipes his mouth with the back of his hand; and I stare at the ridges of veins on his hands, like a rugged landscape.

'I don't like you bitching about Heather. I like Heather.'

'Fine. We all like Heather. Ostensibly. I had to beg her not to say anything. She did say she wouldn't do anything to hurt Von.'

'I don't think it'll hurt Von. She's going out with that aerobics instructor, isn't she? She doesn't stop about him.'

'Yes, but it's all beside the point. The fact is I've been lying to her.'

'Well, don't lie to her. Tell her we're together.'

'We're not together.'

He looks at me through those long black eyelashes; and I see what Judd meant by 'puppy-dog eyes'.

'Not for long,' I say; but he looks even more puppy-dog. 'And I don't want to lie to her any more, which is why I'm . . .'

'Don't you want anything to eat?'

'No thanks, really, I . . .'

'How about some scratchings?'

'Can you stop thinking about your stomach for a second? I want to talk about us. Sorry. I know there's not an us. But . . .'

'Since when was there not an us?'

The barlady comes over with a plate of food for VD – a great hunk of beef on a bed of lettuce. The meat looks like a big dog, rolling around in grass. But my boyfriend appears to think it looks good enough to eat. VD rubs the palms of his hands together; he is ready to feast.

'Hope you enjoy it,' says the barlady, setting down a bowl of oily, pink dressing.

'Oh, I will.'

He grins, and she gives him a look that reads, *If you weren't with the young lady, I'd take you to bed with me.*

'If there was an us,' I say, 'I don't want there to be any more. I only slept with you, because I was all over the place. Charlie had only just left me. And I was *pregnant.*'

'So I took advantage of a poor, pregnant woman. Thanks.'

'Oh VD, you know I like you. I'm just saying, I wasn't thinking straight. I mean, I'm not ready for another relationship. It's taken me this long to get over Charlie.'

'But you're over him now?'

'I don't think about him all the time.'

'But you used to?'

'Yeah, I suppose . . .'

'So, even when we were having sex?'

'*No.*'

VD is thinking. That is why he has stopped gulping down the pint.

'Look, Lucy, I don't know about you . . . I know you're still into Charlie, but I'm . . .'

'I'm not still into Charlie.' And it is true that, for the first time, I do not care that he has gone. I can see that life without him is easier. Emptier, but easier.

'I'm serious about you. I don't give a shit about Von.'

'Well, I *do.*'

'What I meant was, I want to be with you. I've liked you for so long. I know you think I'm just a meathead . . .'

I cannot help it – I stare at his meat.

'I know you're not a meathead,' I say, thinking of him in the park with Maxie and me. Scooping my daughter out

267

of her swing. Buying her ice-cream. Sending the sandpit bully away from her castle. He has so big a body that I have to remind myself that there is more to him than a fine bone structure. 'But OK, I'll be honest, I don't know why you want to be with me anyway. I've got a child. I'm thirty-two. What is it about me?'

I am not being purely rhetorical.

'What is it?' He puts down his knife and fork. 'Well, you're sexy, but you know that. You're brainy, but you know that. You're . . .'

He stops and takes a sip of his bitter, grinning.

'No, it's just because you're sexy.'

'But it can't go on,' I say, pleased, despite myself.

I still have it, I think. I am still the same woman who married the handsomest man in her peer group. I am the same woman who was the first amongst her friends to try anal sex and sharon fruits. I am that woman who achieved a double first at Oxford.

'Why can't it? Can't we just see what happens?'

'I don't know.'

'*Maxie* likes me,' he says, using blackmail, when all else is failing – as I do with Maxie.

'Maxie likes *ice-cream*. You buy her ice-cream.'

'I tell you what,' he says, spooning thousand island dressing on his lettuce. 'Let's not do anything rash 'til this induction course – the one the *Post* are sending us on. Von's in Crete for the next two weeks, anyway. So, if we're still seeing each other when we go away to Wales, we'll tell her then. OK? What d'you say?'

I look behind him at the barlady. She is swivelling a cloth around a glass, holding it up to the light, inspecting it for blemishes.

'I suppose you're right.'

'If we're still together, we'll celebrate in Wales,' says VD, raising his near-empty glass. 'To a whole week away with you.'

'Cheers,' I smile, not altogether convincingly.

It is Saturday evening, and Maxie is at my mother's. Judd is out; and I am baby-sitting for Solomon. 'How's school going?' I ask him, as he stirs a bowl of biscuit mixture.

I have not made biscuits since cookery lessons with Miss O'Connors, but I wanted to give Sol a treat, and I found in the cupboard a packet of Kosen Biscuit Mixture. *Glatt Kosher*.

Even I was able to follow these instructions:

1. *Pour biscuit mixture into bowl.*
2. *Add one egg.*
3. *Stir.*
4. *Spoon biscuit mixture on to greaseproof paper.*
5. *Bake for half an hour, or until golden brown.*

I watch Sol stirring furiously, and think how earth-motherly I am being. Baking biscuits with another woman's son. Solomon does not remember Clare, but, oh, how he wants Mummying.

Indeed, I have begun to mother Solomon – if only because people stare at me if I do nothing to correct his misbehaviour in a supermarket. (The father might be present but I am, when all is said and done, a woman.)

Until this evening, we have not been alone together – Sol and I. But Maxie is at my mother's, and Judd at his creative writing course. I am able to cosset Solomon; and he needs cosseting, I think, taking the bowl from him.

'I think it's stirred enough now,' I say, remembering childhood baking days with Mum, when we would make cakes and biscuits and buns from scratch, always following my mother's own recipe. 'So, you were going to tell me about school?'

Again, he does not reply, staring in awe as I spoon the gluey mixture on to the greaseproof paper.

'What do you *do* in school?'

'Yes.'

'Do you like your teacher – Mrs Cohen?'

'I've got a giraffe on my peg.'

'Who are your friends?'

'Mrs Cohen,' he says, staring at me, as I bend down to tuck the tray inside the oven. Turn the oven-dial to medium-high. 'Are they ready now?'

'They're not ready yet. Half an hour. We've got to wait half an hour.'

'We've got to wait that long?' he says, suddenly anxious, leaning one way, then the other. 'Yes, for them to be ready.'

I pat his head with one of the tiger-patterned oven gloves; and he looks up at me with soft, black eyes, the black almost spilling out.

'Some children have *two* Mummys,' he says; and, before I can take him in my arms for a cuddle: 'Can we take out the biscuits now?'

'I think we should wait a few more minutes. Why don't you go and play with your Brio for a bit?'

He glares at the oven, as if it is cheating him out of biscuits.

'Will they be ready then?' he asks.

'Yes, once you've played. I'll call you,' I say, as he walks away, towards his train set, half of which is missing, because Maxie took some track to Caroline's, who threw the pieces out, thinking they were 'sticks'.

I stare at the blank oven door.

270

'*Lucy,*' says Solomon, leaning against me, interrupting my thoughts.

'They're not ready yet. Why don't you build a Lego castle?'

'Are you thinking about my brother?' he says, sounding as innocent as a foreigner who has just learned English from a tape – the pattern of his speech rising and falling in all of the wrong places.

'Your brother?'

'Are you thinking about Sam?'

And I want to cry then, because I was. I was wondering whether he was happy, lying in his unmarked Jewish grave. I often think of him. Sam. I wonder how he would have grown up; and see that boy, that man, in the street.

I have flashbacks too: I feel him slipping out of me. I remember his agony with the contractions. Laughing as he died. I feel cold with it, sometimes, when it all comes back in a slow-motion series of images.

Blood clot

Ambulance.

Laughing gas.

Then, slip.

'Sam wouldn't have been your brother. You know that, don't you?' I gently ask Solomon.

'I was named after Uncle Solomon, and Sam was my brother.' He thinks about this for a second. 'Sam was Uncle Solomon's brother before he died in the gas chamber. I wanted to play with him when he was born. Lucy – why did he die?'

And I finally understand why all of my Why questions in class at school were answered with the one word: *Because.*

'Why is Miss O'Connors leaving?'

'Because.'

'Why doesn't Miss O'Connors have a husband?'

'Because.'

'Why is Miss O'Connors having a baby?'

'Because.'

But I change the subject, saying, 'You know, your uncles were happy *before* the war; you know that, don't you, Sol?'

'They were happy before the Holocausht.'

'Yes. And you're happy now, aren't you?'

'I'm happy with you,' he says, hugging me hard. I feel as if he will never let me go. 'Mummy Lucy.'

Solomon fell asleep easily this evening. I will have to half-bake biscuits more often. Kids are happier, I think, if they are fed on raw dough. Judd is too concerned with representing all the food groups on their plates. I wish that *my* mother had allowed me to enjoy food. But she talked about it as fuel.

If I asked for more, she would say I first needed to expend some energy.

The doorbell rings, and I wipe my soapy hands on a dishcloth, assuming that Judd has forgotten his key. But it is Charlie; and I had forgotten how much I loved him.

I am nervous as I make drinks – clumsy as I pour out a cup of tea for me and diluted raspberry drink for Charlie. Merely to look at it could rot one's teeth. ('No, it's got real raspberries in it,' says Charlie.) We are both surprised that I have kept a bottle in the storage cupboard.

'The kids hate it.'

'The kids?' he says, taking the spilling glass. Wiping his wet hands on his shirt.

272

'Judd's son's living here too, remember.'

'That must be burdensome.'

'Sol's not a burden,' I say, defensively.

'Well, I hope my daughter's getting enough attention.'

'*How . . . ?*' I cannot believe what I am hearing. I had forgotten how provocative Charlie could be. Now I remember him changing into his posh pyjamas, and going to bed before the end of a dinner party. I remember him sulking if ever I took longer than he did to reach orgasm. Flirting with my midwife.

So I say, 'She gets more bloody attention than she ever did with you here. Now, my *attention's* not divided between Maxie and *you.*'

Charlie lies down on the sofa like a Noël Coward character. He is turned towards me – his audience – as if on a stage set.

'Why are you smiling?' I ask, irritably, sitting down with my mug of tea. All nerves have vanished, now that I remember the old Charlie. The one who walked out on me when I was pregnant. But I cannot look him in the face; I am scared that his beautiful eyes will suck me back into being in love with him.

'I'm just remembering what you're like,' he says, I could swear, fondly.

'Yeah, I'm remembering what *you're* like.'

'I have to hand it to you – you're phenomenal in a row.'

'Wow. A compliment.'

'I miss our rows,' he says, really fondly. It is as if he is saying, '*I miss our dancing on the beach at midnight.*'

'I don't.'

'Not ever?'

I dare myself to look straight at him, and at that flop

273

of dark blond hair. Darker at the roots. His deep-set eyes. Black eyes. Almost as black as Solomon's. A mouth I always wanted to kiss – even in the middle of a violent argument.

'I used to,' I say, relieved at how resistible he is.

'But you've forgotten about me now?' he asks, lazily. 'Now that you're shacked up with *the nanny*.'

It is as if he is saying: *the nancy.*

'Judd?'

'I *knew* you'd get together with him,' he says, decidedly, as if he is answering a TV quiz question correctly.

'I'm not with Judd. He's here because . . .' For a moment, I forget why he is living here. 'He's here because Mrs Leslie was murdered, in the flat below.'

'Yeah, I heard about that. I mean, fucking hell.'

'Fucking hell is right. And that's why Judd's here. In the *spare room.*'

He looks pleased, as if he has won a prize in a TV quiz.

I want to ask him whether he has a girlfriend, but I cannot find a context in which to slip the question. Charlie is busy switching on Judd's computer – asking me whether I am yet on the internet.

'No way,' I say. 'Thanks to you, I've only just caught up with the *television* age.'

'There's nothing wrong with TV. When I met you, you were just a snob,' says the man who thinks people common if they are forced to take advantage of a free health service. 'All that listening to *The Archers*. It was only a soap opera without pictures.'

'Is that what they teach you on your media studies course?' I ask; and he takes the question seriously.

'Yes, in fact,' he says, finally accessing one of Judd's files.

'*Yes,*' he says, in triumph. 'I found the password.'

'What is it?' I ask, genuinely curious.

'What d'you think?' He turns round, and grins a grin I remember, from falling in love with him. I remember it all from meeting Charlie to him leaving me: Rich's flat in High Street Ken; taxis at midnight; needing to see him, just once more; the scratch of the sticks, when we had sex in Epping forest; the flaky crumbs of croissant in my bed in Shepherd's Bush; dressing up to meet his parents; his: 'I love you always' on our wedding day; the two of us laughing like children on a cultural school trip as we walk out of slow, foreign films; Charlie, begging me not to play Swingball, in case it hurts my baby-to-be; the rows; him, suggesting counselling; him, leaving.

'I don't know,' I say, and cannot help smiling.

'*Jewish.*'

'Don't laugh; it's what defines him. It would define you too if half your family had been wiped out in the Holocaust. His parents are dead. What else does he have?'

'All right; I don't want to hear his life history. Oh, what do we have here? "Love in *Lithuania*?"' he laughs, reading from the screen.

'I don't think Judd'll be very happy to find you reading his screenplay. And he'll be back soon.'

'I'm not scared of *Judd*,' he says.

But he *is* scared of Judd; and looks round at the front door, as if it might open before he has switched off the computer.

'You should get connected to the net,' he says, as the computer shuts down, sounding like a dying firework.

'Why should I?'

'It makes everything easier. You can buy anything online.'

'More people trying to sell you things you don't need.'

'It's not just shopping. Everything's easier.'

'What about having babies? That's still as hard,' I say, because I want him to ask after his son, who died because of a placental infection. He lies buried in a Jewish cemetery. I have a map of the burial ground, an arrow pointing to Sam's grave.

'Ah, well, you're wrong there,' says Charlie, leaning forward. 'If you were on the net, you could talk about your miscarriage to people on the other side of the world.'

But not to you, I think.

He flicks through the TV-listings magazines, then leans down and unzips his leather rucksack. He tugs out a bulky present. 'You don't mind if I wake her up, do you?' he asks, standing up, and nodding towards Maxie's door.

'Oh. Maxie's not here. I'm sorry; I thought you knew.'

'But I've brought her a *present*,' he says, as if he was expecting a present. 'Look,' he says, opening it to show me. He has never been able to resist tearing at a parcel. Inside lies a hugely inexpensive doll, naked but for the Christmas wrapping paper.

'I'm sorry; she's at Mum's. But Max'll *love* it.'

I smile at the doll, almost feeling sorry for Charlie, standing there. He is Maxie's father, after all. Then I remember how he wanted me to abort Sam; and how he achieved what he wanted. (One minute Sam was breathing fast inside of me, the next gone. Slip.) I say that he should have phoned in advance.

'So, I have to book an appointment now, for an assignation with my own daughter?'

'To *see* my daughter. Say: *to see my daughter*. It's not an *assignation*.'

'You know, I'd forgotten how controlling you were.'

276

'Oh, here we go.'

'Didn't you ever wonder why I left? Why I needed to go. For my own *sanity.*'

'There was I thinking you were being unselfish and leaving for *my* sanity.'

'You treat me like a two-year-old. You were always so patronizing.'

'It's patronizing, not pay-tronizing.'

I think how everyone who has ever dumped me has called me patronizing. Even Hamish Mclure MP – and he has gone on to be patronizing for a living.

'What's wrong with these?' he asks, eating biscuit after biscuit from the plate. 'They taste like sand.'

'They're kosher,' I say, absent-mindedly.

He puts his handful of biscuits back down, sneering, 'I'd forgotten you were *Jewish.*'

'God, Judd was right. You're an anti-bloody-Semite.'

'I'm anti bloody Semites like *Judd.*'

'Judd's worth ten of you.'

'Oh yes; I forgot. Judd the hero. Judd, who's moved in, to *rescue* you. I bet you don't treat him like a retarded toddler. I bet you let him navigate. Oh, of course. 'Cause this is Judd we're talking about. You don't start rows with him, do you?'

'There's no need for me to argue with Judd. He doesn't leave . . .'

'I told you; I didn't know the bloody eggs were in there.'

'It's not only that. Judd and I might not agree on everything, but we . . .'

'Oh, you'd go for counselling with him, wouldn't you? Bloody Judd.'

'I'm not with Judd,' I say.

'Well, who are you with then, ditz? Because my loyal *mother*,' he sneers, 'says you're going out with *someone*.'

'And why can't I? You left me. You walked out on *me* . . .'

'Because you don't love me; you treat me like Maxie, only worse.'

'I did love you,' I say, feeling myself beginning to cry.

'*Did?*' he sneers.

He kicks the occasional table, and stands up.

'Go on – tell me. Who are you fucking then, if it's not Judd?'

'Well, you're fucking *Catheter*.'

'Caitlin.'

'*Caitlin?*' I think about the name, and why it slices through me, like a knife. It is only a word – Caitlin – but I know I never want to hear that name again.

'Well, I hope you're happy with Caitlin – because I'm *very* happy with VD.'

'VD?'

The colour drains from his face.

'You're with VD?'

'Yes, and it makes a pleasant change, being with such a gentleman. At last – a success story for the public school system.'

'You are such a *slag*.'

He stands up with a suddenness that is out of character, and heaves the rucksack on to his back. 'I only fucking came for my things,' he says.

'So, not to see Maxie then?'

'To see Maxie and to get my things. Not to see an *Essex Girl* I was stupid enough to marry. I mean, bloody hell.'

'Fine.'

He starts opening cupboards at random, lifting out a

heavy box he finds in the storage cupboard, next to the front door. He balances it on his knee as he opens the door.

'What d'you need *that* for?' I ask, staring at the laminator.

'In case I need to laminate anything,' he says, slamming the door behind him.

When Judd comes back, he asks why I am looking so miserable. I tell him that my *husband* was here, wanting to see Maxie.

'You shouldn't have let him in,' he says, going into the kitchen area, and taking out a loaf of challah bread from the cupboard. He tears off a thick piece of bread.

'He is her father.'

'Some father.'

'However crap he might be as a Dad, he's still her Dad.'

He opens the fridge.

I can hear him thinking.

'You're late back,' I say, feeling as if I have hurt him in some way.

'Yeah, I was talking to Chava.'

'At this time you were alone, talking to Chava?'

I think how Yiddish – how *Chava* – I sound; as he takes out a stick of red sausage, chopping it, and slamming the rough slices on to challah bread. He tells me he wanted Chava to read his screenplay. *Love in Lithuania*.

'You wanted her to check it was kosher?'

'Yes, ha ha. Really very funny. No – I'm sending it out to production companies, and Chava asked if she could read it first.'

'What about me? Can I read it?'

279

'You want to read it?' he smiles, leaning against the kitchen counter, and eating the bread and meat in huge bites.

'Of course. Why shouldn't I?'

'Only that you've never wanted to read anything of mine before.'

'Well, I do now.'

Judd sighs, and says that he might be ready to send it to film companies – but he is *certainly* not ready for *Lucy Fletcher* to read it.

'Why not?'

'What, with your acid tongue?' He comes into the living room, leaning against the breakfast bar.

'Oh, well if you don't want my input, don't be disappointed when it ends up on the slushpile,' I say, closing my eyes.

'I'll still have a job here will I?' he says, and I can hear him smiling. He peels some more of the stick of red sausage, eating it in big bites.

'You'll have a job as long as *I* do. I think Hen needs to get rid of a quota of people. He's asked for voluntary redundancies.'

'Well, he won't get rid of you,' says Judd seriously, as he opens the fridge and throws the sausage inside. 'He's obviously really fond of you. Was when I met him, anyway.'

I think of Hen drinking tea with the bag still in it. Offering me a ginger biscuit when he hired me. He was delighted, he said, to have me join the family. He was very happy, he said, to have me on board – and that I had better get out of his office before he mixed any other metaphors.

Judd comes to sit on the armchair, and opens a big,

leather-bound book.

'Is that homework?' I ask.

'It's recommended reading,' he half smiles; and I sigh, self-consciously.

'I wish I had your faith. It'd be so nice, sometimes, to be told what to do.'

'You are being told what to do – but by glossy magazines.'

'They were *Charlie's* subscriptions.'

'So you were being told what to do by *Charlie* who was told what to do by men's magazines . . .'

'Rabbis. Men's magazines,' I muse.

'Somehow, I think you'd be better off listening to me. At least I *have* a brain . . .' he grins.

'Charlie could be very funny,' I say, defensively. 'And people aren't funny unless they're clever. Funny is beyond clever.'

'Well, why did you split up then?' he asks, grimly. 'You could have gone on and on having a laugh together, having *fun* . . .'

'It's not a dirty word . . .'

'All the while pretending you weren't just moving down the conveyor belt towards death.'

'Oh Judd, don't be so . . . So difficult.'

'You want to go back to living with Charlie? Oh, because then the living was easy,' he sneers.

'It's equally hard living with someone who talks about the Holocaust on a daily basis.'

'Well, *I* find it hard to live with someone who won't let something like the Holocaust – which colours everything – touch on their everyday life.'

He returns to his reading, and I watch him, feeling as usual that all I have to do is be close to him, and I will

281

become an intellectual by association.

His expression is intense. I wonder whether he and Chava ever touch. Has she been known to brush past him, on her way to the kitchen? When they study the holy texts, do they sit close together? Does she take his hand as he talks?

It is not that I am envious. Why would I be? (Although I envy how close she is to him.) Only, I wish I could warn Judd against women like Chava. Women who pretend to be pure – all the time poisoning men's minds against me. I can hear her saying, 'What is she, this Lucy? A shiksa. A whore. A *nothing.*'

I wonder how close Chava is to Judd. Are they close enough to – might they? – kiss?

'How is Chava?' I ask Judd now; and he looks up at me, one eyebrow raised, in bemusement.

'How's *Chava*?'

'Yes. How are her feminine, pretty hands?'

He looks at me as if remembering where he is.

'What d'you mean? D'you think she's got pretty hands?'

'Oh, only compared to mine. Mine are *workman*like. Mine are great big farmer's-wife hands. But *Chava*. Such delicate hands, like a peasant girl from the nineteenth century . . .' When I look up, I expect him to be smiling. But I realize, when I see his face whitening, that I have said too much. Sometimes, Judd frightens me. Now, for example.

I watch him thinking, and I am scared, because he knows that I am quoting his diary.

(I will make a joke of it.)

At last, he says something.

'You've been reading those journals of mine.'

'No, I really . . .'

'Don't lie; just tell me. Have you been reading my journals?'

'Only because I'm nosy; and to check you weren't a paedophile.'

He pushes his hands through his hair. 'I can't bel . . .' I stare somewhere, at my bag, which looks like a black cat, and reminds me of the shapes I saw when I was a child before I went to sleep. It reminds me of a time when the curtains were gorillas, and fallen pillows, bears.

'So you read my fucking private *diary*?' He smashes his fist, hard, on the arm of his chair. So hard that his skullcap falls off.

'I'm sorry,' I say, like Maxie, after a tantrum.

He pauses again, to think some more, as I slump even smaller into the sofa.

'How much did you read?' he says, suddenly tensing.

'Don't worry. Hardly much. It got boring as soon as you mentioned *Chava.*'

'So you read until then, about Clare and Chava, but you didn't read on . . .?'

'You'd talked all about Clare, anyway. At length.'

'Did you read on from there?'

'I read until the Chava bit and then you interrupted me. There was nothing that was interesting. Please stop being so angry. It's bad for your heart.'

I look at his pink skullcap on the floor. His name, lovingly crocheted by Chava.

He decides to speak. 'You're impossible to live with.' As he says this, he shakes his head.

'*I'm* impossible . . . ? Bloody hell, I should have listened to Angela when she warned me against living with a Scorpio. She was right. You're so controlling.' I stop, remembering that I am in the wrong. 'Anyway, I've said

I'm sorry. I didn't read much. It's just that I'm a journalist. I'm paid to be curious.'

'About local government *corruption*. You're not paid to be curious about me, just as I'm not paid to be interested in you. I don't give a toss about you and Charlie. I'm *paid* to love Maxie.'

I think how Judd was not paid to soothe me when Charlie left; or to move in with me when Mrs Leslie died; or to be with me when I miscarried; or to organize Sam's funeral. He is not paid to be interested in me.

He is my au pair, that is all. Maxie's nanny.

He is paid to take care of Maxie.

'Well, I'm sorry to have taken advantage of you,' I say, feeling the tears coming.

'I'm just reminding you of my *role*.'

'And you're right – I'm not paying you to be my friend,' I say, as the tears spill. I pay for his childcaring, not for Solomon's hugs – *'I'm happy with you, Mummy Lucy'* – or for Judd's religious teachings. He has hundreds of commandments, the worst of which is the one that forces him to pretend to rabbis' daughters that he is not living with me. I can barely hear Judd when he says, 'I'm sorry. I shouldn't have said that.'

'Why not? It's true, isn't it?' I could easily crease up. I could cry like a two-year-old. Like a two-year-old who has lost control.

'But you know what? I don't give a fuck. Not about you, or anything,' I say, controlling myself. I go into the kitchen area, snapping on the kettle.

'Oh God, I'm sorry,' says Judd, coming in behind me. 'Lucy, I'm so sorry,' he says, and I feel his arm around my shoulder.

His arms tighten around me; and, for a moment, I think it might stop at that. I am enjoying being this close. It is enough. Hugging. If only we could have the type of friendship that involved constant cuddling.

But I look up too soon.

He is looking down at me. Kissing me, and.

And I have never known how to stop sex.

Afterwards, we have to be practical, as there are children involved. Solomon is in the next room, and we cannot be caught half-naked in the kitchen. That is Judd's excuse for dressing so quickly. Handing me my bra.

I grab my pile of clothes and go to the bathroom so that Judd can work out what will happen next. I can hear him tidying up.

I sit on the toilet seat. I can still smell him on my breasts. I will not leave the room until he has gone to bed. I think of his hands on my body.

I lost control, just then. I lost control during the sex. Why was it so good, when there were next to-no acrobatics? I could not concentrate on the task in hand. I lost it.

He made me lose it, I think, shaking.

I am shaking.

'You all right, Lucy?' says a rap on the door.

'Yeah, fine.'

'OK.'

The voice goes away, I think, to his bedroom. But I sit there, still. I do not want to see Judd. Ever again. I do not want to lose control like that.

I am shivering, thinking how one can tell a lot about someone from their bathroom products; and Judd has only the basics – his toothbrush, his toothpaste, his deodorant and his razor. This is in contrast to Charlie, who stocked

Clinique's entire range of male grooming cosmetics. My products lie higgledy-piggledy in a basket; Judd's stand upright.

I realize that I could carry on with this metaphor for some time.

When I come out, wrapped in a towel, the living room is dark and tidy. All I can see is Judd's memorial candle to his mother. Flickering.

So, I think. He has decided that we should sleep on it. *Good decision*, I think.

I go to bed and lie there for a long time, thinking of sleep and relationships, and how I find both difficult.

Yet, once asleep, I am impossible to disturb, and go on sleeping until midday on Sunday. I wake up feeling my face sticky, and stuck together, as a result of the fact that I did not remove my make-up. The first thing I see when I wake up is the time. Then I remember everything.

I do not know how to face Judd. Ever again. I think how I might joke about that one night of passion not being part of his regular duties – although I cannot hear him.

It is quiet and eerily tidy. There is no sign of Solomon, and I am relieved. Gleeful at the thought of an undisturbed hour of children's television.

I reach for the remote control, and wonder why I feel burgled. Then I realize that Judd's books are not there. Usually, they are piled up on the television. They clutter up the flat. And half of Maxie's toys are missing. The half that are, in fact, Solomon's.

The Brio train set has gone. And Solomon's Lego.

The toy-box looks depleted, as does the kitchen. Judd's stuff is missing – his candlesticks, his Kiddush cup, his medicine-tasting wine. His memorial candle. I feel cold as I go into his bedroom. It is immaculate. His duvet has gone. His clothes. Solomon's books.

I close the door to his bedroom. That is when I see a note, addressed to me, on the sideboard – the gist of which is that Judd feels that it would be better if he moved out. After everything. That I was right when I said that the relationship was confusing.

He does not believe in sex before marriage.

I am to tell Maxie that Judd loves her, but that people come and go throughout one's life. And – as I always made clear – he was only her childminder. He was wrong to have crossed that boundary. Maxie should see more of her father. She needs continuity. And if VD provides that, so much the better.

Judd would be lying if he did not admit to feeling terrible. Bloody awful, in fact. He hates having to leave her. He will try to visit her soon, to explain everything.

But he has become too attached. He was wrong to have moved in – although it had felt right at the time. He was beginning to think of Maxie as a daughter. He realized, last night, how much I resented the arrangement. How much I still loved Charlie.

He was wrong to have surrendered to an impulse.

Unlike Clare, I am a good mother. Could I tell Maxie that he loves her? Too much, he thinks, sometimes. But it is better this way. A quick break. There would be less hurt, all round. If he simply went.

If I need anything, he will be at Rabbi Scheur's.

In other words, I think, he will be at Chava's.

Chapter Eleven

I am driving Von to Wales for the induction course. She has been away, so I have been unable to tell her before now that I slept with Judd. She splits open a packet of shortbread biscuits with her teeth, saying that she knew Judd and I would eventually get it together; and I take my eyes off the road to look at her.

'What d'you mean by that?'

'What d'you mean, what do I mean?'

Von says that it was only a matter of time before Judd and I had sex. She knew when we first met. He is too good-looking a bloke. Sensitive enough to take care of children. Strong-minded enough to criticize the way I lived. Really, it was not a matter of whether, but when.

I smile, and feed a tape into the machine, asking Von why she didn't tell me that I fancied Judd. But she says that it could have freaked me out. I was living with him by then. 'Well, we're not living together any more,' I say, pressing Play. 'He's moved out. After we shagged, he left me a note on the kitchen table. Saying that he couldn't cope with . . . Me.'

Von laughs, and asks me whether she can change the music.

'If you must,' I smile.

I was going to tell Von, during this drive to Wales, about VD. But it seems inappropriate now. It would sound as if – while her back was turned – I have been sleeping with just about everybody.

Von tells me not to look so worried. Judd will be back for more. But I say I am not worried about Judd. Not at all. I did fancy him. OK. But I hardly wanted a relationship with him. God, no. I can just imagine *that*. Every time I wanted to touch him, he would be on the phone, checking if it was OK with his Rabbi.

Von laughs, but I can't. I am suddenly too angry, remembering the way Judd left me, leaving only a note. At the time, I was too relieved to feel any hurt.

I tell Von that I don't want to see him again. Ever. Really. He has betrayed my trust. Von changes radio channels again, and says that I have learned a valuable lesson. Never again to employ a fundamentalist Jew as my nanny.

'So. What have you been doing with Maxie?' asks Von, because she thinks of Maxie as an important parcel I am always having to deliver somewhere.

'She's at my Mum's.'

'When d'you have to collect her?'

'Oh no, here we go.'

I have stopped at a traffic light; and a squeegee merchant is waving his squeegee at me, in a threatening manner.

'Just lock the doors,' says Von, lighting a cigarette.

'They *are* locked. It doesn't stop them. No thanks,' I try, as the squeegee merchant dips his squeegee in the bucket. Seconds later, foam drips down the glass. 'Really, no thanks.' The suds are wiped away, just as Von winds down the window; and a hand comes through.

'Von – why did you open the window? Oh, I haven't got any change.' I pull out a pound from my pocket.

'I was getting rid of my ash. Sorry,' she says, as the squeegee merchant takes the coin, all the time leering and winking, as if what Von and I really, really want is to pay him for sexual intercourse.

'So? When d'you have to collect Maxie?'

'Well, as soon as I can. She's been at Mum's for the last two weeks. But I didn't know what else to do. Bloody Judd.'

As soon as I read Judd's note, I rang my mother. She told me to calm down, and ring around au pair agencies. I said that, but, it was a Sunday. Mum sighed, and asked me why I was panicking. I was a Fine. I should show Judd Drexler that I could survive without him. I had kept Charlie on ice, anyway. All I had to do was to find a nanny, for goodness' sake.

'Why d'you think he did leave?' Von laughs.

'Oh, he broke so many of his religious rules by sleeping with me. He's not even really meant to be sharing a flat with me, let alone seeing me naked, let alone touching me, let alone . . .'

'*Fucking* you,' she laughs. 'Or maybe he wasn't ready to live with someone after just one night?'

'Maybe,' I smile. 'Either way, he's really left me in it. I mean, who's going to look after Maxie? He owes me three months' notice.'

'Can't you just get another nanny?' asks Von, singing (almost) along to a song by the Corrs.

I mutter at that, because, in the last two weeks, I have interviewed almost every nanny in north London. But the women were either incompetent, or too well-trained in childcare to get their hands dirty looking after children.

'I will not clean up,' one said. 'I will not be treated like a house-servant.'

In other words, 'I will not be treated like a mother.'

I confided in another that I was anxious about leaving Maxie with a stranger whilst I went back to work. The nanny said that she understood: she had not wanted to leave her last post. The boy would miss her. But she had reasoned it through, and decided that if a child could not be with his nanny, then a really good mother was the next best thing.

I joined an agency for mother's helps, but one would have been more of a hindrance. The other looked like the serial killer, Rose West.

I advertised in local newspapers. Most respondents could not speak English. I interviewed two. The first confided in me that, although she had plenty of nannying experience, she was not really interested in children. Dogs, she liked. The second woman sounded competent – but then she asked me what time she could take her lunch hour.

Last Friday, I rang my mother in a panic.

'Don't worry. Maxie can stay here until you decide what to do,' said Mum.

'Oh, really? Really? *Thank* you. Because I can't take even more time off work. Not when Hen's looking for people to redundancise.'

'That's not a word Lucy.'

'Well, it should be. So, you're sure? About having Max?'

'Of course. That's what mothers are for.'

That, in an ideal world, is what mothers are for.

Mum's all right, Jack, in that she started her career late. We were at school when she set up her slimming business. My brother and I felt secure in our mother's love by the time Slimco was set up.

The business grew with us. It was small when we ran to her with best friend or bullying problems. It was still of a manageable size when Mum was privately coaching me through O and A levels. By the time Marcus and I left home – leaving our mother with an empty nest – Slimco was winning her Essex Businesswoman of the year.

My mother has exceeded all expectations of her. She was expected to cook, and to breed. Her parents thought that she would marry a nice Jewish dentist and fill in her time before motherhood by being, say, a temporary secretary. Her husband thought she should sell her apple strudel.

It was a sin not to.

But I have not had the luxury of such low expectations. My mother wants me to be the editor of a national newspaper. My tutor at college wanted me to enter academia. Charlie wanted me to be a TV newsreader. Dad expects me to be happy. Charlie wanted me to have a twenty-year-old's figure. Maxie expects me to be a stay-at-home mother. VD thinks that I should stop worrying, and get a sense of humour.

I have been seeing a great deal of VD.

We have been to the South Bank to see a play. We have been to the cinema. We have been to The World's End pub in Camden. Oh, and we went to a comedy club. He stayed at my flat for a weekend. I stayed at his flat all of last week.

We had a break from each other this weekend.

I said that I needed to be back in my own flat. The truth was, I needed to be away from his flat. I was sick of being surrounded by his possessions. His tiny stereo system. His gigantic juicer. I wanted to be back with my books, my bed, and my throws. I said that he should try to brighten up his flat; but VD could not see the point of throws. Or hangings.

He said, 'Hang on a minute. You want to put this rug on the *wall*?'

'It's not a rug. It's a tapestry from Bali.'

I now know this of VD: he feels claustrophobic in the theatre; he cannot eat ice-cream; he has sensitive teeth; he thinks that Ibsen is over-rated; he believes that theatre-goers are pretentious; he will not book cinema seats; he prefers to be spontaneous; he buys Big Sized Cokes; he loathes romantic comedy films; he prefers legal dramas; he doesn't only like fast food – he enjoys the odd Chinese; he always feels horny after Chinese food; he *loves* John Grisham; he wants to *be* John Grisham; he wants to *stalk* John Grisham; he actually doesn't think that John Grisham exists; he thinks his books are written by a committee of people; he always buys the Sunday papers on Saturday night in Leicester Square; he loathes London; he wants to live in Leeds; people have time for people in Leeds; his father grew up in Leeds; he does not like deep conversations; he will try anything once; he hates Camden; he hates young people who make him feel old; he loves seeing his step-brother; he doesn't care what people say – he will *always*, in his heart, be a New Romantic; he would count Heather amongst his closest friends; he and Heather sometimes hang out together on their own; he couldn't fuck Heather; he could fuck that *Work* Experience woman; he could fuck most women; he is falling in love with me; he drinks too much; he likes to sit in the front row at comedy clubs; he can laugh at himself; he hates jumped-up comedians; *he* could be a comedian; he knows twenty-four jokes about cats; he can hold nine pints of Stella; he hates his father; he can survive on two hours' sleep a night; he hates himself when he is drunk; his father was a fascist; he *loves* me; he *lovsh* me; his father was a fucker; he always eats a fried breakfast before work; he never takes anything for a hangover; he never means anything he says when he is drunk; he is Mr Joker at work; for years, he has been secretly applying for other jobs; he hates muscles on a woman; he packs a box of food to munch on at work; he cannot understand why he is not working for another newspaper; he likes sex standing up best; he still watches *Top of the Pops*; he refuses to buy a duvet; he needs to sleep in pure cotton; he is an individualist; he is prone to breaking silent, egg-smelling wind during the night; he freezes milk; he likes living with a woman; he likes living with me; he hated and envied Judd when I lived with him.

Von is giving me the latest on her aerobics instructor. He phoned her last night. She had only just got in from Crete. 'Can you imagine Nibs or VD doing something like that? Fuck, no. Craig's . . .'

I pink, worried that, if I reply, I will give something away about VD. His likes, and dislikes. I know too much. I know, for example, that his father was an active member of the British National Party.

Von asks, 'So, are we going to talk about what he's like in bed then?'

I almost crash into the car in front.

I ask her why she is asking such a question.

'What d'you mean, why?' she says. 'Just tell me about Judd between the sheets. Was he any good?'

'*Judd,*' I say, relaxing – remembering the relief of being able to touch him. Finally, having permission to fuck him. 'Oh, you know Judd. He has to be good at every-thing.'

'Did you know *Craig* fancied me?' asks Von, about our aerobics instructor.

'Of course. All men fancy you. That's why I'm mad to hang out with you.'

'Oh, as if you . . .'

'Shit – I could have gone into him.'

The car in front of me leaves the motorway without indicating; and Von tells me about her car-sex theory. She equates the way a person drives with their sexual performance. Von says that a driver who refuses to indicate would not communicate their desires in bed.

I ask Von what it says about her performance that, when she drives, she is forever speeding and screaming at the car in front. She laughs, and says that before she got it together with VD, she knew what he was going to be like between the sheets. Because she had already played passenger in his MG. 'He would only drive in the fast lane – but he was so considerate. I mean, he always made a point of letting in other drivers.'

I blush, and say that her theory works in relation to Susanna. Because she has been too scared to drive since passing her test years ago; and it is interesting that Angela has little to no lane discipline. We both laugh, feeling as smug as scientists with our theory. I speed west past electric pylons which Judd said reminded him of concentration-camp watchtowers.

I am scared that I will never see Judd again. I will never see him loading a washing machine. Or hugging my Maxie. Of course, I should not have taken advantage of him like that. He is religious, for God's sake. According to Jewish law, Judd is not even meant to masturbate for fear of wasting his seed – and he certainly wasted his seed on me. A half-shiksa. A whore.

295

A nothing.

I can only imagine what Chava said, when he confided in her that he had slept with me. Me – a woman who miscarries.

'Change sodding lanes,' screams Von at two lorries chuntering along the middle lane, like a couple of fat old ladies in a supermarket.

There is a gentle knock on the door of my hotel room. I am certain that it is VD, and I wonder whether to pretend that I am not here. But he knocks again, harder this time, and I decide to allow him in – if only to tell him that I have not had a chance to tell Von about our relationship.

'Thought I'd sneak in,' says VD, as I open the door.

'This is a bit silly. Von's in the next room; and I haven't told her yet.'

'Well, tell her tonight.'

'I don't think I can now. The longer I leave it, the more lies I'm telling.'

'So, I'm going to be sneaking into your bedroom all week. Great. It's going to be like a West End farce,' he says, admiring the view of a brick wall from my window.

'But not funny.'

He starts to open cupboard doors, and drawers, to see if I have anything in Room 321 that he doesn't have in Room 426. But, no. He is disappointed to find the same trouser press in the wardrobe. The same broken hairdryer, hanging by a loose cord from the wall, like a life-saving instrument in an NHS hospital.

He takes everything out of the mini-bar, looks longingly at the jar of cashew nuts, then replaces everything. I flick through the course brochure; and read the index:

Page One: Learning the Post's Mission Statement (and making up one of your own).

Page Two: Upskilling. How do I do that?

Page Three: Your Workchurch. How to turn your home into the office, and your office into your home.

Page Four: The internet for everyone. Yes, even you!

Page Five: Outward bound day. How to reach the sun.

'Bloody hell. Why am I here?' I wail, showing him day five.

'Oh, come on. You'll enjoy it.'

'No, we won't.'

'I will.'

He looks at the door.

'Is the door locked?'

'Why?'

'Because,' he says, kissing my neck.

'Look, I don't know.' I push him away from me. 'Von might come looking for us. Can't we wait 'til I've told her?' We lie there, staring up at the bare bulb.

'When are you going to tell her?'

'After the course, I suppose.'

'I can't wait 'til then,' he smiles, throwing the brochure on the floor.

'VD, come on. We're not sixteen.'

'Exactly. We have adult needs.'

'Oh don't do that. Not here.'

'You like it. I know you like it.'

His voice is so muffled that I can barely hear him saying, 'I know you.'

He knows this of me: I like it when he does that; I get

sick of pubs; I enjoy going to the theatre; I always choose vanilla ice-cream (my mother took us to places where there were thirty-two flavours; she would sulk if I chose vanilla); I have good strong teeth, thanks to my mother, who was the daughter of a dentist; I like to book cinema seats in advance; I wear contact lenses; I will not buy from a range of overpriced cinema drinks and confectionery; I adore romantic comedies starring Julia Roberts; I need to sit in the front row to see the screen; I am suspicious of Chinese food; I am suspicious of most foodstuffs; I feel guilty eating pork; I refuse, actually, to eat pork; I have not read any of John Grisham's books; I pity stalked celebrities; I pity successful celebrities; I do not want to be a lonely writer-type; I do not read newspapers; I still have a newspaper delivered; unlike most women, I do not have any cellulite; I will never be tired of London; I think that London has the pace of New York and the romance of Paris; I like to wander London's streets; I am beginning to hate Camden; I feel young again; I aged twenty years when Maxie was born; I lost my freedom when Maxie was born; I love every bit of Maxie's body; I treasure the space she occupies; I think that Charlie looked like a cross between Duran Duran's Nick Rhodes, Hugh Grant, and an antihero in a Victorian novel; I was a Duranie; I was obsessed with Simon Le Bon; I do not trust Heather; I do not trust Work Experience; I want to sit in the back row of comedy clubs; I pity stand-up comedians, having to stand up there, in front of a row of hecklers; I cannot get drunk easily; I will miss the rituals of Judaism, and the feeling of belonging to something; I am more Jewish than I thought; I will miss Solomon, despite his habit of stuffing stale fruit peel inside cushion covers; I will really miss Solomon; I did not mean it when I said that I would really miss Judd; I would miss VD if he left, suddenly; I would miss anyone if they left suddenly; I eat Special K for breakfast; if there is no Special K I will eat Cornflakes for breakfast; I am not secretly scared of anything; I am scared of lots of things; I cannot understand why I am not Chairman of the board of Sainsbury's, or something; I secretly love my job; after sex, Charlie always made feel dirty; I have not seen *Top of the Pops* for years; a part of me is missing when I am not with Maxie; I worry about Maxie dying; Maxie irritates me with her questions; I need to talk to Maxie at least once a day, or I feel that something is missing; I cannot live by myself; I do not think about Judd, unless it is in the context of childcare.

But I lied about Judd; and, of course, the cellulite.

We are about to be divided up into two teams by the course leaders – Suzy and Tim – both of whom I am certain I recognize from pre-school children's television.

'It's the last day. You can smile now, Lucy,' says Tim, as I stand there, cold, thinking how pink my cheeks might be.

'I think Lucy's having fun underneath,' grins Suzy, and VD sniggers. (I remember that I know this of VD: he adores double entendres.)

'Oh, are you, Lucy?' he says.

I am chosen for Team B.

'Is this compulsory?' I ask. Because I have never been a team-player. I know that other people stop me winning. If I win, my team shares my glory. If I lose, I take my share of the team's blame. So I refuse to join in group games. When, last year, Donald wanted Charlie and me to play tennis against him and Charlie's sister, Helen, I said No. I am no fool. Neither was Donald, making me team up with Charlie, who was hopeless at any activity which required energy.

Three Augusts ago I found a stump of Swingball at the

bottom of my parents' garden, hammered into the ground. I wanted us all to play, but Charlie would not leave his garden lounger.

That was a memorable summer. Charlie seemed to care about me then. I was pregnant with Maxie, and he said that I should stop exerting myself or I would lose his baby. The sex was hot and sticky that summer.

It is white-cold in the forest. We are given a map which is all shades of brown. Our goal is to find the Sun, which is drawn into stone on the side of a hill. We are to go via a Cave.

We were all surprised when Von was appointed team leader. She has spent the last four days swearing at Suzy, who she says reminds her of a chipmunk on speed.

Now, Von is insisting that we take the conflict seriously. At Brownies, my best friend, Danielle Carruthers, was the same. As soon as she was given some responsibility, Danielle changed. I, meanwhile, was unable to summon up even enough energy to gain an Enthusiasm badge.

Because I have more in common with Charlie than I choose to admit.

Yet, I was upset when Danielle – her own uniform a mess of badges – was appointed sixer of the Imps. Because she stopped laughing at my jokes about Brown Owl's body odour.

She helped the others to build rope bridges.

'Yes, it is compulsory,' says Von to me, grinning, and asking what she has done to deserve such a team. We will never find our way to the Sun. Not with Rainie so fired up against us.

'If it wasn't for my asthma, I'd be as fit as Rainie,' says Heather, when Von goes to collect our emergency supplies. VD messes Heather's hair.

'She was joking, squirrel,' he says.

'Squirrel?' I repeat.

'Don't you think she looks like a squirrel?'

'I do *not*,' says Heather, grinning, and pretending to punch him.

Von comes back, her shoulders slung with four water bottles. She is carrying a huge rucksack, full of today's lunch and emergency supplies.

Von and VD are looking at the map. They are wearing matching kagouls. Looking at them, I feel dirty. Like VD's secret mistress. They look like a young man and his pretty wife, out rambling. I feel like a filthy whore.

Heather comes between them, to study the map. Under her DKNY track top, she is wearing a T-shirt which reads: Hug Me; and I imagine someone hugging her – all breath slowly squeezing out.

'You don't *have* to join in, Lucy,' she says, catching me staring at her. 'I think Suzy has realized that you're a bit weird. Why don't you pretend you've got period pain, or something?'

'No,' says Von. 'Come on Luce; you were the same when we started working out. "I can't do it"; and now look at you.'

They all three turn to look at me, stuffed into a baggy, green tracksuit.

'What's wrong with you? This is great,' says VD, stretching his pecs.

'Yeah; I love fresh air,' says Heather; and I shiver, thinking how much I would like to be back in the hotel lecture room. On the net, flirting online with New Yorkers in erotic chat-rooms. I am better at flirting electronically – perhaps because I have full access to a computerized thesaurus. *Virtual* men laugh out loud (LOL) at my jokes.

301

Virtual men do not tell me to start running.

'Come on, Lucy. It's only until we find the arrow,' says VD. We have to jog if we are to beat the clock. Rainie's team will jog this stretch. We spent too long studying the map. We have half an hour to find that arrow.

I am surprised to find that I have overtaken Von, who jogs on Hampstead Heath. But I am giving it my all. What is the point, otherwise?

So much so that I am the first to reach the black stream.

Von and I wait for VD, who has stayed behind to walk with Heather. She suffers from asthma. If we want time for lunch, we have just five minutes to locate the arrow. I suggest to Von that we look for the arrow without Heather and VD. But, as team leader, she feels she should wait for the others.

I locate the arrow on the map.

I find the arrow pasted on to the bridge which crosses the stream. Just as I do, I look up to see VD, walking towards us, with Heather. He is, if I am not mistaken, tickling her.

Heather says that I am weird because I wanted to get on and look for the arrow. She thinks we do not need lunch. 'Lunch is for wimps,' agrees VD. Nevertheless, he is anxious to open the bag of supplies, to see what is inside. He says that his stomach is rumbling. Von says that she can hear it.

Heather lies her head on his stomach, to listen. VD pretends to push Heather's head down towards his crotch; and she laughs hysterically. I say that, as we are out in the freezing cold, we might as well search for the stars.

'Well, I can't run,' says Heather, sitting up.

'That's OK,' soothes Von. 'We can walk.'

302

'We don't need to run,' says VD.

I would prefer to run. We can rest when we reach the top of the hill. Heather can walk behind us. But Von is team leader, and has the final word. She decides to put it to a vote. Unsurprisingly, Heather wins. She had VD's vote. I walk ahead of the others, wondering why Von was made leader, when I am the only team-member able to read a map.

I am the one who finds the bag of gold stars. So, I leave a note for Von, telling her that I have the Stars, and that I will meet them in the Cave.

I am left sitting alone in the Cave. At first, I feel smug. I clear the Cave of sticks, so that we can sit down and have lunch. I clean a large log, so that we can use it as a table. I pride myself on winning every competition – no matter how minor.

But I have been now been sitting here in the semi-light of the Cave for half an hour. I am beginning to feel lonely. If I am honest – scared.

By the time Von and VD arrive, with Heather not far behind them, I cannot see the point of this competition. I am the only one taking it seriously.

Yet, I do not want to sit here forever. Having lunch. Watching VD trying to force-feed Kendal mint cake to Heather. 'Come on, Squirrel. You're far too skinny.'

'No, I'm fat. See.' Watching Von's face as Heather tickles him to the ground.

'Oh yeah,' says VD, touching her up. 'A supermodel could fit into your waist.'

'Come on – let's go,' I say.

'Yeah. *Let's*,' says Von, who is hurt by VD and Heather, flirting.

Heather and VD lag behind Von and me on the footpath.

'I see what you mean about *Heather*,' says Von. I half turn to watch VD helping Heather over a stile. I can hear her using the word 'gentleman'.

I mutter something about Heather and all men. But I am not in a strong enough position to say any more. At the end of the footpath, Von and I look at the map together, waiting for the rest of our team. (I point out a steep gradient on the third contour.) Because Von wants VD and Heather to help us look for the spear.

While Von galvanizes them, I sit on a stile. VD asks to see the map. Heather asks to see it too. She stands as close as she can to VD, as he unfolds the map to its full size.

For something to do, I lean down to pluck one of the tall feather-duster flowers, scraping away at the feathers. For some time, I pluck and scrape, enjoying being outside, with the wind on my face.

'I've found the spear,' I hear Heather scream.

'You haven't?' says VD.

'I have. Come and look.'

'Which way is it pointing?'

'I can't find this sodding spear,' says Von, coming towards me.

'Don't worry; I've found it.' Heather runs towards us; she is so thin that, even from here, I can see her ribcage contracting.

'Oh, why do we care about a sodding spear?'

They all turn to look at me. Heather, holding her spear.

'Because we can now go on to get the ropes,' explains VD.

'I know what the rules are. Suzy explained them very clearly. I just don't know why we're following them.' I pluck another feather duster.

'Oh, we're not going to have another deep conversation are we?' asks VD.

'Let's get back to this bloody conflict, shall we?' says Von, as I scrape.

There are *mmmhmms* from Heather and VD.

Heather begins to state the obvious, elegantly. We have found the spear, she says. Now, all we have to do is to look for the ropes, and build a bridge to the cave. 'You're right,' says VD, and they smile at each other as if Von and I are invisible. Heather promises to find the ropes for him. But it is Von who runs off in search of the clue.

Curiously I do not mind sitting here, watching VD and Heather flirt. I even find it interesting, anthropologically. Von is the one who finds the ropes, and I build a rope bridge, for which everyone else takes credit. But, because I was carrying our supplies, I left the stars on the other side of the bridge.

When she hears this, Heather's eyes cut to slits.

The three of them regroup to face me. They stand there, lined up in order of importance.

Von: Fucking hell, Lucy.

Me: After the Cave, I had to carry the supplies. That's why.

VD: Nice one, Luce.

Me: I couldn't carry it all over the bridge.

VD: Whatever, it loses us points. You're not going to be able to say: 'Oh, sorry, Suzy and Tim, but I had to carry the supplies.'

Heather: Is it your period pain, do you think?

Von: We've all had a go carrying things. It was your turn after the Cave.

Me: Great. So my turn comes when we have to cross the rope bridge.

Von: Well, we're not going to win now, are we?

Me: So, if we lose, I promise to take all the blame.

Heather, to Von and VD: I think it's her period. She's always irritable now.

Me: How do you know?

Heather: I have to sit next to you, remember.

This trip is beginning to remind me of one of those constipated Brownie-Guide holidays where I was too afraid to go to the toilet in case someone laughed at my flannel.

VD: Never mind – let's go on. We're not far from the Sun now.

Heather, with her arm around my shoulder: Perhaps you'd like to stay here, Lucy? You might feel better after a rest. Hey, everyone, doesn't Lucy look like Anthea Turner?

Me, under my breath: I'd feel better if you'd piss off.

VD: Meg Ryan, I reckon.

Von: I know why we're called Team B now, anyway.

Me: What's that supposed to mean?

Von: Only that Team A has Rainie and that work experience woman.

Heather: Yeah, but they've got Clay. I'm sure she held them back.

VD: Clay's probably still eating lunch in the Cave.

Von: No. Clay'll be great at some things. She'd have cleared the Cave out, no problem.

Me: I cleared the bloody Cave out.

Von: Only the surface shit. We still had to sit on crap to eat our lunch.

Me: Oh, for God's sake. Why does any of this matter?

I am sitting on the grass, underneath a tree. Knees up. The grass is pale and patchy. It looks as if someone has eaten from it, suddenly and ravenously.

Heather: Because it does.

Von: They'll catch up with us soon. And we had two hours on them.

VD: I vote we go back and steal their clues, so that they can't beat us.

Von, sneering at VD: That's not really how I'd like to win.

VD: So long as we win – who cares?

Von: We could have won if you and Heather hadn't spent the whole day flirting.

I scrape the ground with a twig. The roots of the tree are visible in the earth, like an old man's fingers.

Heather, looking away: We are not flirting. I wouldn't flirt with VD. He looks like my old teddy bear.

VD: Says Ms *Squirrel*.

Von: For God's sake, why don't you just fuck in front of us?

Heather: It's not me that you should be worrying about.

Von: What?

Heather: I didn't mean anything.

Von: No – what are you sodding well saying?

Heather: Only that . . .

Von, looking at VD: Is there something I should know about?

Me: *No*. Let's go on.

Von, to VD: There is, isn't there?

VD, looking at me: Well, yes, actually.

Me: VD. *Please*.

Von: Just what the fuck is going on?

Heather: Just tell her. Why shouldn't she know?

Von: Tell me what?

Heather, looking at VD: Well, I'll tell her then.

Me, standing up: No, you bloody well won't.

Von, bemused, to me: What have you got to do with this?

Heather: She's seeing VD.

Von: She's what? No, she's . . . Is that true, Lucy?

Me, letting the map go limp: Well, it is, but it doesn't . . .

Von: How long have you been . . . together?

Me: Not long.

VD: Not long? It's been nearly two months.

Von: You. Fucking *whore*.

Me, facing Heather. Why did you have to say anything, you bitch?

VD tells me, hey, not to blame Heather. She wouldn't hurt a fly. Von asks me why I am blaming Heather. I am the sodding whore. She thanks Heather for telling her the truth. She is glad that one of her friends isn't a sly cow.

Heather smiles. She stands there stiff in Diesel combats. But her shoulders shake. She says, not to worry, she realizes I am having my period. I ask her how she knows that I am having my period; and she looks to VD for support. For it was VD who told her; he said that he hadn't been getting any for four days now. Von says, ugh, she doesn't want to know.

After a few minutes' silence, VD says, 'Well, come on ladies. This isn't getting us any closer to the Sun.'

A dead leaf blows into my face, which I take personally. I have had such bad luck lately. Last week's induction course was a disaster: I lost my closest friend. I slunk home, as if in disgrace.

Now, it is Monday. Worse, it is Monday morning in Camden, and I am pushing Maxie's heavy buggy uphill, to her new nursery, past blocks of brightly coloured flats

308

that resemble cereal packets, and old people, their hair matted with grey grease.

I have taken the day off work. I pretended that I caught a heavy cold during the induction course. But, really, I need to spend the day with Maxie. It is her first day at Camden's Bunny Hops nursery.

At the bus stop, a handsome man turns to stare as I walk by. But I have reached a stage in life where I know that, if a good-looking man is gazing in my direction, it is probably down to my child.

I ask Maxie to point out the scenery to me, and she announces the 'canal, dirty, Mummy', the 'silly shops', and the big houses along Haverstock Hill. 'Fire engine,' she says, when we hear its bright-red sound in the distance. As we turn off into a cul-de-sac, she points out the 'funny bushes', cut into wedge-like hairstyles. To me, these bushes appear not so much funny as embarrassed. It is as if they have been forced by their parents to have that cut.

'Mummy, when does scenery end?' asks my daughter, who is bored easily. She has the attention span of a Charlie.

'Soon, Max,' I say, crossing the road to avoid saying hello to someone I know. Her name is Susan and she was in my antenatal class. She opted for an elective Caesarean, and was always talking about the benefits of being cut open.

'Where's Judd, Mummy?'

I breathe in, and tell Maxie, for what feels like the thousandth time, that Judd loves her. It is only that he is living in his own flat now. She will soon see him. In the meantime, she is a very lucky girl to be able to go to Bunny Hops.

She is lucky because, as their brochure said:

- We are the only nursery in the whole of the UK to offer your hopping bunny a choice of organic, vegetarian food at lunchtime.
- We teach using the Schtengler-Kennet method. Your hopping bunny's brain is like a sponge – so let it soak up foreign languages and literature.
- We offer a wide variety of extra-curricular subjects including art and music appreciation. We also arrange trips to the opera, and to museums.
- At Bunny Hops we appreciate the fact that Mummy and Daddy Rabbit have to work hard. That is why we provide excellent care for your hopping bunny from eight in the morning until seven at night.

Maxie looks thoughtful. Not for the first time, I feel as if I have finally made it clear: Judd will no longer be taking care of her.

But: 'Mummy,' she says. 'Where's Solomon?'

'Solomon lives with Judd. I told you. You live with Mummy.'

'I want to live with Judd.'

'Well, sorry. You live with Mummy.'

'Is VD my Daddy now, Mummy?' she asks, twisting round to look up at me.

I stop the pushchair.

I try to decide what to say.

But I feel too much like the sort of woman who my mother would shake her head at in the street, when I was a child. 'Poor kids,' she said, passing the woman without a word. 'She has a different man every week. How can they know who their father is?'

'I doubt *she* knows,' my mother's friend said.

Oh, and how I sneered at these 'latchkey children' as Mum would call them. I imagined their loveless lives. I imagined their bedrooms, empty of dolls. One was called Mel Amphrey. She had lifeless hair, and was always losing her marbles.

'You know who your *Daddy* is, Maxie,' I say, pushing again. 'He's the one who gave you that doll. *Charlotte*. I know. I'll arrange for him to see you soon.'

'No want to see Daddy, Mummy. I want to see Judd soon.'

'Hm. Yes. OK.'

'No want VD living us, Mummy?'

'He's not living with us. Mummy and VD are only friends.' Friends who shared Mummy's bed. Friends who were caught kissing, by Maxie.

After that survival day, I thought VD and I were finished. Especially when he came into my hotel bedroom, to watch me pack, and sat on the hard double bed, saying his fantasy had come true. Women fighting over him. Even the mud was there. If only, if only, we had wrestled.

I threw clothes into my case. My make-up bag. I told him that I didn't want to see him. Ever again. Actually.

He asked me what he had done.

I said that that was obvious, and snorted. But VD sat there, seeming pathetic, and said that it was not obvious to him.

I grunted, and said that he had not stopped Heather telling Von that we were together. VD looked as serious as I have ever seen him. He said that he had not stopped Heather speaking for a reason. Unlike me, he wanted everyone to know about us. He wanted to shout it from the rooftops.

I said that he should not use clichés, even in casual conversation.

But he saw me smile, and took my hand. He played with my wedding ring. 'I really like you. You know that, don't you, Luce?'

'Well, you have an odd way of showing it. What was all that flirting about – with Heather? And please don't deny it, or . . .'

'Well, if you really want to know, I was pissed off with you. You haven't let me near you all week.'

'Because I didn't want Von to find out. Not in the way she did, anyway.'

'But she knows now. *So . . .*' He sat beside me, and rested his head on my shoulder. 'What's the problem?'

Maxie and I reach the broken-brick Victorian school building, and I wheel her into the Lilliputian nursery division, pushing the buggy down the cracked pathway and into smells of muddy shoes and slippery mince.

It is Maxie's first day at nursery, so I am to stay with her. That is the school rule, but I would have been loath to go anyway. She seems so very tiny, pushing open those heavy doors, and taking her coat off, all cuteness. I wonder how I can be planning to leave her tomorrow.

I kneel down to see the room through her eyes, filled with giant, colourful toys and assorted children. She keeps her hand in mine and her eyes on the toys. Eventually, the toys have the better of her. She lets go of me, hesitating towards a lonely, rolling toy pram. A naked black doll lies inside it, exposed.

'They could at least dress the poor thing,' laughs a redheaded woman, bringing me back to my surroundings.

'She must be cold,' I agree, smiling.

We sit down on the bright, doll-sized chairs, set out

for visiting adults. Redhead says that her son is starting nursery that day. She does not want to leave him tomorrow. I smile again, relieved to see someone as anxious as I am.

On my other side sits a thin, dark, bored Hungarian woman, whom I recognize from various playgroups. It is her child's first day here too, she says.

'You're her mother?' I ask, surprised. I stare at the child, who has the sort of blonde beauty that even other mothers could love.

'No, not her mother,' says the Hungarian. She laughs, unhappily. 'But she thinks of me as her Mummy. Calls me Mummy, you know?'

She explains that the little girl's 'so-called parents' are on a business holiday, 'to Los Angeles'.

'Isn't that an oxymoron?' says Redhead, smiling sideways at me. She introduces herself, but I forget her name instantly. (Lavinia, Laetitia?) 'A *business* holiday?'

'I do not know this word, moron,' Hungarian says, chippily, and I am relieved to hear it. There is something about her that terrifies me. Her fingernails are as long and blood-red as an animal's.

'You see that child there?' says the Hungarian, pointing to a pretty, black boy, who might have been a girl.

'Mmm,' I say, watching Maxie, who is showing her belly-button to the other children. Like Charlie, or any two-ish-year-old, she is an exhibitionist.

'He's a throwback,' says Hungarian.

'*No?*'

'Oh yes. His parents are white.'

The principal teacher comes over, kneeling down to reach our level, to ask if we mothers are OK.

'Yes, fine,' says Hungarian, speaking for the three of us.

313

'I'm sorry that you have to sit at the side like this,' says the teacher, addressing the Hungarian as if she had appointed herself as our representative. 'Only we feel that – this way – the children are better integrated.'

'We are happy,' says Hungarian, miserably.

As the teacher walks away, she says, 'It is not right, leaving us at the side like this. Ahh, Bethany, you not like it at nursery? I didn't think so.' That small blank beauty of a child, with Benetton blue eyes, has drifted back in her direction.

'See, they hate leaving, for the first time. See how she clings, because she loves me too much? How the mother can do this?' says Hungarian, throwing guilt-inducing looks at me. 'The mother should be the one leaving her child at nursery for the first day, not me. I am just an au pair.'

'I agree with that,' says Redhead, firmly, and her mini redhead comes over, almost on cue.

Redhead explains how she gave up her high-flying job in law as soon as Arthur was born, because he needed his mother then, and, yes, she missed the mental stimulation of work, but to Sinclair Lovett she was quickly replaceable, whereas to Arthur, she was *irreplaceable*. And, yes, she had given up her life, but as a result the bond between Redhead and Arthur was much stronger.

She does not appear convinced by her own argument, however, so I doubt her success as a solicitor.

'So, why is Arthur to start nursery now?' asks Hungarian, accusingly.

I look around for my Maxie, hoping that she will support the cause of the working mother. But she is too busy enjoying herself to worry about my needs.

'I'm pregnant again,' says Redhead, making me feel envious. How full she must feel. Full. Filled. 'Oooh,

314

Bethany's got such beautiful hair,' she says, looking at Hungarian's charge. 'I wish mine was blond.'

At first, I think that she is talking about her hair, but then I realize that she is, in fact, referring to her son.

'He's got great hair. I *love* red hair,' I say, more to the boy than to his mother, if only to lessen his need for counselling at a later stage.

'It is a shame, the colour,' says Hungarian, her consonants firing like black bullets. She stares at the boy sympathetically. I turn to look at Redhead, empathetically. But she is glaring at the Hungarian.

Suddenly everything about her seems orange. Even her ears.

'Well, I don't think, *actually* . . .' she starts.

'No, it's *lovely*,' I urge, truthfully, as Maxie comes over to ask me for some cranberry juice.

'You give her cranberry juice?' asks Hungarian, as I fumble inside my bag. My fingers squash into melted chocolate. '*Cran*-berry juice,' insists Maxie.

'What's wrong with cranberry juice?' asks Redhead, and I smile gratefully up at her, before sticking my fingers back into the chocolate.

'It is so full of sugar,' says Hungarian, disapprovingly.

'*Natural* sugars,' insists Redhead.

'She's allowed ten units a week, tops,' I joke, handing Maxie the chocolate-soaked cup of cranberry juice.

'Tell her rotting teeth that this sugar is natural,' laughs Hungarian, bitterly; and I turn to her, to respond suitably, but am interrupted by the teacher.

'Come on Maxie, Bethany, Arthur. How about drawing me a picture?' says the teacher, who is all cardigan. She leads the three children towards a table splattered with paper and jars of Crayola.

I feel reprimanded, and say so.

'Yes,' says Redhead. 'They're so understanding about the children's feelings, but what about ours, eh? Today's bound to be hard for us. I was almost crying this morning.'

'Yeah,' I agree – although, these days, I am so depressed that I cry most mornings.

'Oh, I don't know why you fussing. You should try to live in Hungary.'

'Hmm.'

That was either me or Redhead. Perhaps both of us, together.

'Here, I don't know why women have children,' says the Hungarian, her lipstick crossing the line of her lips. 'The mother leaves Bethany with me straight away, soon as she was born, with me.'

'Well, maybe she was postnatally depressed,' I interrupt.

'Pwuch, postnatal depression. We don't have postnatal depression in our country. We just get on with it. Anyway, she was out having fun, straight away, the mother.'

'Having fun, or working?' I ask, drily.

'Work, huh, if you call it that,' said Hungarian, even more drily. 'She is a manager of some company. But she should try looking after a toddler for a day. *Then* she would see work.'

'*That* I agree with,' says Redhead, glad of the opportunity to tell us, once more, that she was once a hotshot commercial lawyer. But that caring for Arthur is far more taxing.

Suddenly, the Hungarian changes her tone. She leans towards me, covering her mouth with her hand, and says, her voice muffled: 'You see that child there?

'Yes.'

'Siamese twin.'

316

'*No?*' I say.

'Yes,' says Hungarian. 'Separated at birth, by an operation. The other one died.'

'Really?'

'It is very sad,' she says, but happily.

Arthur runs straight towards us then, like a car coming out of a bottleneck. He holds up his drawing, wanting praise. No, *needing* it.

'God, that is good,' I say, and Hungarian asks if she can see it.

'Well done, Arthur,' says his proud mother.

'What is it of, this picture?' asks Hungarian.

'A spaceship,' says Arthur.

'He's obsessed,' says Redhead, with mock embarrassment.

'You are very clever boy, no?' says Hungarian, ruffling the boy's offending red hair.

'He *is* clever,' admits Redhead, coyly. 'But I think a lot of it's to do with the fact that I've been at home with him, giving him constant mental stimulation.'

Satisfied, Arthur runs off towards a giant plastic seahorse. Hungarian looks the other way, and sneers. 'You don't want that. In my country, the genius – he might as well have a disability. It is not a good thing to encourage.'

'Well, that's ridiculous,' I start, until my child runs up to me with her picture of a black wiggly line. 'Er, yeah, that's great, Max . . . Mind you, I don't think you can see how clever a child will be at this age. Mine's big on, erm, social interaction.'

Mine scowls and sidles away, still clutching her cup of cranberry juice.

'I see your Maxie, before, with that man who look after her,' sneers Hungarian.

'Yes, her nanny was a man,' I say firmly.

'You did not mind him being a man?' she asks. It is as if she is asking: *Did you know that he was a man?*

'No, why should I?'

'Do you think the men, they feel as much as we do?' asks Hungarian.

'Yes.'

'He is Jewish, you know?' she says, and then leans close enough for me to smell her sugary breath. 'You know, I used to work for Jews.'

'*I'm* Jewish,' I say firmly, reasserting the half of me that left with Judd.

'Oh, you do not look . . . Yes, but you are so fair,' she says, as if that makes it not so bad. 'Anyway, it was not the Jewishness that I think,' decides Hungarian, quickly. 'It was the way they . . . Oh, hello again.'

Maxie is by my side, saying: 'No like nursery.' So I explain to her that she does, in fact, like nursery. She likes the toys, and the other children. She likes the tiny tables, spread with white paper and buttery paint. She likes the fact that there will soon be juice and biscuits.

'Like biscuits,' she concedes.

'She has a big – how you say it – appetite, your Maxie. I look after a fatter child before this,' says Hungarian, as Maxie wraps her arms around my legs. Since coming back from her three-week stint at my mother's house, Maxie has taken to clinging on to my legs, like a child on a merry-go-round.

'Well, I've put her on the hip-and-thigh diet,' I joke.

'Why don't you come and get a biscuit?' asks the woolly teacher, taking my daughter's hand.

'But that's blown it,' I say, although I am the only one laughing.

'Fat around the waist, you know,' says Hungarian, thoughtfully. 'The mother had to buy trousers for him in a special shop.'

'What, baby outfits for the fuller-figured?'

'Yes.'

'Maxie's probably got a healthy appetite,' said Redhead, soothingly.

'If anything, too healthy.'

I know that I should not insult my daughter like this – even in jest. She is too young to know that I am being self-deprecating.

'So what do you do?' asks Redhead, patting my knee. 'As a job, I mean?'

I talk about myself then. At length. Hungarian quizzes me as if she is presenting *FastNews*. We discuss methods of childcare, and Hungarian *pwuchs* ours, as her Bethany sits sedated in another corner.

'So you don't feel that you're missing out. I mean, on seeing Maxie grow up?'

'*No.* I see her enough,' I say, remembering how envious I felt when Judd reported her first word.

Ud.

'Well, that's fine then,' says Redhead, touching her pregnant stomach. 'You have just Maxie then, do you?'

'Yes,' I say, thinking: *I have two children, but one died.*

There is then a lunch of lamb and rice – the flavour of each dulled with spice. We parents and carers eat the leftovers.

Hungarian's Bethany comes alive only when the other children nap. After twenty minutes of her au pair cajoling, singing and shouting ('I believe strongly in discipline,' says Hungarian), Bethany finally falls asleep.

'Out like a light,' says Hungarian, without irony.

The children go outside to play. We adults watch them climbing on to the swings and the slides, sitting on the grass, underneath a tree. Maxie builds castles in a sand-pit which resembles a large bowl of granulated brown sugar. Redhead and I are surprised by how much fun we are having. So much so that we are sorry when it is time to go.

'You see that child there?' says Hungarian, as we squeeze our children's limbs into coats. (Redhead has run Arthur to the toilets.) I nod, looking at Hungarian's eyeline.

'Child of an egg donor.'

'*No?* Do you know everything about everyone?' I ask.

'Oh yes.'

She says this with a firmness that is unnerving.

'They *could* clean the seats,' says Redhead, emerging from the toilets.

'Oh, you know nothing. In my country, my friends and my family, we do not complain, but we have nothing,' says Hungarian. 'Dirt is everywhere. We earn in a week what you people earn in a minute. Our shops have nothing in them . . .'

I tell Redhead that we are sure to meet again at the school gates. She says, but, what hours is Maxie doing? I say that – *of course* – Maxie – *because I work* – will be at nursery full-time. Won't Arthur?

Redhead is open-mouthed at the thought. 'No. Just three hours a day. I couldn't leave him any longer. I mean, as a *mother*,' she says.

As if I am not.

Chapter Twelve

I am having Christmas Day lunch with my family. My mother is a Jew, and my father is an atheist. But why should the Fletchers be denied a traditional turkey dinner simply on account of their beliefs? So, we are eating turkey and Brussels sprouts. Roast potatoes and peas. Stuffing. *We* are Mum and Dad. My older brother, Marcus. My old schoolfriend, Tracy. Her daughter, Cordy.

Tracy has dressed up. She is wearing a thick, gold necklace and glittering lipstick. But, still, she looks dirty. Her skin is like damp pastry. Her blonde hair is dyed to the point of death.

'Are there any good films on this year?' she asks.

'The same old rubbish,' says Mum.

'Nah – *Lethal Weapon Two*,' says Marcus, unscrewing the piccalilli.

Tracy has been having her Christmas lunch at the Fletcher house for years. My mother semi-adopted her after she was thrown out of her house when she fell pregnant at fifteen. *Baby Jamie* is now seventeen, and spending Christmas with his girlfriend.

'What about the Lottery programme. Will that be on, d'you think?'

'*Lottery* programme?' echoes two-year-old Cordy.

'I bally hope so,' grunts my brother.

Now that he is thirty, Marcus needs to be a millionaire *more than ever*. That is why he has invested so much of his money in Lottery tickets.

'I'm not sure about this Lottery,' says Dad, readjusting his pink paper crown.

'Only 'cause you ain't ever won anything.'

'It's the poor, buying these Lottery tickets. And where does the money go? To *opera*-lovers.'

'Mummy, can I have more 'tatoes?' asks Cordy.

'*I'm* an opera-lover,' says Mum.

'*I* like Oprah too,' says Tracy.

'Can we – this one Christmas – not discuss politics?' my brother asks.

'Cordy, I'll get you the bloody potatoes. Just sit down,' says Tracy; and Cordy falls back into her seat.

'I just wish you'd feel as strongly as your father. But what do *you* believe in – other than money?'

'I believe in me.'

My brother is halfway through a course of counselling. Hence, the fervently expressed belief in himself. He has been depressed ever since his wife Sally left, to volunteer her services overseas. ('Me, me, me,' mutters Mum.) He will not eat any of his Christmas dinner. He says that he might as well smear the stuff around his waist. He has been on one of Mum's Slimco diets ever since Sally said he was fat, before leaving him for Sierra Leone.

'How *is* Sally?' I ask, because I liked Sally.

'She was a good girl, that one,' smiles my father. 'All she wanted was a baby.'

'Well, all I wanted was my life back,' says Marcus.

He had been through one course of IVF, and did not want

to go through that again. The humiliation of masturbating in a cold blue room in that hospital. The nurses looking at him, because they knew the truth about his painfully low sperm count. Sally, blaming everything on the size of him. It was well known, she said, that fat men had trouble producing sperm; and Sally wanted a baby above anything. Including him.

'Maybe you should do another course of IVF,' I tell Marcus.

'I'm not going another round.'

'If you agreed to do that, she'd come back.'

'I need to take care of me now,' says Marcus, He looks enviously at our plates of food. 'That's why I can't eat all this stodge.'

Mum says she does not know why Marcus is blaming her. She lights a cigarette, saying that she always taught him the difference between good and bad carbohydrates. Marcus put on weight after he started living with the slut. *Sally*. Yes – Mum breathes in the cigarette – she will say what she thinks now that Sally has gone. That girl gave him far too many puddings.

'Nothing wrong with a bit of pudding,' says Dad.

'I like your new curtains, Auntie Judy.'

'Thank you Tracy. At least they cover up the old wallpaper.'

I look at the wallpaper, thinking how there is nothing about my mother's house that reminds me of the terrace I grew up in. That was the old life; this is the new. Minutes after my parents moved here, it was as if Mum's pleated lampshades had always been smooth. Dad's thrillers, hidden. The naked *Radio Times* wrapped, for modesty's sake, in a leather cover.

Cover up. Cover up.

The Slimco house is always clean. Even after one of my visits; and I always set about making a mess. I open cupboards, and the bread bin. I ask Mum what she has in her fridge. These are my rights, as a child in her mother's house.

I am like Maxie when she comes home from nursery. I create havoc because I can. My parents' home is like a hotel. Almost everything is free to take home. It is only that my mother does not present me with a bill at the end of my stay – and I am able to take the bath towels.

When I visit the Slimco house, my mother always follows me, straightening items of furniture. She likes to keep her house clean. There are dustcovers on the furniture in the front room. But the furniture here does not collect dust. There is never any clutter.

Dad is not allowed to have his collections lying around this house. In my childhood home, there was always a tower of my father's old newspapers, dating back to 1902, curling up next to the coal fire. There was always one of Mum's cigarettes, burning away in an ashtray.

'What's wrong with the effing wallpaper?' asks Marcus, looking round.

'It's four years old,' says my mother, going again to empty her ashtray. 'No-one has patterns any more.'

'*I* should get new curtains,' says Tracy. 'Could you pass them potatoes, Marky? What about you, Luce? You still living in that flat near King's Cross?'

'Yeah – and you've just moved, haven't you?'

I am ignoring the fact that she said *King's Cross?* as if she was really saying *the depths of depravity*.

I remember where Tracy lived while I was in the sixth form. It was a flat in the notorious Macadam estate. She lived in the Oates block and, boy, was I terrified walking towards it. It felt so grim, that I was surprised to look up and see sky.

Women wheeled their buggies straight for me, their eyes full of hate.

I could never find the Oates block. It was hidden behind buildings crammed together like junkies in a hallway. And it was eerily quiet – the graffiti on the buildings so tidy that it looked as if it had been painted on by a professional.

Tracy tells us about 6 Hillfield Crescent. It is a former council house, she confesses. But it is now on a private estate. A *cul*-de-sac. It has a waste disposal unit. A bathroom cabinet with mirrored windows. There are mirrors everywhere, to make it look bigger. But it is already big. There are three bedrooms. A *utility* room. A pull-out broom cupboard. (She is going to have to buy a set of brooms from John Lewis.) A study.

'What do *you* bally need with a study?' says Marcus.

'Don' be so sodding cheeky,' she says.

For a moment I see the Tracy I knew at thirteen. The one who wore pink make up, and split pedal pushers which outlined her crotch. The Tracy who swore at me to fuckin' pass 'er the brown bag of cheap cider.

Tracy was, intermittently, my best friend. We leaned against street signs, drinking. Vodka and cider and punch. She snogged Wayne, and I snogged Billy. At parties, she was always the one, drunk, at the bottom of the garden, shouting and unclipping bras from scraggy lines of washing.

It was no surprise to anyone when Tracy fell pregnant at fifteen. Had Gants Road Comp been a typical American high school, Tracy Atherton would have had an entry in the yearbook as the person most likely to end up as a homeless, drunken prostitute. But now she looks at me with pure pity when I say that I cannot afford to buy a house in Primrose Hill.

I try to remember that it is only Tracy looking at me, sympathetically. I am prepared to be generous, because it is only Tracy.

'You know, you probably earn more than I do by temping,' I say, self-deprecating as ever, with Tracy. It is the only way we can be equals.

'Lucy – just how long have you known Tracy?' says Mum, lighting another cigarette.

'About as long as you have.' I smile down at Tracy. 'In other words, forever.'

'Well, why don't you know anything *about* the girl then?'

I know everything there is to know about Tracy the girl. She was often drunk, even in the classroom. She hated her father, and her father's girlfriends. She hated her mother. But she hated her boyfriends even more.

When her Mum was out we went to her house to sit on the kitchen counter, our legs swinging, eating whole packets of Breakaways. Bar after bar. We nibbled the chocolate first. Then we ate the biscuits inside. After that, we would be bored. We had to find things to do.

Tracy once searched through her mother's drawers, taking everything out. She wore the jewellery. I left her, sitting on her mother's bed, her face smeared with her mother's make-up, crying.

I found out later that Wayne was too scared to ask me out. So he asked Tracy out instead. They had sex in her mother's bedroom; I know that. The whole school did. There was a fight when Danielle Carruthers found out.

'*Fight, fight, fight.*'

Tracy was a Kaja. She fought me, for being a Duranie.

Later, she said, 'Sorry about that – I was a bit out of it, y'knowwhaImean?' So we shared a cigarette, smoking out of her Mum's bedroom window. She was crying. Saying that the difference between us, was that I only liked Simon Le Bon. She loved Limahl.

'Hush hush, I-do-I.'

She cut herself, I knew that. Tracy was not looking to slice a vein. She simply enjoyed her secret sessions in the bathroom with a razorblade. She said that I should try it. It felt fab, watching the blood ooze out. But I was not to tell anyone. I was to swear never to tell.

I was not to say anything about her bruises either.

I knew more than I wanted to, about Tracy the girl. But not much about Tracy the woman. Only that she still hates Mr Tartin, our French teacher. Only that she does not trust men. Only that she likes Chris Tarrant. And Bacardi Breezers.

'What d'you mean?' I say, licking my spoon clean of cranberry sauce.

'Don't you ever ask Tracy about her life? Or are you the only one that matters?'

I do not know much about Tracy. I rarely see her alone. We are always with the rest of the posse – none of whom talk about their lives.

When we were at school, I did not want to know the answers. I did not want to know more about the belt she showed me. Her Dad's black belt, hanging innocently in the wardrobe alongside his ties.

Later, I did not want to highlight our differences. I was the student. She was the single mother. I was the career woman. She was the cleaning woman. (I did everything by the book; her father did not believe in books.) She wanted a proper night's sleep; I wanted to go to university. She wanted to earn money enough to pay the rent; I wanted to work for the United Nations. I wanted multi-orgasms; she wanted a father for Jamie.

Besides, I knew all there was to know about Tracy Atherton. She had Jamie when I was in the sixth form. (I remember her rented rooms. Flags of nappies, hanging above the bed. A smell of baked bins.) When I was at Oxford, she worked part-time, as a cleaning woman.

With my mother's help, Tracy took an evening course in secretarial skills. She met Clive through the Lonely Hearts Ads of a London listings magazine. When I started at the *Chronicle*, she temped. When I had Maxie, she had Cordy. But Clive – is it Clive? – had already left to join the army. He is on duty in Northern Ireland.

What more do I need to know about Tracy?

Only, says my mother, that Tracy stopped temping years ago. Only that, she stopped temping to train as a legal secretary. Only that, she is now training to be a legal executive. She could, if she wanted, go on to be a solicitor.

I stare at Tracy in disbelief. I cannot help it.

I tell Tracy that I am amazed at how far she has come. She laughs, and says that she cannot herself believe it. But she likes the law. And Mr Thorp – a senior partner – said she had the brain for it. She did not know that she had the brain for anything. *Neither did I*, I think, remembering her drunkenness during French lessons. I remember Miss Roberts asking us what we wanted to be when we grew up. Tracy said, a dinner lady. I said, a judge.

'So, what about you then, Luce? Have you interviewed any stars yet? What about David Beckham?'

'I write a beauty column,' I say, embarrassedly.

'Oh.' She looks at my mother. 'I thought you was working in London now?'

'I've changed locations. Not jobs.'

'So you're still with local papers then?'

'Lucy doesn't work for ambition's sake,' says my father.

'Well, she should,' says my mother.

'She certainly doesn't work for the bally money,' laughs Marcus.

'Lucy's work friends are like family,' says my father, proudly.

'That's no reason to stay in a job,' says Mum.

'She's been working with the same people for years.'

My mother breathes in the nicotine.

'So it's time to get out,' she says.

'Lucy's office is a community, like a Soviet.'

'Not any more,' I say; and I tell Dad that only editorial staff have survived the sale of the *Chronicle*. Fred and Derky were the first to be forced to take voluntary redundancy. Hen, said that – in the end – he had no choice. He simply could not justify their existence on the payroll.

Derky blamed all of his woes on computers. He could not stop crying in public. Tiny, pathetic tears. Fred was stoical. As he said in his drunken leaving speech, if he wanted to chat, he had his helplines. He had the chat-rooms on the net. He had always paid for his own internet connection. That had helped the paper editorially.

'For example, Lucy was able to read about miscarriages,' he said.

I swallowed, as people stared at me, and it all came back to me, from conception to abortion: the unnatural 'natural' tiredness; the swilling taste of metal fillings; the inability to enjoy a party; the sudden loss of consciousness; the secret drinks; the smugness; the complacency; then, slip.

Emptiness.

Hen saw my face, and quickly interrupted Fred's speech,

to say that we were all now going to be on the net. But he wished Fred well in his redundancy.

Dad is upset when I tell him about the redundancies. He says we should 'mobilize the core workforce'. But I do not think he would have been so sympathetic if he had heard Derky tell his 'Bob' jokes against disabled people.

'Now that we've moved, everything's changed,' I say, sadly.

'Except you,' says my mother.

'The atmosphere's so different.'

In my new office, no-one smiles back. There is laughter, but only at e-mails received. *(LOL.)* Ting. *Ting.* That is my new office sound. No-one says Hello. I am always invisible, walking to a spare desk. The *Post* newsroom is as breezy as a bank.

It all smells of new blond wood.

The editors are the only ones over thirty. The *workforce* are all young, good-looking, and single, with disposable incomes. Their socioeconomic status would have direct-mail marketers screaming for a peek at their address books.

I miss VD and Rainie, both of whom are still based in the Archway office. I so miss Von who has not spoken to me since she stopped speaking to me on the induction course; and Clay, who has taken voluntary redundancy, so that she can focus her energy on her son's nursery-school career. Sometimes, I even miss Heather. She behaves as if we are no longer friends because of the distance between our desks – although we often wave at each other across a crowded room.

My new office is such a strange place. It is no surprise that Heather is popular: she has so much in common with

330

my new workmates – most of whom also wear designer labels on the outside of their clothes; and want to be models, actresses, or whatever. Mostly, whatever.

On our first day in the new office, Heather was caught vomiting by some women from the *North West-End Post* – formerly the *Brent Cross Observer*. She confessed that she had bulimia nervosa. I found it strange to discover that Heather is not naturally thin. It was like finding out that someone very pretty has had extensive plastic surgery.

Word spread about the office. At first, there were sniggers. But, then, there were nods of understanding. Sympathetic glances. Smiles. Perhaps if Heather had been Fergie-fat, her disordered eating would have been thought of as greed. But Heather is Diana-thin.

Her binge-vomiting appeared glamorous.

Now, Heather is Ms Popular. She spends most of her time smoking in the Ladies – talking about sex with other single women, and stripping the subject of any sensuality. They discuss locating the g-spot and the m-spot, as if giving directions in a shopping mall. Or they complain about their loud and ticking biological clocks. I am excluded, because mine is not loud, or ticking.

I sometimes wonder whether I still have one.

Even Susanna is more popular than I am. Her personality has changed since she visited a dermatologist. She has been taking hormone pills, and her skin is virtually clear. Susanna is surprisingly pretty under those boil-like spots. Not only that, but (thanks to the hormone pills – she has shed her bleached moustache.

'Wow. You look different, Susanna,' said VD, when he visited the London office. 'Have you had plastic surgery or something?'

'Only cosmetically.'

The new Susanna jokes. The new Susanna Lowry has more confidence – perhaps because she is seeing our boss, Bill Hempsall. No-one dares upset the boss's girlfriend.

'You didn't tell me,' says Dad, with the same startled expression he had when learning about Gorbachev's Perestroika. 'When did all this happen?'

'I've finished, Mum,' says Cordy.

'You should see this as an opportunity,' says Mum.

I say, 'I hate opportunities. They make me feel tired.'

I sometimes wonder why I bother to go into work. I only have my column to write, and that takes minutes. For the rest of the time, I am on the internet, bitching about people I have never met, like Bill Clinton. I would simply go home, but there is a culture of presenteeism. If I leave the office on time at six, I am made to feel dispensable.

I don't understand this world of New Media. I knew how to behave in the old world.

'For years, I've been telling Lucy she should leave that place. But, I'm only her mother. Why should she listen to me? But, you'll come crying . . .'

As if on cue, Maxie wakes up from a sleep that she fell into screaming, and I am filled with dread, hearing that sound. I will bring her in, and she will throw food on to the floor and hit or kick whoever says No.

'I'll just be a minute,' I say, standing up.

'OK, love,' says Dad, looking worried.

'D'you hear that, Cordy? Maxie's woken up. You're lucky getting her to nap in the daytime, Luce. Cordy can't sleep during the day, can you Cord?'

'Max was up all night, that's why,' says my mother.

'She screamed for bally ages before she dropped off,' says Marcus.

'Mum, can I have more Brussels sprouts?' asks Cordy.

When I go in, Maxie is standing up in the travel cot, screaming in what feels like one long pitch. (She is back in a cot.) Her face is Barbie-pink, and a mess of tears. She has taken off her wet nappy. (She is back in nappies.) The nappy is wrapped around Flumpy's head, like a fat bandage. 'Maxie naughty,' she says. (She is back to baby-talking.)

'Yes, very naughty. Not very nice, is it?' I say, unsticking the nappy, and thanking God that she hadn't pooed, as she had last week, when I came into her bedroom to find a nappy leaking diarrhoea all over the cream carpet.

'Want to get out.'

'OK – out you come. Are you going to be a good girl now?'

'No be good girl. Not.'

Tracy stands up when I come back into the room with Maxie. Mum stuffs out her cigarette in the crystal tray, and takes her from me. She asks Maxie whether she wants some food. And, *and,* she has a surprise for the children. Two foil wrapped chocolate Santa Clauses – both of which my daughter grabs.

'Just one, Maxie. And say thank you Maxie.'

'No say thank you.'

'And one for Cordy.'

Cordy says, 'Fank you Auntie Oody.'

Since Judd left, three months ago, Maxie has been difficult. In my parenting manual, she now fits into all of the categories for the demanding toddler: the super-high-activity toddler; the distractible toddler; the slow-to-adapt toddler; and the initial-withdrawal toddler.

'*My* one,' screams Maxie, grabbing Cordy's Santa Claus.

Maxie is the high-intensity toddler; the unscheduled toddler; the low-sensory-threshold, highly-sensitive-child

333

toddler; and the unhappy toddler. I am having to comfort myself with the childcare manual's assurance that my 'challenging' child will not stay that way. She might even grow up to be a director of industry or a junior cabinet minister.

But secretly I worry that people will think she has a personality disorder, and take her away from me. Because she smears food on the wall. She bites my hand when I try to take the food away. She takes the phone off the hook, and tells VD to go away. She hides when Charlie comes to take her out. She tells me that I am not her Mummy.

Flumpy is her Mummy. Judd is her Mummy.

Maxie is badly behaved; and I cannot take all the blame for that. Although, against the advice of every parenting manual, I bribe Maxie to keep quiet in supermarkets – with food which is filled with additives. I was the same with the dog I had as a child. Whenever High Five performed a trick, I gave him a biscuit. So he began to expect a chocolate sandwich biscuit every time he stood up on two legs. When I ran out of Penguins, High Five began to bite, and had to be put down.

'Issmychoclit.'

Maxie is generally miserable; and I cannot put all the blame for that on her nursery. Her cardiganed teacher says that some children are simply like that – no matter the stimulation. She then listed all the activities provided by Bunny Hops to stimulate our offspring. Look and Listen. Communicate. Hear and Feel. Sing and Talk.

I am tempted sometimes to take Maxie away from nursery. But, like any other highly educated woman, I need a career. Not only that, but I need to earn money for luxuries like BSE-free meat.

'Do you still have that Jewish bloke looking after her?' asks Tracy.

'No,' I say, staring at Maxie, helplessly. 'I wish I did.'

'She should ask him to come back,' says my mother.

'Why should I? *He* left. He's the one who took Solomon away; although I was the only one who could calm him down after a nightmare.'

'Solomon wasn't your child, Lucy.'

'All I'm saying is, I don't want him back. He'd have to crawl back.'

'But it's hard to find good childminders,' says Tracy.

I say, 'On his hands and knees.'

Even now, when my daughter hurts herself, she calls for him. 'Want Judd, Mummy. Want Judd.' She keeps thinking that she sees him in Golders Hill Park – but it is some other man, wearing a similar skullcap.

She pushes other children. She slaps me. So much so that I took her to see the GP. Angela booked me an appointment with her Dr Strom. She sent me in ahead of someone with suspected meningitis. Well, she is the receptionist. It is her right to choose which of the patients need seeing urgently.

When I came out, I stopped to chat to Angela. She was not her usual, happy, self. 'What's bugging you?'

'Oh, nothing much,' she said. Only that illnesses do not interest her as much as they did. Only that she would prefer to be an actress – although there are very few roles for mixed-race fat women. Only that she had found these lumps in her breasts and . . . And that was when I heard the screams.

Maxie's and my own.

'*Maxie*,' I yelled, pulling her away from the shocked child she had pinned to the floor.

'I'm sure it was Poppy's fault too,' said the child's anxious mother. 'Did you take something Poppy?'

'No, no. Oh, I'm so sorry. She's very tired,' I say, wondering whether I should simply wear a T-shirt which reads: 'My child is a terror because she is tired.'

'I'm sorry. Say you're sorry, Poppy.'

'Maxie, that was very, very bad. Stop crying like that. Say you're sorry.'

'It doesn't matter. I'm sure Poppy goaded her.' We both looked at her child, who was clearly traumatized.

'Say you're sorry.'

'Maxie not sorry,' said the ragbag of screaming limbs I carried to Angela's desk.

Angela smiled and said, 'I wouldn't worry, Luce. It's only because she's a Virgo.' And I told her that the doctor said the same, only less optimistically.

I then had to leave, before I had a chance to discuss the lumps in Angela's breasts. How could I be a good friend, when Maxie was having one of her worst tantrums ever?

Or is this one Maxie's worst tantrum ever? Because she will not now let go of Cordy's Santa Claus.

'No want to share,' she says, and her bottom lip goes.

'It's not yours to share. It's Cordy's.'

'No Cordy's. *Maxie's.*'

'You have to share. Everyone shares,' I say.

'I don't *want* to.'

My mother says that I need to give her a reason why everyone shares.

My father says that people share because they want to live in harmony with their neighbours. Giving is a way of receiving. My brother says that people *share* because they want something in return. You lend me your spade, and

336

I'll lend you my wheelbarrow. Giving is a way of receiving something later. My mother says that people share because they are told to. And that is it. I am too soft with Maxie, she says. She needs to know the boundaries.

'What d'you want me to do? Hit her?'

'*Tell* her.'

'Maxie, give Cordy the chocolate,' I say, through gritted teeth.

'I want my chocolate,' says Cordy, her eyelids drooping even lower.

'Don't give me cheek. You'll bloody wait,' says Tracy; and Cordy's face softens into one greyish lump.

'Sorry,' she mumbles, as Maxie stares.

'Louder,' says her mother, as we all stare.

'Sorry.'

In the pause which follows, I half expect them all to break into loud applause.

Christmas Day is not the same without Charlie here. I am sure he would watch *Who Wants To Be A Millionaire?* with my father. Marcus says he does not want to watch other people winning cash. What pleasure is there in that? My father says the pleasure comes from playing the game. 'Yeah, right,' says Marcus, lying on the sofa. Seconds later, I see his eyes closing. As for me, I cannot relax in front of the television. I am too busy preventing Maxie going near my mother's books.

She wants to tear out their spines.

'Has Charlie been in touch?' asks my Dad, as if he is thinking the same. He looks from me to Cordy, who is dressing a rag doll.

'Oh yes. He takes Maxie out every other Sunday.'

'Why every *other* Sunday?' my Mum calls out from the

337

kitchen. Tracy is in there too, helping my mother to load the dishwasher. I keep overhearing them, discussing the importance of salt.

'It's working fine. If he wants to see her more, he can.'

'D'you think you'll ever get back together?' asks Tracy, coming in, to sit on the arm of the sofa.

'Of course not. No way.'

'That's a shame.'

'I'm with someone else anyway.'

'Oh, right. Who's that?'

'VD.'

'He's got what?'

'Vinnie.'

When, every Sunday, Charlie comes to pick up Maxie, he does not come inside. No, he stands at the door, looking handsome. He asks me whether I have packed all he needs for Maxie, and leaves. Conversation is not part of our deal. This is a deal we arranged, months ago, on the phone. Charlie would pick Maxie up at midday and have her back by six. He has not once complained, or been late to bring her back. It was only awkward on one occasion.

That was when VD was there, wandering around in his bathrobe.

'Charlie,' said VD, coming to the door. 'How are you old mate?'

'Very well. Very well,' said Charlie, shaking VD's hand.

VD bent down to face Maxie.

'You going out with your Daddy, are you?' he said.

'Don't want go.'

'I'm early,' said Charlie to me. 'So I'll be back late.'

'Yeah, fine. I'm pleased you like being with her.'

'Well, she's not a baby any more, are you, Max? We can talk to each other now, like human beings.'

338

'Yes.'

'So, I'll be back around eight. Because I'm early.'

'Yes, fine,' I smiled. 'I don't see why you should be penalized for being early.'

Charlie stiffened.

'I don't think you should use words like that in front of Maxie,' he said.

'To be penalized means to be punished,' laughed VD, putting his arm around me.

Charlie turned as pink as Maxie's top.

'I know that. Come on Max. I'll see you at eight then.' He bent down to button up Maxie's coat. 'We're taking you somewhere nice today.'

I have wondered, since then, about the *We're*. Nevertheless, I do not ask Charlie what he does with Maxie on their Sundays. All I know is that Maxie comes back caked in mud and chocolate ice-cream. So she cannot be having that bad a time. Maxie is depressed; and I am pleased that she can still be happy – even though she did once mention being happy with a lady called *Caitlin*.

'I thought you and Charlie were great together,' says Tracy.

'We're even better apart.'

'Well, you never know what'll happen in the future. Him being Maxie's Dad and that.'

'I do know what's going to happen. We'll get a divorce, that's what.' I look at Tracy, who has two, ostensibly fatherless children. I always felt superior to her. But now I wonder whether we still have our differences. Because I too am a single mother. I have lost almost all of my advantages.

'A divorce?' repeats my father.

'So it's good that I know a lawyer.'

'I couldn't do your divorce for you.'

'Has Charlie asked you for a divorce?' asks Mum, sharply; she has Maxie on her lap. She managed to coax her there with a sugar-coated biscuit.

'Can I have one, Auntie Judy?' asks Cordy.

'He hasn't mentioned anything. Not since he left. But VD wants me to ask *him* for one.'

'On what grounds?' asks my father, as if there needs to be one.

'Not between meals,' says Tracy; and Cordy stares at the biscuit, then goes back to her doll. I too stare at the biscuit, thinking how – unlike Tracy – I am the stereotypical single mother. I feed my child sugary foods, and bring men into my bedroom.

'Want another one,' says my stereotypical child-of-a-single-mother.

'*No.*' But I see her face, about to break into a wail. 'Well, just one.'

'It's the age,' says Dad, as I go to get the biscuit tin. 'Did you see that? He needed to ask the *audience.*'

'Cordy's the same age,' I mutter, sitting down. Maxie comes to sit on my lap, so that she can be nearer to the biscuits.

'Yes, but she's got her father at home.'

I look up at Tracy's over-made-up face.

'Is – is it, Clive? Is Clive back?'

'It's Colin. And he never left me, or her. He was in Northern Ireland, that was all. Anyway, he's back now. Back in civvies.'

'Lucy, you so clearly know nothing about Tracy,' says my mother, lighting a cigarette. 'How can you be so self-centred?'

'I just assumed . . . So, where is he? Colin?'

'He likes to be with his mother for Christmas Day.'

I smile.

'How did you get out of going? I had to go to Charlie's family every other year.'

'It was nice having Charlie here,' says my father.

'Well, I'd better go and finish in the kitchen,' sighs my mother, putting the lid on her ashtray. She takes it into the kitchen with her.

'Col doesn't think it's a suitable place for kids. His mother's home, I mean.'

'Why not? No stair-gates?'

'Don't be flippant, Lucy,' calls Mum, from the kitchen.

'It's for mentally ill people,' says Tracy.

I stare at her, trying to find the words with which to apologize. But not knowing where to start.

'Look what I found,' says my mother, coming back in. 'Anyone want the turkey wishbone? Tracy?'

'Yeah, I'll pull it. Come on Lucy – get the other end. Mind you, I shouldn't go against you,' she laughs. 'You've *always* been the one who pulled.'

'I wasn't.'

'Course you were. There was Billy. *I* always liked Billy. And Charlie. He was gorgeous.'

'No? Really?'

Yet I remember how Tracy flirted with Charlie. On our way home from here, last Christmas, Charlie said that he could always go for a *little bit of rough* like Tracy.

'Oh yeah. Charlie looks like a film star, doesn't he? I couldn't believe it when you two got married. It looked like a fairy tale.'

'Lucy likes to surround herself with handsome men,' says my mother, disapprovingly. She looks at my father, and her face softens. 'She's like me in that.'

341

I laugh as we pull the wishbone. Tracy wins – but I expect she wished for less than I did. 'Well done,' I say, generously.

But, oh, how I wanted my wish.

I invited VD to spend Boxing Day with me. But he turned up at my flat with Heather. Now, I cannot understand why she is here, eating the middle of my bread.

'I can't stand the crusts,' she says.

'*Charlie* doesn't eat crusts,' says Caroline, who is here to collect Maxie, politely refusing all my offers of food. 'My son,' she adds, in case there is any misunderstanding.

'How *is* Charlie?' asks Heather.

'Very much as he was,' she says, quietly pinking. 'He's his father's son.'

I think of Donald, and how he must have thanked God that there was to be no Charlie-and-Lucy row this year at his Christmas dinner table.

He must have enjoyed the festive season, in fact. Roger, away in India, being a diplomat. (Years of being a good son to Donald and Caroline prepared Roger for that role.) Charlie, sitting there, spouseless, and sulking. Helen, as silent and beautiful as a Rossetti painting. Her long oil slick of a husband, agreeing *absolutely* with Donald about *everything*.

Poor Caroline. She usually takes comfort from Maxie and me. Her own daughter is a stick of wood, although the wife Donald would have wanted for himself. Sitting there, soundless, with pretty, pre-Raphaelite, red, curls. So lovely a mouth that it is always a surprise to see it open. Or to watch food being deposited inside.

I am not sure what Helen does. Judging from her

conversation, which is limited, I think she spends most of her time having her colon irrigated.

I am so glad that I did not have to make conversation with Helen this year, or that grease-pole of a husband of hers. (We went to my parents' house last year; so it was the Wallis turn.) Even the look of Helen's husband irritates me. I mean, he is so tall that at cinemas and theatres he must find himself in everybody's way.

You're in my way, I always thought. *Generally.*

By contrast, Helen is worryingly beautiful. She is like a freshly painted house in Primrose Hill – i.e. begging to be graffitied. She is everything that Donald would have wanted from a daughter. Or a daughter-in-law, I think.

'Talking of whom,' says Caroline, who is still pink. 'Donald said to say Hello.'

'Say Hello back,' I say; although I doubt that he did.

'He says to remind you about William.'

'William?' I say, taking Heather's plate, covered in challah crusts and crumbs, and put it on to the counter.

'The chap who owns those newspapers? You know Donald was always saying if you ever wanted to switch newspapers, he could ask William to find you something.'

'Oh, *that* William. But Donald hasn't mentioned him recently, has he?' I say, surprised.

'Yesterday. Yes. To be honest, I think he misses you. This idea he has, of you working in the Cotswolds, it's just an excuse. He thinks he needs an *excuse* to see you. He really is like Charlie in that.'

'In what?'

'Couldn't get me a job, could he, this William?' interrupts VD, stretching. He leans over to look at Heather's new computer.

Heather has come, I think, to show off her state-of-the-art laptop computer. But only Caroline was impressed by 'so many buttons'. Heather said earlier that she bought the computer because of its pulling power. I said, but, that she would not know if men were interested in her, or her iBook.

I said this, because VD was showing her laptop a great deal of interest.

I stare at Heather's hands, now, as they flick about the keyboard. Despite myself, I am impressed by her long, red-polished nails, just as I am impressed by the fact that Chinese people speak Chinese. Or that there is so much blood gushing around the body.

'Well, that's it,' she says, shutting the lid. Snap.

'It's got everything, hasn't it?' says Caroline, as Maxie wakes up, screaming.

'That'll be my daughter then,' I say, standing up.

'Right, well, I'll leave you young people to have fun,' says Caroline. 'I'll just take Maxie and go, shall I?'

'Let Max wake up first,' I say, after her.

'Any more of that Jewish bread?' asks VD.

'Oh,' coos Heather, as Caroline returns, holding Maxie. 'Hello little baby,' she says, taking my terrified daughter, and swinging her around in the air.

'Er, I'd better . . .'

I retrieve Maxie, because Heather is still holding her laptop. And I know that, if push comes to shove, Heather will save, not my baby, but her iBook. Maxie wriggles free from me. She reaches round for the pack of crayons, hidden behind the television.

'No,' I say.

'She just wants to draw, Luce,' says VD, coming to put his arms around me.

'Children need to express themselves,' says Heather, because she once read an article saying so.

I say that that would be fine – but Maxie likes to express herself all over the bathroom walls. VD laughs, and hands Maxie the crayons. He has a magazine she can draw on. Maxie stands there, waiting. He puts the car magazine on the occasional table. She actually sits on his lap to draw. Quietly.

'What's happened?' I say, amazed.

'I don't know,' says VD. He strokes Maxie's hair, and she leans back into his lap. 'But don't spoil the moment.'

We sit there for a moment, me beside VD; and I see Heather watching us, enviously.

'What are you doing on New Year's Eve?' she asks me, with malice aforethought.

'Nothing,' I say, because inevitably Von has not invited me to her party.

I feel sick, sometimes, thinking about Von. (She was so rigid about how a friend should behave.) So I try not to think about her too much. She has invited VD to her party; and I insisted he went. I said that I did not see why he should miss out, on my account. 'You've always been the party animal,' I said.

'You can't do *nothing*,' says Heather, because she is a member of the party police, and thinks it antisocial, if not weird, for people to sit in on the eve of a national public holiday.

'I want to do nothing,' I say.

I tell her that I want to watch the BBC's New Year's Eve extravaganza. I want to see celebrities kissing each

345

other at midnight. I want to relive the year's key events through television images. I want to be reminded of when I was twelve and eating family packets of cheese crisps in front of the TV. I crave that warm feeling. Besides, the New Year's Eve programme isn't one you can videotape. Even by the next day, it has lost its atmosphere.

'You are so weird,' says Heather. 'I don't think I've ever seen any of those New Year's Eve programmes.'

'Yeah; they're on at a really bad time,' smiles VD.

'Well, you don't know what you're missing.'

I remember, two years ago, watching the programme with Judd. He had offered to baby-sit, because he refused to celebrate a date on the Christian calendar. But I said that I was not going anywhere. It was during one of Charlie's absences, and I felt depressed. So, I invited Judd over to the flat. We spent the whole evening laughing at celebrities.

'It's a shame that Von didn't invite you to the party,' smiles Heather.

'It's a shame that you decided to tell Von about VD and me.'

'We've been through this, Lucy,' Heather says, patiently. 'I'm her friend too; and I felt that she should know.'

'We have discussed this, Luce,' says VD.

'Oh, I feel like a spare part in all this,' says Caroline, excitedly. 'What is this all about?'

'I was only saying that it was a shame about the party,' says Heather, looking at VD. 'Von's invited some celebrities that she's interviewed.'

Von writes the *Post*'s interview pages, which are syndicated. She is highly regarded by Tobu Frazer. He liked the look of her picture byline, and asked for the interview pages to be expanded. He asked, too, for her picture to be expanded.

So it is now full length.

'Von is doing well, isn't she? Oh Maxie, that is good.'

'Yeah, well, that's because she writes froth. It'd be nice if Frazer was as interested in news.'

'Is he not interested in news?' asks Caroline.

'Nope,' says VD, tearing out pages of the magazine for Maxie. She stares at his hands as he makes paper aeroplanes. 'No-one at the *Post*'s interested in news. Bill Hempsall said as much, didn't he?'

'Yeah, but what's wrong with writing advertorials?' asks Heather. 'They're easier, I think.'

VD grunts and, yet again, I hear about the estate-agency scam he uncovered. How Bill Hempsall refused to upset Turner and Gemple. Given how much they spent on advertising. 'Stop trying to be something you're not, Vincent Derwent,' said Bill Hempsall, laughing. 'Wait 'til you get a job on the *Guardian* for stories like that.'

Yet again, VD mimics Bill Hempsall's laugh. He begins to imagine Bill and Susanna in bed, but stops when he remembers that Caroline is here.

'You don't have to stop because I'm here. I'm not such an old prude, you know.'

'No, I know,' says VD, embarrassed. He shows Maxie how to roll the paper into small balls, so that he can make the four wheels for a paper car.

'Can I have it?' she asks, awed.

'Well, why don't you all just resign in protest?' asks Caroline of VD, because she does not realize that there are people needing to work for an income. She thinks I work only because I need, somehow, to fill my day.

'Because I'd need another job.' He laughs, and hugs Maxie closer to him. 'So, if this William chappie really does know of anything . . . ?'

347

'Of course. I'll ask Donald. I'm sure he'd be impressed by you, er, VD.' *And your public school accent.*

Heather asks a smiling Caroline whether her husband knows anybody in BBC light entertainment.

'No, seriously,' she adds, when Caroline laughs.

Chapter Thirteen

'Judd.'

Seeing him standing there, I feel the cold right through me. Such a moment should be a disappointment, because this is real life. Yet, I am enjoying his presence. It is a second's comfort, like hearing a word or two of Yiddish from a stranger in the street. Then I remember the truth of Judd's presence. That he is here to see Maxie.

'I wanted to return your key, and . . . Where's Max?'

'You've missed her by minutes. If you *care*. She's gone with Caroline. It's *Boxing* Day.'

He does not look the same. So thin, as if the Scheurs have been starving him.

He has stubble in the shape of a beard. I cannot look at him for long, remembering.

'Do sit down,' I say, opting for sarcasm, as he sits in the armchair.

'Thanks.' He leans forward, Judd-energetic, as if desperate to say something.

'Where's Solomon?' I say, interrupting him.

I think of the time when we were a make-believe family of four. We visited London Zoo, and the Aquarium. Strangers gazed at us. They commented on our happy unit.

349

'With . . .'

'Oh never mind,' I interrupt, not wanting to hear how well Chava takes care of Solomon, when I was the one to half-bake him biscuits.

'I wanted to see Maxie.'

'I know why you're here, but it's a bit bloody late.'

'I should have phoned.'

'I meant it's too late to jump back into Maxie's bloody life. I mean, Maxie's life, without the bloody. She needed you *then*. But, oh no, you'd vanished,' I say, remembering how angry I should feel – not only with Judd but with his Judaism. 'And just how would your rabbis have told me to explain that to a two-year-old?'

He is uncomfortable sitting in that easy chair. It is as if, at any moment, he might be asked to leave. Yet, there is fight in him, still.

'You know why I left, Lucy.'

'No, I don't,' I say, thinking how Solomon made me curious about subjects such as train signalling and dinosaurs. Does he think of Chava as his second mother? 'I really don't know *how* you could just leave a child like that, for weeks, with no explanation.'

'I had beliefs. When we . . . It went against . . .'

'Everything you believe in.'

'I left *you*, Lucy,' says Judd. 'Not Maxie.'

That was a slap. I should have readied myself for that. I was too easy in his company. I still feel the sting when I say, 'Yes, you *abandoned* Maxie. I don't give a damn that you left *me*. I'm with *VD*, remember. And the truth is, I'm still married to Charlie, who misses me, and I . . . So, don't flatter yourself that you, that it, meant anything to me.'

He pauses too long. During the pause I notice that he has

350

fragile lines around his eyes. It is as if they will disappear if I say something kind.

'Don't worry, I know what you think of me. I'm just the childminder, aren't I? But I *loved* Maxie, for God's sake . . . *Love*. Don't you think . . . ? It was awful, leaving her. I've looked after that kid since she was a baby. In nappies.'

'Well, she was back *in* nappies after you left. All I'm saying is, you can't just turn up after months and expect to see her. I won't *let* you see her. I mean it. She's only just forgotten who you are,' I lie.

His hair is dirtier than is usual. The colour has darkened during the months he has spent with Chava. He has suddenly aged, as I did when Sam died. Something has aged him, suddenly.

'I was too close to her. You made it bloody clear that Charlie was her father. Not me. *Charlie*. I was only Maxie's childminder. Her *nanny*. You could get rid of me at any moment. Oh, I was well aware of that. And it wasn't just a job for me, looking after Max. She was . . . She felt like my daughter, and I couldn't handle that. I . . .'

It is not like Judd to be lost for words. He is usually certain of his position. He is on one side of the argument, and on the other are those who commit crimes against humanity.

'I was hardly going to *sack* you. You were wonderful with Maxie.'

'No *job's* there a lifetime. I'm sure I was easily replaced.'

'Well, you weren't. She's in a nursery.'

'You put her in a *nursery*?'

'There's no need to sound so horrified. She's in a nursery, not a Romanian orphanage. And what am I supposed to do with her, while I work?'

'Find someone like me.'

'I couldn't *find* anyone like you,' I snap; and my words hang in the air.

They are still hanging there, seconds later.

'Well, I'm a bit otherwise engaged now,' says Judd, smiling. I stare at him, catching the one word – *engaged*.

'That's nice,' I say, hardening myself to hearing Chava's name. It is only a name. But I do not want to know anything about her, or their wedding.

'Don't you want to know *why*?'

I am too busy imagining the wedding canopy. The chuppah. I can hear that sound, of breaking glass; and my thoughts drift away to the bible story of Rachel and Leah – read by Judd to the children.

Jacob worked for Rachel's father for seven years, so that he could win the beautiful Rachel's hand in marriage. But the father tricked him; and he instead married Rachel's sister. The ugly Leah.

'Sexist rubbish,' I said. 'As if a woman's looks are everything.'

Judd said, 'The words *beautiful* and *ugly* refer to Rachel and Leah's souls.'

Now, I can see Judd's face as he lifts the heavy veil, hoping to see Chava, merely to find me. I wish he had warned me of his coming. I would have worn my Don't Fuck With Me leather skirt.

'How are you otherwise engaged?'

'I've sold my screenplay,' smiles Judd.

'You *haven't*?' I say, trying to keep the relief out of my voice. I wish I was wearing my kitten heels.

'You see. You didn't believe in me, did you? But, yeah. I've sold the options to Gaunt. A film production company. They're pretty keen to make it.'

'I know who *Gaunt* are. Bloody hell. They made *Curfew*.'

352

We sit there for a few seconds, enjoying the idea of Judd as a screenplay writer. The atmosphere changes. I am glad that, after all, there is enough success to go around.

I only wish I was wearing mascara.

'You can go to celebrity parties.'

'That really isn't a life I'm interested in.'

'I've missed Solomon.'

'He's missed you,' admits Judd. 'He's having those night-mares again. Still asks after "Mummy Lucy".'

'Did you tell him I wasn't his mother?' I ask, sadly, thinking how much he needed a Mummy figure.

'He doesn't trust me any more. He thinks something terrible's happened to you.'

'How could you do that to him? Why didn't you at least let me say goodbye?'

'Because I had beliefs. For God's sake, I know I went over the top and, yeah, that I rushed into it. But I thought they had all the answers.'

I think of the unkosher butter.

'And now you don't think so?'

'There's a lot of truth to Judaism, but . . .'

'But you don't sound so sure.'

'Erm. Yeah.' He touches his skullcap. 'I'm not as strict now.'

'You're *what*?'

I remember all the times I could have airily said: Oh, I'm not as strict now – rather than, say, throwing melting butter into my bedroom bin. It exhausted me, keeping up with him.

'I'm just not as rigid.'

'But, God, why? Why not?'

'I don't know. Lots of things.' He looks around my

room, as if hurting at the reminiscences. 'There's so much hypocrisy.'

'So you're back to being John Lester are you?'

I try to imagine him as a John, standing in the terraces at a football match. The image comes surprisingly easily, but that is because it is still Judd. He is simply wearing different colours. In my mind, Solomon is beside him, in the same strip as the winning team. The two of them are passionately screaming.

'No, I'm not back to being John,' he says angrily. 'I'll always be a Jew. As will you. One thing has nothing to do with the other.'

'So, was there a moment when you stopped believing? Did you have an epiphany?'

'*No*. Of course not. I still . . . Just that, when I left you, I went to live with the Scheurs.'

'Mmm, you said. In your letter. Bet you didn't tell them you'd just come from me.'

I try to laugh the hurt out of my voice.

'I had to say my landlord had thrown me out.'

'Some chance,' I say, remembering his flat in Mornington Crescent.

'It was fine for a while. I missed Maxie. I missed you,' he said, gently. 'But it felt safe, being with people who knew all the rules.'

'I was learning your rules,' I say, because I too could have a beautiful soul.

'I know.' He laughs and looks at me with undisguised affection. It is full on his face. 'You were better at following my rules than I was the Rabbi's.'

'Did he find butter in your bedroom?' I tease.

'He found me reading stories to Solomon, and changing the words. He told me I couldn't teach Solomon about dinosaurs. Chava has to marry a fat bloke with a beard just because he's from the "right family". You can't . . .'

'Chava has to do what . . .? Marry a fat bloke with a *beard*?'

'Huge beard,' he says, laughing.

'So is that why *you're* growing a beard?'

'I'm not growing a bloody beard.' He puts his hand to his chin. 'I just can't be bothered to shave these days.'

'Well, it must be love.'

'What?'

'Why don't you elope?' I say, thinking of the two of them together.

It hurts as I imagine Judd, helping Chava to pack a bag. Her clothes, going into the bag, still on their hangers. She will not stop to wipe away the tears. They are dripping too fast. There is just time to listen for one last time to her father's lecture tapes. Then, they must hurry.

Judd cannot wait any longer.

'God, just thinking of her kissing that Yaakov,' says Judd, not hearing me. 'It's sick. But the odd thing is, she's not unhappy about it. Well, he's such a learned man,' he says, sarcastically.

'And from such a *good family*,' I add, thinking cruel thoughts about Chava's side-parting. 'So, seriously. Why don't you rescue her from a life of beard rash?'

'She doesn't want to be rescued,' he says, smiling.

'Oh,' I say, pretending disappointment. 'I thought you were going to give me a happy ending.'

'What sort of ending did you want?' he asks, curiously.

'You escaping the Jewish ghetto with Chava.'

'No.' He laughs. 'I don't think so.'

'I did wonder why they'd let you – a single man – live

355

in the same house as a single woman. But, I suppose if she was *engaged.*'

'I wasn't allowed to be alone in the same room as her. I wasn't allowed to touch her.'

'That must have been frustrating for you,' I say, sarcastic again.

'Why?'

'Oh, well, her *delicate hands.*'

He sighs, and smiles. 'I take it you're referring to my *journals*. The ones that document my path to righteousness.

'Of course, if you'd read *on*, you'd know that I realized I didn't love Chava. I was in *love* with the idea of an orthodox Jewish girl. Not *Chava*,' he smiles, before turning serious. 'You'd have known that I've been questioning . . . I haven't been sure about anything for a long time now, probably since your miscarriage. Rabbi Scheur always put me back on track. But I knew I was losing my faith. When Solomon gave the game away to the Rabbi, and said we'd been living with you for months . . .' He half smiles and looks down. 'I don't think Sol was very happy at the Scheurs. He knew what he was saying.'

'Really?'

'He knew what he was doing.'

'And what did the Rabbi say?'

He is furious at the thought.

'He said that I had broken any number of laws, living with you. That you might as well be a shiksa – a non-Jewish woman.'

'I've had worse said about me,' I smile.

'Well, whatever. I had to get out.'

'So, you're not religious at all any more? Is that what you're saying.'

'Let's just say I'm *part*-religious,' he smiled. 'But still Jewish.'

'So where are you living now?'

'I'm back in my flat. They couldn't rent it out.'

'What a surprise,' I say, thinking about him in that basement flat, with its view of red bricks. Moss climbs that wall in a futile attempt at escape.

'And Solomon? Where's he now?'

'Oh, at a schoolfriend's house.'

The doorbell rings, and I press the buzzer, hearing VD's voice through the Intercom. ('Lucy; it's me. Listen; d'you think Caroline was serious about that job?') 'I'll go then, if that's *VD*,' sneers Judd; and it is as if he is talking about venereal disease.

The train rolls into the platform, and I wonder whether I will step out in front of it today. I often wonder this, in perhaps the same futile way that I contemplate calling out *Yes* when the vicar asks whether *anyone has any objections?* during a wedding service.

I sit on the tube, smelling that stir of odours. Where did I put my credit card? My mother said that I should look in all the places I have been to over the last few days. But I have searched under the sofa so many times I am sick of seeing that Christmas '98 *Radio Times*.

I watch the stations come and go, thinking that my credit card is missing, and only Katie could have taken it. Because it went missing last week. After Judd left, I upped her hours. She comes to my flat three times a week, and has had ample opportunity for theft.

I realize this, as I step out at Oxford Circus. Oh, Katie pretends to be so virtuous with all that anti-violence-to-animals (she wears crunchy cardigans and plastic shoes),

357

and anti-field-sports (she wears anti-field-sports T-shirts); yet, secretly, she is a thief.

I could have changed tube lines, coming out at Marble Arch, but I am in no hurry to reach work. So I take the more scenic route, in and out of major department stores, looking at clothes cut to fit the generic woman, rather than, say, me. I think how Katie cleans.

She swirls around a stinking, drenched cloth.

Since the *Chronicle* relocated, in October, I have felt sadder, somehow. Day by day, sadder. It is now January 3, and I am feeling depressed.

It is so windy with black rain spitting. I dare not look strangers in the eye. Too many people want to talk to me. They want to question me for market research. Too many people are foreigners, needing help with directions. Too many people want to give me things. They hand out damp leaflets, or sprays of tester perfume. By the time I reach work, I resemble a monthly magazine, a mess of scents, free samples and throwaway fliers.

I am one of almost a thousand people employed in this glassy building. The windows run down each side of the building, like water. I even believe that those mirrors make me appear important. And more importantly, thin.

I am the stereotype of a busy, rushing career woman, so I do not bother to smile at the stern doorman. *Is that black hair-growth on his ears, or is he wearing a Walkman?* I am one of twenty-two in this short, fat lift – although the lift has a capacity only for twenty. I am squeezed into this small space. The mirrored ceiling adds to my sense of being surrounded. *There is such a smell of wet umbrellas.*

Fortunately, I am on the first floor. All the *Post*'s editorial staff work on this level. We escape the lift like cars racing away from a bottleneck. Everyone collects a mobile phone from a tray. (Tobu Frazer is forward-thinking. He believes that, in a modern office, we should all be mobile.)

There is a huge digital clock on the wall of the office reading *Monday, January 3*, in case one day might merge with another.

As my first task for the day, I cancel my credit card. Then, I cancel Katie. I am too cowardly to tell her in person. Instead, I leave a message on her answering machine. I say that I am sorry but I have been thinking. I have come to the conclusion that I have no further need for a cleaning woman.

I have a typically dull morning. I spend much of it on the internet, discussing toddler-taming with a woman in Ontario. So I am pleased to receive an e-mail from Hen, who is still officially our editor.

To: LucyF@FrazerPost.com
From: Hen@FrazerPost.com
Subject: Meeting with Hen
Lucy, cn u come 2 my wkstation?

In our Archway office, Hen had his own room. It had a semi-opaque door. But he has been reduced to sitting in the newsroom. He no longer has a secretary, because Shirl took voluntary redundancy. I often think of Shirl, and the signs she put up everywhere.

TO WHOM IT MAY CONCERN, PLEASE DO NOT SMOKE IN THE TOILETS.

TO WHOM IT MAY CONCERN, PLEASE DO NOT FLUSH SANITARY WEAR IN THE LAVATORY.

PLEASE DO NOT BANG LID OF PHOTOCOPIER.

PLEASE DO NOT FEED THE FAX MACHINE.

I feel as if I am seeing Hen's legs for the first time. I sit beside his desk, refusing a ginger biscuit from the box he always keeps beside him.

Hen seems so vulnerable these days. He has to take orders from Bill Hempsall, who takes orders from Simon Whyte, who takes orders from John Clarkson, who takes orders from Harry Turner, who takes orders from Tobu Frazer. He has to sit at a desk the same size as Former Work Experience's. She is to his right, listening to every word of our conversation.

Hen *ahems,* uncomfortably, and asks me whether I read Simon's *ahem, memo* about becoming a teleworker. As *The Post Beautiful Life* can be written anywhere, would I, *yes,* consider working from home?

I feel as if Hen is saying, 'We are sending you home'.

Hen – who came to my wedding.

Hen – who found me at that wedding, miserable behind a pillar, because Charlie was dancing slow, with Heather. He said, 'You've got a real relationship, Lucy. Warts 'n' all. That's why it'll work. Besides, one thing I can't stand at weddings is ostentatious displays of affection.'

'Don't look so alarmed, Lucy,' he says now. 'It's only an option. Just one that I thought you'd be interested in.'

'Is it still not possible for me to work part-time?'

'Still not possible I'm afraid.' For a moment, he shows his fear, but recovers in time. '*Post* policy.'

I say that I will consider Hen's offer. But he does not appear to want to leave it at that. Instead, Hen laughs, and scrapes a ginger biscuit. He says that I should not think about it for too long. He heard Simon Whyte tell Bill Hempsall that Tobu Frazer might ditch the idea of teleworking altogether – although it was his idea.

Tobu Frazer's.

I ask how I will work from home, as I have no office equipment. Hen says that I will, of course, be connected to the internet. I ask whether my pay will remain the same;

and Hen says that I will *ahem* be on a much reduced *ahem*, *freelance* salary. I will be paid per word.

So not much, I think.

But I will save on travel expenses, and childcare costs. 'With the amount of free time you'll have, you can look after Maxie from home. Think about it, Lucy. You'll be able to count the advantages.'

1) I can be with Maxie full-time.

2) I can avoid Von, and that odd man from accounts who keeps asking me out.

3) I can be a real mother to Maxie.

'Well, OK. Yes,' I say.

I can take Maxie away from that nursery. I can teach her to talk properly. I can do potty re-training. (There was so much in her nappy this morning, that I was surprised not to find my credit card.) I can teach her the rudiments of French. This is what I think, all bright inside, when I switch off my computer at five. I can be every bit as good a mother as Judd was.

Judd, who has disappeared again.

I will forget about Judd, and teach my daughter about her Jewish roots, I think, as Heather approaches me. She says she has heard, on the grapevine, that I will be leaving.

'Who from?' I ask, knowing that the grapevine does not reach to me.

'Oh, everyone knows.'

'Yeah, well, I'll be writing my column from home. So that I can be with Maxie.'

'Oh.' She looks puzzled, as if trying to remember who I might be referring to. '*Oh*. For a moment, I thought you were talking about my cat.'

'Mmm, but I wasn't.'

Heather tries to look thoughtful, saying, 'No, I approve of that. If women are going to have children, they should *be* with them. I could never work out why you came back to work at all. I mean, you didn't need to.'

'Well, because I . . .'

'If *I* had a baby, I would *never* leave it.'

'Good for you,' I say, walking to the lift.

Heather walks with me. I feel heavy alongside her, as if I am all flesh, and she is all bone.

'It was a shame you missed Von's party.'

'Why? Was it so good?' I ask, pressing the lift button. It lights up, unnecessarily.

'Did VD not tell you?' she says, her eyes as round and silver as compact discs. 'We had *such* a good time.'

'Did you really?'

I stare at her, but she does not flinch. She merely rubs her wedding-ring finger.

'He should have told you.'

'I'm sure there was nothing to tell,' I say, wondering why she always looks so freshly ironed. Even after a bath, it is as if I am trying to cover up my true scent with bottled, potted, smells.

'It's good that you *trust* him so much.'

She always smells so clean. It is not a freshly bathed scent either. With Heather, I am all smells. At the *Chronicle*, that did not matter. Here, I filthy everything.

'For Christ's sake, Heather, VD's more than just the office playboy,' I say, trying to inject some honesty into the conversation.

'I never said he wasn't.'

'Fine. God, where is this lift?'

'You know, you'll have to have a leaving party,' says Heather, moving away.

362

'Mmm.'

'And I hope – despite everything – that I'll be invited,' she laughs.

'Oh, I'm sorry,' I call out with mock sincerity. 'But I'll probably be limited to inviting friends.'

In the lift, Former Work Experience asks me whether I am going down. I nod, as she presses the button, saying that she could not help but overhear my conversation with Hen.

I say Yes, talking brightly about my decision to work from home, to which there are so many obvious advantages. I feel warm towards Work Experience because she is also leaving the office on time.

I always feel as if I am sneaking away when I leave at six to collect my daughter from nursery, scared that someone might spot me. I have a feeling that children are frowned upon at the *Post*. That is why part-time working is not permitted. If I had been serious about making it as a Journalist, I would never have reproduced.

That is the attitude here.

Yet, I have to leave at six. If I am five minutes late to collect my child from nursery, Cardigan acts as if I have abandoned her late at night in a dark forest.

'Your daughter was heartbroken,' she says.

That is the attitude there.

Sometimes, I wish I could be freed from loving Maxie. But at nights, I still risk waking her up so that I can see her one last time before she dies from meningitis.

Work Experience and I are the only two in the lift, our stomachs lurching down.

I confide in her that I would have preferred to have worked part-time.

We walk the wood floor to the door. Work Experience

says that she does not – if she was *absolutely* honest – believe in part-time workers. She does not see why concessions should be made for women with children.

She too – *yes* – would like to work part-time, and take extended 'maternity' leaves, but she has her career to think of. We reach the electric doors, where Experience says that she made a choice not to have children, and she does not see why she should be penalized because of that. She is being sent on a fast-track editor's training course.

'Oh, well done,' I say, as the cold whips through me.

'Are you going to Marble Arch tube?' she asks.

'Oh – yes.'

She pulls her coat neatly closed, and tells me that she is on her way to a press conference. She had to fight for a place on the fast-track editor's scheme, she says. They did not want women. Yes, even in this day and age. They think all women want children.

Could I believe it?

I tell her that she might not want children now, but it will be different when she hits thirty. Then, the urge kicks in.

We reach Marble Arch and I wait for Experience as she buys a tube ticket. She says that she does not see the need for season tickets. 'They're a security I don't want,' she says. 'Who knows where I'll be working next month?'

On our way down the escalator, she says, 'The truth is, I'd love to have kids. In the abstract, yes. I do have that urge you're talking about. But I've made a conscious decision not to give in to it, y'know?'

We wait for a northbound train, and she says that she

364

hopes I have not taken offence. In her opinion, they should not be purging the staff of people like me – people with experience.

'What d'you mean, purging?' I ask, as the train comes speeding into the station. 'I *wanted* to work from home.'

'Well, you saved *Hen* a job anyway,' she says.

'I saved . . . ?' I know that I look annoyed. 'What are you trying to say?'

'Nothing you don't know, Lucy.' We climb on to a packed train. 'Only that Tobu wanted Hen to shed about half of the *Chronicle* staff. And he'd only managed a third.'

'The bastard,' I say, as the train lurches away. I hang on to a strap.

'Hen's not a bastard. He begged Bill to let you work from home. Bill wanted me to write the column. Simon said we should scrap the column altogether.'

'How d'you know all this?' I ask, still annoyed; and she sighs, raising an eyebrow.

'D'you think I sit next to Hen every day for fun?' she asks. 'Believe me, a girl can eat only a certain number of ginger biscuits . . .'

A passenger overhears her, and laughs.

'Simon thinks people aren't putting in the hours. That's why we were all being monitored. Times we come in. Times we leave the building.'

'I get out here,' I say, realizing why I felt I was being watched.

'This is between us, remember? I only told you because you're leaving. You know that, yeah?'

'Thanks for telling me,' I say, as the doors slide open.

'It's not just you, anyway,' she says, as I leave the

train. 'Hen wants to find a way to get rid of Heather now. And VD.'

'VD?' I say, as the doors slam shut.

'Is this your credit card?' Cardigan asks me, when I come to collect my daughter from Bunny Hops. 'Only I found it in Maxie's Barbie bag.'

Chapter Fourteen

My head is decorated with chewing-gum foil covers, and I am sitting under the hood of a salon hairdryer. I am in a chair beside Caroline, who is wearing a sharp-collared electric blue suit.

It was Caroline who persuaded me along to this hair-dresser's, on the third floor of a department store I had not heard of. She said that we should celebrate the New Year and the fact that I have become a lady of leisure.

We really must do lunch, she said.

I said that I am not a lady of leisure. As of last week, when I took Maxie out of Bunny Hops, I am a full-time mother. In my spare time, I clean and cook. I wash and iron. Caroline's horrified pause made me feel like an eighteenth-century aristocrat, telling her mother-in-law that she had entered into domestic service.

'What happened to your woman?' she said, yesterday, on the phone.

'My woman?'

'Your cleaning woman?'

I tell her about the lost credit card. I explain that I tried to re-employ Katie, but that she was no longer interested. She was pleased, in fact, that the job had come to an end.

For too long, she had felt like a go-between – her loyalties divided between Charlie and me. Apparently, Charlie is always asking after me. He once even asked her to spy on VD. But she would never look through another woman's underwear.

'Oh, Lucy,' said Caroline, on the phone. 'How could you let her go? It's so hard to find women these days. Women you can trust with a key.'

'Don't be silly. I can go through any old cleaning agency.'

'Keep your staff. That's all my mother ever said to me,' said Caroline; and I heard the sadness in her voice. But I knew that she was not sad about her mother dying. 'It was bad enough when you lost your nanny. Judd was simply wonderful with Maxie.'

But, chin up.

Chop chop. Clear the decks; and every other cliché. Was it not useful that the hairdressing salon had a crèche for Maxie? I should *rest*. Maybe have my nails done. I should pamper myself for that *very nice chap* VD. ('It's good for you, as a woman, to have a close male friend while you're waiting for Charlie to sort himself out. I've often thought of having one myself.') When was the last time anyone pushed up my cuticles?

Now, the hairdresser comes to talk to my hair; I look up at a powdery face.

She smells like Grandma Pinny when she leans close to pick up dry sections of my hair, scolding its owner for using a hairdryer. She says 'blowdrying' as if it were a dirty word. Then, she outlines a care programme for my hair which would use up all of my energy, and time. When she goes, I begin to relax. So much so that I confide in Caroline about the lumps Angela discovered in her breasts.

'She's the same age as me,' I say, worried. 'God, what if it's cancer?'

'Oh, I'd tell her not to worry. I've had so many lumps, but they all turn out to be benign.'

'Lumps in your breasts?'

'Oh yes, not to worry. Some of them were as big as melon balls.'

I cannot help but laugh at the image. But then I stop, remembering the photo from a book Angela borrowed from Dr Strom's office.

The photo was of a woman who had had a mastectomy. 'They won't be malignant. Breasts are full of lumpy bits,' I said to Angela, staring at the photo-woman. Her flat, knitted scars. 'Even if they're not, it doesn't mean you'll have to have a breast removed.'

But I could not stop staring at that photo.

It was not the omission of the breast that repulsed me as much as the absence of a nipple. Without that finishing touch, the woman seemed incomplete, like a fairy cake begging for a cherry.

'Even *then*, doctors can do *miracles* with reconstructive surgery,' I said, hugging my good friend, and thinking that this should not happen to Angela, who is all breasts. Nothing is certain. Not any more. Everyone lies, what with their coloured-card systems, and their Dr Armstrongs.

'I don't believe in miracles any more,' said Angela, her voice in chime with my thoughts.

I watched tears, disappearing halfway down her cheeks, as she said this; and I thought of the Angela who would believe in anything. She believed that MPs would never take cash for questions. She believed in Charlie and Bill Clinton. She visited the Millennium Dome, and admired every single Zone.

I handed Angela a tissue, telling her she had to tell the doctor. Then, I quoted Judd, who had often quoted Israel's first Prime Minister, David Ben-Gurion. 'If you can't believe in miracles, then you're not being a realist.'

I feel cold at the thought of Judd as the hairdresser sits an elderly woman beside me. The dryer comes down like the lid of a helicopter over her head. An underwhelming smell of excrement wafts over to me. I lean my head nearer to Caroline, and ask whether she has talked to Donald about a job for VD.

'Oh yes. I talked to him that very night. Donald said that you should come up to the house. He'll introduce you to William.'

'It's not for me. I meant for VD.'

'I know. But Donald said he'd sooner talk to you about it.'

'Caroline, please. I'm serious. Between you and me – absolutely – I think he's going to be made redundant.'

'That nice chap? But he's a Lingdown boy, isn't he?'

'I don't think the world quite works like that any more. Or at least I hope it doesn't. I mean, it doesn't matter where VD went to school.'

But: 'Of course it does,' says Caroline, stroking the pencil-length grooves on her face. 'I'll talk to Donald again. We'll set up a meeting with William for VD.' She pats my hand. 'Don't worry.'

At last, the old lady is moved to another hairdryer. The smell moves, in one solid lump, with her.

I have reached a stage in my life where I am delighted by letters addressed to The Occupier. Because my friends all work, and I feel as if I see no-one. In the streets, no-one sees me, and the days are distinguishable only by playgroup and children's-television schedules.

Such is the life of the stay-at-home mother.

I have been a saint of a full-time mother since the start of January. It is now the middle of February, and I have made some progress. Maxie is out of nappies; and her cot. She has gone up a level in jigsaw puzzles. In the supermarket, she has learned not to upset other customers, or tin displays.

'What a good girl you are,' said the cashier yesterday.

I have learned that, when children are good, they are very, very good. But when they are naughty, their parents are terrible.

'Do you love me, Max?' I asked her, last night, as I wriggled her into her night-clothes. She thought hard about that one.

'Love *Flumpy*,' she decided.

'Well, I love *you*,' I said, kissing her warm, sticky skin.

'What's that?' she asked, putting her hand on my face.

'I don't know. Probably a blemish.'

'Can I kiss Mummy's blemish?'

'You sure can,' I said, as she kissed the spot. 'Mummy's blemishes are all yours.'

'I'm happy, Mummy,' she said.

'Good.'

(But I am not as happy.)

Oh, I know that I am a lucky woman, having money enough not to work. But . . . Perhaps I am easily bored. It is only that I tire of singing the same nursery rhyme all day long. Reading the same old scary fairy tales.

To break the monotony of story-time, I often read the pages backwards. That way, there are happy endings. Little Red Riding Hood is safe at home. Sleeping Beauty is fast asleep. Cinderella has escaped the trappings of marrying into the Royal Family.

I wonder now how Judd coped with full-time nannying. He did not once complain of losing his sense of self – which is how I feel. I have come to the conclusion that good parenting means keeping Maxie alive. *Excellent* parenting involves exhausting the child during the day so that she sleeps well at night.

'Perhaps Judd had less of a sense of self to lose,' said Ysanne, on the phone.

'Judd – not strong-minded?' I smiled, thinking of Judd's strength. His body.

Naked. The mole on his right shoulder, reminding me that, despite everything, he was a flawed human being.

I do not – these days – see much of my college friends. I e-mail them before they need to rush off to an important meeting. They are all three so busy now. Sophie often works fifteen-hour days, every day; and Ysanne's website is worth millions. (But, not really.) Ruth has been promoted to be a policy officer for the Labour Party.

'Are you enjoying working from home?' asked Ruth, when she rang to tell me the good news.

'Well, my column takes two minutes. So, really, I'm just at home with Maxie.'

'I couldn't *do* that,' said Ruth. 'I need to bounce ideas off people.'

I thought of Ruth's work friends, all of whom refuse to talk to me, on any deep level, because I have not published a book. I thought of Ruth's own book, out last week, about the politics of childcare for working women in the UK. It was clear from page one that Ruth did not have much contact with children.

'Have you spoken to Soph lately?' asked Ruth.

'Once,' I said, thinking of that shiny bar in the City.

Sophie talked to her mobile phone, rather than to me. She said things like: 'Well, you're just going to have to sell Italy.' I sat there, feeling small, and looking around at the gleaming wood. There were signs all over the wall saying: *Sorry, no children.*

Sorry, no mothers.

Mothers are banned from so many places. We are collected together and shoved into tiny, toy-strewn huts. We have no right to enter pubs, or cinemas. We are asked to leave art galleries. We are shushed in the adult section of a library.

That is why we stay indoors, and bore each other about rashes, potties and vaccinations, during coffee mornings.

Our children play at the other end of the room. We have no right to join in. We complicate their games. We like beginnings, middles, and ends. We add rules. We stay-at-homes want to be boss, because, oh, we remember a time when men turned to us during a meeting and said, 'What do *you* think, Lucy?'

Maxie will not allow me to meet her imaginary friends. 'No play Mummy,' she says, talking to an empty space.

In this household, invisible people have priority.

My daughter is too busy to play with me, so, I watch TV; and I know that I have entered a different demographic group, because the adverts breaking up the programmes are targeted at consumers who want nappy strength or cures for incontinence.

When she is asleep, I write my column. There is always the same view through the window opposite my computer. It is an oblong patch of Camden that I have come to love and loathe. That front lawn opposite is always badly brushed. That slit of dull sky forever lifeless, like old skin streaked with blue veins. Underneath, people rush to pass by my window. There are only men in uniform clamping cars to look like crippled children.

No-one ever looks up.

In the evening, I turn the TV up at full volume to drown out the sounds of my new downstairs neighbours' arguments. They are always arguing about something. Hearing them through the ceiling, I feel as if I died. My ghost is hovering above my old life. There I am, listening to some of my best rows with Charlie, yet unable to participate.

The woman half of the couple irritates me.

She tried last week to act like a neighbour in a weak TV drama, inviting herself upstairs for biscuits and tea. But there was, really, nothing to gossip about, and I wanted her to go away – so that I could watch the end of *EastEnders*. Bianca is similar to me, in that she too has aborted her baby.

I am often alone; and perhaps that is why I am so happy to now see VD. I bought him an array of cheap men's grooming products for Valentine's Day; and he has come bearing a box of Maltesers for me, still in the newsagent's brown bag, as well as a Kit Kat for Maxie.

Charlie only ever gave me one Valentine's Day card, and that was stolen from my box of sixty variety cards. As a result of his lack of romanticism, I always pretended that I did not believe in such days, spoiled as they were by the commercialism.

'Hello, little one. I haven't seen you for over a *week,*' says VD to my child, who is being dumbed down by children's television. But at least she comes alive when she sees the Kit Kat.

'So, how's the flat? And the *job*?'

'Fantastic. The *Gazette* group still believes in real reporting, unlike . . . Wow, you shouldn't have,' says VD, unwrapping the grooming products. I stand over him, saying that they are more expensive than they smell. He sniffs the soap, arguing that overpriced Valentine's Day gifts are unnecessary, because he loves me every day. I have made him happy.

I led him to a new job, where he is happy.

VD met my father-in-law in January. Donald felt him fit enough to introduce to his friend, William. *William* felt him fit enough to introduce to his friend, Hugh. *Hugh* felt him fit enough to be news editor of the *Chipping Norton Gazette*. He had the job – but only if he was prepared to start immediately.

'It's all who you know, isn't it?' said VD, as if that was a good thing.

We discussed his options. He could either stay and be boiled alive with no prospects at the *Post*, or commute to the Cotswolds, and be faced with opportunities.

'So. Tell me about your new life,' I say. He has been away for almost two weeks. In order to properly settle into life in the Cotswolds, Hugh invited VD to stay with him, in Chipping Norton.

'Oh, it's fantastic,' he says, trying to describe how much responsibility he has. I snuggle against his chest, thinking how young and sexy he makes me feel. Less like a mother. When I am with him, I remember the feeling of irresponsibility.

'That sounds brilliant,' I say, telling VD that Angela had her test results today.

'Oh – and what did she get?' he asks, misunderstanding.

'She didn't *get* anything,' I say, pausing. 'She hasn't got cancer.'

'That's great,' he says; although he is uncomfortable

with Angela. Despite my trying to educate him, VD does not believe in lesbianism. He thinks lesbians are women wanting shagging to their senses.

'You've had your ear pierced,' I say, staring at the diamond stud.

'What d'you think?' he asks; and I laugh, because he is so big a man that he looks, to me, like an oak tree wrapped in fairy lights.

'A bit George Michael. Don't tell me *Hugh* told you to have that done? Or *Donald*?'

'No. Heather did.'

'Heather?' I say, standing up.

'Mmm. Yeah.'

I ask VD what Heather was doing, just passing by Chipping *Norton*. VD twists the earring. He says she has been at a loose end since losing her job at the *Post*.

'So she can commute every day to see *you* now?' I say, spitefully. 'Just when did she come?'

'Last weekend.'

'But *I* wanted to see you then. You said you'd have to fit in with Hugh's plans.'

'She just showed up. She thinks I might be able to get her a job. Which I might.'

'And did she stay the night? At *Hugh's*?'

'We were in separate bedrooms.'

'*I* wouldn't have surprised you on your . . . ? I mean, how did she have Hugh's address? Maxie, stop watching that now,' I call out, reaching for one of the remote controls. 'You've got chocolate all over your face. Come and get ready because Ranny Rine's collecting you soon.'

'No want Ranny Rine,' she says, as I try to move her away from the warm glow of television.

'Yes, want Ranny Rine,' I say. 'You're going to stay

there for the night. While Mummy and VD celebrate Valentine's *Day.'*

'So. Lucy,' starts VD, as if he has something important to ask me. 'Did you sleep with Judd?'

I pause, as he half laughs, scraping the label off the soap. The white spots on his nails reveal a great need for calcium.

'I haven't seen Judd for months.'

'You haven't answered my question.' He puts down the strong-smelling soap.

'What question? Come on Max.'

'Did you sleep with Judd when you were going out with me?'

He says this lightly, but I can hear him breathing. It is not a pleasant sound from so big a bear of a man.

'Why d'you think that?' I say, above *Sesame Street.*

'You told Von that you'd slept with Judd. And she mentioned it to Heather.'

'You shouldn't listen to *Heather,*' I say; but I am a hopeless liar.

'Why not? At least Heather's interested in my life. She doesn't just talk about herself. Or her friends' medical problems with *lesbianism.'*

'Don't be such a . . .'

'Unlike you, Heather asks me *questions.'*

'*I* ask you questions.' It is only that I know VD now. I know that he has athlete's foot. I know that he shaves the space between his eyebrows. I know that he uses face packs, and salon conditioner for very dry hair. He has calcium spots. 'I thought we'd passed that stage.'

We have passed the stage where I am shy about seeing him semi-naked. We have reached a stage in our relation-ship where we know what our menu orders will be. He

377

likes steak; I like fresh salmon. We have reached a stage in our relationship where we can discuss names for our future children. He likes Claire; I like Genevieve.

'So did I,' says VD, pathetically. 'I thought you cared about me.'

'Of course I do. I'm going out with you, for God's sake.'

'But in your spare time, you sleep with other men,' he half whispers.

Maxie is staring at the television, apparently oblivious to the argument. But she sucks hard on that beaker of cranberry juice.

'Don't talk to me like that, you . . .'

'Mummy shouting,' says Maxie, miserably.

'Why d'you still see so much of Heather anyway?'

'Did you or did you not sleep with Judd?'

'Yes. I bloody well did.'

He stands up, still holding the soap. *'You fucking . . .'* he shouts, throwing down the soap; and, for a moment, I think he is going to cry. I hold a frightened Maxie, as he tells me that he wanted *me*.

Not Heather.

He was – is – was in love with me; and I do not know how hard it has been for him. Bloody hell, I have another man's child. For fuck's sake. But . . . He sensed the distance between us.

Despite what I think, he's not stupid. How could he . . . ? But, yes, he loved me, for all I patronized him. Thought he was an idiot. He wanted me. He waited long enough. He thought Heather was being a jealous bitch when she told him I had slept with Judd. He was an idiot. He waited until Charlie moved out, before he . . .

But I cannot find the words with which to interrupt him.

So he speaks again. He says that he knows how I feel. He knows that I am in love with another man. I am still in love with Charlie. I am never envious when he flirts with Heather.

He knows that a part of me is relieved that he has found a job out of London. It puts some distance between us. He realizes that I am confused. So he will give me time to think. He will bloody give me time to think; and I know that I should say something, but it would feel as if I was talking to a script.

'Heather was right,' he mutters, walking to the door, straight for it, as if he is striding on to a rugby pitch. 'I probably am better off without you.'

'She *meant*, you're better off with her,' I say.

'And maybe she's right.'

'Well, why aren't you *with* her, then?' I scream at the slammed shut door.

'That's what I want to know?'

I want to know that: and I want to know why, within a year, three men have walked out on me; and I want to know when my mother stopped being the youngest mother at the school gates; why I lost Sam when the doctors found nothing wrong with me or the foetus; why Maxie is crying; why I cannot hang on to anything. I want to know when the rules changed. I want to know when I stopped being clever, and started to be academic; I want to know why I am still eating kosher; when I stopped having faith in my mother; why I lost a friend who redefined friendship for me; why I failed to become a judge; and why I am crying. I want to know how everything I had last year slipped away. *Slip*.

I am no good alone, so I am pleased to see Caroline. She

is here to take Maxie. She watches with awe, as I fold up the buggy, then asks if I would mind Charlie coming tomorrow to "the house"?

'I said that you were going to drive up, to collect Maxie; and *he* said that he would come too. He wanted to talk to you on neutral ground,' she says, excitedly. 'And he didn't want to come here, and risk bumping into VD.'

No chance of that any more, I think, sadly. I wonder what Charlie could want to talk to me about. A divorce, perhaps? So that he can forever be with Caitlin?

I remember Charlie saying how the two of us would be together forever. He said that it was inevitable. We would retire to the Cotswolds, to live. We would one day be like his parents. I think of this as Caroline leaves. 'Don't worry about us,' she says, trying to appear in control, but unable to hold on to a Maxie, who looks like a wriggling pile of dirty laundry.

'When you're older and sprouting facial hair . . .' grinned Charlie, when I scolded him last year for forgetting another Valentine's Day.

'I'll still be mocking Valentines for their commercialism,' I said-sung.

'You can push me in my zimmer-frame.'

I said, 'Charlie, people don't *push* zimmer-frames.'

I am so upset that I call Angela, and ask her to come over. I say that we can celebrate the fatty tissue in her breasts.

'Here's to *one* benign tumour,' she says, filling my glass with white wine.

'Thanks,' I say, leaning against the kitchen counter.

'And here's to the other,' she says, pouring wine into her own. I have never known her so angry. She is not soft any more – merely fat.

Angela takes the glasses of wine through to the living

room, and, *on second thoughts*, the bottle. She sits at one end of the sofa, facing in. I open a family packet of kosher crisps pouring them into a bowl.

'Why are you still eating kosher?' she asks, examining the packet, as I sit next to her on the sofa.

'I'm not strictly kosher. But I want to feel . . . It didn't take *Judd* to make me Jewish.'

'Whatever – they're inedible.'

'I suppose I'm used to them.'

Angela has finished her glass of wine, so I catch up. She goes into the kitchen area, flapping open and shut cupboards to find some food. 'Try the storage cupboard,' I say. 'Next to the door.' There, Angela finds some packets of cakes, past their sell-by date. Cakes Charlie liked. They are covered in pink icing. They are filled with pink icing.

Despite the date stamp, Angela opens the packet. 'I need sugar, after what's just happened,' she says, eating a cake in one bite.

'But it's *good* what's happened.'

'The test results were good. But Felice just finished with me. So . . . pretty crap really.'

'Oh Angela.'

She sits down again, twisting sections of her hair into pasta twirls. She tells me that Felice was waiting for her to get the results. Then, she could happily end the relationship. If she had had *cancer*, it would have been a different story.

'Oh, Angela,' I say again. 'What shit.'

She refills our glasses, twisting the length of her hair into a rope. She feels OK, she says. But it will be hard, seeing Felice, every day, on the television.

'So, listen to the radio,' I say, picking up the empty wine bottle. I go to get another one. 'She was crap anyway,' I say, behind me.

'Bloody *crap,*' says Angela, who is slightly tipsy. Despite her size, she is easily drunk. It takes me a lot more alcohol, despite my comparative size. My *size* being either fattish or thinnish, depending on my mood. I have learned to accept that I will – despite my Slimco mother – never quite shed the excess *ish.*

'*Fucking* crap.'

'She thought it was enough just to be thin,' she says.

'And perhaps it is – for that type of audience.' I watch Angela as she eats another cake. Even after all these years, I am surprised that she is called *Angela*; it is more of a thin person's name.

'She was so pretty though . . .'

Angela stops eating the icing on her cake, to cry. I quickly pour more wine, reminding her that we were supposed to be celebrating tonight. Not losing drinking time over Felice or VD.

'Bloody men,' I say, forgetting.

'Bloody *men and women,*' she reminds me, asking what happened with VD. I tell her that he was upset that I had slept with Judd. He loved me. He thought I patron-ized him.

Angela hands me the phone. She almost pulls the cord out, stretching it across to me. 'Phone him,' she says. 'Poor guy. He's not your usual bastard. I honestly think he might have been *the one* . . .'

'Don't be silly. There's no such person. Romantic heroes are only ever fictional; they're invented to sell potboilers.'

'*Seriously. Phone* him.'

I dial the number I now know by heart. I do not know why I am calling, or what I might say. I think I am wishing that someone other than VD will answer. VD, who collects toy cars, and is free enough to break wind at bedtime. But, before I can apologize for having slept with Judd, I hear someone laughing in the background. It is Heather. She sounds like a member of a live studio audience.

'Why didn't you leave a message on the machine?' asks Angela, looking up at me with the blank, know-nothing, eyes of the childless woman.

'Because he was there – with Heather.'

'Oh, Lucy,' she says.

'So, no better than Felice then, is he?' I say, and I feel sadder than I should. I am thinking of VD's kitchen corkboard, splashed with pictures by his stepbrother, Ben. There is a ticket to Silverstone up there, and a photograph of me. It looks nothing like me.

Angela smiles sadly; and we say everything women say to each other in our situation.

– We say that we are better off without Felice and VD.

– We say that other women are welcome to them.

– We say that VD was probably gay.

– We say that Felice was probably not gay.

– We say that we should finish the second bottle.

– We say thash VD had athlete's foot.

– We say that Feleesh dyed her hair.

– We say we should finish the third bottle.

We tell VD and Felice anecdotes. We tell ex-boy/girl-friend anecdotes. I talk about Charlie and the eggs. We drink and drink. She talks about a woman called Ginny who was allergic to pubic hair. Every time Ginny went down on Angela, she violently sneezed. 'It was quite nice actually,' says Angela.

I feel sad, remembering how often VD said that he loved me. He used the warm word, *love*, so often that

383

it began to feel commonplace. I now feel that I have a right to hear it in everyday conversation. It became a modern convenience, like central heating; and I miss its glow.

Meanwhile, Angela and I remember what to say to each other, as women in our situation.

– We say that, lishen to this one, VD shaved the space between his eyebrowsh.

– We say that, no, no, Felice wash worse. She shaved off all her pyubic hair.

– So did Anshela see what I meant when I sesh he was gay?

– Did I see whashshe meant when she said she was *hardly* a leshbian?

We are lying in a heap together on the sofa. I am not sure where my limbs end, and Angela's begin. All I know is that I cannot stop thinking about Judd, leaving me this evening. *VD*. I meant VD. Angela laughs, and says that I have so many lovers, they are beginning to merge into one another.

She says, but, penishes will only ever be breast substitutes.

VD, I say. I meant VD. But it was Jush who was the bastarrrd. Judd. Sorry, Judd. He made Maxie and me fall in love with with and then he pished off. Like that. Just when he got to me. Jush when . . .

Angela says they are alllll bastards – women. They coushnt just fuck you and leave you, like men do, they have to hang arounsh afterwards, telling you thash they still love you, and can they still share your flat, and ush your conditioner.

No, no, I say. Women are wonderful creashures from heaven. It is the men who fuck us about. I shoulbe with Anshela. Anshela, who acsh on instinct. Feelings are everything with Angila. She ignores the rules. Rishe now, we're only friends. Merely friendsh. But I want to breathe the same air as.

My lovely Anshe.

Chapter Fifteen

I wake up in agony the next morning, staring at the empty bottles and cake wrappers. I feel as if I have a strange tongue in my mouth. I have someone else's arms and legs. Someone very heavy.

There must be a house on my head, I think, moving my right arm. I look at the cake wrappers, groaning with shame, as I remember Angela. *Oh God.* I kissed her neck. Last night. I nuzzled her neck. She kissed my mouth, and I moved away in horror, saying: *'Oh shit, no, I couldn't. No. Bloody hell. Not with a woman.'*

I realized how to stop sex.

I go to the bathroom mirror, staring at my reflection. It well displays my misery. I did not remove my Valentine's Day eye-liner, and I now look like a charcoal drawing. My eyes feel as if they have swallowed every one of my eyelashes.

I wonder, with a breath, whether I have lost Angela. Angela, who is everybody's friend. She was prepared to be friends with cash-for-questions MPs.

'You've got my support,' she shouted to Neil Hamilton, when he was shown on television, outside the High Court.

I feel ashamed, recalling how quickly Angela stood up,

rubbing her mouth clean of brown lipstick, and picking up her tapestry bag. The clasp was bigger than the bag itself. She felt for the keys in her pocket, looking around, as if to check she was leaving with everything.

I can remember only fragments of our increasingly sober conversation.

– How cruel are you to make a pass at me, now, after all these yearsh, when . . .

– *I wanted to see, thatwas all. Oh Anshe, I'm sorry.*

– I've always only ever seen you as a friend . . .

– *I thought it might be what you wanted; I'm so sorry.*

– So you pitied me? Well, don't, because I could never fancy you.

– *I couldn't go through with it; you don't know how sorry I am.*

– You're all skin and bone.

I remember, through the haze of a hangover, how quickly after that, she left.

How quickly I passed out. The telephone rings, hurting my head, as I am about to leave the flat, and I hope It is Angela. Then I wonder as I always do when Maxie is away from me – whether it is someone calling to say that my baby is dead.

But, ohmyhead, it is Judd.

'Lucy. Look, I've been doing a lot of thinking. And . . .'

'I'm on my way out,' I say, frostily. 'I have to pick up Maxie from Caroline's.'

'How is she?' I think how gentle his voice is. Mine is loud and rasping.

'As if you give a damn,' I say.

'I wanted to see you both.'

'I told you when you came over, there's no need for any *aftercare* service.'

'Lucy, please.'

'This is a really bad time.'

In retrospect, I should not have put down the phone. But I was so angry; and I am still angry, en route to Caroline's. (He should leave me alone.) He should not have slept with me if it was morally wrong. I did not ask him to make love to me. It was not included in his employment contract.

I am angry until I leave the motorway, and drive through the calm, smug green of the Cotswolds. I head through small villages, their every building reaching up and pointing to the church. Only here can I rid my head of Judd.

I drive through the village centre. Even after all these years, I am surprised to see a place so untouched by the modern world. It is three o'clock on a Friday afternoon, yet Caroline's shop is all shutters.

The trees resemble spears of broccoli, planted in an unnaturally straight line. There are pink curtains and cakes in the shop windows, old-fashioned *Naughty But Nice* signs above plates of full-fat cream cakes and generously sugared Victoria sponges.

No matter how hard I tried to disassociate the village from Charlie, still I see him everywhere. In that tea shoppe, ordering orangeade and a marshmallow ice-cream cone, sprinkled with hundreds and thousands. Throwing sweet wrappers into that thick, black stream. I am sad that we will be discussing the divorce here. I want only good memories of this village. I want only fond memories of the Wallis house.

The Wallis driveway appears as shyly as my mother-in-law. She stands there, half waving; and I remember how nervous I was when I met Caroline and Donald for the first time.

'Don't worry, they'll be nice to you,' Charlie smiled, as I drove along the gravel of the driveway, creating tracks.

'They're nice to everyone,' said Charlie, smiling, and slamming the door of my car, hard. 'But, knowing the 'rents, they're bound to hate you.'

'Hello there,' says Caroline now, coming towards me in her country outfit: pressed grey slacks tucked into clean green wellies. 'I saw you from the house.'

'Hi,' I say, switching on the immobilizer. 'How's Max been?'

'Oh, good. Very good.' She smiles that no-teeth smile. 'She's asleep at the moment, because she was up 'til late last night, playing with the old Aga. Come in. I've made tea. Scones with cream. From the shop.'

'What time's Charlie coming?' I ask, breathing in. The air is as fresh and cold as a surprise.

'He just said *the afternoon,*' Caroline says, still smiling as if she is hiding something.

I walk around a ladder which climbs Caroline's wall. I am still superstitious, despite Judd's best efforts to persuade me that tales of black cats and suchlike were invented by the heathen, illiterate, peasant classes in the absence of any government information.

'He must be freezing,' I say, referring to a man in a T-shirt up the ladder.

'Oh no, they don't feel the cold,' said Caroline, briskly. She is still smiling as she pushes open the front door.

There are strange noises. At first, I think they are coming from the television, but then I realize that it is the birds outside, singing live.

I follow my mother-in-law into the open house, past a painting of Helen and into the milky warm smell of the mahogany-and-tapestry living room, where Donald sits behind a local newspaper. It is the paper where VD now works as news editor.

'Oh, hello,' I say; and Donald looks up in surprise, as if he cannot quite work out where I fit into his life.

'Yes,' he says, at last, and smiles a broad smile. 'The little girl's here, is she?'

'Of *course* Maxie's here,' blushes Caroline.

'I didn't know I'd be seeing Lucinda, that's all. It's been months, Lucinda.'

I smile back at Donald, remembering him saying, in his wedding speech, that I would be welcomed, like a breath of fresh air, into the Wallis family. But Sarah Ferguson was talked about in similar terms when she joined the royals. Only after her separation from the Duke of York was she described as: 'Vulgar, vulgar, vulgar'.

'Hello Donald,' I say.

'I kept hearing your child through that machine,' he says, pointing to the Tomy intercom. 'I thought Caroline had the radio on, it was so loud.'

I laugh politely, and sit down. I am surprised to see the photograph on their sideboard of Charlie and me. It is our official wedding day photograph. It flatters me. I am laughing, as is Charlie.

My dress is like silk; and I am slender. Yet, I am always disappointed to see that photograph. I felt like a goddess on the day, but there is the photographic evidence. I was not a goddess – just me in a white dress.

'Thanks so much for introducing VD to William,' I say, remembering.

'*No*,' says Donald, still smiling. 'Good chap that. A Lingfield boy. No doubt about it. And he's doing well. Probably be left to edit the thing in a couple of months.'

Caroline comes in with a tray of tea-things. She sets it down, almost upsetting the milk jug.

'He's very happy,' I say, as always, surprised by the clumsy brown teapot. I expect tea in Charlie's house to be served in delicate china.

'How do you *know* Vincent?' asks Donald, slumping backwards. He looks like Charlie, sitting like that.

'Didn't you know? VD and I were . . .'

'VD,' tuts Donald. 'The man's not a sexually transmitted *disease.*'

'*Donald*,' scolds Caroline; but he ignores her, as usual.

'He was my . . .'

'They are friends,' says Caroline, emphatically.

'He was actually my boyfriend,' I explain.

'But I saw VD last week with a young lady,' says Donald, confused. 'I thought he was teamed up with her.'

'Vincent and Lucy are very close friends. But now Charlie's sorted himself out . . .'

'Good chap, that Vinnie. Good, old-fashioned, news-paper man. Well, according to Hugh.'

'We're not together any more,' I say, more to Caroline than to Donald.

'You're not?'

A smile stretches across her face; and I feel as if I have announced my engagement to her son.

'Oh, I am pleased. Just as Charlie's arranged his affairs.'

'I invited Vincent *here*, Caroline,' says Donald. 'I thought we could tell him a bit about the place.'

'I suppose we are good for knowing people,' says Caroline, filling with pride.

'Vincent's not one of these fly-by-nights – God, brew it, woman,' adds Donald. 'Good tea is brewed properly.'

Caroline takes the pot and shakes it vigorously.

'You don't *shake* it,' says Donald. 'For God's *sake*, woman. Give it to me.' He removes the lid and peers inside. 'That'll do. Come on; pour it into cups. I think you've stretched Lucy's patience far enough. Have a scone, Lucy.'

'Thank you.'

I take one of the scones and split it unevenly. Crumbs fall on to the mahogany occasional table. I try to ignore the mental image I have of my mother, who is saying, '*Starch, Lucy. Starch*'.

'Yes, you might see him actually, Lucy,' says Donald. 'I invited him for this afternoon.'

'You invited him for . . . ?' says Caroline.

I look at the door, as if VD might walk through it. I think of him walking in here with Heather. They will sit on the velvet chaise longue, giggling.

'He's popping in, that's all,' says Donald, waiting for Caroline to butter him a fat scone.

'Well, you should have said something,' says Caroline, buttering Donald's scone.

'What does it matter to you? You've made this messy spread anyway.'

'I bought the scones for *Charlie*. He's coming to see Lucy.'

'Wants money, does he?' says Donald, drily. He is waiting for Caroline, whose knife hovers, to spread cream on the scone.

'What time is VD-er-Vincent coming?' I ask.

'This afternoon,' says Donald. 'Scone, Caroline. *Scone.*'

'Mmm,' says Caroline, dolloping cream on to Donald's scone.

'Coming round more, lately, hasn't he, Charlie,' says Donald. 'Because he's short of cash, of course.'

'No. It's because of Lucy.'

'"I love Lucy,"' laughs Donald. 'Like the situation comedy.'

'There's nothing comical about a marriage breaking up,' says Caroline, wide-eyed.

'Why we had children, I don't know. They're like cars,' says Donald, scraping butter from his scone, and tutting. 'Their value can only go down.'

'Oh, one *needs* children,' says Caroline, as if continuing a discussion about cars. 'One would be lonely, otherwise.'

'What d'you mean? I wonder when Vincent's going to be here,' grunts Donald, sneering at the sight of his wife taking a tiny bite out of a whole, plain scone. He looks at me, and smiles. 'The only ones we see are other people's.'

'Oh, that'll be Charlie,' says Caroline, standing up, as the doorbell rings. She shakes crumbs away from her skirt.

'It could be Vincent,' grunts Donald, as she leaves the room. 'It could be *anyone*.'

I don't know why I am scared. But I am. I am in fright, as Maxie was when I left her alone at nursery school. I am scared at the mere idea of seeing Charlie here, in a house where Charlie first said he loved me. We were in his old bedroom, which was empty. There were only some old suitcases in the corner, waiting to go somewhere. (I thought of my old bedroom, filled as it was with reminders of myself.) We lay on the fading, quilted bedspread – and Charlie said: 'I could even love you, you know, if you weren't so bloody smug.' He wanted to take me to Venice, and propose on a gondola. I said, 'That sounds like a lovely surprise.'

Charlie sulked, because of my facetiousness.

Now, Donald and I seem to have an unspoken agreement to keep quiet until the door is answered. We both

393

listen to Caroline's soft-soled footsteps. There is a squeal and a sound of fur and falling, as she trips over the dog. '*Pooter*,' she says.

Charlie did not stop sulking until I gave him the surprise plane tickets to Venice. We stayed in a small bed-and-breakfast next to the canal. Charlie complained about our room. He flirted with the chambermaid.

He said, 'That's what the bedders are there for.'

I said, 'Where d'you think you are? In a Tom Sharpe novel?'

I hear the front door opening, and Caroline does not speak at first. During the politeness of her pause, I know that it is Charlie. I can imagine him standing there, seemingly bored, as if revisiting Brideshead.

He will not be alone. No, he will be with Caitlin. She will be all Alice-band and pie-crust collar, in the manner of a 1980s Sloane Ranger. A horsey woman, hung with real pearls. She will have strong views *against* country footpaths and *for* the hereditary peerage system, saying in a loud, Thatcherite voice that she is tired of waiting for me to give Charlie a divorce. She wants their wedding day to coincide with the shooting season.

Charlie will have altered his personality to fit Caitlin's. He will have forgotten all of the feminism I was careful to teach him. He will stride in, making jokes against pheasants, and women.

He will, in fact, have turned into Donald.

'Well, how lovely to see you,' says Caroline's voice. 'I mean, what a lovely surprise. I take it you know that Lucy's here? Come *in*, and sorry about the dog.'

I pause for a second. She would not speak in such a way to Charlie. So it is not Charlie, but VD.

VD, who loves me all the time, and without any of

Charlie's caveats.

We have a chance to sort out our differences; and maybe it is time to believe in romantic heroes. Men who look as they should, in black-and-white movies. I could believe in VD. He was prepared to be a father to Maxie. He was prepared to take his time, so that I could orgasm. He wanted me, rather than Heather. That was clear. He used the word *love* unsparingly.

He was so big a man; and I think of my head on his shoulder.

I cannot hear VD's reply. But I do hear his soft voice. And I panic, because I cannot remember how to talk to him. How did I talk to a man like VD, who played rugby on a Sunday morning, and went to church with his step-family each Christmas Eve? He is too big a man for me to talk to.

I reach only to his shoulder.

The living-room door opens fully, and I tip the crumbs away from my Agnes B leather skirt. Caroline's voice is tinkling at whatever VD is saying.

But God, it is Judd standing there.

Judd. A juxtaposition in this English country house.

A Jew, walking on to a Noël Coward set.

'Judd. What are you doing here?' I say, so disorientated by his presence that I almost ask whether there is something wrong with Maxie.

'I just wanted to talk to you,' he mumbles; and I would blush and shiver if I was in a less public situation, because it is such a shock to see him.

'Donald Wallis,' says Donald, standing up with his arm outstretched to shake, as Charlie always did when first meeting a grown-up.

'Oh, yeah. Judd Drexler.'

It is strange, watching Judd and Donald shake hands.

Judd does so with barely disguised bitterness, and I wonder whether he is thinking about the upper classes and their congenital anti-Semitism. It is as if he feels freezing cold in this over-heated living room. He seems desperate to grab his coat to leave.

I could imagine Donald shaking hands with VD. That would have seemed more natural. It would have been as if such an encounter was long overdue.

But this, this is different.

Over our cream tea, Judd brings up the subject of the Holocaust, saying how the Allies had refused to bomb the gas chambers during the war. He says that the British were basically anti-Semitic. Donald says that it only takes a madman such as Hitler to gain power and people find it in themselves to murder, or ignore the murder, of an entire race.

'Oh, not me,' Caroline says, as ever trying to lighten the conversation, but finding the wrong words.

'Oh no, not *you*, woman,' said Donald, as if this was a bad thing. 'No. You couldn't even put down the old dog, you. Made such a meal out of the whole thing.'

'*I've* seen *Schindler's List*,' says Caroline, her skin bleaching white at the strain of changing the subject. 'Did you enjoy that, Judd?'

'Oh yes, very much,' replies Judd, sarcastically. 'I'm just waiting for the sequel, where the concentration camps victims are then imprisoned in displacement camps, or – if they *do* find a boat going to Israel – refused entry by the British, and forced to drown.'

'*Judd*,' I say, realizing that he is not even wearing a skullcap.

'Hang on. Let me tell them about *Schindler's List 3*. In this one, some Holocaust victims have, by a miracle, reached the promised land. But, oh, they are mocked as "soap" by swaggering Israeli military men. And cut to the States, where survivors are told to stop whinging on about losing their entire families to the ovens, because Americans have had a hard time too – first with the depression, and, after that, with war rationing.'

Caroline touches her face as if she has been slapped. I wonder about intervening – I might tell Judd that he is being rude – but the moment passes politely enough. Donald gulps in time, and says that he is not overly racialist. Not compared to some of his colleagues. No, he thinks that Jews and blacks . . .

'Coloureds,' interrupts Caroline, quietly.

Donald ignores Caroline, saying that Jews And Blacks have their place. Britain needs its blacks for its Olympic gold medals. And, as for Jews, well, kept in check, they are probably good for the economy.

'Donald,' interrupts Caroline.

'What is wrong, woman?'

Caroline says she feels Judd has a point about the Holocaust. What had Jewish people done, she says, except for the fact that they were Jews? Donald laughs, well aware that Judd will take exception to Caroline's exception.

Jewish as I now feel, I am not a part of the conversation. I want it over with, so that Judd and I can be alone. I want to ask him why he is wearing the Chinos he wore in his less religious days. Chinos, and a black top, similar to one of Charlie's.

But it is not only his clothes that are different. When I knew Judd, it was as if he was not made of flesh, like the rest of us. Perhaps it was because he wrapped himself

397

up so, in the smart garb of Jewish orthodoxy. Even in the summer, he wore hug-big, black winter coats.

He did not notice temperatures, or fashion; and there was never any sign that Judd had a body underneath that rigid uniform. Even when he shared my living space, he did not occupy much of it. He did not, to my knowledge, defecate. Certainly, he did not stink out the toilet, as Charlie did often, and powerfully.

Now, it is as if he is trapped by a body, like the rest of us. I can see through that skinny-rib top to the thick muscles, like ropes, on his arms. Despite the firmness of his expressed opinions, he appears vulnerable. For the first time, I can envisage him growing old. I can see his arms losing their muscle; his heart, collapsing. I find myself staring at his Chino'd crotch and thinking of him bowing, even there, to nature's laws. His testicles, eaten away by cancer. Quickly looking up, it is hard to escape the inevitable feeling that he might even, given time, lose his brilliant and questioning mind.

My mother-in-law offers to butter Judd a scone. He raises an eyebrow, but accepts. I so want to tell him that Donald and Caroline do not usually have cream teas on Friday afternoon. Normally, it is only Caroline here in the house, pottering.

'What do *you* think, Lucy?' Donald asks me, playfully. Because, sometimes, Donald can be as playful as Charlie.

'Oh, don't involve me,' I say. 'I'm neutral.'

'Yeah,' smiles Judd. 'And so was Switzerland.'

After tea, Donald mutters something about the garden, says to Judd that it 'was good to meet you', and leaves the room. Caroline clears away the tea, dropping spoons, and apologizing.

'*Good*. Keep your staff,' Caroline whispers loudly to me, before she goes.

When we are alone, Judd says, 'Yeah, Donald's all very nice, but fifty years ago, he'd have been happy to have us shoved into gas chambers.'

'Judd, that was terrible.'

I try to feel the anger I felt when he left me, but, oh, I am pleased to see him here, looking around in that same manner I did when I first visited the Wallis 'cottage'.

'So I'm not *Charlie*,' he says.

'I don't want you to be Charlie. Just don't be rude in other people's homes.'

'Or *VD*. Being polite at any price. Anyway, I don't know their code.'

'Manners, that's all. You give us Jews a bad name.'

'Lumping yourself in with us now, are you? So, is Maxie here?' he says; because, of course, he came to see Maxie, not me.

'She's asleep upstairs.'

'Oh.'

'Is Solomon in school?' I ask, presuming that he wants to arrange to see Maxie on a regular basis, and wondering whether VD will want formal access to Maxie too. (I have too many fathers for a single daughter.)

'Mmm,' he smiles and I think of Solomon's black eyes. 'Why aren't you at work?'

'*Oh*. So you thought I'd be at work when you called . . .'

'I wanted to leave a message before I spoke to you.'

I sip my cold cup of tea, which has begun to taste lemony.

'That doesn't make sense.'

'And just what does?' he smirks. 'So, really, why aren't you at work?'

'I stopped working in January.'

'You stopped?' He narrows his eyes, as if trying to see me in a different way. 'But you loved that job. Why?'

'I loved it until we changed offices,' I say, sipping. 'Then, everything changed. And, anyway, Maxie was terrible after you left. She needed me there full-time. But I want a *life* again,' I say, sadly.

'What d'you mean? You have the perfect existence. Recently modernized flat in desirable area. A husband who still desires you. Friends who are there for you, if you'll be there for them too. A boyfriend. Parents who are still alive. The mother of all mothers. A child who . . .'

'Enough already,' I interrupt, in a mock Yiddish accent. 'You're describing what I thought I had. Now, I have nothing and I stay at home all day, with Maxie.'

'I've told you. Apply for a place on one of those courses. You can still be a good mother to Maxie, and work. The BBC loves women like you. Strident, pretty, Oxbridge graduates.' He stops for a second, as if he wishes he could snatch back the word *pretty*.

'She was *terrible* when I worked.'

'She'd had a shock. I'd left her.' He stares at the table. 'There was that certainty gone. I'd be there every day; and suddenly she lost that. I was at the core of her existence, remember. She probably felt as if she couldn't hang on to anyone or anything afterwards.'

'You've just had a scone.'

I am shocked at the thought. It reminds me of the time I came downstairs in my flannel nightie, and watched my mother eating from a cut-glass bowl of chocolate mousse. 'You're allowed treats with Slimco,' she said as she saw me standing there, feeling the cold breathing up my legs. Yet, she hid the spoon under a serviette.

Judd says, 'It *was* offered to me. It was only polite to eat it.'

'But it wasn't kosher. You must have *known* it wasn't kosher.'

'Erm. Yeah. I told you; I'm not as strict now.'

I cannot help but smile, as I watch his gaze go back to Charlie's portrait. I see him take in my husband as Little Lord Fauntleroy. It bothered me when I first saw Charlie like that. I felt as if I had violated him. He was so sweet, and then along came Essex girl.

I look at Judd, who is the very opposite. Straight away, you can see the foreign in him. He might be fair, but there is no mistaking the fact that he is a Jew, with such sallow skin. The nose.

'So, you're as irreligious as I am now, are you?' I ask, trying to divert his attention from the picture of Charlie. I am hoping that Charlie will not come now. Or worse – VD.

'Almost,' he smiles. 'But still as Jewish as you are.'

'So, how's VD?' he asks, and there is sadness in his voice.

'I'm not seeing him any more. He found out I'd er. That we'd . . .'

'That we'd?' he asks, trying to hide the smile.

'Slept together,' I mutter.

'Made love?'

I look straight at Judd, and at that slightly broken nose, like a boxer's, which slightly spoils his (very) good looks. His blue, pale eyes are so probing that my own glance down at his lower half. I feel my face burn, as a noise comes through the baby intercom.

'Maxie?' he asks, gently.

'That'll be her,' I say.

'I can't wait to see her.'

'You don't *deserve* to see her,' I say, because I remember her face when she saw that he had gone. The door opens, shyly.

Caroline comes in. She is like a housemaid in a hotel, and I half expect her to ask whether it would be all right if she now turned down the bed.

'I'll go up to Maxie, shall I?'

'Thanks, Caroline.' I pick up my huge haversack of a bag, filled with all the accessories of motherhood, as I look at Judd. 'I'll be going pretty soon.'

'But what about *Charlie*? He should be here any *moment*,' she says, her face falling into lines.

Judd says, 'Charlie's coming here?'

'He's coming to discuss divorce.'

'Not necessarily,' says Caroline.

But I can see her thinking; and she is upset. 'Is that right, Lucy?'

I have upset my mother-in-law. She thought that Charlie and I would be like her and Donald. Living together, but without that tiny, overused word called love. Charlie, having affairs with women called Caitlin. She put on lipstick, to celebrate our reunion. It is the wrong colour for her lips, but still.

'Well, I'd imagine that's why he's coming.'

'Do you really think he wants to talk about *divorce*?'

'Of course he does, Caroline. What did you think?'

'But I made Donald phone, and postpone VD's visit,' she says, her face hardening and softening in spots as she looks at me.

'It's your house,' I mumble.

'Oh, you must be so angry with me. I really thought –. .'

'Honestly, Caroline,' I say, smiling.

'And to think you could have talked it through with VD. And he's such a nice chap.'

For a moment, I wonder whether she is about to cry. But Caroline only ever cries after a particularly moving television programme.

'I haven't got anything to say to VD.'

'Nicer to you than my son ever was.'

'Really, don't worry,' I say. 'VD was right. We don't . . . I don't love him.'

Maxie's voice on the baby intercom sounds more urgent. 'I'll pop up and get her then,' says Caroline, as if she is resigned to her fate. Grandmothering a child with hardly any connection to her son.

'What about Charlie? Do you still . . . ? Love Charlie?' asks Judd, when we are alone. The word *love* feels different, coming as it does from Judd. VD's constant use of the term expanded its scope. It embraced every warm feeling. From Judd, the word feels physical. *Do you still suffer from your love for Charlie?*

'What about you? Are you here to see Maxie? Because I told you, you can't keep leaving her.'

'I wouldn't leave her again.'

'So, what d'you *want* to do? Move back in as the au pair stroke screenplay-writer?'

He smiles.

'I wouldn't mind – if you promised not to read my journals.'

'God, I won't do that again. That ruined everything. That led to us . . .' I stop to blush at that. 'We might still be friends . . . If I hadn't read those bloody diaries.'

'You wish we hadn't?' That smile is so gentle; I can see why Maxie misses him so.

'I only hope your *screenplay's* better than your journals.

If I'd read any more, I'd have died with boredom.'

'If you'd have read *on*, you'd have learned that I love you. That I'm *in* love with you. That it killed me, living with you. That, sometimes, you're so beautiful, I . . .'

I am not here as the door opens, and Maxie walks in. She sees Judd, and, oh, she runs straight to him. *'Judd.'* It is like the scene in *Kramer versus Kramer* when Billy runs to his mother. *'Maxie.'*

'I love you too, you know,' I mumble. I know that, in retrospect, I will repeat my words for comic effect. But, right now, I am serious.

'What did you say?' he asks, as the doorbell rings.

'I'm not saying it again.'

'And what about Charlie?' he asks, as the doorbell rings again.

'Judd, I know what it is to love someone.' *If this is love, it hurts so much.* 'I'm hardly a virgin in that department.'

I hear the unmistakable sound of Charlie, walking in. 'Bloody dog,' he says; and there is Caroline's muffled reply. Charlie's loud voice tells Caroline not to be such a romantic. 'I'm here to . . . about solicitors.'

'That'll be Charlie then,' he says, holding Maxie close.

'Yup.'

'I love Mummy-and-Judd,' says Maxie, as if we are one word.

'I love Maxie-and-Lucy.'

'Maxie-and-Lucy-and-Solomon,' I insist.

'The whole bleeding lot of you.'

'Hey, you should write this down,' I say. 'You can use it for your screenplay.'

'No thanks,' says Judd, and I can hear him smile. 'This is all much too schmaltzy.'